AT HER MERCY

There were no roads on which to turn, just another stretch of pine. Kate looked at the girl and then the road, afraid to say the wrong thing, afraid of more pain. *No more pain, please!*

"There! Go through the trees!"

Kate steered to the graveled shoulder, then down a slight embankment and up again. She had read that if a kidnapper gets you in a car you are in serious trouble. If the kidnapper gets you into a private place, you are as good as dead. A guy on Oprah had said that. He knew the statistics. He had been a police officer. He'd seen dead women in the woods.

Kate's jaw chattered furiously. Her calves twitched.

"Get in there!"

Kate glanced at her door. If she popped the handle and rolled out she could run. The girl would have to get out her side and run around the car.

But she had the gun. She said she would kill her.

The guy on Oprah said if you run in a back-and-forth pattern you are less likely to be shot and killed, just maybe shot and wounded.

But the girl had the gun.

Wire Mesh Mothers

Elizabeth Massie

LEISURE BOOKS NEW YORK CITY

A LEISURE BOOK®

May 2001

Published by

Dorchester Publishing Co., Inc.
276 Fifth Avenue
New York, NY 10001

ISBN 0-8439-4869-8

Printed in the United States of America.

Visit us on the web at www.dorchesterpub.com.

This one is for my family—Barb, Charlie, and Jenni Lawson, Butch and Kim Spilman, Patricia Spilman, Joe Bruce, Erin and Ben Rothman, Brian Massie, and the memory of my sister Becky Bruce and father Bill Spilman. You are the best.

Wire Mesh Mothers

Chapter One

The orphaned cotton bits, blown loose from the butchered fields of December, scattered themselves across the chipped blacktop of the county roads outside the small town of Pippins, Virginia. They danced their ice dance, dodging automobile tires, winding up for the most part dead along the roadsides and wrapped like suicidal ghosts about the bases of splintery mailbox posts. Sometimes kids played in the harvested fields, picking the remnant fiber, stuffing it down the fronts of their shirts to make big boobs like Miss Carole, the Sunday School teacher down at the Riverside Church of Christ of Nazareth, or making lightweight snowmen by rolling the pieces together into big balls and then pinning the pieces together with thistle thorns. It didn't snow much in Pippins, and real snowmen were hard to come by in the winter.

Usually, though, the kids found other places to play because the plant stubble was so thick and so harsh sneakers couldn't keep out the pain. And so the cotton bits were alone to explore their small world, disguising themselves as things they weren't, playing dress-up, playing make-believe.

Looking like snow. Or turkey down.

Or thick white ashes from a distant crematorium.

Chapter Two

Mistie Dawn Henderson wore her nightgown to school. It was a lightweight pink acetate nightie, with torn lace at the sleeves and neck. Mistie liked the gown; it was pretty and it felt good on her skin. So when she woke up December tenth and found her father snoring face-down on the carpet and her mother leaning over her ashtray on a stool in the kitchen, one hand clutching the Winston, the other shading her face from the light that crept through the thin window shades, Mistie had slipped on socks and shoes and her winter coat, then gone out to wait for the bus down at the entrance to the trailer park.

Mrs. Colvin, who lived in the trailer next door to Mistie, saw her trudging past. She'd slammed up her storm window and called out, "Mistie Dawn, you tell your daddy I'm sick and tired of his music late at night. I didn't get one speck of sleep and now what am I supposed to do? My windows was shut and even then I

11

felt like I was rocking on the damn sea. I got nerves! He knows it! What am I supposed to do, answer me that? You hear me, Mistie Dawn? Say something!" Her voice cracked and went up a few notes. Mistie stuck her hands into her coat pockets, tucked her head, and kept walking, down the graveled road between the mobile homes. To either side she could see painted plaster and concrete lawn ornaments, staring at her with their pupil-less eyes. Tiny gardens were dead and brown; it was winter, after all. Bits of cotton from nearby fields had snagged themselves on rose branches and azalea twigs. The few trees between the lots were as naked as those women in the movies Daddy rented on weekends. There weren't any other kids out of their trailers yet; it was still early.

"I'll have the law on him quick as a dog, and we'll see how much music he can play behind bars," Mrs. Colvin shouted. "You want your daddy behind bars? What you think of that, huh?"

Mistie didn't think much of that. People were always threatening to call the cops on her daddy or her mama for one reason or another, but most of them didn't do it because, as Daddy said, two could play that game and most neighbors had something under their sticky ole carpet if he decided to do a little digging. On the few occasions police did pay visits on the Hendersons, Daddy was polite and agreeable and the cops would say, "Well, okay, then, don't let it happen again." Whatever the "it" was at the time. Cops were rubber dicks, Mistie's daddy would laugh. It was the social services that stuck in Daddy's craw. Social services had chased Mistie's family across a few state borders in the past when they got the idea that the Hendersons didn't take good care of Mistie. Mistie didn't really know what being taken care of was exactly, except that in each place they'd lived, ladies in skirts and heels had eventually come around to their trailer or their apartment or their rental house to talk to Mistie about her daddy and what he was up to. But the Hendersons would pack up and leave once those ladies started sniffing about. At least social services gave up easily, Daddy said with a smile. Not enough workers, Mama would laugh. But, damn, they sure were a bother.

When Valerie died back in Kentucky, Daddy had taken her way away from their apartment and buried her somewhere. Nobody best find her, he said, because if the cops and social services got into it, they'd make it seem like Valerie being dead was the family's fault and then everybody would go to jail, even Mistie. If anybody asked, Valerie'd had a bad liver, Daddy'd said. Wasn't his fault she had a bad liver but somebody would try to make it his fault like they did everything else. Mistie had promised never to talk about Valerie so the family wouldn't have to go to jail.

Mistie had been five when Valerie had died; since then they'd lived nine months in Tennessee, a half year in North Carolina, and then Virginia. Most of Mistie's memories of her sister had disappeared with the body; all she had now was a coloring book Valerie had colored in, one with Teletubbies in it. Sometimes, Mistie dreamed of her sister playing with a little cloud of black flies in the summer sun, but she never saw Valerie's face in those dreams.

When the Hendersons got themselves settled in MeadowView Trailer Park in Pippins, Virginia, Daddy had gotten a job working on a cotton farm in the summer and spring and fall. He stayed home at the trailer in the winter. Mama started selling sweet-smelling soap and shampoos from a catalog. Mistie liked the soap and shampoo but Mama never let her buy any and then after a month she threw the catalog in the trash and said nobody wanted that junk anyway. Just a few weeks after that the baby Mama was going to have came out too early. Mama showed it to Mistie as it floated in the toilet, a red blob with a tiny headlike thing and stringy stuff hanging off it, swirling in the water as Mama let Mistie push the lever to flush it away.

Mistie sat on the bank beside the road. She pulled up a dead weed and wrapped the stem around the base of the spiky seedpod.

"Mama had a baby and its head popped off," she said to herself. She pulled the bent stem forward, and the little pod popped off and up into the air. Mistie smiled. She picked another weed and popped off the seedpod.

A few minutes later, other trailer park children began to gather by the road. They threw gravel back and forth at each other. Mistie got hit on the head and arms a couple times, but she didn't throw any back. It didn't really hurt. She stopped playing with the weeds and sat with one fist inside the other.

A high school boy in T-shirt and no coat in spite of the freezing temperature took out a pack of cigarettes and lit two, one for himself and one for his seventh grade girlfriend. He leaned on the gray split-rail fencing separating the mobile park from the grassy bank by the road and sucked on the cigarette. The morning sun caught the smoke and strummed it like a silent guitar.

"Hey, girl," he said.

Mistie said nothing.

"Hey." He held the cigarette in his teeth, picked up a bit of gravel and tossed it at Mistie. It bounced off her chest. "I said hey, girl. You look like shit. Don't your mama care nothing about brushing your hair?"

Mistie said nothing.

"You all's white trash, don't you know? My grand-mama says you Hendersons as white trashy as they come. Says why don't you go back to Tennessee or Mexico or wherever the hell you come from."

Mistie said nothing.

"Leave her alone," said the seventh grade girlfriend.

"Where your books, girl? You never take books to school. You lose 'em or what? Don't you want to learn nothing?" The boy laughed, nudged his girlfriend, who popped a large bubble of gum, and shook his head. "What's that bruise on your neck? How'd you get a bruise on your neck?"

Mistie touched her neck but felt nothing. Did she have a bruise? Maybe. She fell asleep watching TV last night and rolled off the couch. Maybe she got a bruise when she hit the floor.

"You screwed up, you know that?" the boy contin-ued. "Fucked up in the head. It's from your daddy play-ing that loud music at night. Mrs. Colvin's gonna get you all kicked out of the court. She told us. We gonna have us a party when you gone."

Mistie looked down the paved road to where she couldn't see anymore because of the curve in the road and the trees clustered by the road. She listened for the rumbling of the school bus, but couldn't hear it over the shouting and fighting of the kids around her.

"Fucked up in the head," the boy was saying beside her. "Really fucked up, your whole family is fucked up

15

and they ought to be taken out back someday . . ."

It trailed. The voices of the other kids closed in upon themselves, faded. The road and trees narrowed and vanished, the light swallowed up in grayness. Comfortable, cottony nothingness cushioned her; a familiar humming pulse played behind her eyes. She rocked in its arms.

Something heavy slammed her in the back. Sights raced in like water over the rim of a flooded bathtub. Sunlight stabbed her; noises jammed their picks into her ears.

"Bus is here, you retard," said the high school boy. Mistie blinked and looked at him. He'd already finished his cigarette and was stubbing it out on the gravel with the toe of his cowboy boot. The girlfriend was tugging on his arm and tossing Mistie a look of tempered tolerance. Other kids were pushing around Mistie, swinging book bags and purses, climbing up the steel steps and into the big yellow vehicle.

Mistie took the handrail and pulled herself up the steps. The bus smelled of mildew and cleanser and stinky feet. The bus driver, a man whose name she didn't know but who was always the bus driver, gave her a scowl. Then he said to the high school boy behind her, "Lose the cigarettes, Ricky, or you're off the bus for the next two weeks."

Ricky planted the heel of his hand between Mistie's shoulder blades and shoved her around the bar and into the aisle. Her breath went out with a whoosh, but she choked and caught it back, saying nothing. "Ain't got no smoke," said Ricky. "Want to search me? Want to strip search me?" He winked at the high school girls on the bus. "You a queer or what?"

"Talk like that'll get you off the bus for a month," said the bus driver.

"Like I really care," said Ricky. He pushed past Mistie and strode to the back of the bus where he dropped onto a vinyl-covered seat. Other high schoolers, sitting nearby, turned around and drew together, heads going down, talking loudly but incoherently.

Mistie found a seat halfway back by herself. There was a pencil stub on the seat. She flicked it to the floor. "Mama had a baby and its head popped off."

This was the only bus in the county that had a cross-grade population. It transported kids from all three schools, Pippins Elementary, Curtis Middle, and Southampton High. The high school kids who rode this bus hated it, and let everyone know. At least they had the shortest ride, only three miles, and then they were gone, leaving the younger kids catching their breaths and rolling their eyes at each other.

A little ways down the road, the bus shuddered to a stop in front of a row of small, once colorful box houses. A lot of these houses had kids. Bent bikes and upturned plastic wading pools littered yards. Some of the chain-link fences were torn down and most of the grass in most of the yards was gone, leaving cold-packed dirt and ruts. Five cars and two pickups in various stages of disrepair sat in the driveway of the pink house. In the side yard of the gray house, frozen sheets swayed stiffly on the line.

There was a girl who lived in the purple house whom Mistie liked. Her name was Tessa Kessler. Tessa and Mistie were in the same second grade class at Pippins Elementary. Tessa was pretty, with bouncy blond hair and a lot of new clothes. She wore makeup sometimes, and she missed a lot of school because she had to baby-sit her little brother when her mama ran down to Roanoke Rapids in North Carolina to shop. Tessa got to be in pageants on weekends. She looked like Princess Silverlace on that show on Nick.

Kids from the box houses filed onto the bus. Mistie pulled her foot clear of the aisle as they came, and watched for Tessa. A first grader sat down by Mistie, bearing a blue plastic lunch box and a scowl. He looked as though he'd been crying. Sooty rivulets zigzagged down his face. Mistie was disappointed, because if Tessa was coming to school, maybe she would have sat with Mistie.

But Mistie didn't ask the boy to move. She shifted in her seat, slouched against the side of the bus, and stared out the window at the green house. From the front of the bus, she could hear the door hissing closed, and the grinding of the bus gears as the bus driver settled in for the remainder of the trip.

Then the front door of the purple house opened with a jerk, and Tessa was jumping from the stoop to the narrow concrete sidewalk, a denim book bag dangling from her elbow. Mistie sat straight, watching.

The bus driver said something over the din of students, and the bus door clanked open. Tessa rushed through the open chain-link gate, past her sagging mailbox, and jumped onto the bus steps. Mistie clenched one fist; the other went inside her coat and stroked the satiny nightgown.

"Mama had a baby."

The boy by Mistie farted and scooted his butt around to let the smell escape.

Tessa dropped into a seat near the front, beside an-

18

other little girl. The bus honked its hor.
car, then pulled onto the road. The boy b
pulled a set of Pokemon cards from his pock
gan to shuffle through them, mumbling to him
his brother had bent up the best ones. Mistie found a
tear on the back of the seat in front of her. She watched
it, bouncing up and down and sideways, making her
pleasantly dizzy, until the bus was at Pippins Elementary, and it was time to get off.

Chapter Three

Tony's crotch burned from the tug of last year's too-tight jeans, but the sensation wasn't sexual. It was irritating, and something that a sifting of position could put temporarily past notice. Her head itched under her hat, but she didn't reach up to scratch it. It could be sweat or excitement or maybe even head lice—her little sister was home today with a case of the nits—but right now in the grander scheme of things it didn't matter. Her dark brown hair was already a short crew cut, with half-inch bangs in the front, so if it was lice making her itch, the idea of shaving the rest of it off later wasn't a big deal. But, regardless, sweat or cooties, she kept her hands down and away from her head. A test of will-power.

She was in the backseat of the car, against the door on the right. Buddy was in the front. He was driving, sort of. Buddy didn't have a license, and he didn't know much past how to push the accelerator and that you had to stay on the right side of the road. Buddy was fourteen with thin blond hair that reached his shoulders. His hat was a Redskins ball cap he got from the Exxon Convenience Mart on Route 58.

On the passenger's side up front was Leroy. Leroy was sixteen and the oldest so he thought he was too good to drive. Let baby boys do that, he'd say. He also thought since he was oldest, he was smartest. That was a crock of shit. Leroy wore a really old tattered knit hat that said *I'm a Pepper,* whatever the hell that was supposed to mean. He also sported bent sunglasses. Around Leroy's neck were old dog tags that belonged to someone in his family, but he didn't know whom. They had been flattened on a railroad track years before he was born and the letters were way past legible. Looking at Leroy was like looking at a scrawny snowman with big black coal eyes jabbed into his forehead.

In the middle between Buddy and Leroy was DeeWee. DeeWee was ugly and retarded, but he was Leroy's fourteen-year-old brother so he always came along. DeeWee's hat was just like Leroy's, only green. The gang didn't do colors, although they knew from the TV that gangs out in California and other big cities did. The Pippins gang wore hats. They called themselves the Pippins Hot Heads.

Next to the left window in the back was Whitey. Whitey was black but he got burned once and it left a long white scar on the side of his neck. Whitey had an old beret he'd stolen from his uncle. Whitey was almost as old as Leroy, but Leroy didn't let it matter. Whitey didn't let it matter, either. Leroy was boss.

Between Whitey and Tony was Little Joe. Little Joe thought he was a cowboy, just like the country singers

21

on channel 47. Little Joe had bright red hair and freckles and was from Louisiana. He used to wear a cowboy hat but Tony cut it up with a razor one time. So Little Joe was reduced to a red stocking cap advertising Castrol Motor Oil. He also wore a belt buckle with Johnny Cash's face on it that he polished with spit.

It was almost 11:30 in the morning. The Pippins Hot Heads had been riding around since just after ten, trying to keep warm since the car's heater didn't work very well, shooting road signs and a bum-legged skunk with Leroy's BB gun, drinking the beer Tony had stolen from her mom, and having a halfhearted on-again off-again belching contest. Everyone's breath was cotton smoke on the cold air in the car. Tony could see spit in Little Joe's breath smoke and it pissed her off. Idiot should learn to breathe without spitting; it was gross.

Today's car was a green-and-rust Chevelle. It was Whitey's aunt's but she didn't go to work today, she was in bed with the cramps, so she didn't know it was making the rounds. The thing groaned and thumped and smelled of private, auntish things like perfume and sex. The sex smell pissed Tony off even more than Little Joe's spit did.

"Shit, Little Joe, get them goddamn boots away from me!" Tony shouted suddenly, slamming her heel onto the top of his foot. "Keep them away from me!"

"Ow!" whined Little Joe. "Can't just cut my damn legs off just to give you room. Where you want me to put my feet? Whitey ain't complaining."

Whitey turned his attention from the flat countryside out the window and looked at Little Joe. "That's 'cause I got control of myself. Tony don't know nothing 'bout control. If I was Tony, I'd tore 'em off long ago."

"I'm ready to cut your feet off inside those boots and throw 'em all out the window!" swore Tony. "Those boots's pussy, Little Joe."

Little Joe's eyes drew into slits and he slumped against the back of the seat. "Fuck." But slowly he pulled his feet together as closely as he could. "Ain't pussy."

"They's pussy and they's queer, too," said Leroy from the front seat. He fingered the buttons on the radio, sending a mad barrage of song clips yelping out through the speakers in the rear. "We'll find you a good pair of shoes soon, baby boy, and you can kiss them high heels good-bye."

"These boots cost a lot," said Little Joe. But his voice was almost a whisper, and Tony was the only one who heard him. Little Joe was the bottom of the Hot Heads pecking order and knew it.

"Damn radio," Leroy hissed. "Can't get nothing but old shit and preachin'. And on a Tuesday."

" 'S bent antenna," said Buddy. "It wasn't bent we'd get something better, maybe from up at Richmond."

Leroy drove his fist into the on button; the music died. "Yeah," he said, "if we had a good antenna we could get Richmond stations with rap and shit. Whitey, tell your aunt get her antenna fixed."

Whitey grunted, then let out a long, crisp belch that threw DeeWee into a temporary fit of laughter.

They drove a few more minutes, down a stretch of frozen country road, with no sound other than Little Joe's raspy breathing and Buddy's occasional sniffs and curses. Silently Tony counted the rails of the fences they passed so she wouldn't jump out of her skin. The day was frosty and clear. It was December tenth. Good little boys and girls were in school. But not the Pippins Hot Heads. They were in a beat-up Chevelle, driving around the county looking for something to do. Usually, if they could get a car, the something to do was stealing folks' mail, then smashing their mailboxes and whacking cows in the butt with a crowbar to watch them run. When that got wearisome, they'd pool their cash for a couple gallons of gas at the Exxon, swing by Whitey's trailer at MeadowView for some of the doughnut sticks his aunt always had hidden in an upper kitchen cabinet, and go eat behind the old chimney in the woods back of the trailer park.

Here, in the farmland back roads between the tiny towns of Pippins and Capron, fifteen miles from Emporia and Interstate 95 that ran north to Richmond and south into North Carolina, it was real easy to hang out and not go to school. There weren't many police around except for troopers and not many of those, either, and they watched Route 58 most of the time, watching for speeders. The Hot Heads rarely talked to anybody else, and if, while pumping gas or pocketing candy at the Exxon, someone actually demanded to know why they weren't in school, the gang just said they were home schoolers. Worked every time. Home schoolers were good, Christian kids.

Tony squinted and kept up with the rails on the side of the road. Fifty-seven, fifty-eight, fifty-nine, sixty, sixty-one, sixty-two, sixty-three. Boredom and rage burned her spine with a furious heat.

The need to teach that bitch Martin a lesson clawed the tendons in her neck.

"Buddy, Buddy, stop," said DeeWee. "Gotta pee." Tony peered over the seat and grimaced. DeeWee was holding himself through his pants, pulling and tugging as if he were manning a fire hose. Buddy pulled the car to the side of the road. The cotton field next to the road was flat and broad with a small barn squatting in the corner. The barn was a pretty cool place in the summer because you could have damn good parties once you scraped the spiders from their hiding places. One time, a couple months ago, the Hot Heads had caught two middle schoolers making out in one of the barn's stalls. The Hot Heads had made the two strip naked and run barefoot across the stubbly pasture to wherever, anywhere but the Hot Heads' barn.

Tony had kicked the girl just outside the barn door and the girl had come down in the sharp cotton stalks on her pretty little made-up face with its fucking pink lipstick and blue eye shadow. Stalks, right in her face and in her hands, making her bleed, kinda like Jesus after Pilate got through with him. It was beautiful. Tony had then stomped the girl on the neck, hard—*stomp stomp stomp!* Oh, it felt *wonderful!*—until Leroy pulled her off; then the girl had choked, gagged, then scrambled up and run, stumbling, after her white-assed boyfriend. It had been good for a laugh, then it was into Tony's mama's beer and the doughnut sticks.

It took DeeWee a full eighty-three seconds to wiz, zip, and get back into the car. He smelled like pee. He had probably leaked on himself. The car pulled back onto the road. They drove another quarter mile, past the strobing fence posts along a small cattle farm.

Forty-three, forty-four, forty-five, forty-six.

Tony couldn't stand it anymore. "Stop the car."

"Nuh-uh, ain't stoppin'," said Buddy. "You shoulda peed when DeeWee peed."

25

Elizabeth Massie

"Stop the goddamn car, Buddy."

Leroy hawked, rolled the window down, and spit. Most of it caught the rear window like a clear streak of bird shit.

"You ain't my boss," said Buddy, but his foot came up a bit on the accelerator, and the car slowed a fraction. He glanced at Leroy. "Tony ain't boss," he complained. Leroy shook his head but said nothing. When Tony used the *tone,* he paid attention. He knew he'd better.

"Gotta pee, gotta pee, Tony gotta wee wee!" sang DeeWee.

"Gotta shut your mouth hole, DeeWee." Tony leaned over the back of the seat and put her teeth at Buddy's ear. She said slowly, "Stop . . . the . . . fucking . . . car."

"Back off, Tony," said Leroy. But then he said, "Pull it over, Buddy."

Buddy cursed and pulled the car over. It bit the gravel and then a baby rabbit that didn't move fast enough into the poison ivy by the fencing. The car engine died.

Leroy turned and his knee came up on the seat, ramming into DeeWee's side. DeeWee squawked. "What the hell's wrong with you, Tony?" Tony could see his nose twitching. That was good. He was nervous. Tony liked it when he was nervous like that.

"I had enough of this shit," she said.

"What shit?"

"Us. You see us? You know what you're seeing? Don't you want to just puke when you see us?"

Whitey sneezed.

"What you talking about?" said Leroy.

26

"Just what I said. We're shit. We're fucking babies, all this baby trash we do."

Leroy's eye hitched, but he held his ground. "What trash you talking about? Think them cows thought we was just a bunch of bitin' flies when we hit their butts with them BBs? We drew blood! Think them folks thought the tooth fairy took their mail to never-never land?"

"Bitin' flies!" giggled DeeWee. "Cows thought we was bitin' flies!"

Tony scoffed, "Think Little Joe's boots is baby? Huh? I'll give you baby. That BB gun. Like that little kid in that movie they been showin' over and over on channel forty-five. He wanted a BB gun for Christmas. Oh, ain't he just so bad, now? Asked Santa for the gun. BB gun's a Santa gun."

"You saying I got this gun from Santa?" said Leroy. He pulled off his sunglasses. His dark, snowman eyes looked even darker.

"You ain't making sense," said Whitey tentatively.

"And you pissin' me off," said Leroy. "Ain't nothing I can't hit with my BB gun. I can take off your pimply nose with it. I can take out your whole face if I wanted to, whiny baby. Bang-bang-bang, out like a star at the carnival shooting gallery. Nothing left but that shitty haircut on top your scalp."

"Don't ever call me whiny baby," Tony said.

Leroy popped open the door. A tiny piece of cotton blew in on a breeze. "You want out right now, Tony? I'll pull your ass over the seat and throw you out. Thought you was cool like a guy, Tony. You just whiny like a brat."

"Whiny little brat," said Buddy.

27

"Who asked you into this?" Tony knocked Buddy's cap off and yanked a fistful of hair from his scalp. Blood beaded on the raw flesh. Buddy yelped and grabbed his head.

"Hold your tongue," Tony said. "Or I'll pull that out, too!" She threw the hair into Buddy's lap. Some still clung to her fingers and she wiped it off on Buddy's headrest. Whimpering, Buddy held the wad of hair to his head as if he might be able to put it back.

"Listen to me, everybody," said Tony. "We should be doin' big stuff. Real stuff. Or we should just go back to suckin' Mama's titties for all the good we are."

"Like what stuff?"

"I been thinkin' about a robbery."

Leroy blew air through his teeth. "Big deal, Tony. We steal stuff all the time."

"Not like that. Not stealing. Robbin'. There's a difference, case you didn't know. Show the firepower, rob 'em blind. Leave our mark on something besides cow asses. Do armed robbery."

"Arm robbery! Steal a arm!" laughed DeeWee.

"Who we gonna rob?" said Whitey. "There ain't nothin' around here. And we ain't got no cars that could make it all the way to Richmond or over to Portsmouth."

Tony felt the blood stir in the backs of her hands. Hot, cold. Hot, cold. That new nigger at the Exxon would shit her lacy little drawers. Out the dirty window dry grasses strummed the air and the clouds boiled in the white sky; Tony could smell the shit and the sweat. "It'll be the best," she said. "Stick 'em up! Hand it over! Money in the bag, now, you stupid bitch!"

"What bitch?" said Leroy.

"Possum!" shouted DeeWee.

A scraggly opossum had appeared on the roadside gravel. It waddled into some brush near the car.

Tony's head was itching again, and she fought to keep her hand from scratching. "Bitch at a bank," she said with a shrug, not caring to share her personal vendetta with the other Hot Heads because it didn't matter. She'd kill two birds with one stone with the robbery she had planned.

"Bitch at the store, the gas station, whatever, crying, 'Oh, help me, help me! Lord, save me! Take what you want and leave me alone!' Fucking pussies."

Little Joe's booted foot slipped down onto Tony's and she slammed it back with a kick to his shin so hard she could hear the denim rip. Little Joe grimaced but made no sound.

"Well," said Buddy. He looked at Leroy for direction.

"Well, well, well," giggled DeeWee.

Leroy pulled the passenger door shut. He rubbed his mouth. "You know," he said. "Ain't too bad a idea, even if I didn't come up with it myself."

"A good idea?" said Buddy. "Sure, we just get our asses blowed off and for what? Some packs of cigarettes?"

"Back on the road, Buddy," said Leroy.

"Leroy . . . ," said Buddy.

"Drive!"

The car pulled back onto the road. Nobody said anything for a few minutes. They passed a row of small signs, sitting deep in weeds. Each one bore a single word. JESUS. LOVES. YOU. REPENT. OR. BURN. IN. HELL.

"Hell!" giggled DeeWee, pointing at the final sign.

Another minute of silence. Tony sat back against the seat and grabbed her elbows with her hands. She pulled her arms tightly into her stomach until she couldn't catch her breath. Let Leroy think it over. He was as bored as she was. He hated things as much as she did.

One, two, three, four, five, six, seven . . .

Then Leroy said, "Tony's right. We gotta do something to show we got balls."

"Tony ain't got balls," said DeeWee. "Girls got holes!"

"What we gonna rob?" asked Little Joe. "Pippins ain't got nothing but the grocery, the Exxon, churches, and the old engine shop. And Capron ain't got more than Pippins."

Something crawled from Tony's ear to the nape of her neck. Maybe it was lice after all. She pinched her elbows to keep from scratching. "Exxon's got a money machine we could whack off the wall. Got a cash register, too, and only Mrs. Martin works there in the day. We know the place. Ain't no surprises. She don't have a gun. We'd hold all the cards."

DeeWee picked something out of his nose and rubbed it on his sleeve.

"We'll make the news," said Tony. "Be on TV. Kids other places always making news for stuff they do. And their mamas, oh, shit, there they stand with their head up their asses lookin' all surprised. They stand there lookin' at the TV camera, wiping their eyes, crying, 'I had no idea she would do that! Oh! It's so terrible!' Fuck it, it'd be great!" Ecstatic laughter bubbled up in the back of Tony's throat; she swallowed it back.

In the rearview outside the passenger window, Tony saw Leroy's jaw clench in and out and in and out.

"Yeah, this is good, man, this is good. But we gotta wear something they don't know who we is."

"No shit," said Tony. "I coulda told you that. You gave me time I woulda told you that."

"Gotta get real guns."

"That we do."

"What if we get caught?" said Buddy.

"Stay home, that the way you feel. We don't need you."

The car reached an intersection and Buddy, for once, stopped at the stop sign. Straight ahead was more countryside, leading to the town of Pippins. To the right, down a couple tenths of a mile, was the Presbyterian church and the Riverside Holiness church, side by side as if they really got along, which they didn't since the Presbyterians had Halloween parties for their kids and the Holiness folks believed it to be of the devil. To the left was a field with cattle and the road leading to the row of houses where Tony lived.

"Who's got a real gun?" asked Leroy.

"My great-uncle Henry does," said Little Joe. "Under his mattress. Got some kinda pistol."

"Ammo?" asked Tony.

"Who has a pistol and no ammo? Morons, that's who!"

"He home now, your great-uncle?"

Little Joe sat up straight, like he finally felt he had something worth offering. "He don't go to work 'til two o'clock. But then ain't nobody home 'til after five."

"I got a gun at home, too," said Tony. "Revolver. Was my dad's."

"Well, then," said Leroy.

DeeWee said, "Well, then!" He giggled.

"Buddy, drop us all off at our places," said Leroy. "Everybody find a disguise to wear. Then Buddy'll pick everybody back up 'bout four o'clock. We'll go do us a Exxon store. We won't let nobody know who we are, but we gonna show 'em what we are!"

"But we didn't get our doughnut sticks yet," said Whitey.

Tony grabbed Whitey's ear across Little Joe's lap and pulled it until he shrieked.

"Shut your mouth about the doughnuts, don't you care about important things?" Tony said. "And find a good disguise. Make yourself look like a white boy or Mexican boy or Chinese boy or something."

Tony let go of Whitey's ear, gave Little Joe's boots another kick, sat back, and looked out at the world through the snotty-slicked window. Her heart raced; the blood in her fingers was fiery. She counted the pulses and got to nearly two hundred before the car slowed down in front of her little house and it was time to get out.

Gonna do. For once in our lives, we're gonna do! Won't Mam just love this? Won't the Martin bitch just dump in her prissy little drawers?

Tony's pants tugged and her head itched, but this time they felt good.

Chapter Four

It was the urine on the floor that threw everything over the edge, a small puddle, intentionally leaked there by Willie Harrold, a fine, upstanding student in the fourth grade. Willie was short, with black hair, blue eyes, and groping hands. He had quite the history, little Willie. He explored the forms beneath the shirts of every fourth grade female who happened to wander within his reach. Willie bit kindergarteners on the playground, then said he didn't. He cussed and stole anything small enough to fit into his book bag or pockets. And to keep Willie free to continue his antics, his father swore a lawsuit every time Willie was removed from the mainstream of the classroom and put into a study carrel or seated on the bench outside the principal's office.

"Look what Willie did!" Marion Kiddel shouted from her desk. Kate McDolen, who had been standing at the front of the room in her peach sweater and gray wool skirt, writing on the chalkboard—fine, yellow

33

chalk dust coating her hands, showing once again that adjectives described things, that adjectives like "happy" and "sunny" and "snowy" and "soft" made writing stories much more *fun!*—spun about on her toe. She stared where Marion was pointing.

Some of the students were in their seats, also staring. Most of the students were up and giggling, glancing between the teacher and the culprit. Jenny Wise, slumped in her desk near the door, had actually looked up from the fingernail polish she'd been picking at and was paying attention.

"He went on the floor, just standing there like a dog and went on the floor!" This was Christopher May. He was Willie's best friend. His prime pleasure in life was heralding Willie's accomplishments.

Willie himself had his arms crossed and his mouth open in a wide grin, revealing the crooked teeth his daddy didn't have time to have fixed at the free dental clinic because he was too busy with lawyers, working up lawsuits against the school system.

Happy. Sunny.

Insane.

Kate felt her fingers crush around the stub of yellow chalk.

Impotent.

The arthritic spot in her jaw clicked. She said, "Sit down, everyone. Right now."

Almost everyone slid into their seats. A few students on the periphery of the classroom remained standing. They didn't want to miss the view. Christopher dropped into his seat, not taking his gaze off Willie.

Standard question, coming up. Standard, worthless

teacher question. "Willie," Kate asked. "Why did you do that?"

And Willie's standard, broken-record response. "Do what?"

Jaws clenched, as tightly as her fingers on the chalk. Fuzzy, furious stars rising in the corner of her vision. Her sweater no longer keeping out the chill of the classroom air in December. "I asked you a question."

Willie grinned. "I didn't do nothing. Why you always picking on me?"

Jenny scrunched her eyebrows. Another girl giggled, then put her hand over her mouth. Christopher popped his lips and bounced the heel of his shoe off the floor, enthralled with the diversion. The showdown rarely varied from its usual choreography. It was an old movie known well by the students. The ending never changed. Willie did whatever he pleased. Ms. McDolen kept her cool and sent Willie to the office after a heated argument. Show over. Willie one, Ms. McDolen zip.

Hopeless. Impotent.

Kate took ten slow breaths. A routine that was supposed to work. *Take a few moments, breathe slowly, and you can put things into perspective. Things need to be in perspective.* Teachers were patient, understanding. Teachers always knew how to maintain control, regardless of the circumstances. Teachers were good with perspectives. It's what they were paid for, it's what they were trained for. God bless teachers.

God bless us, every one.

Willie looked at Christopher and grinned.

"Go to the office, Willie," said Kate. The veins in the backs of her hands tingled the way they did when she took three cold tablets instead of two. *I hate this. This is wrong. It's always wrong.*

Willie licked his finger off, then wiped it on his jeans leg. "Can't make me," he said. "My daddy said you can't make me leave 'cause it's against my rights. I gotta get my education."

"Go to the office now."

"You can't make me."

What is wrong with me? Why can't I ever get this right? He's a child, for heaven's sake, a little delinquent, but I'm the adult here.

" 'Gainst my rights. You can't boss me, you can't touch me, neither."

This is insane.

"Can't touch me! Can't touch me!"

I can't do this anymore. I've tried, God, for three years I've tried, and I just can't do it anymore.

Kate McDolen, trained professional, patient teacher, leader and guide to young minds, felt the snap in her neck. Felt the electric clotting behind her eyes, static and immense. The chalk dropped from her fingers and bounced, once, on the floor by her Easy Spirit pumps.

Willie sniffed, a harsh, challenging sound.

When she spoke this time, her heartbeat was in her mouth. Her tongue tasted of metal. "Willie. Go. Now." *Here's your last chance, Willie. Here it is. Take it.*

Please, just this once, Willie.

Willie, grinning, "I'm sick of you trying to tell me what to do. Call my daddy and see what he says."

"Go."

"Ain't going." The smile given to Christopher, the nasal snicker.

You little shit, just go!

36

"Ain't going ain't going ain't going ain't going!" A shrug.

Maybe it was the shrug more than it was the pee.

But in that second Kate was rushing from her desk in a whirl of sweater and skirt and chalky fingers and she was slamming her fist against little Willie Harrold's grinning face and sending that little grinning face with the body to which it was attached to the floor like a roped calf in a rodeo. The boy fell on his butt, crumpled onto his back, and slid several feet, thumping into a couple of the nearby desks on his way. When he gasped and looked up, there was a streak of blood on his face.

A slight alteration in the usual Willie-Kate dance. Just a minor change of routine.

"Whoa!" shouted Christopher.

"Mrs. McDolen!" screamed Marion Kiddel.

Kate stared at the boy on the floor. She was panting as if she'd just run a mile. The teacher in her said she should offer him her hand and help him up and then proceed to figure out how the hell to remedy this situation. To apologize, to do some quick double-talk to gloss over the situation. But she couldn't.

Not this time.

Her heart drove against her ribs like the gloves of a prizefighter hammering home his final blows.

Kate turned on her heel, walked back to her desk, and said, "Marion, go to the office and tell Mr. Byron that I need him immediately." Her voice was steeled and far away in her ear.

And as she returned to the chalkboard and picked up a nice, new stick of chalk, to continue her lesson on adjectives, the only one she could think of was "fucked."

37

Chapter Five

"What is that you're wearing?" asked Mistie's teacher.

Mistie looked down at herself. She had on her coat. She had on her pretty nightie. Princess Silverlace had a pink gown like this.

The other children at the math table stopped playing with the colorful little base-ten logs and stared at her. They never talked much to Mistie except to tell her when to get in line or when to get away from them.

"Mistie?" repeated the teacher. "Let me see."

Mistie stood still while the teacher pulled back the coat and looked at the nightie. "My goodness, just what is that?"

Mistie put her finger in her ear.

"Mistie, what are you wearing?"

Mistie thought of Princess Silverlace on Nick. Princess Silverlace was beautiful like Tessa except she was older and taller and she had a crown that glittered gold and silver. She wore a long, pink, and sparkly gown.

She had a throne in a castle and everybody loved her. People gave her presents because they loved her and she did good things for the people because she loved them. Mistie watched it when her daddy wasn't around. When he was around he would say, "What's that shit? I didn't work out gettin' cable to waste it on this crap," and turn the channel.

"Is that your nightgown?" asked the teacher.

Mistie rubbed the acetate and it felt good.

"Mistie, I'm writing a note. I want you to take it to the office and give it to the secretary. Do you understand me?"

Mistie nodded. She knew where the office was. It was a bright place with grown-ups. It had a bench and it had potted plants.

The teacher scribbled something on paper at her desk. She put the note into Mistie's hand. Mistie didn't read it. She wasn't good at reading.

"That's all, Mistie. Go on."

Mistie went on.

Chapter Six

The teachers' lounge was empty. Most of the teachers regularly ate in the cafeteria with their students, even though they were allowed a duty-free day once a week. Today was no different. It was 12:24 P.M. The fourth and fifth grades were at lunch working their way through potato barrels, oily green beans, and oven-fried chicken. It wasn't Kate's duty-free day but she'd hastily traded with another fourth grade teacher, Benita Little, who didn't care one way or another because she not only ate in the cafeteria with her students every day, she actually sat with them instead of at the teachers' table by the stage.

Kate had eaten lunch with her students every day for the first two years. But not this year.

Through the lounge wall was muffled cafeteria commotion, the buzz of one hundred twenty-some students and an occasional ping of the bell from the teachers' table, indicating the noise level was too high. In the corner of the lounge, the Pepsi machine hummed. The photocopy machine in the office down the hall chunked and clunked as it plagiarized a coloring book for one of the kindergarten teachers.

But the most insistent noise came from Kate's head.

Mr. Byron and Willie's father will talk with you tomorrow morning at seven-thirty.

Kate closed her eyes, took her head in both hands, and shook it like she shook the Pepsi machine when it ate her quarters. The humming in her mind rattled arhythmically, then settled down again to the excruciating clamor.

Mr. Byron called Willie's father because Willie cut his face on the leg of a desk when you knocked him down and he needed stitches. We have a serious situation on our hands. Willie's mother and father will be here tomorrow at seven-thirty sharp. You must have that accident report filled out and everything in order before they get here.

The principal, Mr. Byron, had come to the classroom a few minutes after the incident, with Marion Kiddel bouncing beside him, her teeth chewing her lower lip, her eyes huge. "Here he is, Mrs. McDolen," she'd said, in case poor Mrs. McDolen had gone so crazy that she could no longer recognize her superior. Willie was shrieking that he was dying, that Mrs. McDolen had killed him, and the rest of the students in the class were too stunned to do anything but stare at the wreckage and wait to see what was going to happen. Willie had been escorted by the principal back to the office, but right before lunch, he had returned to Kate's room.

"Willie's family is going to require more than an apology," Mr. Byron had said, taking her aside as her students lined up to go to lunch. In one hand he had clenched a blank accident report form, and the other hand was drawn up around a pen and shaking like a bad Bob Dole impersonation. "They've been waiting to take us to task on something serious, Mrs. McDolen. I think we just handed it to them on a silver platter."

I don't need this. This is wrong, completely wrong.

"Damn it all."

"Say what, hon?" It was the secretary, Miriam Calhoun, peering into the lounge. She was waiting to use the women's restroom across the hall, a popular meditation spot. She was young, with fluttery eyes and Pentecostal hair. Today, her vest and pants ensemble was a dark green Christmas thing, with red threading through the fabric that made it look, from this distance, like little blood vessels all over the material.

"Nothing," said Kate, trying a smile. "Just muttering to myself." But of course it wasn't nothing, and of course Miriam knew it wasn't nothing. Without a doubt she'd heard what had happened in Kate's classroom this morning. Every staff and faculty member would know by now. Word of mishaps and confrontations circulated the school as quickly as a case of chicken pox.

Miriam grinned a pseudo-sympathetic and knowing grin. Kate sat straight to belie her panic, crossed her legs, and drew her short auburn hair up behind her ears. On the center of the table were piles of educational magazines. She picked up one, *Elementary Education Today,* and let it fall open to where it would, which was a blow-in ad for sets of no-fail, individually paced cards for reluctant readers called "Ready-To-Read."

She stared at the happy multicultural cartoon students, boys and girls, making a rainbow border around the card, assuring any interested teacher that yes, Asians and Caucasians and Afro-Americans and Hispanic children alike will find this program so inspirational that it makes them want to hold hands in a circle and smile.

"How are you going to get them to read your cards when the biggest thrill in their lives is a puddle of urine on the floor?" she whispered. She shoved the magazine away.

No, she thought. *I refuse to sit there with the parents and try to be professional while they cuss me out, demand my head on a platter, and tell me they pay my salary. Well, I don't need the damn salary. And I won't lower myself to fight their battle in court to redeem myself. I know how that works. It doesn't work, that's how it works.*

Her lungs ached. Tears tickled the backs of her eyes, and angrily she dug them away. She wouldn't lose tears over this.

I won't go through with it. I will not do this.

Outside the window was the parking lot. Teachers' cars, a bus on the far side, getting gas at the single pump near the Dumpster, a UPS truck by the mailbox, waiting to pull back onto the road. Stray bits of white cotton fiber, blown here from the vast, harvested fields near the school, clung to the base of the hedges like lost baby ghosts.

Take it in, Kate. As Romeo said, "Eyes, look your last." They are going to fire you. It doesn't matter who you are, they are going to bring you down like wolves after a deer. Kiss this place good-bye. So typical, Kate.

43

What have you accomplished lately? Yes, please, do tell.

"Cut it out, Kate," she said, catching her chin in her hand and squeezing it just enough to make it sting. "Stop it, I can fix this. There is nothing that cannot be fixed. I'm college-educated, master's degree, for Christ's sake. Willie's father didn't finish grade school. I just have to think it through. They cannot have the best of me." She got up, plugged a couple coins into the Pepsi machine, then returned to her chair, can in hand. She popped the top and took a drink.

"I tripped and bumped into Willie. I may have looked like I pushed him, but I bumped him."

Yeah, sure. And that second grader Mistie Henderson isn't being abused in spite of her bruises and behavior and Mr. Byron isn't sneaking down to the nature trail after school with our sweet school secretary Miriam and Susan Jansen, our music teacher, didn't have a nose job over the summer.

"This is ridiculous," she whispered.

Her face fell into flat palms.

"Lord, girl, what went on in your class today?"

One palm slid away enough to reveal Deidra Kirtley, third-grade teacher, standing by the table with her arm around a set of dog-eared science workbooks. Deidra was the closest thing Kate had to a friend at school. She was an attractive, chunky lady of fifty-something, dark skinned and quick witted. She was loud, abrupt, and confident. And she didn't seem to care that Kate was a McDolen.

A number of the Pippins Elementary teachers silently and sometimes not so silently resented Kate because she didn't have to teach, she did it because she had wanted something to do when her son had gone off to a private school in Pennsylvania. Kate had come in three years ago at the age of thirty-eight, with a brand-new master's degree and all sorts of shiny and bright teaching concepts. And they had rolled their eyes. Oh, all over the school did the eyes roll.

Kate had tried to ignore it, to laugh it off. She could sometimes even see herself from their vantage points—a thin, plain-faced woman who dressed just a bit more formally than they, who didn't have their disillusionment but didn't have their experience, either. Most of the teachers in Pippins were natives of the area. They'd attended Pippins Elementary, Curtis Middle, and Southampton High and then Franklin State College thirty miles to the east. They had returned like salmon to their place of birth to marry, reproduce, grow old, and educate subsequent generations. They knew the territory, knew the ropes, knew the populace and its intricate weavings of love and war. They knew why a child from the Via family shouldn't be seated next to a child from the Spradlin family. They knew not to sing happy birthday to any of the McCaffrey kids because they were Jehovah's Witnesses and not to ask much about the absences of certain fathers at parent conferences because they were in prison over in Mecklenburg. They knew which mothers baked the best cakes and cookies for the Spring Fling, and knew which mothers not to ask because their offerings were often embedded with dog hairs or mealy bugs.

Kate did not know these things instinctively. She tried to absorb what she could, she listened in on teachers' lounge banter, she tried her own brand of humor out on her fellows when the chance arose, but found herself always at the periphery, always not quite in the inner educational circle, never invited to the small gatherings on Fridays at one of the restaurants in Emporia, gatherings that were heralded by little computer-printed announcements and stuck into certain mailboxes on Thursday afternoon, gatherings that were referred to as "BMW Meetings." Bitch, moan, and whine. They sounded like fun. There wasn't much going on at the McDolen home recently, what with Donnie gone off to school and Donald finding myriad reasons not to spend much time at home.

Most often, however, Kate didn't have the time to ponder her lack of complete acceptance at Pippins Elementary. She was too tangled up with the day-to-day of teaching. Mothering had been hard; teaching was no easier. She tried to follow student IEPs to the letter. She tried to focus on the weekly fourth grade team meetings in which the team leader, Patty Ryder, constantly wasted time by telling boring stories about her on-the-side career of raising purebred miniature poodles. She spent untold hours hunting down science equipment that never was in the storeroom and grading homework papers that were more often than not a waste of pencil lead.

But other times, being on the outskirts hurt. Other times, it just seemed like the latest on the failure hit parade that was Kate's recent life.

Deidra, however, would talk to anybody.

"You've heard, every agonizing detail," said Kate.

"I've heard all right. I just thought your take on it might be . . . interesting."

"It was an accident. I tripped on my heels. They caught in the carpet."

"You don't have carpet."

"I tripped on a crack in the tile floor."

"Yep. Tripped with your fist balled up and swinging. I can see that right now."

Kate felt her toes begin to dance inside her shoes. "Don't you have students somewhere?"

"They're in music. Got another twenty minutes."

"I really don't care to talk about it."

Deidra sat next to Kate. She placed her elbows on the table and put her folded hands beneath her chin. "It's not like you'll be fired or anything."

"No?" said Kate. "This could become a mother of a legal battle. Did you teach Willie Harrold?"

Deidra nodded. "I did at that."

"He peed on the floor," Kate said. "Peed, Deidra. Stood there and just let it go."

"Pee washes up, you know."

Kate groaned.

"Okay, so he peed?"

"And I punched him. He sliced his face on a desk edge and bled like a stuck pig. Let's add some blood to the equation, and see how it adds up."

"Call the Southampton County Education Association rep yet? That's what they're there for. You are a member."

"I'm a member. But I haven't called. I'm not sure how to explain it. It's bad, it's really bad."

"There're worse things in life."

Kate rubbed her eye. "Possibly. But you know the bottom line of this whole thing? I don't want to explain it. I shouldn't have to explain it. This was Willie Harrold, Deidra. Saying his name should be enough."

"You could quit." Deidra perked up. "Turn in your

resignation. You don't need this do-do, pardon my French. If I were you, I'd quit in a heartbeat. It's not like you . . ." She stopped herself and then got up to get a pack of Van-O-Lunch cookies from the machine by the Pepsis.

"Not like I what?" asked Kate.

"Kate." Deidra sat and dumped out two of the little rock-hard cookies. "You never seemed to really enjoy this place very much, is all I'm saying. You work so hard and yet you seem so miserable. You could be doing anything else. Having teas for the socially elite of the county. Golfing in Emporia. Raising horses or poodles and showing them in New York. Painting, quilting, learning to stain antiques. Getting all prettied up for your lawyer husband when he comes home. He's a great-looking man, hon. Why you think this is the place to spend free time is beyond me."

"I got a teaching degree because I wanted to make a difference."

"What did you do before you were a teacher? You did something with your time."

"I have a son, don't forget. And I did some charity work. Giving cans of food to the food bank, giving clothes to the Salvation Army, that kind of thing. I like to make a difference, Deidra."

"Is teaching the only way to make a difference? You have to ask yourself if it really is the path for you."

Kate took a sip. The soda was as bitter as dandelion juice.

"Your husband's family has been in Southampton County forever," said Deidra. "Hell, some of my great-greats were slaves to his great-greats."

"Sorry."

Deidra shrugged. "I'm not looking for that. What I'm saying is that the McDolens owned most of this county one hundred fifty years ago. They've sold off a good amount, but still, in the minds of the locals, they are the lords of the land. You married into that. You married into money, honey. Hell, if I were you, I'd be doing something else."

Kate took another drink, and held it in her mouth until it warmed. She put her can down. "I'm not a quitter."

Deidra chuckled. "Quitting is in the eye of the beholder. Choose your battles. I wouldn't choose to go down in a brawl with the Harrolds if I had other options."

"I care about kids."

"I didn't say you didn't."

"But kids cuss constantly, Deidre, and they aren't just randomly cussing, they cuss *us*. They don't do homework. They won't do class work. They sit there in their own little worlds, with God knows what brewing inside those heads. Sure, there are a few who listen, who do what I ask, but it's few and far between. Nine-year-old girls dressed like twenty-year-olds on the make. Eight-year-old boys already spouting racist rhetoric."

"Yes," said Deidra. "Whatever. I'd quit if I were you."

"It wouldn't matter if I did. They can still stick me for assault."

I ought to quit. I ought to get the hell out of Dodge. She's right. I don't need this job.

Deidra seemed to consider this. Then, "Call your

husband yet? If anyone can find pull to get out of something like this, you can."

"No."

"Damn, girl, get on that phone now while you can. He'll get it fixed. Not many of us here in this poor little county have someone in the family who has the power to clean up messes for us. Hey, your kids leaving lunch in a couple minutes? No problem. I'll watch them for you. I'll take them back to your classroom if your call runs over. Go on, now."

"I . . ." Kate said. Why not? She thought. Call him. Let him do something for her for once in his life. Then, "Sure, yes, thanks." It was a worthless effort, but at least it would get her out of the conversation with Deidra and give her a few extra minutes.

In the office, Miriam was back at her desk, typing something into her computer with a tidy little clickety-clack of her polished nails. Mr. Byron's office door was shut. On the bench near the teacher mailboxes, second-grader Mistie Henderson, dressed in a thin gown with a cardigan sweater, squirmed and played with her fingers. Kate knew this child. She'd heard Mistie's teacher discussing this girl before school in the lounge. Mistie stuck crayons up her vagina. Mistie rubbed herself against tables and chairs and had been discovered several times in the girls' bathroom, benignly watching her face in the mirror as she squeezed her own neck with her hands. Twice, she had grabbed the crotch of Vernon Via, the school's physical education teacher. Joe Angelone, the guidance counselor, had promised to schedule a conference with Mistie's parents, but so far, hadn't quite gotten around to it.

"Why is Mistie in here?" Kate whispered to Miriam.

Miriam kept typing, but her lips pursed. "Wearing a nightgown. Got no panties on. Joe found a sweater and some clear underwear in lost and found. Called her parents. Her mother said she'd bring out a dress. It's been twenty minutes. No mother. I wouldn't be surprised if she doesn't show. She never does. I'll send her back to class in a few minutes."

"Oh."

There were only two phones available to teachers. One was on Miriam's desk and the other was in the guidance counselor's office. Kate didn't want to talk in front of Miriam, so she knocked on Joe Angelone's door. He called her in. He was a man in his mid-thirties, with thinning brown hair and wire-rimmed glasses. He was seated at his cluttered desk, examining a brightly painted wooden mask, turning it over in his hands and sighing.

"Our new artist-in-residence," he said, holding up the mask. "Isn't she wonderful? Her family is from Kenya, and we have her for a whole month. All grades except fourth and fifth, sorry. She's going to teach mask design. We'll have the best display at the Southampton Schools Art Fair."

"I need to make a call."

Joe rubbed his thumb on the mask's blue nose. "I found her. She's from Norfolk. Has work in galleries all over the United States, I understand. I'd pat my own back if I could twist my arm that far." He chuckled and his eyes winked behind the lenses. "I've always been able to get the best artists to come to Pippins Elementary. I beat out the middle schools and high schools every year. I bet they wish they had my connections."

"I bet. I need the phone."

"Well, please make it short. I've got a lot of work to do." Joe pushed back from his desk and stood. He went out into the office, carrying the mask with him. He stood within earshot, still admiring the mask with such awe that it looked as if he thought he was holding God in his hands.

Kate turned her back to the door, lifted the receiver, and for a moment considered actually calling Donald. Maybe Deidra was right. Maybe he would help her.

A brief fantasy played in her mind. Donald, leaving his office in Emporia and driving all the way to school to take her in his arms, give her a hug, and tell her it would be all right. Donald, pouring her coffee in the teachers' lounge and listening with a sympathetic ear, then telling her he understood and he would do everything he could because she was his life partner, his love.

Keeping her finger on the cradle's button, she punched in her home number, pretended to let it ring, and put the receiver back down.

Kate went back to the lounge. Deidra was still there, grading science workbooks.

"Call?"

"Mmm. He wasn't in his office. Left a message." Kate sat, rolled the base of her Pepsi can around on the table.

"Doesn't he have a pager?"

"No," said Kate.

"Cell phone, then, surely?"

"Yeah, but he never remembers to turn it on." She grinned suddenly and broadly. It hurt her cheeks to smile this hard. "Don't worry about me. I'll figure out what to do. It's probably not as big a deal as I'm making it."

Deidra looked back at the workbook. Her voice

cooled. She knew she was being brushed off. "Call SCEA. They have strategies. Maybe something will fit in your case."

"You bet."

When Deidra left the lounge, Kate opened the window and poured the rest of her Pepsi out onto the ground. It sizzled, fizzled, and went flat in the grass. A well-bundled mother, crossing the parking lot to her car, turned at the sound of the opening window and squinted through the winter sunlight. Her perfectly round shades made her look like Little Orphan Annie.

With Donald's income and the mortgageless house on the hill, what was the point of continuing to teach? True, the Harrolds could and probably still would pursue legal avenues to hold her feet to the fire and make her pay for the attack on their sweet little child. But if she quit, she could spend the daylight hours hiding out in her sunroom, reading Anne Tyler, drinking Pepsi, and gazing at the collection of Patricia Spilman watercolors over the fireplace.

"Indeed," Kate said to the Little Orphan Annie mother, who was now in her car, turning over the engine. The car coughed, sputtered black exhaust, then coasted away, out to the main road. "What's the point of staying, indeed? My illusion of doing something worthwhile has yet again been blown to the sky. Kate has failed once more. Big, fat, whooping surprise."

She went across the hall to the restroom. As she pushed open the door to go in, she glanced back toward the office, past Miriam who continued to pound delicately at the computer keys, to the little girl Mistie on the bench in her nightgown and borrowed cardigan sweater.

Alone, trembling slightly but seeming unaware of her discomfort. Her eyes flicking back and forth from the door to the ceiling to the floor to her hands. Her feet, wiggling in the cheap little shoes. She reminded Kate of a puppy she'd encountered once when she was in college, a puppy she'd watched shiver in the rain behind an apartment complex, no doghouse, no shelter, a chain so heavy it could hardly move, a collar so tight it was embedded in the flesh. But so accustomed to neglect that it didn't even whine.

By the time Kate had to return to the cafeteria to gather the masses and take them back to class for math, a strange little seed of thought had found its way into Kate's mind. A painful seed, taunting, insistent, frightening. A course of action, a course of deliverance, void of the SCEA and Donald and Mr. Byron and Willie Harrold's parents.

Do it.

Don't be ridiculous.

It's not ridiculous. Do it. What the hell have you got to lose?

The students—sans Willie, for Willie was gone home with his daddy to plot the course of Mrs. McDolen's impending doom—were surprisingly somber and quiet as Kate wrote the first of the division problems on the board.

Of course it's ridiculous. You've never had such an absurd idea in your life.

Maybe. Maybe not.

As the rest of the afternoon stumbled along, the seed sent out its probing web of rhizomes, irrevocably linking her to what she was going to do when the last bell of the day rang. Her heart lurched; her arm hairs stood at attention.

Do it. If you lived in Nazi Germany and had a chance to rescue one life, you would do it. You could be that hero. You will be that hero.

She forced herself to focus on the math problems, but beneath it all she'd never been so excited in her entire life.

Chapter Seven

"Mam," said Tony.

The woman on the sofa made a snuffling sound, then turned over, her face to the back, a filthy throw pillow clutched to her chest. She was dressed in sweatpants and a T-shirt. Her hair, gray and long, was pulled back into a limp ponytail. She stunk like she was having her period.

"Mam!"

The woman said, "What you want? Can't you see I'm trying to sleep?"

"Darlene's out back playing in the sinkhole."

"So?"

"So you told her not to. You told her to keep her nitty head inside so the neighbors wouldn't think she was skipping out school again."

"She ain't hurting nothing. Mine yer own business."

"No problem," said Tony. She went back into the kitchen and pulled a beer from the refrigerator. She

56

took a long swig, then looked out the grease-iced kitchen window at her ten-year-old sister in the sink-hole. Darlene was digging with a tree branch. Going to China or something. Little puffs of frosty ground arched up and out of the hole every so often. Maybe she'd fall in and nobody would be able to get her out and the Chinamen would put her in prison and torture her and make her build fireworks for Americans. Tony smiled around the beer can.

Tony's home was the yellow house on Rainbow Lane. A developer had bought a chunk of farmland off Donald McDolen and had put up a row of ten box houses. One was white, one pink. Others were blue, yellow, green, lavender, peach, aqua, gray, and teal. Each house had started out with chain-link fencing, a small storage shed, and a deck off the kitchen in the back. Now, the houses had taken on the personalities of the owners, much like dogs begin to look like their masters. Mrs. Sanford in the white house had maintained the fence and deck and had put in rosebushes and a gray stone patio. The Campbell family in the teal house didn't have a fence or deck anymore. Their teenagers had torn it down. The lavender house belonged to the Kesslers, whose daughter did beauty pageants all over the state. And the peach house was now a crack house, with its ratty shades always drawn and a steady flow of customers coming and going in cars with smudged license plates and windows smoked over. People in the neighborhood tried to keep pets, but as soon as Tony could get her hands on them, they would be sliced and diced and thrown out in the woods. Nobody knew she did it; everybody blamed the crack house customers.

There were two bedrooms in Tony's house. One was her mother's and Darlene's, although Lorilynn Petinske seemed to prefer the sofa in the living room. The other bedroom belonged to Tony and the nine-year-old disabled twins, Judy and Jody. Judy and Jody were disabled because they couldn't behave in school, and so for the past year, Lorilynn Petinske had gotten monthly checks for the girls to stay home. Tony didn't know where Judy and Jody were now, probably over at the pink house. The bedroom had a double bed where Judy and Jody slept and a cot where Tony slept. There was only enough walking room to sidle between the bed and the cot to get to the closet or the dresser. The visible floor space was littered with dirty underwear and crumpled school papers.

"Angela," called Tony's mom.

Tony didn't answer. She refused to answer to that name. Her mother knew it.

"Angela!"

Tony stepped across the tops of the cot and the bed, then dropped down to the floor in front of the closet. She wrangled back the warped sliding door. She had to have something that would make her unrecognizable at the Exxon. The thrill was to do it and to have everyone wonder and tremble, not to be caught. There were several old Kmart cardboard storage crates in the closet that had accordioned with age and the weight of accumulated clothes and junk. These boxes held stuff that Tony's mother considered valuable. Tony had been through them many times, had removed and sold a tarnished pocket watch, some costume jewelry, and an old black silk parasol that had belonged to Tony's great-grandmother. She'd taken the Swiss army knife and stashed it in her dresser drawer beneath her jeans. She'd smashed and then burned the small collection of porno movies and *Playgirl* magazines she'd discovered at the bottom of the box, a collection that had clearly belonged to her mother.

Most of the stuff, however, was just clothes. Tony's first school dress. Judy's and Jody's matching knit baby bonnets. A cotton apron Darlene had tried to hand-stitch when she'd been in Brownies for half a year. Other assorted outgrown clothes that for some reason, Mam had felt were worth hanging on to.

One box was crammed with clothes that had belonged to Tony's grandfather. Her mother's father. Trousers, a pair of cracked and musty shoes, two flattened hats, a couple starched, faded shirts, a moth-chewed gray knit vest. They smelled of silverfish and thirty-year-old sweat. Mam, who wasn't real crazy about Granddad, hadn't thrown them out because she said it was an insult to the dead to do that.

Tony pulled out Granddad's box and tossed it onto the double bed. Granddad had not been a large man, unlike Buddy's gramps who had a gut like a wheelbarrow and a beanbag butt. She put on the beige slacks and drew them up tightly with the old vinyl belt. She added a long-sleeved checkered shirt, the vest, and the black shoes. Her feet swam in the shoes, so she found three pairs of socks in the dresser and put them on and tied up the black laces. The socks kept the shoes from slipping. She studied herself in the full mirror on the back of the bathroom door, and then pulled one of the flattened hats down over her eyes. She found the knife in the drawer beneath her jeans and stuck it in the side of her shoe, working the handle up under the leg of the trousers. She tore a strip of cloth off one of the blouses Darlene had left on the floor and used it to tie the handle in place, snug, against her ankle.

She found her mother's sunglasses on top of the fridge. She put them on. They were cheap and the bridge cut her nose.

"Angela, goddman it!" called her mother from the living room.

Tony tried to see herself in the window glass over the sink. From what she could tell, she looked a little like herself, a lot like her father. That was good. Her father, Burton, had been a real man. He'd left when Tony was six but that was okay because he didn't really want to, Mam had made him go. She had found a new boyfriend and told Burton to get out, she never wanted to see him again. Tony understood why he didn't try to stay. Burton had been a real man and a real man could never have put up with the shit on the sofa in the living room.

Tony dumped her mother's black vinyl purse out on the kitchen table and collected up the three tubes of Shop-Rite lipstick. These went into the shirt breast pocket. War paint for the Hot Heads.

"Angela, you're in there, I hear you!"

Tony shoved a kitchen chair over to the stove and climbed up to get the shoe box from the back of the tiny cabinet over the stove. The box was covered with chew marks and inside were little black mouse turds. Also inside were Burton's revolver and a small paper bag of bullets. Burton had lost the revolver in the divorce along with the sofa and his television. Tony had tried the weapon out several times in the woods behind the houses of Rainbow Lane, drilling holes in trees and downing groundhogs and starlings. It had a good feel to it, the wooden veneer on the handle slick and easy to grip. She put the revolver in a pocket of the slacks and patted it. It felt like a hard-on.

As she was pulling the small paper bag of bullets out of the cabinet, her fingers lost hold and the bag fell and bounced on the stove, and the folded top popped open. The three bullets in the bag rolled out, skipped over the lip of the stove, and disappeared into the black maw of the crack between the stove and the solid sink counter.

"Fuck!" swore Tony. She grabbed at the air as if she might actually draw the bullets back out of their hiding place, but came up empty.

"Tony!" Mam at last relented, her voice dissolving, changing from demanding bitch to whiny child. "I need a beer, honey. Please?"

Tony tried to rock the stove to move it backward, but it was too heavy. She yanked the long-handled barbecue fork from the utensil drawer, got on her knees, and scraped the narrow space with the prongs. Nothing came out.

"Goddamn it!" Tony kicked the stove, tried to rock it again. It didn't budge. She slammed both fists against the white enamel surface of the stove, and kicked it with her granddad's shoe.

"Tony, honey? You out there in the kitchen? Please bring me a beer. My throat's so dry I can hardly breathe."

Tony shoved the kitchen chair back into place and took another beer from the fridge. She popped the tab, then found the can of Bug-Be-Gone spray in the cabinet under the sink. She spritzed down the hole in the can, not too much, just enough to make Mam sick, then swirled it around and wiped the top with the wet dish-rag.

You're a fucking bug, Mam, a lazy ass mosquito, sucking everybody dry.

Tony took the can to Mam, who thanked her meekly, then left by the back door, stomping in Granddad's shoes across the warping redwood deck and down the steps. Darlene glanced up from the sinkhole, stuck out her tongue, and kept on digging. Tony walked down the brown graveled drive to the road with the empty revolver in her pocket. It was already after three-thirty. Leroy and Buddy wouldn't be long.

As a sharp winter wind blew up around her legs, Tony wished she'd brought her heavy coat. But she wasn't going to go back into the house with that stinking new nigger. She wouldn't step foot inside that dump again until she'd done what she had to do.

She licked beer and salty sweat from her upper lip, jammed her hands into her trouser pockets, leaned against the yellow house's sagging chain-link fence, and counted, counted, counted, until the Chevelle showed up.

Chapter Eight

The teacher was going to take her on a ride. Mistie didn't know this woman, but she'd seen her on the school playground sometimes. The teacher wore bright lipstick and had pointy eyebrows and smelled good like the soaps and hand lotion Mama had tried to sell from that pretty catalog long time ago. The teacher had told Mistie what her name was but Mistie had forgotten it.

Now, the two of them were in the teacher's classroom. Mistie sat in a desk the teacher had pushed behind her own desk. The desk wasn't like the second grade desks. This one was bigger and there were papers and books inside. "Sit there," the teacher had said. "Don't get up, okay? Can you sit still for just a few minutes? I need to get a few things before we go."

And so Mistie sat at the desk, looking alternately at the dots on the ceiling and the rows of little clay houses in the classroom windowsills. Some of the clay houses were painted, some of them were plain. Some were cracked. Some looked like they hadn't been finished.

The teacher said, "We're studying ancient man. Those are supposed to be early native homes from the Southwest." The teacher was talking really fast and her voice went up and down like a cat when you squeezed its stomach. "Some of the boys and girls did a very nice job, don't you think?"

Mistie didn't. She looked at the ceiling again. Her stomach growled. She poked at it, making it growl some more.

The teacher had a big cloth tote bag with writing on it and a picture of an apple. The teacher crammed in books and a few things out of her desk drawer. "My senior annual," she said, holding up a blue and orange book. "I can't leave this behind. I graduated from the University of Virginia nearly twenty years ago, can you believe that? Yes, I'm just an old Wahoo. Wa-hoo-wa. Well."

Mistie put her hand between her legs and rubbed hard until it got hot.

"Mistie, don't do that," said the teacher. "Please. Okay? Mistie? Here, here's a Tootsie Pop I took from one of my students. It's raspberry I think. Hard to tell raspberry from cherry in this light. Here."

Mistie took the sucker, unwrapped it, and stuck it in her mouth.

"Okay, all right," said the teacher. Her lips kept moving around as if she were tasting something sour. "A little food and some drinks, then the bank, and we'll be off. It's going to be a nice trip, Mistie. Oh, it's going to be fantastic. You'll see. We're both going to have a wonderful, wonderful time." She paused, placed her hands on her hips, and glanced about. There was sweat over her eyebrows. It looked like the sweat on Mistie's daddy's eyebrows at night. "Now, what else do I need, is this it? What time is it? I think we can go now. Most everyone is out of here by now. Mistie, button your coat, please. It's very cold outside."

Mistie stood and buttoned her coat. She took the sucker out, looked at it, then bit the red orb off and spit it into the air. "Mama had a baby and its head popped off," she said.

"Oh?" said the teacher. "Fine, then. Let's go." She reached for Mistie's hand but Mistie didn't want to hold her hand. But when the teacher said, "Come, follow me. And be just like Elmer Fudd, okay? Ever see him on cartoons? Be vewry, vewry quiet."

Mistie was.

Chapter Nine

It was a few minutes before four o'clock. As Kate had hoped, most of the faculty and staff had left for the afternoon, hitting the road for home and putting as much space between themselves and the school as possible in the least amount of time. Mr. Byron's pickup was still in his reserved spot nearest the flagpole, but then, he was required to stay until five. The gray Toyota next to it belonged to Miriam Calhoun. She would stay as late as Mr. Byron stayed. There were three other cars belonging to teachers. Some liked to stay after and grade papers. Kate used to be like that.

Kate's own white Volvo was one of the three, sitting on the far side of the parking lot because she'd arrived too late that morning to get one of the choice spots near the front. Kate led Mistie out the back of the school, by the exterior of the gym, the cafeteria, and the row of metal trash bins. There Kate paused and peeked around the wall. She almost laughed aloud, but bit it back. *Good for you, Nancy Drew!* she thought.

When Kate was quite certain there was no one on the long front walk or milling about the lot, she hustled the girl to the Volvo, pulled open the back door, and helped Mistie inside. "Just sit way down," she whispered in as calm a voice as she could manage. "Sit way down for just a little while. You can get up in a little while, promise. Okay? Mistie?"

Mistie didn't seem to understand. Kate demonstrated, slumping low and peeking back at Mistie around the side of her seat. "Like this. Pretend you're real short."

Mistie didn't argue, and she scooted down far enough that Kate was pretty sure the top of her head couldn't be seen from anyone outside the car.

"Good," said Kate. "Thanks." She patted the girl on the head. The hair was sticky. On the floor of the back was a quilt Kate kept in the car in case she'd ever been caught in a blizzard, which she hadn't. Kate carefully draped the quilt over the girl. "We're being secret, okay?"

Mistie didn't say anything, but didn't seem to mind the quilt.

The strange little girl had been amazingly easy to collect when the bell had rung. She'd been lagging behind most of the other students, her coat on backward. Kate had motioned Mistie aside when the bus duty teacher wasn't looking and said, "Won't you come to my class for a few minutes?" The dulled eyes didn't seem to register the request, but the body did. Mistie Henderson had obediently followed Kate down the hall and had sat in the desk while Kate had snatched up a few important items. Her grade book and some teacher manuals so it would appear she'd planned on returning the next day. Some change from her desk drawer for quick drinks later tonight. Her university yearbook, *Corks and Curls*, which she'd brought to school last week when notice of the upcoming twentieth reunion had arrived in the mail. During brief moments of free time, Kate had been flipping through the pages trying to reassociate herself with names and faces for the get-together in May. Donald thought they should certainly go, and she wanted to. One of the few things they'd agreed on in a long time. She'd gazed at Donald's photo. Handsome, sandy blond, member of the pep band and intramural track team. God, but he'd been a charmer, a romancer, a fast-spending, generous man who had seemed to Kate to be all the right things. Kate had gazed at her own picture. A slight grin, hair straight and past her shoulders, her chin tipped up just a bit at the encouragement of the photographer. And then the photos of Alice and Bill, smiling placidly from a sea of other smiling fourth-year faces.

As her students had started to work on some problems she'd posted on the overhead projector, she'd pulled out the yearbook and looked at Alice again, then Bill. They knew what she was thinking, and they thought it was a splendid idea. Their approval had made the plan more than possible to Kate; it had seemed probable.

Canada was about a sixteen-hour drive straight north except through Pennsylvania, which, for some reason, didn't have any major highways leading north through the middle of the state; she'd have to go west and up. With enough high-octane soft drinks and coffee, Kate knew she could make it without sleep, though it would be one hell of a haul. The Volvo's tank was full of gas, so any stop would be way north of here, somewhere in never-never land where no one knew her or the Volvo or the child.

The Christmas cards Kate got yearly from Alice and Bill Harrison had the return address of Bracebridge Run, outside Toronto. Chatty cards all, speaking of a lovely home full of adopted, handicapped children and adopted, stray pets. Alice and Bill had been friends of Kate's during their university years. They had been social activists then and were social activists still. Wild children they were themselves, hippie holdovers at the University of Virginia when hippies had been out of fashion for nearly ten years. They'd worn long hair and flowing blouses and sandals and handmade clay beads around their necks and on their wrists. They'd been laughed at by the preps, the jocks, and the intellectuals who'd dominated the campus, but it all rolled off their backs like water on duck feathers.

Alice had gotten Kate interested and involved in some wonderful causes back in those days. Kate, a shy and quiet girl from a comfortably wealthy and politically disinterested family in Norfolk, had become involved in Amnesty International, the University Environmental League, and Friends of Animals—a very new movement at the time. She'd called home about her adventures; her sixteen-year-old sister Amy had said, "Just don't get arrested," and her father, chief accountant at Elizabeth River Financial, had told her, "Honey, we love you. But do remember why you're there, and that has more to do with books and papers than anything else."

One particularly thrilling event was the clandestine

rescue of a mangy, malnourished dog from the back-yard of a skanky tar-paper shack outside town, then spiriting the pup to Kate's dorm room to keep until Alice could arrange a proper home. Kate had kept the dog in her room for three days. The dog had smelled terribly. It had been covered with fleas and mites. One eye was puss-rimmed. But she'd minded the dog until one of the local Friends of Animals had agreed to take him in.

Kate had felt light-headed and giddy over the rescue. She'd done something incredibly worthwhile. She'd saved a life, just like the underground railroad did for the slaves before the American Civil War and the underground hiding places did for the Jews during World War II. Amy would have been amazed at the way her older sister had broken the law to help a defenseless being.

The Friends of Animals held an event nearly every weekend, protesting outside a slaughterhouse in Albemarle County—"Meat? Would you eat your brother, your sister?"—printing up and distributing brochures denouncing animal testing in the university's biology department. Kate savored every daring moment. She felt a new life in her blood. She had discovered the thrill of doing.

And then she'd met Donald McDolen.

She had fallen in love. She'd skipped Friends meetings, had even returned to eating chicken and burgers on her dates with Donald. The Friends denounced Kate as a backsliding hypocrite, but Bill and Alice remained her friends.

Three days after graduation, Kate and Donald had married. And so it went. And so it had become.

Kate knew Alice and Bill would help her. They would be proud of Kate, reclaiming her power to do right. They would hail the delivering angel.

In the driver's seat, Kate pulled the rearview around to look at herself. She forced her eyes to relax. She knew how to perform. She'd kept her cool during conferences with parents when their bodies reeked and their breaths came out like fumes from rotten blast furnaces. She knew how to play the role. No one would suspect the woman at the wheel to be a kidnapper.

"Mistie, you okay back there? We're going on a little ride and soon you can sit up front with me. All right?"

Mistie sneezed, and Kate took that as a sign she hadn't suffocated to death under the quilt. She hoped Mistie had covered her nose but doubted it. Kate turned on the radio to FM-92.1. Oldies. "Build Me Up, Buttercup."

The rearview was snapped back into position, the key was turned in the ignition. The car drove out of the lot, sliding down to the road as easily as a kid on a water park inner tube. Kate steered right onto Route 58 into the setting sun. She squinted and lowered the visor. She noticed her fingers were locked around the steering wheel like a drowning woman's fingers locked about a stick. She forced them to loosen. Her knuckles were cold.

Chapter Ten

"What the hell you waiting for?" called Darlene from the sinkhole. Tony glanced back from the roadside and gave her sister the finger, though her hand was cold and she couldn't really feel the finger wiggle.

"Ha! Where you goin' dressed like that? You look like a clown! It ain't Halloween, dumb ass!"

Tony turned away. She used to enjoy getting into it with her sister, loved to argue with her and then punch her into the ground, but anymore it was a waste of time. Darlene was stupid as a slug. Let her get into it with the twins. Darlene was so brainless, while an argument with Judy or Jody could keep her busy for hours.

But Tony had much more important matters at hand.

Overhead, the sky had grown heavy and thick with impending sleet. The air smelled wet and metallic. Tony shook her head, and she could feel the blood ringing just behind her ears. Her arms and legs ached with the cold, but the revolver in her pocket was hot. The knife in her shoe was rubbing a blister, and it felt good.

Tony wasn't exactly sure of the time because she didn't wear a watch, though she had one. It was in her bedroom in the dresser with other stupid trash her family had given her for Christmases. It was a girly watch, a nasty, pink-banded watch with some sort of orange swirly pearly shit on the face. She'd been given it four years ago when she was eleven. Back when she still let them call her Angela. Back before she knew the truth of the matter, the reality of the world. Fuck it all, she'd been ignorant.

A low-riding station wagon drove by, slowed, and turned into the driveway of the peach house. Tony stared at it, imagining it bursting into flames and blowing bits of crack heads all over the yard. The car door popped open after a few seconds. A thin, slow-moving man and a thin, slow-moving woman climbed out. They weren't old—maybe early twenties—but walked as if they'd been hit with a bat for the last forty years. They whacked on the splintery door, stood shifting foot to foot in the cold. The woman was wearing a thin sweater and no coat. The door at last opened and the heads went inside.

Tony bet there was a baby somewhere, left behind at the camper where these two walking trash bags lived. Maybe two babies. Little crack-addicted babies who cried all the time. Tony's skin crawled at the thought.

A pickup truck passed on the road, and a red El Camino. This car honked and Tony gave it the finger. She didn't know them and didn't want to.

"Who's honkin'?" called Darlene.

Tony ignored her.

Just as it began to sleet, the sex-stinking Chevelle

pulled up. Through the foggy glass, Tony could hear Whitey say, "Wait 'til you see what we got, Tony!"

The rear car door popped open. Tony climbed in. Darlene, up in the sinkhole, watched with snide disinterest as her older sister, dressed like a clown, pulled away.

Chapter Eleven

"You all right, Mistie?" Kate asked again, then reached one hand back over the seat to make sure the girl was there and hadn't somehow seeped out through the door crack or melted into the cushion. The lump was there, squirming mildly under the quilt. Kate nodded to herself and said, "Okay, then."

The windshield was struck with a plop of sleet. Then another.

"Oh, now, isn't this just dandy?"

Another. She turned on the windshield wipers. On the radio, the Monkees' "Auntie Grizelda" was playing. A little too frantic for the moment at hand. She switched it off.

The McDolen house was five and three-tenths miles from the school, off Route 58 and up a long, spruce and dogwood-lined drive, which Kate's husband had paved when they'd moved in nearly four years ago. The house was an elegant brick structure, built by Donald's grandfather Owen Bennett McDolen in the late 1920s. While everyone else in the area was scrambling to survive the Great Depression, raising extra vegetables in their gardens to can and pickle and stash in pantries in case things never got any better, God forbid, moving in with other family members in the county when upkeep on their small farms was too much to maintain financially, making corn moonshine to sell on the side for cash money when cash money had become a thing of legend, and fearing fear itself, the McDolen family went on with life as usual in their brown brick manor house. They hired black jazz musicians—all the daring rage at the time for rich white folks—to travel from Richmond to Pippins to entertain at birthdays and other festive gatherings. They kept a firm hand and close eye on the bottom thirty to make sure the trainhopping hobos didn't set up their tents on McDolen property. They bided their time on money they'd hidden in wall safes and under mattresses and in foreign banks.

Kate had never been especially crazy about the house. The bricks were in eternal need of replacement as Owen had thought old bricks brought from England would be the most elegant when construction had begun. Elegant perhaps, but hardly hearty. They'd been made with too much sand, and time had eroded many of them, requiring constant replacements. The interior echoed regardless of the area carpets, and there was no air-conditioning in the summer because it would "ruin the ambiance." The basement smelled of old biscuits and there was a spooky subterranean maid's room, full of old books and magazines that continuously bred nests of field mice and centipedes.

Kate and Donald had lived several places since they'd married—Charlottesville, Richmond, and Alexandria—as Donald completed his education as a lawyer, passed the bar, and joined a firm for a short stint with big-city legalities. But Donald had always wanted to come back to the place of his childhood. He was the only son. It fell to him, he said, to keep the home place in the family. And so to Pippins they had moved, hi-ho-the-dairy-oh, to Pippins they had moved. Donnie, who had been born in Richmond, was a little apprehensive at the idea of living in the country; he made Kate promise he wouldn't have to wear overalls and clodhopper boots to school.

Donald set up his practice in the nearby town of Emporia and was kept as busy as he cared to be. His clients were most often businesses who wanted to buy up farmland on which to build their respective industries. Donald McDolen knew the land and the people and the mind-sets. Because of Donald McDolen, there was a new Wal-Mart between Emporia and Pippins, and a Little Debbie factory north of Capron.

Kate's car circled up the driveway past the spruce and dogwoods, skidded slightly on a patch of sleet, and stopped at the front porch. She turned off the engine, then pulled the blanket off Mistie. The girl's face was slick with snot. Kate's stomach clenched but then she shook the disgust away.

"I have to stop here for just a minute," she said. "A quick pop in, pop out, then we're gone. Do you have to use the bathroom? This is the best place if you have to go. We have a nice bathroom. Lilac soap. Mmmm."

The little girl rubbed her nose.

"Do you, Mistie?"

77

The little girl shook her head.

"Are you sure?"

The girl stared at Kate. Kate blew a puff of air through her teeth.

"Well, you should come with me in the house, though, I guess," said Kate. "Do you want to come in with me for a minute? It's warm inside the house."

Mistie shook her head.

Kate clenched her fists, then let them out. Sure, fine. It would be easier to go in and out without having to coax the girl along the way. Easier, faster. And no possible Mistie fingerprints left at the scene.

Good Lord, what am I doing? The right thing, that's what. Shut up about the fingerprints.

"All right then, but stay in the car. We're going on a really fun trip. A long trip but a really fun one. But if you get out of the car you can't go. You'll miss the fun. Understand?"

Mistie scratched her nose and rolled her lips in between her teeth. Kate took that for a yes. "I'll be right back."

The heavy oak front door opened at the turn of Kate's key. She swung into the foyer, dripping sleet, and dropped the key ring into her coat pocket. It was then she realized how hot her hands were. She had been driving without gloves, but her hands were pulsing with a quick and urgent heat. She rubbed them vigorously.

"What am I doing?" She chuckled aloud. She touched her lips. They, too, were hot. "What the hell indeed."

On the foyer table beneath the bevel-edged mirror was a lush, scarlet poinsettia with a white satin bow, purchased last Saturday at the Let's Be Buds Flower Shop in Emporia. Just above the plant on the wall in a tidy cluster were three small watercolors of dogwoods blooming by a Blue Ridge stream. Kate collected watercolors done by Virginia artists. It was one of the few things she did, it seemed, of which Donald still approved.

Kate pulled a pad of *Mc*-embossed notepaper from the drawer in the small table. She removed a black pen and uncapped it.

Donald, she wrote. *Don't wait dinner for me. I had a bit of a problem at school today. No biggie. I'm off for a drive. Won't be long. Don't wait up.*

She drew heavy lines through the note, then stuffed it into her coat pocket.

On the next sheet she wrote, *Donald, I had a bit of a blowout at school. Some minor student trouble. Nothing for you to worry about. But I'm going to take a couple personal days off and go see some sights. I should have waited for you to get home before I left but when was the last time you cared about where I was or what I was doing, anyway?*

She tore up the note.

Kate peered out the door-side window. The little girl was still in place. The quilt in the backseat was moving slightly.

Donald would be home around seven. His work took him away from the house early and sent him home late. Six days a week. Sundays he golfed with friends if the weather was nice and played poker with the friends if not. Her son, Donald Junior, was still in Philadelphia at Ricketts-Heyden School until Christmas break next Thursday. He was a boarder. He needed Ricketts-

Heyden. And Kate and Donald needed him to be at Ricketts-Hayden.

Back at the hall table, Kate scribbled, *Donald, I'll be gone awhile. You know I've needed time alone since the incident in July. Now's the time. Food's in fridge. Kate.*

That was the answer. That would keep Donald from looking for her for a while. He'd leave it alone. He hated any mention of the incident in July.

Lord, help me.

She propped the note against the poinsettia, aware that she was leaving her own fingerprints on the pen and foyer table, and then letting out a short burst of laughter at that preposterous concern. She backed up to the front door to make sure the note was clearly visible to someone coming home. It was.

She crossed her arms then, and looked around herself. The mahogany, carpeted stairway. The arched entrance to the grand living room. The wide hallway lined with various paintings and portraits. The crystal chandelier over the foyer, the one Donnie had thought magical as a child; he would chase the colorful sparks it threw to the floor as if chasing leprechauns. The smell of cigar smoke and last night's baked ham and the furniture wax Belinda used throughout the house when she came to clean twice a week.

She remembered.

Donnie sitting on the third step from the bottom, arms crossed, staring out the front door as Donald loaded the trunk and cases into the Volvo's trunk. At fifteen, he was already his father's height, six-one.

There was a hint of stubble around his chin, but Kate had not said a thing. It was not the day for that.

"I would be happy to come along," Kate offered. She was standing by the foyer table, watching between her son on the steps and the front door. "You know I would."

"Don't come," said Donnie simply. He did not look at her. His green eyes were shadowed in thick, black brows; his father's brows. His mouth was set in the line Donald often wore when determined, or distracted, or angry.

"All right." Kate took a long breath. "As soon as you have it, call with your mailing address. I'll send you lots of mail. When I was a girl and went to camp, my father sent mail nearly every day. Mail really helped me get over my homesickness."

"I'm not going to camp."

"I know."

"I won't be homesick."

"No, you probably won't, you're pretty old for that, I suppose. But if you are, this is something my father told me when I went to camp. Find someone who feels worse than you and do something nice for him. Then you'll feel better. Okay?"

"I'm not going to camp."

Kate sighed. Donnie wasn't going to camp. He was leaving for boarding school in Philadelphia. He would enroll as a sophomore. He would be allowed to come home to visit on only three occasions—Thanksgiving, Christmas, Easter. No weekend excursions allowed. Ricketts-Heyden was not for rich little boys preparing for Harvard or Yale. It was a school for rich little boys who'd been trouble to their families or in trouble with the law. Rich little boys like Donald Peter McDolen, Jr., who had discovered girls in eighth grade, drugs in ninth.

At first Donnie had used the old McDolen stable for his trysts; Kate had found cast-off condoms, empty cartons of Kools, several stubby roaches, and Donnie's lost Algebra book when she'd ventured into the stable to collect some old leather harnesses she'd planned on using to decorate the family room in an old-country motif.

She confronted Donald with the evidence when he'd come home that evening. But Donald had only laughed and said at least Donnie was practicing safe sex. And the drugs? Kate had asked. What about the drugs? Donald said it was only pot, for heaven's sake, they'd tried pot in college.

"This is different. He's our son, not us," said Kate.

Donnie continued his antics in spite of Kate's warnings and threats. He moved his activities from the stable to the house. Not only did he entertain high school girls in his bedroom, but he began his own pot distribution center. When Donnie was arrested during the second semester of ninth grade with some stash on him at the school, Donald the father was forced to become Donald the lawyer. A private plea was arranged; if Donnie was given the help he needed, the charges would be dropped. Donnie would remain an upstanding citizen and the McDolen name would be untarnished.

Donald found Ricketts-Heyden with a couple phone calls. Donnie was enrolled within the week, to begin in June.

"I'll miss you," Kate said to her son on the stairs.

"You'll get over it."

Donald opened the front door and called, "Hurry up, the car's running. Kiss you mother good-bye and let's get going."

Donnie had not kissed his mother good-bye. He hadn't even looked at her as he'd stood from the stairs, shoved his hands into the pockets of his jeans, and walked out the door.

The weeks that followed were quicksand; thick, sluggish days where she couldn't even read a magazine article or a page from a novel without losing concentration. Her gaze slid off the print. She found herself zoning in and out of focus when Donald talked to her. She didn't answer the phone, believing it to be her mother wanting to know what happened, or the school calling to say Donnie had killed himself or somebody else.

At her yearly pap exam in Emporia in August she began to cry and couldn't stop. The nurse practitioner asked Kate if she was depressed. *Depressed?* she'd thought. *I don't know, I'm just so tired.*

So unbelievably tired.

She was sent home with a prescription for Zoloft. She was too distracted to take it. Donald said, "You have to do something, Kate. I can't stand to see you hanging around all day in your pajamas. When did you last shower?"

"When did you last care?" she'd asked him over dinner. "You don't see me often enough to know what the hell I do or don't do."

The following day, Stuart Gordonson called to tell her there was a forth grade opening starting in September at Pippins Elementary School and she would be the perfect candidate for the position.

Ah, but Donald had been quick and to the point.

She remembered.

With a new surge of conviction, Kate yanked open the front hall closet, grabbed a handful of spare scarves, a knit hat, and two of the seven assorted umbrellas, then raced out through the sleet to the waiting car.

Chapter Twelve

There was wet pattering on the back window. Mistie pulled the blanket away from one eye and looked at the glass. Thick streaks of ice were striking the window and sliding down like Daddy's tobacco juice on the side of the refrigerator when he missed the can. Only Daddy's tobacco juice wasn't clear like the ice, it was brown. But it slid the same, not in a straight line but zigzaggy, all the way down to the floor. Mistie had tried chewing tobacco one time. Her daddy said it'd be good for her since it was a vegetable and kids should like vegetables. She didn't like it and gagged, so he'd made her swallow it all down.

"That'll show you," he'd said.

Mistie's stomach growled and she pushed her knuckles into it until it stopped. She burped. She wondered where the teacher was taking her. Maybe to a carnival. Maybe to Wal-Mart. They had balloons at Wal-Mart, and ice cream. Princess Silverlace liked strawberry ice cream the best.

She put her finger into her nose and pulled out a dry crust. She stared at it, then said, "Mama had a baby and its head popped off." She flicked the crust out from beneath the blanket and onto the floor. She wished the teacher would hurry up.

And then the front door popped open and she could smell the teacher's hand lotion before she heard the teacher's seat squeak beneath her.

Chapter Thirteen

"Show us what you got first before we show you what we got," said Whitey. The Hot Heads were in their usual seating places, except for DeeWee, who got left home. DeeWee would forget what they'd said in the car earlier, but DeeWee might not forget what they did if he was there to see it happen. And DeeWee, even Leroy would admit, couldn't keep his mouth shut if God Himself came down to earth with a staple gun.

Leroy was dressed in a hooded sweatshirt and a bulky black coat Tony had never seen. He had a pair of scratched plastic sunglasses that looked like they came from a Burger King kid's meal. Buddy had on a hunter cap with the flaps pulled down and a fake fur coat that looked like a mauled grizzly. He'd sprayed his face with what smelled like the gold glitter spray his sister used to make her normally dirty blond hair look like something special. He hadn't sprayed the eyes, though, and they popped white through the red.

Whitey wore a wrinkled trench coat, a scarf around his neck, and a pair of fuzzy mittens. Little Joe had lost all traces of cowboy. He wore a windbreaker, some Farm Bureau rubber boots, and a pair of eyeglasses that had the lenses punched out.

The Chevelle lurched forward as Buddy's foot slipped on the gas, then off, then back on again. He cussed at the sleet. The Chevelle's passenger windshield wiper was broken, and it spasmed like a dying grasshopper against the glass. The icy downpour picked up in intensity. Tony ran her hand under her nose to catch a leak.

"Show us what you got," repeated Whitey.

"You show me first," Tony said.

"Bull, us first," said Leroy from the front. "You had this idea. This is your goddamn circus. You show us what you got."

"Got this knife," said Tony, lifting her foot for all to see.

"Knife?"

"Swiss army," said Tony. "For backup." She pulled out the revolver and waved it around. Little Joe ducked when the mouth of the barrel came to rest at his forehead.

"Cut it out!" he wailed.

"Mrs. Martin gonna cry just like you," mused Tony. She grinned and put the revolver back into her pocket. Her head was itching again, beneath Granddad's flattened hat. Again, she let it itch. It felt, well, fucking glorious.

"That's a big-ass gun, Tony," said Leroy.

"I'm the only one big enough to handle it," she said. And then to Whitey, "Now show me."

Whitey produced a pistol. Tony didn't know one pistol brand from another but it was small. At least it wasn't rusted or bent up.

"Got ammo for this?" said Tony.

"Asshole," said Whitey.

"Didn't do anything to your face," said Tony with a nod of her head. "People know them burned-up cheeks anywhere."

"Yeah? Watch." Whitey tugged the scarf up to show how it fit over his nose and chin. Muffled through the knit he said, "Just shut your fat lips."

"What else we got?" Tony asked. "Little Joe, you said your great-uncle had a gun at home."

"He was home," said Little Joe. "Couldn't get it."

Tony slapped his glasses off. Little Joe put them back on. "Then what about you, Buddy? Leroy?"

There was silence a moment, and Leroy said, "Still got the BB gun, okay? So what? Nobody else found guns. You want to make a big deal, fine, I'll throw you out the car. With what you and Whitey got nobody at the Exxon'll know what's bullets and what's BBs."

Tony shook her head, but she knew Leroy was probably right. Mrs. Martin was a squirrely, middle-aged woman who chain-smoked and flirted with the guy who drove the gasoline truck. She would just shit her pants and cower behind the counter where she belonged. She would remember enough details for the police and news reporters who would show up in the wake of the crime so the Hot Heads would find their way into the papers and maybe onto the evening news. "Oh," Tony could hear her squeal. "It was a hideous gang! Five of them, teenagers, tough talking, armed! They didn't take no for an answer, and they took every penny from the cash register." *No fucking pennies*, Tony thought. In her mind Mrs. Martin backed up, started again. "They took every dollar from the cash register and shot up the place! Just look at this place! I'm lucky to have come out with my life. And they're out there, they'll do it again, you can bet on it! You have to warn everybody! What did they look like? Well, I can't say exactly, they had disguises. Sorry. They just seemed too smart to let anyone know who they were!" Maybe she would get fired, that would be good. But remembering the dread on her face and the smell of pee in her panties was the best reward of all.

Bitch'd never call Tony a little girl again.

Buddy took a sharp left onto the main drag, Route 58, that led to the Exxon. Everyone in the car flopped to the left. Everybody cussed. Buddy muttered, "Oops."

The car passed another cotton field, a cattle field, and then the huge house on the hill that belonged to the McDolen family. Then a couple farmhouses and pockets of trees. The trees were coated with sleet, and the small ones at roadside shimmered like glass in the passing wake of the Chevelle.

"What are we gonna do after we rob the Exxon?" asked Little Joe.

"Celebrate," said Tony. "Take what we got and celebrate in the old barn. Listen to the car radio for when they start talking about it on the news. Plan our next robbery. We can't just do one and let it go. We'll have a reputation we gotta keep. We're grown up now."

"Fuck," said Little Joe. His voice sounded higher now, like something was squeezing his diaphragm and pushing the air up through his windpipe before he was ready for it.

The Exxon was ahead on the left side of the road, sitting at the back of a graveled, grassy parking lot and a single aisle of pumps. The tall glass sign for the price of gas had been blown out in a wind last week, throwing shards everywhere, and was still not repaired. The metal plates with the numbers were propped up against the door to the station bathroom along with some stray two-by-fours. Didn't matter; nobody ever used the Exxon bathroom because it had snakes in it. A lone car sat in the gravel, not near the pumps but near the plate-glass window of the building. Tony didn't know the car; it was a white, new-looking four-door. She didn't care who it was, though. One more witness to enjoy the fun with Mrs. Martin.

Buddy made a deep sound in his throat, then coughed. Tony figured he was scared shitless. Her own heart had picked up a painful rhythm that she knew as pure joy. Any chill she'd felt for not having a coat was long gone. "Go around the Dumpsters," she said, leaning forward to Buddy's ear. "You're the getaway. You stay in the car."

Buddy let out a long breath. "Yeah?"

"Yeah."

He tried to look pissed. It didn't work. "Well, okay, then, shit, just leave me behind."

Leroy was already pulling the hood of his sweatshirt up around his head and drawing the strings in until very little of his face showed. He slammed an old knit hat down over top of the hood.

The Chevelle was steered across the gravel lot and around the back of the Dumpsters. There were four of them, painted sky blue and stenciled in bold white,

PROPERTY OF BROWN'S WASTE MANAGEMENT. NO
TRESPASSING. There was a tight squeeze between the
Dumpsters and the scrub pines behind them—there
was a high-pitched scraping sound as several low
branches took a bite out of the Chevelle's coat—but
Buddy eased into position so it would take a simple heel
to the gas pedal to get the car across the edge of the
gravel and back onto the road.

The engine died, but Buddy left the key in.

"Okay, now wait," said Tony. She retrieved the tubes
of lipstick. Wrenching down the rearview so she could
see, she covered her face in a sunburst pattern of
stripes, starting at her nose and moving outward. "Now
you," she said to Whitey. She kneeled over Little Joe
and covered Whitey's scarred face with big polka dots.
Whitey held still and silent, as if he were being blessed.
It made Tony feel strange, the way they suddenly
trusted her so close to them. Little Joe was given zig-
zags with the second tube. He worked around to see
himself in the rearview.

"Cool," he said. "I like that!"

Tony almost smiled.

Leroy turned without being asked. Tony gave him
random swirls. Tony, Leroy, Little Joe, Buddy, and
Whitey looked at each other. For the most fleeting moment Tony thought she should say something to them,
like they were the best, or they were cool, but it was
too fucking personal. She pulled the revolver out of her
trousers and handed it to Whitey.

"Trade you," she said.

"What? Why?" Whitey looked excited to have the
chance to hold the larger gun, but there was an edge
of suspicion to his voice.

Tony shrugged. "So I'm trying to be nice for once. Want it or not, Scarface?"

Whitey gave Tony his pistol in exchange for the revolver. He slid it into the pocket of his trench coat. "Cool," he said. Then, "But I don't wanna shoot nobody."

"Don't have to," said Tony. "We'll scare 'em to death, just looking at us. Scare the living shit out of 'em."

"Yeah, okay."

Tony let her finger slide along the trigger for a moment; then she turned away and cracked it open. This baby was loaded. The itching beneath her hat flared hot and insistent. She grinned. "Take whatever you want, but don't shoot 'less you have to," she said. "Save the ammo. But fuck the place up good."

Leroy snatched up the BB gun from the floor and slid it inside his sweatshirt. The tip of the barrel poked out at the bottom.

Three doors popped open. The gang stepped out into the cold December sleet.

Chapter Fourteen

Mistie Henderson groaned suddenly, a throaty sound that was more canine than human.

Kate's foot lifted instinctively from the accelerator. "Oh, God," Kate whispered. Then, "Mistie, you okay?"

The groan again, followed by a soft whimper.

Kate had just steered from her driveway back onto Route 58, heading west. Fifteen miles ahead was the intersection for Interstate 95 at Emporia. The sleet was harder now and the tarmac was already covered with a slushy sheen. She would have to drive more slowly than she'd imagined to get to Interstate 95 heading north. With some luck the sleet would not follow her very far. It was her turn for luck. It was way past her turn for luck.

"Mistie?" repeated Kate. The car slowed. *God, don't let anything be wrong with this child. Not now, not when I'm getting ready to help her, please just this once help me, just this once, okay? Hear me?* "Mistie, do I need to pull over? Are you sick? You aren't sick, are you?"

Mistie was silent. Kate licked her top lip. "Are you sick?"

Silence.

"Are you hurt?"

Nothing.

"Scared?"

Silence. The car stopped in the middle of the sleet-covered road. Kate could see no one coming in either direction. The windshield wipers plopped back and forth.

"Hungry? Are you hungry, Mistie?"

This brought on a small whimper and a whine.

A painful rush of air escaped Kate's lips. Hungry was okay. Hungry wasn't too bad at all. Thank God for hunger! "So are you hungry, Mistie? Is that it?"

The little whine.

Kate turned on the defrost. Her anxiety was steaming up the windshield. She pressed on the gas; the car began to move. "I'm sorry I didn't think about that before I left the house. Why didn't I think about that? I could have packed a little lunch for the road." Of course the child would be hungry. Children get hungry. Donnie was always hungry; as soon as they'd get into the car to go somewhere he was either hungry or had to go to the bathroom. Why hadn't she grabbed something from the kitchen before leaving? Kate fumbled in her purse, came up with an unopened bag of peanuts she'd thrown in there a couple weeks ago. She reached back and said, "Here, Mistie, can you stay down and catch this? Mmm, peanuts!" She tossed it over the back of the seat.

There was a slow scrabbling noise in the back. Kate turned the wipers on full blast and they battled the sleet and each other. Small clear spots were forming where the defrost was cutting the fog.

Then a groan, clearly unhappy.

"You don't like peanuts?"

There was a swishing sound as if the girl was shaking her head beneath the blanket.

Please, just eat the peanuts. It's not like you're used to expensive treats, come on. "They're good, fresh. I just got them a couple days ago in a multipack."

Silence. Then a soft, gurgling whine.

"Can you wait just a bit, then, for something else? We've not even gotten through Pippins, and we have a long way to go, Mistie."

The swishing sound again. Kate's throat clicking with frustration. Her forehead was speared with a painful lance. She steered the car over next to a sagging wire fence by a dead cotton field.

"Mistie," she said. She looked back over the seat and tossed the blanket aside. The child was sitting low and staring at the floor. Her pale hair was a fragile, tangled spiderweb. Kate was struck with a memory of Donnie on a family vacation when he was seven. He'd been a pale-haired child as well, and handsome, taking after Donald's side of the family. Donnie had had so much potential. He had blown it. She had blown it. All God's children had blown that one.

But that was another story entirely.

"Mistie," said Kate. "Tell you what. There's an Exxon up the road. We can stop for just a minute and I'll get some snacks for the road. I'm okay on gas, but I think we need to fill up our own stomach tanks! Ha! We can get a real supper later, once we've been on the road awhile. What do you think?"

Mistie didn't think much, or wasn't sharing. Kate dropped the blanket back over the child and gingerly petted the head beneath the fabric. The girl's mute obeisance made Kate's stomach clench.

The sleet hesitated as if catching its breath, then came down again, harder, colder. Kate flicked on the heater and was greeted with a blast of hot air on her legs between her shoes and the hem of her coat.

The Exxon was only a few miles up the road. Pippins' only gas station, hangout to Pippins' odds and ends. She never felt totally comfortable in the place and had only stopped by for a few dollars of gas when she'd found herself low. She preferred to drive to Emporia to the Wilco. But the Exxon was the closet place that sold anything that even slightly resembled food. If Mistie had something to eat . . . What the hell did she like to eat? Kate would either have to get her to talk or just buy a shitload of whatever and hope there would be stuff she liked in the load. Then they'd be good for a least a good long stretch on the road. They had to get out of Virginia ASAP. Once in Maryland, or hopefully Pennsylvania, they could find a couple small roads to take and then they could do a potty break.

If I get enough food at the Exxon, Kate thought, *we can just eat in the car the whole way to Canada. Yeah, that's it. A little bit of everything, then we're gone.* A shiver cut through her body—excitement, terror, pure joy. She took a long breath and let it out.

There were no cars at the Exxon. Well, not counting the banged-up woodie wagon that the woman who worked there drove, on the right side of the building near a thicket of weeds. Perfect. Some song Kate didn't know faded on the station, and then the oldie "For What It's Worth" began. Kate began to sing along, not exactly sure of all of the words but sure of the emotion and the demands behind them.

Freedom!

She steered into the graveled lot of the gas station, and stopped by the door. The closer the better. Quick in, quick out. Her stomach fluttered, then twisted. A child saved. A soul saved. A spirit saved. She felt young again, she felt brimming with hope and possibilities. She wrapped one of the scarves around her neck—a red plaid one Amy had given her back in college—and said, "Mistie, just stay under that quilt a little longer, and then you can come out. I'm getting a few yummy things. Right back."

A VDOT snow scraper hummed past on the icy road. Kate ducked down beside her car. She'd never ducked behind anything in her life, well, except when she was a first-year student at the University of Virginia and she'd gone as a member of the pep band to make their mark with spray-paint cans on Beta Bridge. A Charlottesville police car had approached, slowly, and everyone else had merely put paint cans behind their backs and stood looking innocent while Kate had leapt down the bank, twisting her ankle, and waited, panting, behind a prickly patch of thistles until the police car had gone on. Donald wasn't in the pep band that year. She'd had a crush on a sax player named Ben but that had never gone anywhere.

The scraper gone by, she trotted to the door, stepping full center into one slushy puddle up to her ankle. She shook her foot and pushed through the Exxon door.

There was a soft tingle over the doorsill. A fly, stupid and dazed from being born at the wrong place and the wrong time, dove at her ear from the light fixture above and she slapped it away.

A deep breath. A quick perusal of the four narrow, food- and knickknack-packed aisles. Paddy-whack, give the dog a bone. A shopping basket would have been good but she knew she could hold a lot. She was a teacher, for heaven's sake, used to juggling more papers, books, and odds and ends than a carnival performer. No, she *had* been a teacher. Now she was a felon. Or a soon-to-be felon. But a good felon. A felon with a cause. James Dean would have applauded. So would Alice and Bill.

Down at the other side of the convenience store, the woman who worked there picked at her teeth as she slumped over an open spread of some newsprinty tabloid.

Kate scooped up a loaf of bread, two cans of deviled ham, a roll of paper towels, a pack of plastic utensils, and an overpriced can opener. She skirted quickly around to the side where the glass-fronted drink coolers sat. She selected two Big-Gulp Pepsis and then a small bottle of apple juice. When she got to the front, she pawed up a handful of Toostie Rolls, Nestle's Crunch Bars, and Twix. She dropped everything onto the counter in front of the woman with the tabloid. One Pepsi fell over, rolled off the counter, and Kate retrieved it with a chuckle. "Just like children," she muttered. "Always taking off when they think you aren't looking."

"Mmm," said the woman. Her Exxon-logo-blazened name tag identified her as Mary Jane. She pushed the tabloid aside and picked up her price scanner. "Picnic in December, is it?"

"Oh, well," said Kate. "I guess."

One plucked eyebrow went up and the shelf bangs bobbed with a single nod. The scanner beeped on the utensils, paper towels, Pepsis. She had to run it over the bread twice, then the deviled ham, juice, can opener, candy.

The door to the convenience store opened.

Kate's shoulders stiffened. *Hurry up hurry up hurry up!* She pulled a ten-dollar bill from her purse and held it over the counter, ready for Mary Jane's total. She turned and looked at her wet foot, turned it over and back, keeping her face less than visible to whoever else had come in.

"Damn kids," mumbled Mary Jane. She blew air through her teeth, causing her shelf bangs to tremble. "I know they been shopliftin' this place. Hey!" she called. "You brats oughta be in school!"

One voice, clearly male, clearly young, called back, "We're home schoolers!"

Another voice, also male but a bit lower, said, "School been out a hour, lady. Goddamn idiot."

"Don't you cuss in my store! And what's that on your faces?"

Snickers. Kate glanced over her shoulder and saw what seemed to be a carnival entourage or a group of gypsies. Of course there hadn't been gypsies in the Pippins area since last March when a three-county alert had gone out that transient thieves disguised as roof layers and blacktop spreaders were roaming about, sidetracking old ladies in their yards with promises of extra low priced fix-it jobs while others in their groups sneaked into the backs of the houses and stole the old ladies blind. Of course, these kids looked like old-fashioned gypsies who rode in horse wagons and told fortunes, not the ones who drove extended cab trucks with buckets of tar and carried faux business cards. These kids had painted their faces and were dressed in a way most teenagers would have preferred death to being seen.

Sweat sprang out on Kate's neck and she shrugged against it.

"Okay?" asked Mary Jane. "You look a bit woozy." She popped open a plastic bag with a flick of her wrist and put the Pepsis in first.

Kate nodded. "I'm fine." She could feel the kids . . . how many were there? Three? Twenty? . . . walking around the store, poking through the shelved items. *Pay and get out. Keep your head low. They won't see you, they won't notice you. You're the last thing they care about. These are just kids. They aren't interested in adults, they're interested in themselves. They're having some sort of initiation and couldn't care less about anyone else.*

The rest of the items were plopped into the bag, bread on top, amazingly enough since Mary Jane had her attention focused on the kids in the store.

"How much?" Kate prodded.

"Ah," said Mary Jane. She glanced at the register. "Eleven twenty-three."

Damn. Kate fumbled for her wallet, her fingers digging past checkbook, lipstick, compact, address book. She found it, flicked open the change compartment and clawed out five quarters. She slammed them down beside the ten. "Keep the change."

"Oh, well, two cents, thanks," said Mary Jane. She tried to smile to show Kate she was joking. Kate tried to smile back. She snatched the bag and worked her way down the center aisle, watching her dry shoe and wet shoe. One of the kids stepped around the end of the aisle in front of the door, and Kate glanced up so she wouldn't run into him.

Her.

It was a girl, she thought, someone who looked slightly familiar through the red stripes. This girl was about fifteen, thin, hard looking, with short black hair and old, baggy men's clothing. No coat. Her eyes were shaded beneath a flattened fedora, but even in the shadow they seemed to boil with hate.

And then Kate was past the girl and out the door. The bell overhead tingled.

It was still sleeting, steady and thick. Kate lost her balance on the slick stoop. The bag jerked and ripped, and the Pepsis and deviled ham dropped to the icy gravel.

Chapter Fifteen

Tony fingered the pistol in her pocket, the only piece in the store with bullets, and tasted expectation on her tongue. The scrawny woman who had been buying stuff had just gone outside, the door slapping shut behind her, but that didn't matter, Tony didn't need anybody more than Mrs. Martin in the store. This show was for her, even if she'd never know it.

Yesterday afternoon when Tony had come in the Exxon with her mother to buy beer, Mrs. Martin had been talking on the phone and scratching herself a strip of "Holiday Hurrah!" lottery tickets on the counter. She scratched and rubbed, flicking off the little crumbs of waxy ticket residue as she went. Tony's mom had said Tony could pick out a snack. Tony selected a box of Little Debbie oatmeal cakes. She and her mom went to the counter, then Mam said, "Forgot the Frosted Flakes."

Mam had gone back for the cereal. Tony had stood

at the counter, one hand on the box of oatmeal cakes, one hand on top of the case of beer.

Mrs. Martin had put the receiver down on the counter and she'd jerked the beer out from under Tony, snarling, "You ain't old enough to buy beer, little girl!"

Little girl. There were few words that stung Tony like those two words.

It was all she could do to clench her fists and not drive one down the old woman's throat.

Little girl!

She grabbed the beer back, letting one set of fingers scrape the woman's forearm as she did. The woman squawked and reached for Tony, who skipped back several feet, still clutching the beer.

"Don't you never grab nothing from me, little girl!" said Mrs. Martin.

Oh, just you wait, bitch, Tony thought.

Then Mam had come up with the Frosted Flakes and a carton of vanilla ice cream and the confrontation ended. Mrs. Martin had hung up the phone and rung up Mam's total.

This is for you, Mrs. Martin, Tony thought as she put her hands on her hips and strode forward through the center of the store. Little Joe and Leroy were making their way up the left aisle, joking with each other and playing with packages of disposable diapers and cans of motor oil on the shelves, clearly unsure of what they were supposed to do but ready for the word. Whitey, who thought he had a fine-ass revolver at his beck and call, was moving up the right aisle, humming something that sounded a little like "Turkey in the Straw." Knowing Whitey, it could be the kids' song or maybe it was some gospel thing. Whitey's mom sang in a gos-

104

pel group, and Whitey, when he wasn't spending evenings with the Hot Heads, sometimes went along as a backup tenor.

Mrs. Martin stood at the front counter, her elbows planted against the counter, her eyebrows pinched in a prissy, pencil-drawn line. She was wearing a festive Santa pin with a string to pull to light up the eyes.

"You kids got money?" Her voice was higher than usual, betraying genuine, growing concern. "Got no money you best get your behinds out of here 'cause I ain't puttin' up with no nonsense!"

"Mmm, doughnut sticks," said Whitey from the other side of the store. There was the sound of crinkley plastic wrap being collected and thrust into pockets.

"Answer me!" demanded Mrs. Martin. "I'll call the police, don't think I won't! You're nothing but trouble, you've shoplifted from here before and I won't take it anymore!"

Tony reached the counter. The woman's eyes widened and she stepped back, but not far enough. Tony smiled, shrugged, then grabbed the front of Mrs. Martin's sweater and yanked her forward over the counter. She pressed the mouth of the pistol to the Exxon name tag. "Hey, little girl," she laughed loudly. "How's it hangin'? Oh, it ain't, is it? You're just a fucking pussy!"

The Hot Heads took the laughter as the sign. Leroy pulled out his BB gun and waved it in the air, then began slugging jars from the shelves with the butt end. The jars burst on the tile floor. "This is a stickup! This is a stickup!" crowed Little Joe, and he did a karate-like kick and sent a small display of videos-to-rent flying like geese out of a pond. Whitey ripped open a box of trash bags and yanked one out. He began shoveling goods into it—paper cups, bottles of aspirin, boxes of Hostess cupcakes, cans of Spam, some die-cast John Deere toy tractors.

Mrs. Martin stared, gog-eyed, her pointy eyebrows twitching. Tony licked her lips and tasted the fear steaming off the woman. "Open the cash register," Tony said. "I want everything in there."

"I can't," whispered Mrs. Martin. "It locks at four o'clock and . . ."

Tony leaned over and bit the woman's cheek. The skin split and Tony could taste the hot blood. The woman wailed and tried to jerk free. "You're lying," Tony said through the flesh. "You are, aren't you?"

Mrs. Martin sputtered, "Yes." Tony opened her mouth and straightened, the gun never wavering from Mary Jane's little tag of identification. Keeping the rest of her body perfectly still, the woman reached over with one hand and punched keys; the register opened with a *ding*.

"Get it all out, and no pennies," said Tony. "Put it in a bag. Don't get a freakin' bag with holes. Half the bags here got holes in 'em."

Mrs. Martin was trembling so badly she had to dip her hand in three times before she could come up with the bills. Her cheek was a welt of teeth marks and blood. It seemed to be swelling nicely. Tony waited, smiling. Behind her, the racket was increasing. Whitey was indeed singing "Turkey in the Straw" at the top of his lungs. Little Joe had moved from cowboy yodels to Indian whoops. Glass shattered. There was a loud thumping, and Tony guessed it to be the ATM machine being whacked off the wall.

"I know you, don't I," said Mrs. Martin as she

crammed money into the bag. Her voice was tremulous but determined. "I seen your face here before."

"No," said Tony. "You think you do, but you don't have a clue. I'm just a mirage. Just your own ignorance come back to bite you in the behind. Now give me the bag."

Mrs. Martin passed the bag over the counter. Tony called, "Somebody get up here and get this bag, I got a wrinkled old bag of my own that I can't let go quite yet!"

Little Joe bounced up to the counter. His lipstick war paint was already smudging, bleeding down his face in a pool of sweat. He snatched up the bag, tied the plastic handles tightly, and stuck it into his windbreaker. He zipped the jacket up to his chin. "Yeah!" he wailed. "Oh, yeah! Can't nobody touch us! Whoooo! Too hot to handle!"

Tony couldn't see Leroy pounding on the ATM machine; it was down behind the left counters. But she could hear him whacking and cussing, "Fucking box won't open!"

But what Tony *could* see was the most beautiful sight she'd ever witnessed. The store was in total destruction. Complete ruin, as if a bomb had hit dead center and blown out in all directions. Little bitch Martin got to see it all, got to see how worthless she was, how impotent, how weak, before a handful of Hot Heads. Tony aimed her gun at the ceiling and squeezed off two shots. The pistol kicked slightly in her hand. The fluorescent light exploded and showered shards upon them all. The job, christened with sparkling glass. She could see the news at eleven tonight, photos of the busted lights, the box-strewn floor. The headline of the *Em-*

poria News-Record tomorrow morning, BAND OF TEENAGED THUGS DESTROY STORE. WHO WERE THEY?

Mrs. Martin wailed; she looked at the phone on the counter by the lottery tickets and Tony said, "Oh, you wish."

"Yeee!" squealed Little Joe. "Whoooooo! Ya ya ya ya!" He leaped like a warrior all around the glass, grinding his shoes into it and flapping his arms. "We gonna celebrate! Yessir! We gonna celebrate! Praise the Lord!"

Tony couldn't help but laugh. A thick bubble forced its way up her throat and she let it out. It felt fantastic.

And then the door to the rear storeroom could be heard thumping open, and there was a call, "Hey, Mary Jane! Damn, but it's messy outside!" He was there then, standing in the storeroom doorway behind Mary Jane. The gasoline delivery man. He wore an oily brown jacket, a pair of brown gloves, and a matching brown hat. He stared, his eyes as bright and wide as new wheel covers. He swore something unintelligible, and before Tony could even think of how to handle two instead of one he was leaping forward, knocking Mrs. Martin away from Tony and Tony back from the counter.

"No!" Tony yelled as her feet went out from under her and she crashed to the floor on her shoulder. She heard and felt the joint pop at the same time, and her vision swirled in sparks of silver and white. The pistol skittered from her hand and slid beneath the rack of sunglasses at the end of the aisle. She rolled over and drove herself forward on her knees, grabbing for the gun. Her fingers came up short. *No fucker is going to stop me! No goddamn pussy-licking gas man is going to . . .*

The gasoline man roared and Tony glanced up. He was coming over the counter, arms wide, hat flying. Mrs. Martin screamed like a dog getting its tail cut off.

"Motherfucker, no!" Tony shouted, and as she crouched out of the way of the man's looming bulk there was a piercing blast from the middle of the store and the man lurched in midair, hit the floor on his toes, staggered, and fell backward on his ass. He clutched his chest and gurgled. His teeth snapped together loudly. In the center of his gasoline-delivering brown uniform jacket, a flower of wet red blossomed.

"What the hell!" Leroy and Little Joe were there by Tony now, staring at the dying gasoline man, and then back down the center aisle where Whitey stood, still holding the gun out with both hands and pointing it straight ahead. A tendril of smoke haloed the weapon.

Whitey pulled the scarf down from his mouth. A string of drool came with it. "I shot him."

"Damn!" said Leroy.

Mrs. Martin appeared over the counter, her painted fingernails scratching against the countertop. She looked at the gasoline man and then at Tony. "Oh, God, you little bitch, he's dying!"

Tony staggered to her feet. Her shoulder throbbed, hot and furious. "I didn't shoot him, whore!" *There were no bullets in that gun, the bullets all fell behind the stove! Whitey could not have shot that man!* "I didn't shoot him!"

In a flash, the rats deserted the sinking ship.

Leroy released the case of beer he had under his arm and darted for the door. Little Joe and Whitey followed.

Tony spun to run, but the gasoline man's hand shot out and grabbed her by the shoe. Tony bellowed and stomped the hand, kicked it, but the dying gasoline man held tight. *How can he hold tight, he's dying?* she thought.

Then, *Shoe's on too tight, too many goddamned socks!*

"Let go, motherfucker!"

On the other side of the counter, Mrs. Martin was fumbling with the telephone, her breaths coming in great Indian whoops that would have made DeeWee laugh.

"Let go!" Tony stomped the hand, then raised the revolver and aimed it at the man's wrist. "Now!"

He looked up at her with red-rimmed, maniacal eyes and tried to say something. Blood puddled out the corners of his mouth.

Tony pulled the trigger. The hand split and fell away, spraying her foot with hot crimson. It trembled, a fat and fleshy crab strumming the tile. Mrs. Martin screamed anew, dropped the receiver, then cried, "I'm callin'! I'm getting the police!"

Tony stomped the hand one last time and raced for the door, hurdling the wreckage and shoving the hot pistol into her granddad's trousers.

Chapter Sixteen

By the time she had captured all the runaway snacks, sans a Twix that had slid across the sleety lot into the twilight zone that was the weeds behind the gas price signs, Kate's knees were soaking wet and her head was hurting. The Pepsis had rolled under the Volvo along with the deviled ham. The bread, which had flopped out in another direction, had become an unintentional kneeling pad under Kate's weight. She'd clawed up all the things and tossed them through the passenger's front door. As she dropped into the driver's seat, a gasoline delivery truck had pulled into the parking lot. It drove around the side of the station.

Just get out of here now, things are okay, nobody will remember I was in the store, at least not until I'm out of the country. I'm forgettable. That's a good thing right now. Forgettable is good this time, Donald. Wouldn't you just be surprised?

"Mistie, I'm back," she said. She swiped her wet forehead with her sleeve, plucked the deviled ham from under the accelerator where it was hiding, and dropped it on the passenger-side floor with the other stuff. "Bag ripped, the silly!"

The expected silence. Kate looked over the back of her seat. Mistie had moved, but was still under the blanket. The girl had made a pooch along the hem and her nose was poking out just a hair. "Got lots of things you might like. I just bet you like Pepsi!"

The girl said nothing. Kate kicked off her shoes, aiming them at the passenger-side floor. Her toes would dry out, she didn't mind driving with stocking feet. *In fact,* she thought, *this may be the last time I wear panty hose at all. What would I need them for? Once I take Mistie to Alice and Bill's house, I just may drive west across Canada and get a job at a rock shop or craft shop. That would be fun, and I could wear comfortable clothes all the time.*

Her breath eased out, making a funny squeaking noise.

She turned on the engine. On the radio, the announcer said, ". . . With chances of wintry mix ninety percent through tonight and tomorrow. Clearing tomorrow afternoon with highs near thirty-five. And please, parents, do not call about school closings, as we haven't yet received any word from the county and will let you know as soon as we do." Kate turned the radio off. Too much sound right now.

A whine from the back.

Kate's hands clenched the steering wheel; adrenaline stung her arms. *Enough whining! God! Okay, get this taken care of now, get her settled, then nothing else will stop us, nothing else save a bathroom somewhere off the main road in Northern Virginia or even Mary-land, with luck.*

"I'll give you a Nestle's Crunch and some Pepsi," she said. Clearly that was satisfactory, for a small, snot-sticky hand came out from under the blanket. "Eat the candy bar but don't drink yet, until I tell you it's time to sit up. You might spill."

The fingers wrapped around the candy and drew in beneath the blanket. A sigh of seeming contentment. Kate looked through the windshield. Nobody else was on the road. They were smart; the weather was pathetic. *Thank you, God, for sleet.*

There was a loud, popping sound of thunder some-where nearby, somewhere outside the car. Kate flinched. Thunder? Impossible. Just a car backfiring somewhere behind the gas station, back past the weeds where there was a trailer park.

Kate eased the Volvo around the pumps to the edge of the driveway and looked both ways beyond the splays of trees clustered at the roadside.

A tractor was approaching the station from the east, an old-fashioned rusty blue with the close-set front wheels and exposed engine. It was heading in the same direction Kate wanted to drive. In tow was a long flat-bed with elephantine rolls of winter hay. She could pull out and pass him but he was going so slowly he might, at some future date when pressed by authorities, re-member that, yes, he saw that teacher's white Volvo leaving the Exxon and remember exactly *when* he saw that teacher's car leaving the Exxon—he knew it was, because he was traveling all of twenty miles an hour and could read the license plate as she sped past.

"Damn!" hissed Kate. She rolled the car back several

yards and steered over to the row of Dumpsters to wait. To Mistie, "That was 'Sam.' Did you hear me? What the Sam Hill is a farmer doing out in this sleet? I hope he doesn't catch cold!" Kate checked her watch as the tractor ambled past on the road. Give the man a full minute's head start and then she could drive out of the gas station. She could get on the road and past him without any unnecessary attention.

In the back was a soft sound of wrapping paper shredding. "Hang in there, Mistie, you having fun?" said Kate softly. "I'm having fun, are you? This really is great, an adventure for both of us . . ."

And then she heard shouts. She looked back to see three of the gypsy-dressed kids stumbling across the gravel toward the Dumpsters, arms flailing. Kate's heart stopped. She gripped the wheel. They know what I've done! They *know!*

God God God God!

Kate grabbed for the gearshift, hand shaking madly. She jammed the stick into reverse to pull back from the Dumpsters. *God God God!*

The kids ran around the Dumpsters and fell into a rusty car on the other side. Kate's dry mouth opened with a click. She held her foot on the brake, watching. *What?* The rusted car revved, bucked, and lurched forward from its hiding place and sped to the road. Black smoke trailed. The car nearly struck the tractor's flat-bed, swerved around it and scraped the back door on the corner, then vanished beyond the trees.

Kate looked back at the gas station, then back to the road. *What was that about?*

Mistie sneezed, another one clearly not covered with a hand or handkerchief. Kate would buy some upholstery cleaner in Ontario; give that backseat a good, solid once-over. "Well, that farmer won't think twice about a white car passing him now," she said. "I think those kids were giving Mrs. Martin a hard time in there, I'm afraid. I'd go back, but we have to get."

Kate took a Pepsi from the seat beside her and cranked off the top, hand still shaking. "I need a drink," she chuckled. She drew on the bottle several times, then sighed, recapped the bottle, and said, "That's it, nothing else is delaying us. Promise. You've been under that blasted blanket too long and it won't be long before . . ."

The passenger door was wrenched open. Kate flailed about to see a red-striped face with steel gray eyes shadowed beneath a flattened fedora. The mouth of a gun was inches from her face.

"Bitch!" said the striped face as the rest of the body slid in to the car. "Don't say a fucking word! Drive!"

Chapter Seventeen

The Nestle's Crunch tasted good. It was warm and mushy beneath Mistie's fingers and sweet on her tongue. There was quilt lint in the chocolate, but it didn't matter because the chocolate was good on her hands and on her tongue. She liked being under the blanket because she liked to hide. It was fun to hide. She liked to hide at home in the metal shed behind the trailer or in the big potato bin in the kitchen when it was empty of potatoes.

The teacher talked a lot. She had a voice that went up and down like those flutes the fourth graders tried to play at the assembly last week.

There was a drink on the floor, a plastic bottle with a white top. The teacher said not to drink it yet. Mistie didn't mind, she had chocolate to play with. She patted her tongue with the stick and sucked on it, then rubbed it on her palms. Warm, soft.

Then there was another voice up front. Mistie paused and listened. It was a girl. The girl got into the car, said the "fuck" word and then "Drive."

The teacher did.

Chapter Eighteen

The woman at the wheel stared at Tony until Tony cocked the trigger; then she eased the car to the edge of the lot and turned on her left blinker.

"Go right," said Tony.

"Right?" The woman said the word as if she'd never heard it before. But then she steered right without another word. Tony rolled her upper lip in between her teeth and bit until it hurt. Right. They'd turned right, driving on Route 58. So where was she going to go now? She went right only because the woman wanted to go left.

Where the hell do I go?

"Where am I going?" the woman asked without looking away from the road. It sounded as if there were a roach in her throat and she were trying to talk around it. "I saw your buddies leaving without you. They sure were in a hurry, weren't they? Where should I drop you off?"

"You aren't dropping me off anywhere."

The woman's jaw tightened, though her eyes twitched at the corners. She was going to try to be brave, in control. What a foolish, ridiculous female! "Then what . . . ," the woman began.

Tony slammed the gun into the woman's ear; her head snapped to the side and she grabbed her face, groaning in surprise. The car swerved madly on the ice.

"Drive!" yelled Tony.

The woman took the steering wheel with her left hand, holding her ear with her right.

"Now you know what 'right' is, don't you?" said Tony.

The woman gasped, heaved, and looked like a groundhog with its foot caught in a trap.

"Don't you?"

"Yes." Her voice was tiny.

On the radio, some oldies shit that Tony's mother sometimes listened to. Something about everybody smiling on their brother. Tony pounded the power switch with her fist. The song died in the air.

"Turn right on Route 35 before you get to Courtland."

The woman licked her lips. She flinched as if the jaw on the right side of her head had cracked. "Where are we going?" she managed.

"Don't ask," said Tony.

I have no idea, maybe to the ocean, let's go to the ocean and catch a boat to China, my little nitty sister is probably there already, she was digging in the sinkhole, we all can go to China and make fireworks!

The woman's jaw was working slightly; she was trying to think of what to say next. Tony rubbed her nose with her free hand and a smear of lipstick came away with it. She thought of the blood on the gasoline man's shirt, of the blood on his crucified hand.

They came up behind an empty flatbed truck bearing the obligatory orange triangle in the rear.

"Pass it," said Tony.

"All right," said the woman.

The car pulled around the truck. As they came even with the driver of the truck, Tony said, "Don't even move funny when he looks over here or I'll kill you in a heartbeat."

The woman's gaze flickered in Tony's direction, then back to the road. Tony lowered the gun to the woman's waist and noticed her own hand shaking. She took the gun in both hands to steady it. Her head itched, her neck itched, her stomach reeled against the waistband of Granddad's trousers. In the back of her throat, a stinging like needles.

They eased over in front of the truck. The woman looked up at the rearview as if she could blink the truck driver a warning, a plea.

The stinging in Tony's throat, flaming hot. Her stomach pitching madly. Sweat breaking out on her lip, her arms, the bridge of her nose. She took long breaths through her teeth.

"Drive faster," Tony said. She rolled down the window. The freezing air caught her hat and blew it into the backseat. She gulped icy breaths.

There were no bullets in that gun, and now we've got some asshole murdered.

"It's slick on the road," said the woman. "If I drive any faster we might slide off the road."

Tony counted her breaths. There were stars swimming just behind her eyeballs. *Shut up, bitch.*

"Could you please close the window? The windshield is fogging up."

Shut up, bitch!

It rushed forward, the smell of smoke, the taste of blood, the sight of the fat crabby hand blown apart, and Tony leaned over and heaved it out on a loaf of crushed Sunbeam bread on the passenger-side floor.

Chapter Nineteen

The moment the girl leaned over and vomited on the floor, Kate thought, *I can get the gun! I can knock it away and grab it!*

The girl held her stomach with her left hand and kept the gun pointed across her chest with her right.

Snatch it!

Kate saw herself shoving at the gun with the palm of her hand, and letting go of the steering wheel to take hold of it as it hovered for a second, pointing at the radio. She saw the gun in her own hand, turning around to aim at the girl, then forcing her out of the car.

Good-bye! Run, girl, run!

The jagged pain in her head made the world wobble; the smell of fresh vomit made her stomach turn and constrict.

God, help me!

Kate shoved at the gun. The girl sat up abruptly, face spattered in puke, and grabbed the handle with both hands, swinging it back around and shoving the barrel against Kate's cheekbone.

"Don't hit me again!" Kate cried. "Please!" Her molar, loosened from the first blow, creaked in the socket and flared hot in her head.

"Get the hell off this road, bitch!"

There were no roads on which to turn, just another stretch of pines. Kate looked at the girl and then the road, afraid to say the wrong thing, afraid of more pain. *No more pain, please!*

"There! Go through the trees!"

Kate steered to the graveled shoulder, then down a slight embankment and up again. She had read that if a kidnapper gets you in a car you are in serious trouble. If the kidnapper gets you into a private place, you are as good as dead. The guy on Oprah had said that. He knew the statistics. He had been a police officer. He'd seen dead women in the woods.

Kate's jaw chattered furiously. Her calves twitched.

"Get in there!"

Kate glanced at her door. If she popped the handle and rolled out she could run. The girl would have to get out her side and run around the car.

But she had the gun. She said she would kill her.

The guy on Oprah said if you run in a back-and-forth pattern you are less likely to be shot and killed, just maybe shot and wounded.

But the girl had the gun.

Kate's legs were so weak she could barely press the gas. She steered the Volvo through the rash of pine trees. Branches scraped the sides as if trying to open the doors themselves. The underside of the car thwapped over ruts and downed limbs. The world grew darker as the trees grew denser and taller.

Let her have the car, that's it, just give her the car!

But Mistie's in the backseat. What would she do to Mistie?

Oh, my God, this is wrong, this is not what is supposed to happen. I was doing the right thing for the first time in years and what are You doing to me, God?

A sharp, pointed branch drove itself into the front windshield, cracking it like a hammer. Kate stifled a cry. She yanked the wheel to the left and the branch gouged the passenger-side window with a banshee's wail.

"Stop here!" said the girl.

Kate let up on the gas. The car rolled a few more feet and then settled at a tilt in a soft patch of humus. A startled pair of cardinals took to the air in a blur of red. Kate touched her molar with her tongue. It wobbled. It tasted raw and bitter.

Slowly, Kate unlocked her fingers from around the steering wheel. She was a teacher, damn it all. This was a child to her right. A *child.* A little girl who was likely as scared as Kate was. This was not out of control, not yet. There was time now to set this right.

I'm a teacher. I can do this.

Kate took a breath, and turned to the girl. She said, "I know you are frightened. We both are. We've gotten into a situation that seems pretty terrible right now, but it's not too late to start over and set things straight."

The girl tipped her head and a strange smile spread across her crusted lips. Her eyes narrowed, but she said nothing.

Yes. She'll understand, thought Kate. *Keep talking.*

You're good at that. Thank God Mistie is obedient. The girl will never know she was there.

"I would be happy to drive you wherever you want to go," said Kate. "I have no reason to say anything about this little . . . fiasco . . . to anyone. I'm just glad we are both all right. We've both had a fright. People do silly things when they are scared. Women do. Young girls do. It happens."

The girl ran her free hand across her mouth, scratching off the drying puke. She wiped it from her fingers onto the dashboard.

"Did you say young girls?" she said.

"I suppose I should say young woman. You're not a young girl, are you?"

The girl put her foot up on the dashboard in the dry puke. Her shoe was an old man's leather shoe. She spit on it, and rubbed what looked like blood from the toe with the heel of her hand, then licked the hand.

"I'm a teacher," Kate pressed. "A teacher and a mother. I want you to know I hold no ill will toward you. I know children, teenagers. I know sometimes they do things they later wished they hadn't. Well, everyone does that, in fact. Things they wish they hadn't. Things they wish they could go back and do over. I don't hold grudges. Let's put this all behind us. Where can I drive you?"

"You're a teacher? Teach where?"

"Pippins Elementary."

The girl stared for a moment. Then she nodded, her head bobbing up and down on her neck like a felt-covered toy dog in the rear of a jacked-up automobile. The movement was chilling. She said, "Hey, teacher, show me your woolly."

125

Kate said, "Show you what?"

"You heard me."

"I don't know what you mean."

"You're a teacher at Pippins and you don't know kids' rhymes?"

"Kids' rhymes?"

"You know 'Little Bo Peep'?"

"Yes. Of course."

"You know 'Old McDonald'?"

"Yes."

"Say it. Say 'Old McDonald.' "

Kate swallowed dry air. "Well. Okay. 'Old McDonald had a farm, ee-yi-ee-yi-oh.' We're really wasting time. . . ."

The girl jabbed the gun into Kate's neck.

"On that farm he had a cow, ee-yi-ee-yi-oh."

"Say the 'Mary Had a Little Lamb.' "

"Mary had a little lamb, his fleece was white as snow, and everywhere that Mary went the lamb was sure to go."

"Yeah. Now say the 'Aunt Molly.' "

A fresh lance of pain shot through Kate's jaw to her eyes. Her molar pounded as if trying to drive itself up by the roots. Tears sprang, but she blinked them back. Play the little game with this girl and then it'll be done with. Play cool and she would let Kate go. Of course she would let Kate go.

"I don't know the 'Aunt Molly,' " she said honestly.

"I bet," said the girl. She put her hand on Kate's knee, and pushed the skirt and coat hem up to Kate's thigh. "Think real hard." Chills of fear sprang up under the fine nylon of her panty hose.

Kate slid her leg out from under the girl's touch, but

the girl grabbed Kate's knee and pulled it back. Cold air rushed up between her legs. "Think real hard," the girl repeated. "Come on. 'Went downtown to see Aunt Molly . . .' Say it. You know it."

"I don't. I . . . I've never heard it before."

"We used to say it over at the elementary school on the playground. Weren't you listening?"

"I . . . no."

" 'Went downtown to see Aunt Molly, paid two cents to see her woolly. Hair so black I couldn't see the crack. Made her give me my two cents back.' Used to sing it to make the girls mad, me and Whitey and Buddy."

"Listen," said Kate. "Let's be reasonable. Let's . . ."

"Reasonable? You said I was a young girl. Little girls ain't reasonable, are they?"

"You're a young lady. I misspoke."

"You don't know what I am. But I want to see what you are. Show me your woolly."

"Wait," Kate lifted her left hand carefully. "First promise me you'll put the gun away. You'll get out of the car like this never happened and walk off. You won't look back, you'll . . ."

"I don't have to promise you shit," said the girl. "Pull down your fucking underpants."

Kate reached for the hem of her skirt, which was already to her hip. She took hold to hike it to her waist. She couldn't.

"I can't."

The girl pulled a knife from her ankle and flicked it open against the steering wheel, the gun never wavering. The knife snapped into place with a little click. The blade spit dull sparks in the gray light of the pine woods outside.

"No, no, no, no, please," said Kate. "Wait!"

The girl knocked Kate's legs farther apart with her fist and thrust the knife to the crotch of her panty hose. Kate could feel the very tip on her mound.

No no no no no! Kate slammed herself back against the seat, her knees instinctively coming together, but then a flash of sharp heat on her left inner thigh caused her to open them again.

"I'll cut you again, you motherfucking shit, just try me," said the girl. "You got couple holes now, I'll give you a couple more."

Kate, sobbing now, "Please, don't, wait, okay, wait!" Her heels dug into the floor mat but there was nowhere to go. "Stop this. You don't need to do this!"

The girl slit open the panty hose at the center, then across the tops of both legs. She sliced the navy blue cotton briefs free at both hips and, with the blade, peeled them away. Kate felt the cold air on her exposed flesh and hair.

"Fuckin' what I thought," said the girl. "You're just another cunt!"

Kate closed her eyes. *This will be over soon. This will. It can't go on much longer.*

"Close your legs," said the girl. "You smell like a whore!"

Kate closed her legs. She could feel the blood from the nicked thigh, like a warm oil, smearing the other. "All right," she said through bile and salt. "You saw what you wanted to see. Now, let me go. There is nothing I can do for you."

"You gonna drive me."

"Yes, I said I'd be happy to drop you off somewhere. Just tell me where you live or where you want to go."

"Not drop off. You drop me off you'll just tell on me like you did that time."

What time? What time?

The girl picked a Tootsie Roll from the floor, wiped the vomit off on Kate's shoulder, and tore the wrapper off with her teeth. She took a bite and chewed thoughtfully. The dark wax stripes on her face were smudged. Drops of sweat dotted the line of her dark eyebrows. The gray eyes steady on Kate, the thoughts behind them indecipherable.

Try again. I can do this.

"Where do you need me to drive you, what is your name, I'm sorry, did you tell me your name?"

"Didn't tell you." Chewing, slowly.

"Where do you want me to drive you?"

"Texas."

"You don't mean the state of Texas."

Quietly this time, as if confident in her complete control of the situation, tapping the side of the gun with her pinky as it moved in a slow wave up and down along Kate's torso. "Don't tell me what I don't mean."

"I have some cash. Enough, I think, to buy a bus ticket to Texas. There's a station in Emporia. I could get you to Emporia. Do you have relatives in Texas?"

"Do teachers ever shut their fat lips?"

Kate rolled her lips in between her teeth.

"Texas, and you're driving me. But first you're cleaning up this vomit shit. Mothers like to clean, don't they? See 'em on television all the time, happy to be cleaning vomit, happy to be cleaning toilets, happy to be cleaning their babies' smelly butts."

The girl glanced over the back at the quilt. "Wipe it up with that."

"No, I may have some Wipe-Its in the glove box if you'll just look . . ."

The girl said, "Fuck that," and pulled up the quilt.

The girl looked at Mistie. She looked at Kate and shook her head. The gun imitated the head, shaking slowly.

Tsk, tsk, tsk.

She said, "Well, now, what the fuck you got hiding here, little Miss Teacher?"

Chapter Twenty

The girl said the "f" word again and stared at Mistie.
The girl looked scary to Mistie, with red all over her
face. Mistie remembered on the *Princess Silverlace*
show once that a bad witch tried to cast a spell on
the princess and steal all her people's cattle. The
witch had disguised herself with paint and feathers so
people would think she was a goose. She looked just
like this girl except there were no feathers. Maybe
this girl was a bad witch. Maybe she was going to put
a spell on Mistie now that the blanket was pulled
away.

Mistie put her hands over her face. She could smell
the chocolate on her palms and she licked them. Maybe
the girl would go away if she didn't move. Sometimes
her daddy went away if she didn't move. Mostly he
didn't go away but sometimes he did.

Don't move.
Be vwery, vwery quiet.

Chapter Twenty-one

She remembered.

Fifth grade, three years ago. The oldest in the class at twelve because she had failed third grade for not coming to school enough. The official record had said she'd missed sixty-seven days. Tony's mam had protested briefly that her daughter was sick and had good excuses for missing, but then let it go. To protest a retention with any conviction required coming in and talking to the teacher, the guidance counselor, and the principal. That was too much for Mam. That would take a good couple hours out of her day. That would cut into her beer and her *The Price Is Right* and her sofa time.

Retained, then, Tony—still Angela—was the tallest girl in the class. The others were a good four inches shorter, a year dumber, and, the only good thing for them, flatter. They didn't like Angela and she didn't like them. They called her lezbo behind her back because she hated makeup and never wore skirts. She called them hussies, cunts, pussies, whatever caught her fancy at the moment, to their faces. She spent a lot of time on the bench in the office.

Angela made friends with a couple boys in the class, Buddy and Whitey. Buddy was a goof-ass who couldn't read very well. Whitey was a black kid with a burned-up face. They were almost her age but not quite. She told them what to do and they usually did.

It was during Spring Fling. Spring Fling was an annual PTA fund-raiser, a minicarnival held the last Friday in May. Classes were let out after lunch, and the kids who had brought money were free to run around the school grounds, buying cupcakes at the kindergarten bake sale or tossing nickels to win stuffed animals at the third grade booth. There was face painting and a water balloon toss. There was a popcorn vendor set up by the cafeteria workers and PTA moms selling lopsided clumps of cotton candy on white paper cones. Kids who didn't have money wandered around begging the other kids for a loan, manned the various grade-level booths, or plopped themselves down on the playground swings and slide and pretended they didn't care.

The day was hot, hotter than a set of fried jumper cables, and Angela, who had brought three dollars she'd swiped from her mother's wallet, was spent out and was now perched atop the wooden climbing tower. She wore a pair of cutoffs, a baggy T-shirt to hide her embarrassingly mature chest, and rubber flip-flops. From her vantage point a good fifteen feet above the ground, she could watch the comings and goings of the kids who still had money. Over at the water balloon toss on the blacktop two boys had gotten into a scuffle and the teacher was breaking it up. There was a long line at the face-painting booth, little guys bouncing in sneakers and waving the little American flags bought at the fifth-grade flea market booth. A clump of fifth graders had won packs of baseball cards and they'd found shade by the special education trailer for a swap meet. Scents of cotton candy and butter and hot earth drifted across the playground.

"Somebody lost a balloon!" called Buddy. He was below Angela, sitting in the shadows under the tower. He didn't have any money, either. He had tried to borrow some from Angela but she wouldn't share.

The balloon was bright pink, and had lost just enough helium to keep it barely above kid's-head level. A breeze spun it in lazy circles, its string trailing like a kite tail, across the blacktop and over the grassy playground to the wooden climbing tower.

"Look, balloon!" Buddy repeated.

"I see it," said Angela.

The balloon whirled and dipped, raised up and drifted low. Written on one side was the name of the sponsor who'd donated the balloons to Pippins Elementary, *Southeastern Citizen's Bank*. Angela leaned out from the tower, holding tight with one hand, and grabbed the string as it flitted by.

"Got it!" She slid down the corkscrew slide in the center of the tower with the balloon in her lap and joined Buddy in the shadows. He was sitting on his butt in the grass, chewing on clover. There was green drool at the corners of his mouth.

"You look sick," said Angela.

"Yeah. Let's suck the helium."

Angela bit at the knot on the string, pulling it loose and spitting it off onto her leg. She put the lip of the balloon in her mouth and inhaled deeply, just like she did with her mother's cigarettes. The funny taste of rubber filled her lungs. She pulled the balloon away, pinching the lip shut, and said, "Hello. My name is Angela Petinske. What's your name?" It was a foreign voice, pinched and cartoony.

Buddy howled. He grabbed for the balloon and Angela slapped him away. Then she handed it to him. He sucked helium.

"My name is Buddy Via and I hate school, don't you? Ha ha ha ha!" he said.

They took turns sucking and speaking, each one trying to make their sentence a little longer than the last. Angela felt light-headed and good. Screw the Spring Fling and the pussies who got their faces painted. This was better.

Until a teacher outside the tower said, "Rob, is that the girl?"

Angela jumped a mile and let go of the balloon. It sputtered and wheezed, then dropped beside her lap like a dead, pink puppy. Outside in the sunlight stood the new fourth grade teacher Mrs. McDolen and a little boy with a ball cap and brand-new Nikes. His eyebrows were drawn together and his index finger was shaking in Angela's direction.

Angela didn't wait. She jumped to her feet and stared through the wooden slats of the tower. "What you saying, boy? The girl who what? Huh?" Buddy sat, watching, in the grass.

"Come out here so we may speak," said the teacher calmly.

135

May speak. Only teachers talked like that. It drove a burr into Angela's spine. She crawled out through the slats and stood, arms to her side and feet slightly apart. "Okay. Speak," she said.

"Watch your tone," said the teacher. "Rob said you stole his balloon."

Angela's mouth dropped open. "That's total bull!" she said. "I found it!"

The teacher held out her hand while Rob twisted the toe of his Nike in the dirt. Angela was suddenly conscious of her flip-flops and wanted to stomp him in the head with them.

Buddy poked the deflated balloon out through the slats. Angela would not pick it up. The teacher did. "I see clearly now," she said, turning it over, "Look. Rob's got his name on it."

"Huh!" said Angela.

"Ooh, Angela, stealin' a little boy's balloon," taunted Buddy.

Angela looked at the balloon. In small, black marker was written *Rob Forrester*. She shrugged.

"So? He lost it," said Angela. "Finder's keepers."

"I dinn lose it," whined Rob. "You took it!"

The teacher pushed a strand of her hair behind her ear and put her hands on her hips. Angela put her hands on her hips. "Don't mock me," said the teacher.

"Don't mock me," said Angela. " 'Cause I didn't steal nothing."

"You did!" wailed Rob.

"Bullshit!" said Angela.

The teacher looked as shocked as if she'd stepped into a pile of that very stuff.

Five minutes later, Angela was sitting on the bench

in the office. Ten minutes later, she was in the office with the principal, listening to him talk about respect for peers and adults and then to him tell her she would sit in detention all day Monday.

Angela gave the bitch Mrs. McDolen the hairy eyeball for the remainder of the school year, all six days of it. And then she went on to Curtis Middle School and never had to look at her again.

Until now.

She remembered.

This was the teacher. Sitting at the wheel of her rich-ass white car in her rich-ass shoes, looking surprised that there was a little girl hiding under a quilt in her backseat. This would be good.

"I see now," Tony said.

The teacher's mouth opened and closed. Her eyes were wide and twitching.

"What you into, teacher? Little girls? Got a little girl in the back of your car for when you get an urge?"

"How dare you!"

Tony slapped the teacher soundly across the mouth. The teacher sobbed, once, then bared her teeth like a dog. It was hysterical and Tony laughed aloud.

Then she studied the girl in the backseat. She was about seven or so, a mess, all snotty and sweaty and wearing some kind of trash. She was covered in brown goo, what Tony hoped was candy and not something else.

"What are you doing in here?" Tony asked.

The little girl rubbed her crotch.

"Oh, yeah, I see," said Tony. She turned back around

and put both feet on the dashboard. She tapped the teacher on the arm with the pistol. "You got a little secret there, huh, teacher woman?"

The teacher was scrambling for something to say. It crawled all over her face, and then, "I was taking her home for the afternoon. Her mother gave me permission to . . ."

"Yeah," said Tony. "Whatever. You can tell me later. We'll save that up, how about that? Good bedtime story."

"No," said the teacher. "No, listen to me now."

"I don't have to. You know how to get to Texas?"

"I . . . well, of course, but . . ."

"Drive."

The teacher backed the car around, and then maneuvered through the thick of pines back to Route 58. On the road, the teacher didn't even have to ask which way to turn. She went right, and drove in silence to the turnoff onto Route 35 a mile outside Courtland. She put on her blinker and turned south. Eight miles to North Carolina. A couple thousand at least to Texas.

Burton was in Texas. He had moved there long ago when Lorilynn Petinske had sent him away without his pistol or his sofa.

Tony leaned against the passenger's door and studied her two traveling mates. Two fucked-up females.

And Tony in charge, completely, for the first time in her life.

This was going to be the most excitement she'd ever had. This was going to be a ride to remember.

Chapter Twenty-two

Real life.
  This is real life. It is happening.
  Kate checked the rearview mirror, then glanced over at the teenager leaning on the passenger's door. They had crossed into North Carolina several minutes ago. The girl had been silent all those many minutes. On both sides of the road, pines held sentinel, oblivious to the insanity passing them by. It was after five, and the gray sky was darkening with the nearing of dusk. Kate turned on the headlights, but the girl shook her head and Kate turned them back off. The sleet on the road was slush now.

  If ever there was a time that things shouldn't be real life, this would be it. If ever there was a time for a quick and amazing rescue out of the wild blue yonder, by Arnold or Bruce or even one of those motorcycle guys from *CHiPS*, it was now. Kate knew the late-night movies and old TV shows. With Donald gone late so often, she'd learned the stations and their various offerings from nine to midnight.

In the backseat, Mistie was playing with the wrappers from several Tootsie Rolls. The girl had tossed them to her, and had laughed when Mistie had unwrapped all three and put all three in her mouth at once. Mistie didn't seem bothered by the laughter. She didn't looked startled anymore by the presence of the teenager. She only seemed intent on consuming the rolls of chocolate.

In the barren patches between the forests, little houses had prepared for evening. Porch lights dotted doorways; shades had been drawn. Many of the homes were outlined in Christmas lights. Some small bushes were likewise decorated, and there were the expected plastic nativities, and shiny reindeer loping motionlessly across lawns. Smoke curled from chimneys and stacks, rising just above the roofs and holding there in swirls of tainted ribbon, awaiting the next sleet or snow. In side-yard corrals horses and cows, coats sugarcoated in sleet, nosed through the remnants of hay bales and melting salt blocks, snuffling up the last before morning. Inside the doorway of one well-lit garage, two young men in heavy coats tinkered on a truck while a toddler stared out at the cold and at the white Volvo hissing by.

It was all real life.

None less so than the rest.

None less so than the gun in the girl's lap, the gun that was trained on Kate's ribs, the gun that had made a torment of the side of her jaw. No less than the stinging cut between her legs or the dried blood or the panty hose that had been slit apart and now hung around her knees.

There was no rescue. There would be no rescue, though Kate deserved rescue. She had done the right thing. She had captured a butterfly and had meant to set it free. She had put herself on the line for the child in the back. Surely such things were meant to be rewarded. Kate was a good person. She wasn't some stupid, dim-witted woman. She wasn't some trashy trailer park bimbo.

Rescue in this case was well deserved.

And yet any rescue would just be another pit.

Another few minutes, driven in silence, due south. Then the girl said, "How much money you got on you?"

How much do I have? Kate wondered. *How much? Did I cash a check yesterday? I was going to, I don't know.* "I'm not sure," she said.

"You said enough for a bus ticket. Get out your wallet. Pass it over."

Kate glanced about for her purse. Where was it? There, on the floor under the girl's legs. She snatched it from the floor and put it beside her. The car wobbled a bit with the lack of attention, then straightened. She knew her purse by heart. Without looking she unzipped it and felt around. Her fingers identified lipstick, the tiny address book, ink pens, compact, blush, eyeliner. And then her kidskin wallet. She pulled it out and flung it at the girl.

The girl shook the gun. "Don't ever throw anything at me. You aren't my fucking mother. You want me to throw something at you? You wanna *know* what I might throw at you?"

"No," said Kate.

Silence as the girl dug through the contents of the wallet. From the corner of her eye, Kate could see the photos of Donald and Donald, Jr., scattering. Receipts from her credit card that she'd not yet filed, coupons she'd clipped for her grocery trip to Emporia—Swiffers, Bic disposable razors, 409 spray cleanser—loose stamps, MasterCard, Emporia library card, Food Lion MVP card, some dried four-leaf clovers she'd found in her yard last summer.

"Got a lot of shit," said the girl. "Fucking pack rat."

Kate said nothing.

"And only twenty-two dollars and a couple nickels. You're a McDolen, you have lots of money. Where's your bank?"

"Emporia."

"We can't go back to Emporia. You got a ATM card here, you can get money anywhere, right? You can get it in Saudi Arabia, even, I've seen it on TV."

"ATM," said Mistie in the back. Her voice rose like the little Arab child in the commercial who lead the stranded tourists across the desert to salvation. "ATM, ATM!" Then she went quiet again.

"What's the next town?"

"I don't know," said Kate. "Roanoke Rapids, maybe."

"How far's that?"

"I don't know."

"You better know."

"I'm not even sure it's on this road. I've only driven there by way of Interstate 95. Maybe it's not even on this road."

"Teachers are supposed to know stuff," said the girl. "What the hell's wrong with you? Oh, yeah, I remember. You're a cunt. A smelly old cunt. Turn on those headlights before we run into something."

Kate turned on the lights.

They took a long curve, and then a slope downhill, and there was an outcropping of houses and a gas station and the spires of several churches poking up through the trees. Streetlights sprinkled the air like fireflies. A green sign on the right side of the road read GUMBERRY.

"Bet they have a bank," said the girl. "Find their bank."

"They might not . . . ," began Kate but then clamped her mouth closed. Maybe they would have a bank. Maybe the bank would even have an ATM machine. Kate could withdraw all the cash she had on hand and bribe the girl to let her go with Mistie. Hell, she could drive the girl to Raleigh, buy her a plane ticket to Texas, and give her a thousand dollars spending cash on top of that. Then she and Mistie would turn again to the north, wounded and tired but back on track.

Kate's heart clenched in hope. *Please, a bank in Gumberry.*

They found no bank in Gumberry. They passed through the center of town in an eye's blink, and then were back in the country with the pines and the gray sky and the darkness.

Just one little bank. I can get out of all this mess with one little bank. Kate pressed on the gas; the car picked up speed. The girl didn't seem to mind. Mistie, her mouth full of Toosties, said something that sounded like "Mama had a lady and its head hopped off."

A few minutes later, Garysburg, the size of Gumberry. Nearly identical houses, churches. *What do these people do, barter?* Streetlights. A few antique shops. No bank. Kate thought. Her heart had picked up a rhythm with the humming of the tires. She was on the last leg of the race, and if she crossed the finish line, things would turn out just fine.

Dark countryside. Barns, trees. A sign for Weldon, three miles. Beneath that a sign for Interstate 95, four miles. Where there was a town and an on-ramp, there would be banks. Travelers needed banks. They never took enough money with them on vacation. Some smart bank would have set up operations in Weldon, for certain.

"Mistie," Kate ventured. "You okay back there?"

A sneeze. Nothing more.

A straight stretch, the sky lighter up ahead promising civilization of some sort. Kate realized her hands were clenched so tightly around the wheel they were numb. The hose at her knees chafed, and she thought, *Just a few more minutes and the tide will turn. I'm an adult. I'm a teacher. I'm a good, sensible person. I have the power.*

The car passed the town limits of Weldon. The houses, a small school, grocery store, Methodist church, Baptist church, blinker light, yellow-yellow-yellow, indicating the center of town. A bank.

Kate slammed on the brakes. The girl growled, "Watch it! Damn!"

There was a green, glowing HONOR sign over top of one that read BANK OF NORTH CAROLINA. *Excellent, yes! Money will talk! Thank you, God, thank you.*

Kate's fingers drained numb to cold to hot. She turned into the near-empty parking lot. A single car was in the drive-through, the driver punching numbers. She held a respectable distance to wait her turn. A sign on the brick bank wall read "HAVE YOU OPENED NEXT YEAR'S CHRISTMAS CLUB? SEE INSIDE FOR DETAILS!"

"Listen," Kate began. Her words were slow on her tongue and muffled in her ear, like a mosquito embedded in the wax, humming in a low-pitched key. The heat crawled from her fingers to hands, hands to arms, arms to chest. Her teeth buzzed. Her loose molar popped and clicked. She felt she was outside herself, not herself, watching herself calmly work her way out of a hideous circumstance. "I've been thinking. You need to get to Texas, for some reason."

"Friends," said the girl, with a tone of pride. "I got lots of friends down there. I bet I got a lot more friends than you, teacher."

"You need to get to Texas, I need to go home. I think I have enough money in my account to get you a plane ticket from Raleigh to wherever you want to go in Texas. Dallas? Austin? El Paso?"

The girl rubbed her nose. She didn't respond. That was okay, she hadn't told Kate to shut up yet. She wasn't waving the gun.

"Wherever, I don't need to know," said Kate. "I'll take out every penny I have in the account."

"No fucking pennies."

"No, well, it comes out in bills, not coins. I'll withdraw everything I have and give it to you. We'll drive to Raleigh, about another forty-five minutes."

The car at the ATM machine roared away, spewing blue exhaust. Kate held her foot on the brake; the Volvo purred.

"Forty-five minutes, tops. There is an airport. You can get a plane ticket and be in Texas in a matter of hours. You'll even have enough to catch a cab from the airport once you get there."

The girl sniffed, looked back at Mistie, then at Kate. Her expression was impossible to read in the darkness of the car's interior.

"That's the most reasonable, don't you think?"

"You'll tell on me. You're a teacher. Teachers tell."

"I won't."

"You told already on me. You don't remember."

"I don't remember but I'm sorry if I did."

"You did."

"Okay, I'm sorry I did."

"Just get the money."

Kate rolled the car to the ATM machine. She held out her hand to the girl. "I need my card. It's the blue and gold one on the floor by the deviled ham."

The girl gave her the card. Kate pressed the tab on the armrest; the window eased down. "Do we have a deal, then? I don't even know your name. That's one in your favor, I guess, plus I don't break promises."

The girl took a long breath. One of her feet slipped down off the dash and onto the floor amid the scattered snacks. The foot on the dash began shaking. "Maybe," she said. "Maybe we can do it that way."

Kate turned to the window. She didn't want the girl to see the sheer relief and hope on her face. *Mistie, I did it. Mrs. McDolen pulled us through. We'll get to Canada, you just wait and see. It's beautiful up there. Places to run and play. People who will love you and protect you.*

She pushed her card into the slot. The slot pushed it back out again.

"Whoa," she said.

Card in. Card out. She leaned out of the window to read the small print on the screen. *We're Sorry. This machine is temporarily out of order.*

Kate shoved the card at the slot; it spit the card out into her hand.

"What's the matter?" said the girl. "Where's my money?"

My money, you little shit! It's my money and I can't get it.

The gun jabbed Kate in the arm. "Where's my money?"

Stop it!

Card in, spit out. Mistie in the back, humming a tune of some sort. "Daaa-da-da-daaaaa, da-da-da-daaa." Kate vaguely recognized it as the theme song *The Simpsons*.

The girl grabbed Kate by the ear and twisted. A roar of electricity blew through Kate's brain.

"Where's my money?"

"Leave me alone!" Kate's arms flew up around her head and she ducked down into a protective ball. "Leave me alone! What is wrong with you? What the hell is the matter with you?" Her foot slipped off the brake and the car lurched forward, crunching the driver's rearview inward. The car struck a curb outside the drive-through and hopped up onto the concrete and stopped.

The girl slapped Kate on top of her head. "Sit up!" she said. "Where's my money?"

"It's broken," said Kate into her forearms. *I won't cry, goddamn it, I will not let her see me cry.* "Everything is broken."

"You got that right," said the girl. "No money? Well,

flying's for pussies anyway. I wanna drive."

"You want to drive? Take my car! Let us out!"

The girl blew out an exasperated puff of air. "Hell no. I think you two make good company. You and your little doll baby in the back. We'll have lots of time to talk. It'll be fun."

"Please let us go."

I can't do this, this is insane!

"We'll play games, you, me, and Baby Doll."

Kate reached for the door handle and yanked it open, then she was falling out of the car to the concrete and struggling to stand. She was pushing up, up with her hands, her Easy Spirit pumps trying to find purchase on the wet surface, and she was running then, flying, away from the car and the green HONOR sign and the humming floodlights.

She remembered.

In bed in the hospital sixteen years ago, second floor, white walls and sheets, shaved belly and privates, a white light overhead that never winks, never rests, a monitor beeping in her ear, kicking, kicking against the pain and the fear. The nurse saying, "Don't yell, you're scaring the other patients. Don't grab those side rails, breathe. Quit fighting, just breathe." The pain huge like her belly, going nowhere but spinning circles through her flesh, pushing but nothing helps, nothing stops the pain and it won't let her catch her breath, crying doing no good, then thinking, *I will run away!*

Falling from the bed to the startled grunt of the attending nurse; waddling down the hall trailing a broken IV, running away from the pain, going home, going anywhere but this place of sweat and torment. *I'll come back another day, I just can't do this now, leave me alone! I'm going home!*

Being stopped at the stairs by a male nurse who takes her arm and coos, "Mrs. McDolen, you're in labor, you can't leave! Come back now, you're scaring everyone. Stop acting like a child!"

The wheelchair under her ass, plop, back to the room as the pain builds and hammers her insides and she thinks, *Let me go home! I can't do this!*

And the doctor comes in, stares between her legs and puts his fingers in there, and checks the monitor and says, "It's not coming, let's get it out."

Yes! Get it out!

They get it out with a shot to her spine and a cloth draped in front of her face and a scalpel.

She remembered.

A call came from behind, "I got her out, you want me to cut her?"

Kate stumbled. She was on the other side of the road, in between cars in some disheveled automotive lot. The streetlight at the walk made the figures across the street appear blue. Blue like babies without enough oxygen. Blue like the deep blue sea where sailors and lovers go to drown.

"I'll cut her! Look!"

Kate looked. The girl had taken Mistie out of the backseat of the car, and they stood arm in arm like a friendly couple of kids, only the older girl was holding her knife, and it was opened and it was poised at the little girl's neck.

Two cars passed in rapid succession, spraying melted sleet, *whiz whiz*, headlights catching Mistie and the girl, the girl lifting her hand and waving casually. The red-eyed taillights grew smaller and disappeared up the road.

"Here, teacher, teacher, teacher! Come on back!"

The knife was visible again, taunting and twirling. Mistie held still, staring at the knife and then at her shoes. No struggle there.

Kate walked back across the road. A stray cat followed her halfway, and she yelled it away beneath the car where it had been hiding.

Chapter Twenty-three

The girl held her by her arm outside in the dark cold and called across the street, "Here, teacher, teacher, teacher!"

Mistie stared at the knife in the girl's hand. It was sharp like the one Daddy used to cut open apples and things. She wished the girl would let go. She didn't like people touching her. It was scary, people's hands and the way they got sweaty and sticky; the things the hands held sometimes.

She shut her eyes tightly and imagined television with Princess Silverlace in her pink gown and the sparkling gifts being laid at her feet. The princess smiled at the people who stood at her throne. She smiled at Mistie. Mistie smiled back. The princess held out her hand, not to take Mistie's but to welcome her to come up and try out the throne. Mistie walked up the carpeted steps and sat down. The chair was huge and gold, and the cushion on which she sat was soft and fuzzy, like what God's lap would be if God had a lap.

"Mistie, get in the car."

Mistie opened her eyes. The teacher was back again, standing beside her. It had started to drizzle, and the teacher's face was streaked with wet. Mistie could no longer smell the teacher's sweet hand lotion.

"Mistie," repeated the girl with the knife. "Get in the car."

Mistie looked at her feet, the teacher, the sky. There were no stars tonight.

"There's another Twix in the car," said the teacher. Mistie went to the car and climbed in.

Chapter Twenty-four

The teacher drove south. Sometime soon they would have to stop and let the baby doll go to the bathroom. Tony, herself, was feeling the early pressures of a bladder that would soon be uncomfortably full. She leaned against the car door, eating some of the squashed bread from the floor. Every so often she rolled down her window and tossed out the crusts.

"I like birds," she said simply.

A while ago, maybe ten minutes, maybe thirty, Tony told the teacher to pull off at a roadside trash pile. It was brush laced with trash, a spot country folks had obviously decided made a decent and convenient dump. Tony ordered the teacher to use the quilt and water from a small, muddy puddle to wash down the dash and the passenger-side floor. The teacher had then tossed the quilt and the floor mat onto the trash pile along with the empty bread bag and candy wrappers the baby doll had scattered in the back. Tony threw in the photos and credit card and receipts from the teacher's wallet, and found pleasure in grinding them into the slimy rubbish with the toe of her granddad's shoe. Then Tony told the teacher she might as well add the panty hose and underwear to the pile and she did, slowly and ceremoniously covering them up with sticks and some slimy brown paper bags as if she were performing a burial.

Tony had used the same puddle and a scarf she'd spotted in the back of the teacher's car to clean off as much of the lipstick as she could. There was still wax in her eyebrows and along her hairline but that would come out later. Later in Texas at Burton's house. On Burton's ranch. She wished she had something else to wear besides Granddad's old moth-chewed clothes, but she'd deal with that later, too. She wanted to look good for Burton. He was a wealthy man, he was a powerful man, and she didn't want to disappoint him.

The car, now smelling less strongly of vomit, paralleled the interstate on a small road whose route number Tony didn't know and didn't care. The remaining snacks were stuffed in the glove box and those that didn't fit bounced along on the backseat beside the kid.

The teacher had changed her tune big time since her failed escape back at the bank. She'd gotten real quiet. This amused Tony. She imagined the teacher was Mam at the wheel, sitting with a crumpled skirt and crumpled coat, no panties, bruised face. Mam, her fat ass cheeks sticking to the inside of her skirt, saying nothing until Tony gave her permission. Then Tony imagined it was Mrs. Martin back at the Exxon, driving to Texas under Tony's order. Scared shitless, afraid to move an inch to one side or the other.

Tony licked the corners of her mouth, drawing in some renegade bread crumbs. She rubbed the barrel of the gun with her thumb. Burton had rubbed his thumb here, she was sure. He had been a tall man with near-black hair and near-black eyes, handsome and muscular. He'd been able to hold Tony and Darlene up over his head, one in each hand, and spin them around until they laughed themselves sick.

She looked at the teacher. The woman stared straight ahead at the night road. She looked out the window. A sign flashing by—Route 301 South. Another, twenty-nine miles to Rocky Mount. She looked in the back where little Baby Doll had fallen asleep in her torn pink nightie and sweater and her coat. Her hair was plastered across her forehead, making it look as though she'd just blown in on a tornado. That was one screwed-up kid. Maybe seven years old, maybe eight. She didn't say much, but hummed to herself and played with herself. What was the teacher doing with this kid in the back of her car, covered up in a quilt? She said she was taking the kid home for the afternoon. What a crock. A McDolen would never take a kid in a torn nightgown home for an afternoon. They owned most of the county.

Tony looked at the blood on her shoe. She looked at the teacher. She said, "Truth or dare?"

The teacher's eyebrows flinched slightly, but she didn't look over. That was no fun. Tony waggled the pistol. "Look at me. Truth or dare?"

The teacher glanced at Tony. "What is that?"

"You never played truth or dare? Where the hell you been?"

The teacher shook her head. Her nose seemed to be

running, but she wasn't wiping it away. That was gross, especially for a teacher.

"I ask you something and you have to tell me the truth or take a dare," said Tony.

The teacher's cheek hitched. She said nothing.

"Talk to me."

"What do you want me to say?"

"We're gonna play truth or dare."

"Fine. Whatever you say."

"You gotta tell me the truth or you gotta take a dare." Tony reached under her hat and scratched her head. It was itching again. This time, it was good to scratch.

"I'll tell you whatever you want to hear. You have the gun."

"Shit, that ain't the way it works. Besides, I'll know if you're telling the truth or making something up." When the Hot Heads played truth or dare in the old barn, Tony could always tell when Whitey or Little Joe was lying. DeeWee, of course, wasn't allowed to play because he even believed the story about the aliens living over in Capron in an old tobacco barn and the story about the three-legged dog-ghost that haunted Route 58 on Halloween night.

"Hear me?"

The teacher nodded.

"Okay, you want to tell the truth or take the dare?"

"What's the dare?"

"You don't find out until you choose what you're going to do. Answer or take the dare?"

"What do you want me to chose?"

Tony said, "Don't start with me."

"Truth."

"Good," said Tony. "Truth. And it better be the

damned truth. Why is that kid in the back of your car? Why was she hiding under a blanket? Don't try to tell me she was comin' home with you for a visit or I'll do the teeth on the other side of your face and you'll be suckin' tomato soup through a straw. I'll do it."

"I know."

The teacher glanced in the rearview and shifted a bit on her seat. Tony had no fear she would try anything insane like popping the door to hop out anymore. She knew Tony would hurt Baby Doll if she did. And Tony knew she would, too.

"I—" began the teacher. "I wanted to do something for her."

"Not good enough. You have to tell everything."

A fork appeared in the road ahead, a dark looming maw of trees and rock, and the teacher let up on the gas. The teacher looked at Tony. The face was full of stony, resigned hatred. It was a good thing to see.

"Take the left one," said Tony. The teacher steered left. "Now, tell me."

Slowly, as if choosing her words with great care, "I wanted to help her. She doesn't have much, you can probably tell. She wore a nightgown to school and she was clearly freezing. Mr. Angelone found a sweater for her in the lost and found."

In the back, Mistie groaned a bit in sleep, then went quiet.

"I thought I could do a little better than that."

"What do you mean?"

"I thought I could give her some of the clothes at my place, clothes my . . . daughter had grown out of. Some pants, maybe, some sweatshirts and maybe a jumper or two."

Tony pondered this. This might be something a McDolen would do, give old clothes away. It made more sense than inviting the kid to visit for an afternoon tea.

Tony drew one leg up beneath her, and bit at a hangnail on the index finger of her free hand. "Why was she hiding in the back of your car? What were you hiding her for?"

The teacher said, "The bag of snacks tore outside the store. I had to get them from under the car. When I finally got in, Mistie was nervous. I'd left her alone. I admit that was a mistake. Then I pulled over to the Dumpsters to get her something to eat. She seemed so hungry. I don't know if she gets sweets much at home, I figured it couldn't hurt. Then we saw kids running out of the store, they were yelling quite loudly, and they drove away in a car that was behind the dumps. Your friends' car. The commotion scared Mistie. She crawled under the quilt. She's a very shy child."

Tony watched the teacher's face for signs she was lying. If she was, it was a really good lie. Were teachers trained to lie like that, without time to think about it?

"Huh," said Tony. "Guess her mom's gonna be wonderin' what the hell happened to her baby, isn't she?"

"I suppose so."

"She know what kinda car you got?"

The teacher shrugged. "I could call her. I don't have a cell phone but I've got quarters for a pay phone."

"Right! And tell her what?"

The teacher shrugged.

"Guess you're in trouble now, huh?"

"I suppose so."

"That's really funny." Tony took her hat off and

158

scratched harder. It wasn't nits, no way, it was excitement. It was all the good stuff from today, crawling around underneath her skin ready to pop out. "Don't you think that's funny? Kids get in trouble all the time and teachers never do. Grown-ups never do. Well, hardly. I think kids should all get a gun and a knife like I got. We'd tell 'em what's right and what's wrong. We wouldn't let teachers or mothers do some of the shit they do."

Tony rolled down the window a little. She stuck her fingertips through the crack and wiggled them. The air was misty and cold. "What time is it?"

"Clock's right there."

"You tell me, bitch."

"Six-fourteen."

"I want supper. That bread was shit."

The teacher's lips moved slightly, then went still.

"What did you say? You better say it out loud."

"I said that bread was supper."

"You lie like a log! McDolens don't eat regular bread for supper. You eat steak and caviar and shit like that. Right?"

"Right. I'm sorry. I should have clarified my comment. The bread is for the maid's supper."

"You have a maid?"

"Of course."

"Lazy ass, got to have a maid."

"We have a very nice maid."

"We just passed a sign says McDonald's up ahead in Wilson. Three miles. You got more'n twenty bucks. I want a Quarter Pounder and big fries. Hey, Baby Doll!" She reached over and shook the kid. The kid whined and opened her eyes. They were squinty and red rimmed.

"Want some McDonald's?"

The kid nodded, then shut her eyes again.

"Do the drive-through. Act like we're a family. We're the kids. You're the old hag."

"Fine."

Tony frowned. This was losing its fun. The teacher wasn't crying anymore. She wasn't begging or arguing or trying to explain anything.

"Truth or dare?" said Tony.

"I suppose you want truth."

"No!" Tony pinched a bit of skin on the woman's neck. Tears sprang into her eyes but she said nothing. "No, what do you want?"

"Truth."

Tony let go. "What do you think happened back in the Exxon? Why do you think I was runnin' out of there so fast?"

"I thought I heard a backfire. Maybe it was a gunshot or two. Am I right?"

Tony grinned. "You got it! Yep, we shot up stuff! Guess what we shot?"

"Windows?"

"What else?"

"Somebody?"

"Yep! Guess who?"

"Mary Ann?"

"Who's Mary Ann? Oh, that cunt Martin? No, but it should have been. Pop, blow off her boobs just like that! Guess again."

"One of your friends?"

"The gasoline man. We killed him. Shot him in the

chest, blam! Blood all over. Look at my shoe. Got his blood on my shoe."

The teacher's eyes closed, then opened. She was really bothered. That was good. That was great! Tony scratched her head furiously, and counted to sixty three times until they made it into the town of Wilson.

Chapter Twenty-five

The girl sat on a pile of wooden pallets behind the abandoned Dairy Rite, holding the pistol at Kate's head as Kate squatted by a denuded, twisted dogwood tree to pee. The sky had broken open; the moon was visible now, a white eye laced with tenuous threads of cloud and gray smoke from a nearby farmhouse. The car was cooling and ticking against the back of the old building. Mistie sat inside the opened back car door, crossing and uncrossing her feet and looking at her fingers.

"Watch for snakes in those weeds there," laughed the girl. "One'll probably jump up and bite you on your little new nigger ass!"

Kate said nothing. Snakes hibernated in December, thank God for the smallest of favors, but she wasn't going to correct the girl.

"Know what a new nigger is?"

Kate shook her head. She was exhausted, her mind fogged. Her legs were bristled with the cold.

"It ain't black folks. I got no problem with black folks, yellow folks, white folks, whatever. New niggers is women. Like you. Like my mam. Lazy-ass, worthless, stinking wastes of air."

Kate nodded.

"New niggers expect everybody to do for 'em. They are shiftless, needy, whining all the time. Make me want to puke."

Kate let go the stream of hot liquid; she felt spatters strike her calves and go cold immediately.

It was after midnight; once they had reached Fayetteville the girl had insisted they circle east and north and then south again, a good additional forty-some miles, to throw off anyone who might be on the trail of the gasoline man's killer. They had stopped once to let Mistie go to the bathroom behind some cedars, and the girl had relieved herself right afterward, after tying Kate and Mistie together with two of Kate's winter scarf collection.

Now they were in the country, a mile and a half outside the town of Dillon, South Carolina, behind the Dairy Rite with its soaped-over windows and its peeling paint. The girl had yammered on and on about what great fun it would be to spend the night in a motel and then the next day the motel owners see in the paper that they had housed a famous murderer from Virginia, but when it came down to it, the girl decided they would spend the night in the Volvo behind the Dairy Rite because, after all, they were fugitives and fugitives couldn't afford to tempt fate.

There was nothing with which to wipe. Kate cringed for a moment, then used her hand. She didn't dare ask the girl if she could go in her purse for a tissue. She

163

pulled down her skirt and wrapped her coat about her waist.

I'll never be warm again. Donald is warm tonight, back home. Donnie is warm at school. What did Donald think about the note? Did he believe me? He's a lawyer, he's supposed to question everything.

"Okay," said the girl. "You and the kid are gonna sleep in the back." She waved with the gun. Kate climbed into the backseat, nudging Mistie over with her hand. The backseat was damp and smelled of urine; Mistie had wet herself when she'd fallen asleep several hours back. Kate made sure her coat was securely underneath herself.

The girl took Kate's scarves from the front. She ordered Mistie to tie Kate's hands behind her back with one. Mistie whimpered but did as she was told. The job was loose, but it gave the girl the chance to tighten them herself without Kate being able to lash out. Then the girl tied Mistie's in the same fashion, and bound their feet at the ankles. Kate couldn't imagine sleeping like this.

Claustrophobia, she thought. *I never knew what it was like*. She tried to work her wrists, but there was no flex room at all.

The girl locked the back doors, then placed wooden pallets upright against each door. "I'm a light sleeper," she said. "If for some reason you get out of those ties, which I don't think you will, I'll hear those pallets hit the ground and your brain'll be in sights of my gun before you can count to one-half."

Mistie drew up her knees, twisted and wiggled against her bound arms, and looked at Kate. She said, "Ow."

"I know, Mistie," said Kate. "I'm so sorry. This won't go on forever."

"I can make it go on long as I want to," said the girl. She slipped into the driver's seat and put one foot up on either side of the steering wheel. "Truth or dare?"

"I'm exhausted." Kate stretched her legs out to the other side of the floor, underneath Mistie. "If you want me to drive tomorrow, I need sleep."

"One more," said the girl. "Then I'll think about letting you alone. Truth or dare?"

Truth, she thought, you can't handle the truth. A small portion of her brain thought that was funny, but the rest was too numbed to know why. "Truth."

"Good!" The girl scratched her head. "Okay. When did you first get fucked?"

Kate felt the hairs on her neck bristle. "We've got a child in the car."

"Yeah, so?"

"Please don't say that, and don't ask me that."

The girl shook her head. "Women are such pussies, aren't you? God! Truth, or I got a dare for you."

"Please," said Kate. Breath, another breath. "Okay, my husband. Our wedding night."

The girl struck Kate across the forehead with the pistol, tearing a strip of skin away. "I think you're lying to me! I think you was horny as a rabbit."

"I was raised Catholic," said Kate. *Don't cry, oh, please don't cry.* Her head blazed and she could feel the blood oozing into her eyelashes. "I don't believe in sex outside of marriage."

"Huh," said the girl, but she considered this. "Maybe so. Maybe not. But you were itching for him to get in your pants, I bet. New niggers like dicks in their pants.

Maybe 'cause they wish they had one, themselves. You wish you had a dong?"

The car felt as if it were swaying, as if it were on a ferry, moving out to sea. Kate let her mind flow with it, and for a moment she saw the waves and could smell the brine, and see the stars sparkling on the water. She had a blanket around her shoulders to keep off the sea chill, and it was soft and white and drawing her to sleep.

"Hey!" The voice was right outside her mind. She opened her eyes to see the girl's face in her own, inches away.

"You going to sleep?"

"I think so. I can't help it."

"Fucker," said the girl. "Go to sleep, then. We'll get started really early tomorrow." The girl pulled away, back to the front, but made sure Kate could see the pistol in her hand.

And then Kate shut her eyes again and slumped against the seat and she was on the boat under the stars. The blanket was comforting and peaceful and she looked out at the water and thought, *I will float on forever. Away, away, and forever.*

Chapter Twenty-six

Mistie wanted to go home. Yesterday at school the teacher had said they were going to do something fun, but the girl with the gun had gotten in the car and made them do other things. Nothing had been fun.

The girl was really mean, meaner than Daddy sometimes. She hit the teacher and hurt her. She hadn't hurt Mistie yet but maybe she would. Mistie wanted to go home and watch television. She wanted to watch *Princess Silverlace*. She wanted to watch *Sesame Street* and count with the Count. She wanted to sit behind the trailer and play with the seedpods and repeat the little saying her sister Valerie thought was so funny, "Mama had a baby and its head popped off." She wanted to sleep on her bed. She wanted to see Tessa Kessler and sit beside her on the bus.

Last night the girl had tied Mistie's hands behind her back. She couldn't sleep like that, and whined until the girl woke up and said, "You little brat, you're keeping me awake!" But she untied Mistie's hands from the back and tied them in the front. That was better, but Mistie still could hardly sleep.

In the morning she told the teacher to drive into a town and go through the Burger King drive-in. That was okay. The girl didn't ask the teacher what she wanted but she did ask Mistie. Mistie said, "I don't know," and the girl laughed and said, "You got vocal cords after all!" and she got Mistie a biscuit with sausage and egg on top. Mistie hated egg, and let the yellow, greasy bits drop to the floor, but she ate the biscuit and the sausage and drank the cup of Coke, too.

Then the teacher drove to a bank and this time the teacher got some money out of a machine and the girl said, "We set for Texas! Yee-hah!"

Mistie didn't know where Texas was, but hoped it was near MeadowView Trailer Park so she could go home and watch TV.

Chapter Twenty-seven

They found a Texaco in Bloomville, South Carolina, another tiny town on another back road the girl insisted they take. She had said, "Get gas there. It's a Texaco. Bet they named it for Texas!"

Kate pulled up to the gas tank and turned off the engine. Immediately the girl took the keys from the ignition and stuck her thumb through the key ring.

"Make it quick," she said to Kate. Kate nodded; got out. Her feet were cold inside the Easy Spirits. What she wouldn't give for a pair of socks, a pair of Dockers, a sweatshirt instead of this stupid teacher's outfit. The peach sweater was scratchy now, and the gray skirt wrinkled and binding.

In the back, Mistie entertained herself by pulling yarn threads out of one of Kate's scarves, a green and white striped one, and wrapping them around her fingers until they turned white. There was a growing tangle of yarn on the floor of the backseat. She'd wet herself again last night.

The girl opened her own door, but sat in place with the gun in her lap. Her feet were up on the dash, and they wiggled back and forth, making squeaking sounds.

As she brushed her shirt back into some semblance of its former self, Kate checked herself in the reflection of the driver's window. She looked as though she'd been through a war. The side of her face was bruised, her forehead crossed with a long, tacky gouge that was slowly evolving into a scab. There were streaks of mud on her cheeks and chin. Her ear still stung where the girl had tried to twist it off. Her legs, unshaven for two days, were prickly. Her armpits, gone without deodorant for two days, were rank. Her hair was crusted with dried sweat.

There were a few natives outside the Texaco, two men in mechanic blue with knit caps and gloves, a young woman in a faux-fur parka with a toddler on her hip, and an old man in a heavy coat and a pair of rubber boots sitting atop a plastic Coke crate in front of the double garage doors. Over the closed garage doors hung a sign, MARTIN'S AUTO REPAIRS. WE USE ONLY FISHER AUTO PARTS. On the other side of the garage doors, by the corner of the building, was a Coke machine.

The wind had picked up since dawn, and the temperature was down to near freezing. Kate had to alternate hands to hold the cold pump handle long enough to fill the Volvo's tank. She watched her breaths puff on the air, little exclamation points crying out impotently.

Think, she told herself sternly. *Think it out. Concentrate on the idea you had last night.*

My story made sense. It made sense I was taking her home to give her some clothes. That was good, that was really a good one. The girl believed me. Others will, too.

The girl got out of the car and leaned against the back door. Her arms were crossed over her chest. How she could keep from shivering in the pants and striped shirt was beyond Kate. The girl watched Kate steadily. The gun, Kate knew, was in her trousers pocket, the knife on her ankle.

I will tell them Mistie missed the bus. I saw her wandering the halls, saw her in that nightgown and thought it was terribly sad. "Mr. Byron, I had some old clothes I was going to give her. Yes, agreed, it was wrong not to call someone and let them know she'd missed the bus. I was on my way home and planned on calling as soon as I got there. Mea culpa, Mr. Byron. Yes, well, that means, 'my fault.' No, it's not English. I had no idea we could be car-jacked. Thank God for everyone who assisted in our rescue. You'll have to come over to the house for an appreciation party."

All she needed was a moment. All she needed was one person to hear her and believe her.

Kate glanced at the South Carolinians by the garage doors. She looked at the meter on the pump. Half full, already up to fifteen dollars. The two-hundred-dollar withdrawal she'd made at a bank this morning—ridiculous bank; it wasn't her bank so the maximum withdrawal was two hundred—wasn't going to last long.

The girl's what, fourteen, fifteen, maybe sixteen? I

*will get out of this. I will get out of this. She thinks like
a child. I think like an adult.*

"I need caffeine," Kate said. Her voice sounded
steady, calm.

The girl raised one brow. "You had coffee at Burger
King."

"That's not enough," said Kate, trying to bring a lev-
ity into her words. With dismay, she saw the mechanics
and the mother go inside the store. But the old man on
the drink crate remained. He reached down slowly to
tuck his pants leg back inside the rubber boot. He
would help. He had to help. "Teachers drink coffee like
water," she continued. "I suppose it's an addiction of
sorts. I sure could use a drink, a Pepsi, Dr Pepper,
whatever."

"I could use a million bucks, so what?"

"You've got some quarters. I'll just get one quickly,
and come back. I'll get you one, too."

The girl glanced inside the car where Mistie was busy
unraveling the scarf. "She's so weird," she said in disgusted amazement. "She plays with everything. Her
food, her crotch. Makes me sick. She's nothing but a
typical new nigger in training, huh?"

Kate said nothing. She waited. Waited. Her heart
picked up speed, but she didn't let it show on her face.
Then the girl said, "Okay, and get one of them news-
papers from the machine there on the porch. I wanna
see something."

A few more squeezes and the nozzle clicked off, the
gas tank full at $23.93. Kate waited like a child with
her hand out as the girl fished quarters from her shirt
pocket. Kate imagined herself leaping upward in a Tae
Bo kick. She'd seen those women on TV, and knew they

would have been out of this situation in a second. She imagined herself slamming the girl's chest with a sudden and well-aimed foot, knocking the girl's breath from her lungs and legs from under her body with one move.

Just like you did with Willie Harrold.

Willie.

She immediately forgot about the girl squalling on the ground, and remembered Willie.

Willie's Daddy was probably at the school this very moment, insisting that Mr. Byron and Joe Angelone find out why the hell that coward Mrs. McDolen didn't show up for school. The phone would be ringing back at the McDolen house, unless Donald had read the note and had given the school the heads-up on his wife's sudden absence. *Donald, what are you thinking now?* Kate's stomach fluttered.

No, stop it, you can do this. Deep breath. Yes. Okay.

She trembled fiercely; dread and hope. She rubbed her arms to cover the tremors and said, "Brr, it's incredibly cold out here. Nearly forgotten it's almost Christmas."

"You watch your ass," said the girl, pressing six quarters into Kate's palm. " 'Cause I'm sure keepin' an eye on it, ugly as it is. False move, the kid'll die."

Kate nodded. She strode to the newspaper box and casually dropped in the quarters, took the paper and rolled it up under her arm, collected the dime in change. She looked at the old man on the crate. He was picking his teeth with a little stick.

Okay, now. Okay.

She walked to the drink machine. Her whole body shook; her calves knotted and twitched. She tucked one hand inside the other to keep from dropping the coins.

Here's your chance. Now. God, help me.

The old man on the drink crate, a mere two yards away, looked in her direction, smiled, and nodded. Kate put in one quarter, and listened as it fell through the machine works with a soft little *clink*.

Without turning to the man, she whispered, "Listen to me, please. I'm being kidnapped."

A second quarter into the machine. *Clink*. A taste of blood at the back of her mouth. Maybe she'd bitten her tongue, she couldn't tell.

"Call the Virginia State Police after we leave." Each word painfully dry. "Get my license plate number. Please. I'm in danger. I need your help."

She pressed the Pepsi button, and a can dropped into the retrieve slot. She bent to pick it up and put it into her coat pocket. Next quarter; *clink*.

"Don't do anything now. Just get the license number. Call the state police. Help me, please."

Second quarter, *clink*, Dr Pepper button pressed, *clunk*, can in the slot.

"Do you understand what I'm saying?" She reached for the Dr Pepper and put it in with the Pepsi. "I hope so." She turned back toward the car.

The girl stood in front of her, arms crossed. "I understand, all right." A look of sheer hatred, of sheer disbelief and wonderment, all rolled into one. Then, loudly, "Let me help you with those, Mom. You're always trying to do something nice for others, let me do something nice for you." She waggled her hand. Kate gave her the Dr Pepper and the newspaper.

No no no no no!

The old man on the Coke crate grinned and nodded.

The girl tipped her head toward the car, indicating Kate go on ahead. Kate moved on. The front door to the Texaco station banged open, and the young mother came out, calling, "George! Damn it, George, turn your hearing aid back on, old man, there's a phone call from your wife. Get in here!"

The old man looked confused until the young mother pointed at her ear; then he nodded and smiled.

"In the fucking car," hissed the girl.

Kate climbed in. She couldn't feel her hand on the door handle as she pulled it closed beside her. Through the windshield she saw the old man get up from the drink crate and waddle into the station after the young mother.

The girl dropped into the passenger's seat and yanked the door shut. "I've left the gas money on the tank. They'll find it. Now drive until I say don't drive. You goddamn, stupid, fucking bitch. Just wait, oh, yeah, just you wait!"

I am a stupid bitch at that, thought Kate, her heart lunging against her ribs. The remnants of the breakfast biscuit, eaten well over an hour ago, turned sour and repulsive in her stomach.

Another lesson in vocabulary.

Stupid.

Fucking.

Bitch.

Chapter Twenty-eight

There was a lake not far from Bloomville, South Carolina, due northwest from the Texaco station, passing over Interstate 95, and then through the towns of Summerton and Rimini. It was a huge lake, Lake Marion according to the signs, lined with tall trees and cabins, punctuated with boat ramps that led down to the water's edge.

Tony instructed Kate to follow the road along the lake's side. She'd know what she needed when she saw it. Minutes later she spied a cleared utility line and furrowed drive that traveled beneath the overhead wires. "There," said Tony, and the teacher turned the car onto the line. She rolled the window down and let fly, one at a time, the pages of the *Clarendon Courier*, the ten-page rag masquerading as a newspaper. There had been not one mention of the events in Southampton County, Virginia. Not one tiny article, not even a blurb. There was weather, and sports (the local high school football team had won their final game, 22–6), and a half-page photo spread of the "Miss Clarendon Holiday Pageant" winners (little girls in frilly gowns and tiaras), and a local sheriff's report of speeding tickets and driving without licenses and bad checks.

The Virginia armed robbery was clearly not big enough news. The Virginia murder of a gasoline man was clearly not important to South Carolinians.

About a half mile bouncing along the rocky stretch they came to a chain strung across a dirt road. There were thick pines and cedars on both sides. A sign hammered to the wooden post read CAMP LAKEVIEW. CLOSED. TRESPASSERS WILL BE PROSECUTED. GOD BLESS.

"Here," said Tony. "This looks right."

The teacher stopped the car in front of the chain. The teacher had said nothing since the Texaco; back to being a quiet little pussy. Oh, but she wouldn't be quiet for much longer. What Tony had in mind involved some good old-fashioned screaming.

An empty camp would be just the place.

"Break the chain," said Tony.

At last the teacher spoke. "How?"

"With the car, idiot. How do you even stand up straight without somebody telling you?"

The teacher shook her head but didn't argue. Tony wished she would argue. She felt like slapping the woman's face. That was okay, she'd save it all up. It was going to be a good, fun time.

The teacher backed the car up as far as she could go across the utility line to the heavy woods on the other side. She floored the gas pedal and the car lurched forward. It struck the chain with the front grille, bucking

177

momentarily, and then could go no farther.

"Again," said Tony.

The teacher backed the car and drove forward again, slamming into the chain with a satisfying sound of headlights smashing and metal fighting back. The hood popped open. Baby Doll, in the back with her tangle of scarf yard, gasped.

Tony said, "Fun, huh? Again."

Once more the teacher backed the car and floored it forward blindly. The chain stopped them short. The teacher floored the accelerator and the car inched forward. Dirt sprayed out behind as the wheels cut the ground.

"Shit," said Tony. "Stop for a second."

The teacher let up on the gas and put the car in park. Tony rolled down her window and stuck her head out. The chain was holding firm, but one of the wooden posts to which it was attached had snapped and was bowing over, splinters sticking out like a porcupine's tail.

"Everybody out," said Tony. The teacher climbed out but the kid stayed inside, her hands over her ears. Tony pulled open the kid's door, and yanked her out by the collar. She whimpered but did not struggle, then stood by the car with her arms wrapped around herself.

"We can kick it over," said Tony. "C'mon."

Tony and the teacher took turns striking the post with the bottom of their shoes, though the teacher's prissy-pot pumps missed more often than they connected. Tony remembered stomping the girl outside the barn after the Hot Heads had caught her fucking her boyfriend. With a grunt, Tony landed a square blow just above the crack and the post toppled, taking its end of the chain with it to the ground. Tony sniffed and wiped her nose. The snot was nearly frozen. She was going to need a coat soon. She wondered if it ever got cold in Texas. She forced the car's hood back down until it latched. "Okay. Let's get in there."

The rutted camp road took its scenic time reaching the lake. The place appeared to be some sort of churchy, Jesus getaway, with a designated MESS HALL, CHAPEL, an outdoor amphitheater made of rough-hewn logs, and wooden crosses planted in various spots along the drive. There were no cabins for campers, but large, rectangular platforms covered in pine needles and dead leaves.

"What are those?" Tony asked aloud.

"That's where the tents go," said the teacher.

"How do you know?"

"I used to be in Girl Scouts."

"Huh," said Tony. "Big shit."

The next curve in the road brought Lake Marion into view. It was stark blue through the trees, still and slick like a slice of sky cut and pasted between two layers of earth. Several Canada geese floated on the smooth surface, bobbing their heads up and down as if showing this was their space, bug out, folks.

The slope to the lake was gentle, sandy, littered with moss and mud and spotted with a small grouping of picnic tables. "Park there," said Tony, pointing to the slope. "Turn off the car."

The teacher eased to the top of the slope and cut the engine. She stared ahead, her face grim.

"This is a fine place," said Tony. "Ain't nobody around. Don't you think it's fine?"

The teacher didn't nod. The kid in the back sneezed.

"Well!" said Tony. "I think we'll stay here for a while. Get our heads back on straight. Here." She handed the teacher the red plaid scarf. "Tie your feet together, real tight. I'm going out for firewood so we can play Girl Scouts. You can show me how to build a fire, okay? But I don't want you taking off again or doing anything else stupid."

The teacher wrapped her ankles together with the scarf. Then, as before, Tony told the kid to tie the teacher's hands behind her back while she pointed the gun at the teacher's temple. Tony doubled-checked and tightened them a bit more. She could smell the fear and helplessness burning off the woman. She licked her lips to taste it on her tongue.

The teacher secured and seething in the front, Tony bound the kid in the back. Ankles. Hands. She wondered why the kid never tried to fight. If this had been Tony, she would have gone down biting and kicking. The kid kept her eyes closed as Tony tied her up; then she curled up on the seat.

Tony sat down on one of the picnic table benches, brushing away a plop of bird poop first with the back of her hand. For church kids, these sure were skilled vandals. There were names and initials carved everywhere in the wood. Hearts, crosses, even an occasional profanity. Well, church-kid profanity. *Hell's bells!* said one. *Go to the devil!* said another.

How far to Texas? She knew it was south of Virginia, and west. They were going in the right direction, but how much farther? Besides some new clothes, she would get a map as soon as she could. She would look up Lamesa. That's where Burton Petinske lived.

She knew because he'd sent her a birthday card when

she'd turned twelve. It was a few weeks late, but it came all the same. The card was a toothy German shepherd sitting on top of a crushed birthday cake, and inside it said, *I would have sent you birthday greetings on time, but when Old Killer decides to wait, we all wait!* Inside the card was a photo of Burton sitting on a fence with horses and cattle in the background. His note said *How do you like your old dad now?*

Tony had liked it plenty. Her dad was a rancher, with lots of land and animals. Thank God he wasn't in a cowboy hat like Little Joe, but he looked fine up there on the fence, his eyes staring straight at the camera, his arms muscular beneath the short sleeves of his tee. He'd looked just like an actor Tony had seen in a late-night movie on channel 45. The movie was *Desire Under the Elms*. The actor was Tony Perkins, not the *Good Morning America* weather guy but the guy she'd seen in *Psycho* over at Buddy's house once. He was cool, calm, brave, and handsome. He didn't let anything get in the way of what had to be done, not even a fucking baby. He did what he had to do without thinking twice.

That's when Tony decided she was Tony and not Angela. She told everybody once about her new name, and never answered to her pussy name again. She hadn't told anyone why she'd changed, though her mam, Darlene, and her sixth grade teacher were the only ones who asked.

With her new name she was stronger. She began to bind up her breasts with an Ace bandage. Her already boyish style of clothing became more severe, more like the real Tony would dress. Like her father would. Plain. Rugged. Nothing but blacks, browns, and blues. She'd cut her shoulder-length hair to above her ears. She started skipping school more than ever before.

She was destined for something great, she could feel it in her blood.

Tony's head was itching. She dug her stubby nails into the scalp and raked until it felt better. She wondered if Darlene and her old nitty head had gone back to school today. She wondered if Mam was curious as to where her oldest daughter had gone.

Over in the car, the teacher was looking at her through the window glass. Maybe wondering when Tony was going for the firewood. No, probably wondering how long she would have to travel with Tony. How much longer she would be tormented.

"I bet you are wondering," said Tony. "Hell, I'll set you straight on that right now." She hopped from the picnic table, trotted to the car, and pulled the front door open.

Chapter Twenty-nine

The girl ran toward the car, a bizarre and elated expression on her face. She looked as though a spirit had whispered something quite amazing into her ear and she couldn't wait to share the message. She tugged open the driver's door and rolled the window down halfway. Then she reached across Kate, clicked the key backward one turn, and shoved the gearshift into neutral.

What? God, not this . . . !

Kate bucked in her seat, and drove her face forward, catching her teeth in the girl's upper arm and biting down through the shirt.

"Bitch!" cried the girl, and she bit Kate back on the face. Kate wailed as the skin parted, but her teeth held tightly. *I will not let you do this, you can't kill us this way!*

The girl stood straight and struck Kate around the ears with her free fist, then jabbed at Kate's eyes with

183

her thumb. Stars split Kate's vision, followed immediately by searing heat. She opened her mouth and let go of the arm. Her head whipped down and away.

God, no!

The girl had her hands on the car door now and was pushing it shut. Kate rolled to the left, trying to fall out before the door clicked in place.

"Mistie!" she screamed. "We have to get out!"

The door struck her with force and drove her back inside. The girl grinned through the partially opened window. Kate shoved herself against the door again, and twisted about, trying to catch her elbow against the door handle.

It's not locked, I can get it open!

The girl laughed, then opened the back door long enough to roll the window down partway. She slammed the door shut and then went to the back of the car.

"Bye-bye, kids!" she said. "It's been fun, but not fun enough!" In the rearview, Kate could see the girl leaning against the trunk and pushing. The car inched forward, then stopped. The girl shouted, "Yeah!" and pushed again. The car hesitated, then moved. It dipped its nose toward the lake, and slowly crept down the slope.

"Mistie!" screamed Kate. In the back, the girl was staring out the window, eyes huge. "Mistie, oh, my God! I'm so sorry!"

Kate lay on the seat and kicked at the window. Her Easy Spirit heels slipped on the glass; she shook them off and kicked again with her bare feet. Her bare feet had no strength in them, and they only squeaked and streaked on the surface of the glass.

The car picked up speed. Kate could see the lake looming up, dark blue, immense, like a tidal wave ready to take them down.

"No!" Kate screamed again, kicking, kicking, kicking. She flopped over and tried to shove her head through the half-opened window, but the girl had been careful. It was not wide enough for Kate's shoulders. She looked over the back. Mistie had drawn up her knees and had buried her face in her lap.

Outside, back up the slope, the girl clapped her hands and stomped her feet.

The car struck the water, almost softly, but enough to send a spray across the side windows. The Volvo paused, bobbed, then drifted out until it was away from the bank, floating. Sinking.

"Mistie, I'm so sorry! I wanted to save you! God, help us!" Kate kicked the window again. Again. Her ankle twisted but she kicked again. She held her breath as she did. How long could she hold her breath? How long would she be under the water until she couldn't hold it anymore? How long until she would take a breath of lake water, and then another?

What did it feel like to drown?

Kate screamed. Mistie whimpered. Above it all, the cheering of the girl on the land behind them.

The front of the car dipped forward. Kate closed her eyes, catching her breath, holding it, then opening her eyes again to find the window and to stomp it.

Water seeped in under the dashboard, dripping furiously onto the floor mats. The car dipped farther forward like a deer taking a drink. The drips became a steady flow.

I'm going to drown first. Me, then Mistie. God, will

185

I go to hell? Is the road to hell really paved with good intentions?

The water through the front, faster now.

Does it hurt to drown? Did Susan Smith's little boys suffer a long time?

Mistie's breath hitched, and then the whimpering, louder now. Kate gasped, swallowed, gasped again, as the water outside climbed to window level. She could see the green muck of the lake, bits of algae, bits of grass and tiny sticks and other moving things, creatures too tiny to distinguish, patting against the glass, impatient for company.

"No!"

Kate kicked. The water rose to just below the window opening and suddenly she knew what it was like not to breathe. She couldn't catch her breath. It was too hot, too closed in, the air squeezed too tightly inside the car.

She sobbed, throwing her shoulder against the window. Maybe glass was more fragile under water. Maybe it would break once the car was filled.

I won't be able to see!

The car leaned forward, more sharply now, and Kate struggled to get her heels against the floor to stay upright. Water poured in through the front of the window into her lap. She slammed her head into the window, sending sparks into her brain, driving dark splinters into her consciousness.

In the backseat a quivering voice, louder than Kate would have ever expected.

"Now I lay me down to sleep, I pray the Lord my soul to keep."

Kate had prayed that with Donnie when he was little.

186

"If I should die before I wake, I pray the Lord my soul to take."

"Mistie, I'm so sorry!"

The floor in the front was flooded now, the water coming up over Kate's legs and to her waist. There was a slice of daylight over the rear of her window, the rest submerged.

Breathe breathe breathe, then hold your breath. Breathe breathe breathe breathe!

The front tires of the car struck lake bottom. It was clearly no deeper than five feet here. But that couldn't matter, it wouldn't matter, for children drown in five inches of water and bound women drown in five feet.

The back of the car started to settle. Water poured in through Mistie's window, and Kate turned to see the girl's face squeezed up, and her teeth gritted against the horror.

The water reached Kate's shoulders, chin, nose. She tilted her head back and gulped air. Then it covered her and she thought, *How long until I'm dead?*

There was a thump, a muffled rush. In the blur of lake water Kate turned to see the back door opening and arms reaching in. The arms took Mistie by the chin and pulled her out through the door as the back was completely submerged. The girl's legs trailed, kicking weakly. Kate twisted herself about and tried to hoist herself over the seat and into the back. The door was still open, flapping lazily as the car found its place of final rest on the soft lake floor.

Her eyes stinging in the lake muck, her lungs throbbing, Kate wriggled into the back.

Help me help me help me!

She tucked her body, and snapped it outward, trying

187

to move as a fish, an eel, to swim up and away. Her feet slipped on the floor, the seat, seeking purchase. The pressure in her lungs won out; she gulped water and gagged.

No!

A hand then, catching her by the hair and steering her out through the door, up into the light and the crest of the water and the *air!*

Kate's head broke the surface and she opened her mouth to drink the air and it hurt and it was incredibly pure and whole. *Air!*

She was dragged on her back, bobbing, until her heels caught in a tangle of water grasses. She arched, bringing her legs down and her body upright. The lake bottom was slick, soft. She stumbled, fell forward into the water, and the hand grabbed her hair again and turned her over again. She coughed and spat.

"Guess you forgot about those scarves, huh?" The girl's voice was close to Kate's ear. Matter-of-fact. Kate was dragged through the water plants, the mud, up, up.

Up.

And the world swelled, ebbed, folded, and went black.

Chapter Thirty

The campfire was pretty decent. The picnic table was old wood, and seasoned better than a lot of the stuff Mam bought to burn in their woodstove. There was nothing with which to break the table into smaller pieces, so she'd put dried pine needles underneath, with sticks collected by the teacher and Baby Doll on top of that. She'd picked up a pack of matches from the lot by the pumps back at the Texaco, a half pack with most of the red tips washed away in some past rain. But several were still potent, and the needles caught fire with little urging.

Tony had instructed the teacher to light and tend the fire, Girl Scout that she was. She'd done so without hesitation or argument, kneeling on the ground in her soaking wet clothes and fanning the little blaze with the palm of her hand. The flame had grown steadily until the underside of the table had given up the ghost and had accepted its fate. Now, there was quite a bonfire, and the three sat as close as they could without scorching themselves, crossed-legged.

The kid's shoes and socks were off and drying near the blaze. So were Tony's granddad's shoes and her pairs of socks. The teacher's winter scarves hung from the forked twigs of a green stick planted in the ground near the fire.

Tony had suggested the teacher take off her coat at least, to let it dry, but the teacher hadn't seemed to understand the suggestion, or really didn't care, so Tony let it go.

The sun was out, and there was no wind, which was a small favor. The geese were gone from the lake, replaced by a flock of mallards, ugly brown-headed females and pretty green-headed males. Tony wasn't sure of the time, because the clock was in the lake with the car. Maybe one, maybe two in the afternoon. She was hungry, and the smell of the wood smoke made her think of barbecued sandwiches and beer. Followed by some doughnut sticks.

"Truth or dare?" Tony said to the teacher.

The teacher was watching the fire, little twin tongues of flame dancing on the shiny surface of her eyes. Her hair was flattened against her face, framing the bones and making her look even older than she was. Her shoes were missing, lost somewhere amid the fish and the snapping turtles of Lake Marion. She didn't look like a teacher anymore. She looked like a whore who'd seen the bad end of her pimp. Tony grinned at the idea.

"I said truth or dare," Tony repeated.

The teacher did not say anything to Tony. She did not even look her way.

Tony lifted the gun from her knee and waved it at

the teacher. "Hey, you forget how this works? Did your little baptism erase your mind?"

The teacher's mouth opened, but no sound came out. It shut again.

Beside the teacher, the kid played with a batch of dried grasses she'd picked. She was intent on the chore of wrapping the stems about the seedpods, yanking the stems, and watching the pods snap off and fly into the air.

"Mama had a baby," she said dully, "and its head popped off." After each popped pod, she reached down to rub herself between her legs. Tony cringed.

"Truth. Or. Dare," Tony said, her attention back on the teacher, each word punctuated as if speaking to a foreigner.

The teacher's mouth opened, closed, opened. "Truth." It was more a mouthing than an actual word.

"Okay, then," said Tony. "Tell me. What was it like in the car? What did it feel like to think you were going to die?"

The teacher's hands came slowly from her lap, sliding up her arms to latch on to her elbows. One eye closed, then the other, then they both opened. The woman looked like a fucking, brain-dead monkey. One good scare and she was reduced to nothing more than a sack of wet clothes by a burning picnic table.

Tony cocked the pistol and pointed it at the teacher's foot. "I could also blow your big toe away if I wanted. Maybe all your toes if I wanted. And I'm starting to want."

The teacher's hands began rubbing the elbows. "Was hell."

"Yeah? Cool. Hell like how?"

A silent breath. A shiver. Eyes closing and opening. "Like . . . hell."

"Did it hurt?"

The eyebrows furrowed as if she wasn't sure what the word hurt meant. Her lip hitched. She shrugged, one shoulder lifting, then dropping more in a spasm than a conscious move.

Tony slammed her fist against the teacher's jaw, knocking her to her side in the pine needles. The woman lay panting, stirring crumbs of dead leaves with her breath. "Hurt," she said. "Yes."

Satisfied, Tony sat straight and crossed her legs again. "I didn't know if I was going to let you drown or not until that last minute," she said. "Oh, I rolled the windows down to let the water in faster, not to save you or anything. 'Cause what do I need with you two? I can drive a car if I want to. I know how."

The teacher remained on her side, staring into the fire. Her face was pinkening with the heat. She was going to have a sunburn.

"But I'm a fugitive," Tony continued. "Wanted for armed robbery and murder. It's a good cover having a teacher and kid along for the ride. So, I decided pull 'em out of the car. I'm a good swimmer, if you didn't notice. And I wasn't even a Girl Scout."

The teacher looked like she was going to go to sleep or pass out.

"Hey!" Tony kicked the woman in the side. "Hey, don't you dare!"

The teacher opened her eyes.

"Sit up. We've got things to do. Places to go and people to meet, my dad used to say. You hear me? Hey!" She kicked the woman again.

The teacher nodded, imperceptibly, into the leaf dust.

"All right, then!" said Tony. She held her hand close to the fire, and felt the sizzle on her palm. "All right, then."

Chapter Thirty-one

Her new clothes were funny and big. She felt as if she was playing dress-up. She used to play dress-up when she lived back in Kentucky, climbing inside her mother's petticoat and walking around in front of the mirror until Daddy said, "Get out of here, your mama and I got stuff to do. Watch the television!"

Mistie didn't remember much about Kentucky, but she did remember dress-up. She did remember TV. There were good shows on all day, and she didn't go to school because she was too young so she got to watch all the time except when Daddy got home. Cartoons, game shows, talk shows. The Hendersons didn't get cable like some of the other people in the apartment building, but Mistie knew how to move the wire antenna around on top of the set to get rid of most of the lines and the fuzz on the screen.

When the family moved to MeadowView, they got cable. Daddy hooked up something he said he wasn't supposed to do, but damn it, he swore, communication was supposed to be free, the Constitution said so, so cable was supposed to be free, too. Mama said Daddy probably was right. Mistie liked TV even better in Pippins than in Kentucky. Fifty-five channels, not counting the ones where they sold jewelry all the time and where the guys just stood in front of a bunch of people and talked about books.

She missed TV. She wanted to go home and watch *Princess Silverlace* and *Cat Dog* and *Sesame Street* and *Power Puff Girls*.

The girl and the teacher had used a rock to break a window out of one of the cabins. The girl had said, "This is the camp director's cabin, it's gotta have something we can use in there!" And wham! She threw a rock in the window and the teacher threw a rock in the window. Then the girl had said to Mistie, "Climb in there and unlock the door, Baby Doll."

Baby Doll. The mean girl called her Baby Doll. That was a nice name. Mistie climbed inside with help from the teacher and found a light switch. She turned it on and looked around. There was a bed, a dresser, a closet, a television. She turned the television on but there was nothing but squiggly lines.

"Hey!" The shout came from outside, through the broken window glass. "Open the goddamned door!"

Mistie looked at the window glass on the floor. It was sharp but pretty, like gems on a crown. She looked at the bed. It looked a lot like Mama and Daddy's bed except the cover was smoothed out and made up. Daddy and Mama slept together in a bed in the trailer. Mistie slept in a room by herself on a mattress on the floor. Sometimes when Mama was out of the trailer and

Mistie was home, Daddy would come to Mistie's room, kneel on the mattress, and say, "C'mon, honey, give me some sugar 'cause your mama don't love me no more." He would rub her between her legs and kiss her on the mouth. He tasted like tobacco juice. One time when she gagged he got mad and spit into her mouth and made her swallow it down.

"Now!" said the girl outside the window. "Or I'll crawl in there after you. Don't think I can't squeeze through this little hole!"

Mistie rubbed herself and looked at the bed. *Little hole.* Sometimes Daddy said something like that. He'd pull up her nightie and say, "I can get in that little, sweet hole. It's much better than your mama's. She's a frigid old bat. Don't you grow up to be no frigid bat." If Mistie was good and let him stick her and kiss her, then Daddy would let her watch whatever she wanted on TV for the rest of the night. He wouldn't even cuss over *Princess Silverlace.*

The girl had her head in the window hole, and her shoulders were nearly through. She was grunting. Mistie went out of the bedroom and into a dark, pine-paneled living room. There was a front door with a latch. She stared at the latch, not sure what to do with it. She pawed it, and tugged it. Then she turned the steel button and heard a *clack.* A second later, the door was thrown open by the girl. Mistie stumbled back several steps.

"This place got food and clothes?" the girl asked Mistie, then shook her head. "Why would I ask you?" The gun was in her hand. She waved it out the door and the teacher came in. The teacher hadn't said anything for a long time. She looked as if she were sleeping, but with her eyes open and standing up.

"Baby Doll, sit on that sofa there," said the girl, flicking her chin toward a brown, scratchy couch. Mistie dropped to the seat. It was soft and she rolled to the middle between the cushions. There was a clock on the wall near a fireplace. It was a black cat with eyes that went back and forth and a tail that did the same.

The teacher and the girl went into the bedroom. Mistie heard the girl say, "Oh, yeah, this works." They came out with an armload of clothes. The girl threw some at Mistie. They fell short and hit the floor.

"Figured the director would have a few things here. Wouldn't carry everything back and forth each year. Put those on."

Mistie picked the clothes off the floor. There was a pair of sweatpants with a drawstring at the waist. There was a sweatshirt with Tweety Bird on the front. There was a denim jacket. All of them were too big for her.

Mistie looked at the girl. What about her nightie?

The girl had kicked off her shoes and socks and was pulling on a pair of white socks. The teacher wasn't doing anything but looking at the floor, clothes over her own arm.

"Change!" said the girl. "You want to go in the lake again?"

Mistie took off her wet coat and the wet cardigan. She wriggled out of the wet underpants Mr. Angelone had given her at school. She didn't want to take off her wet nightie. She pulled on the sweatpants underneath the gown and drew them up as tightly as she could around her waist. She tried to tie the strings together but they wouldn't stay. Then she pushed up the pants legs so she could walk.

The teacher hadn't moved. "What's wrong?" asked the girl. "Afraid to let me see your body? Think it's disgusting? It is. But you better change or you can just freeze to death out there. Your choice. We've got some walking to do."

The teacher put the clothes she was holding on the back of the sofa. She took off her coat and dropped it to the floor. She pulled on a pair of red kneesocks. Then, she picked up the jeans and stepped into them as if she thought they, or she, might break if she moved too quickly. She pulled them up to her waist and snapped them closed. They were large, but not so big they fell off. She unzipped her skirt down the back, stepped out of it, then pulled her sweater off over her head and added it to the wet pile on the floor. She was wearing a white bra. It had streaks of brown-green on it. Lake water.

Mistie's mama had big titties. The teacher did, too, all round and poking out from her chest. Mistie stared. She didn't think teachers had titties. Titties were things Daddys liked to suck and play with. Why would a teacher have titties?

Mistie looked at the girl. She had taken off her wet trousers and was already in a pair of loose, tan corduroy pants. She was trying to put on a *WWJD* sweatshirt underneath the striped shirt without taking off the striped shirt or putting down the gun. Mistie tugged the Tweety sweatshirt on over the nightie. The pink fabric was clinging and damp on her skin, but it still felt good. She put on the denim jacket, and then her socks and shoes. Her pants legs fell down. She sat and rolled them up.

The girl struggled with the sweatshirt and gun. She got her arms out of the shirtsleeves, one at a time, and unbuttoned the top few buttons so she could slip the sweatshirt on over her head and down through the shirt. It looked like a magic guy Mistie had seen on TV, trying to get out of a straitjacket. For a brief second the girl's arms went up as she threaded the sweatshirt through the neck hole, and Mistie could see that the girl didn't have a bra on, but some sort of bandage wrapped around her chest. Maybe she had shot herself when Mistie was asleep?

The teacher was now dressed, with a vinyl zipper jacket over her own *Camp Lakeview* sweatshirt. She had sandals on over her knee socks. The girl had a long, green slippery raincoat and hiking boots.

Off the living room was a small kitchen with an empty refrigerator but stocked pantry. The girl instructed Mistie and the teacher to fill a canvas duffel bag with as many cans of food as they could. A can opener from a splintery kitchen drawer was tossed in with it all. With one last inspection, the girl found the TV buzzing in the bedroom and drove her foot through the screen. It sputtered and sparked, then died. They left the camp for the road.

Mistie couldn't keep up at first. The clothes were big and bulky, and the string around her waist kept coming untied, the pants kept riding down about her hips, and the pants leg rolls kept unrolling. This wasn't fun like playing dress-up in Mama's slip.

The girl walked in the back, behind Mistie and the teacher. Mistie could hear her breathing and sometimes scratching her head and playing with the gun. Mistie wondered where they were walking to. Mistie wondered if Mama was home and if she was watching TV. Mistie wondered when she would go home.

Suddenly, the girl said, "Hold up there, Baby Doll, I'm sick of watching you trippin' all over the place." The girl took a knife out of her sock and cut Mistie's pants legs off just above her ankle. "Now you can keep up and stop the damn stumbling. Okay?"

Mistie sniffed.

"Okay?"

Mistie nodded.

"Okay, then." She tipped her head for Mistie to get going. Mistie tripped over a stone in the road and kept on walking.

Chapter Thirty-two

The cab of the truck was crowded and hot, the seat lumpy, the floor gooey with spilled coffee. Tony sat by the door. Mistie was in the teacher's lap in the middle. The driver, Bobby "Blessing" Sanford, was at the wheel. His radio was turned on to a gospel station, and it was all Tony could do to keep from reaching over and twisting the knob to shut it off. Blessing liked to sing, and he liked to sing about Jesus.

"And he walks with me and he talks with me," he sang, a half note above the key on the radio, "an' he tells me I am his oooown. And the joy we share as we tarry therrrrrrre. No one has, ever, known."

The old man took his Styrofoam coffee cup from the dash-mounted drink holder and slurped down a few swigs. He had dentures, and they popped audibly as he smacked his lips in caffeine-laced pleasure.

The organ on the radio ground out the interlude between verses. Tony looked out at the road ahead, pitch-black, studded with headlights from oncoming traffic, and said, "Hey, man. Could you turn that music off? I'm not feeling so good."

Blessing wiped his mouth with the sleeve of his jacket and said, "Listenin' to the Lord's music should make you feel better."

"Yeah, well," said Tony. She wanted to play the man's game as long as she could, as far southwest as she could. Blessing thought Tony, the teacher, and Baby Doll were a family of Pentecostals catching a ride to a Christmas revival in San Antonio. Their car had broken down, so Tony had told him, and they were hitching as far as they could get.

Tony had spotted Blessing's rig in Pinewood, a small town past northwest of Lake Marion. At the center of the town two roads intersected, the larger of the two an east–west stretch on which several logging and milk trucks rumbled back and forth. Tony had imagined stealing a car—she'd taught herself to hot-wire when Leroy's dad's car wouldn't start last June—but then the sight of Blessing's truck parked in front of the Pinewood Bar and Grill changed her mind.

The cab was silver with a hand-painted montage of Christian symbols and scenes from the Bible. On the right side of the hood stood Adam, fig leaf intact; on the left stood Eve, fig leaf likewise tastefully in place. In between them a huge, walleyed snake coiled up a spindly apple tree and flashed his tongue at the woman. In a cloud over Adam, the eye of God in a triangle glared down at the couple. In a cloud over Eve, a disembodied Jesus' arm was extended, complete with bloody, nailed palm. The door on the driver's side had Jesus on the cross and Jacob on the ladder, with the name *Bobby "Blessing" Sanford, Saved Soul* painted in purple bubble letters at a jaunty angle. A collection of bumper stickers lined the base of the cab. *"Honk for Jesus." "No God. No Peace. Know God. Know Peace." "Golgotha Mini-Golf, Cave City, KY."*

Tony knew instantly how to work this one. She herded the teacher and the kid across the road to the bar and grill, and instructed them to sit on the bench outside the door. There was no hesitation; they'd walked nearly five miles that afternoon, and even Tony's feet were stinging inside the hiking boots. Tony poised herself under the corner light, which was just now humming into life in the twilight. She could see the passenger's door from this vantage point. Jesus walking on water and a flock of angels whirling about his head like a halo of lopsided hummingbirds.

Within a half hour, a lumpy old man with a pox-scarred face came out of the restaurant, Styrofoam coffee cup and truck keys in hand.

"Excuse me, sir," Tony said.

The man paused at the front of the cab and turned to face Tony. "Who, me?"

"Yes, sir, sorry if I startled you. I see you're a God-fearing man."

The man nodded, looking uncertain. He might have been mugged in the past, Tony suspected. But three females, how bad could that be?

"Me, my mom and sister need a ride," she said, moving away from the light and closer to the cab. "Our car broke down back up the road a ways. Blew a rod. Scared us nearly to death. All that smoke." Tony forced her lips up into a wide grin.

203

"That's terrible. Thank the Lord you didn't get hurt. Did you get hurt?"

"Oh, no, sir, the Lord was watching, that's for sure."

"You wanting a ride to a shop for a tow?"

"No, thank you. The car's a goner. Not worth fixing. But we're heading to Texas, if you're going anywhere near there."

"Texas!" The man's face opened up and, at last, he smiled. "That's a far piece, child. I always liked Texas, myself. What's in Texas?"

"Holiness Christmas revival."

"I thought Holiness didn't celebrate Christmas."

"That's Witnesses, sir."

"Mmm. You're right. I'm a Primitive Baptist, myself."

"Yes, sir."

"I'm heading up to Columbia, then getting on twenty to Atlanta, down eighty-five and then sixty-five to Mobile. Far as I go, I'm afraid."

Tony moved a few steps closer, sizing him up. He had no money on him, except for change from his coffee. But maybe there was a stash in the truck. One big mistake she'd made was letting the car go down in the lake with the teacher's cash card. "Do you have room for three extra folks? We don't take up much room. We'll squeeze up real tight. We'll be real quiet, too, if you like."

Bobby "Blessing" Sanford looked cautious again, until Tony opened her raincoat and showed him the *WWJD* sweatshirt. Then he nodded and said, "Hop in, sisters. Happy to help out."

As Blessing clambered into the driver's seat, Tony hurried to the bench and directed the teacher and Baby

Doll to the passenger door. "Get in," she told them in a whisper. "Don't say a fucking word unless I tell you to."

She reached up over Jesus' ecstatic, smug, "I-can-walk-on-water-and-you-can't" face and yanked the door open. The teacher went in first, then the kid. Tony climbed in last and shoved the kid onto the teacher's lap.

Blessing started up the engine, then frowned at the teacher. "Ma'am, your daughter says ya'll weren't hurt in that blowout, but you look right banged up."

"Oh," said Tony, shifting her butt around, trying to find a spot on the cushion that didn't feel like a spring was ready to chew through the vinyl, "well, a little banged up but I meant nothing serious. Like brain damage or broken bones or anything. Right, Mom?"

The teacher blinked slowly, and Tony said, "Right, Mom?" and touched her pocket where the gun was, and the teacher saw it because she nodded and said quietly, "Yes."

"My," said Blessing. "Want me to pray for you, ma'am?"

"Yeah," said Tony, "but can we do it on the road?"

She scratched at the itch on her scalp, then folded her hands primly in her lap. And smiled. Damn, did she smile. It pissed her off, hard as she had to smile to get the old geezer to steer his rig out to the road.

"Sure thing," said Blessing. Gears grated, the cab jerked, and a plastic cross hanging from the rearview swung back and struck Baby Doll in the forehead. She looked at it as if she'd never seen such a thing.

Once straightened out and at a decent clip on the highway, Blessing said, "Let us pray! Dear Lord! Put your hands on this woman and heal them wounds on her face! Help this family get to Texas safely and soundly."

"Thank you . . . ," said Tony.

"And bring your angels to watch over them and keep them. And the cherubim and the seraphim! All those heavenly bodies what work for you, Lord! Glory, hallelujah."

"Glory," said Tony.

"In the name of our Lord Jesus Christ we pray, He who shed His blood for the salvation of the world!"

Shut up!

"Amen."

"Thank you, sir."

They rode in silence for a short distance; then Blessing turned on the radio and spun the dial past everything tolerable to a religious station.

Tony grit her teeth to keep her mind off Blessing and his off-tune renditions of every church tune that God's disc jockey felt moved to play.

She thought about Burton. He lived in Lamesa, though she wasn't sure where. The birthday card had a post office address. Of course, ranchers would have hired hands go into town for their mail. They couldn't take chances that their mail would sit by a roadside in a box where gangs of local kids could drive by and steal it and then shoot the box up with a BB gun.

She thought about Leroy and his BB gun. What was Leroy doing now? Was he arrested? Was Little Joe? Mrs. Martin would have called the cops as soon as she could get her act together. Two, three minutes, tops. The police would arrive for the statement five minutes later. Was that enough time for the Hot Heads to escape in the Chevelle? Would Mrs. Martin be clear-headed enough to know what she was supposed to tell the cops?

Tony's mind circled back around to Whitey. His expression as he stood in the middle of the pile of shit that had been the Exxon convenience store, holding the revolver that wasn't supposed to have any bullets in it. She must have left bullets in the chamber last time she'd shot groundhogs behind Rainbow Lane. She hadn't checked inside. Stupid. Whitey was the one who had shot the gasoline man.

What was that like, seeing a dead man down your barrel? Was it like watching a white car bobbing in lake water while two people screamed inside? One way, no. The gun was fast and the lake was slow. But Tony's skin had broken out in little bumps as she'd watched. Tony had imagined the teacher trying to kick her way to freedom, trying to hold her breath and sucking in water over and over again. She had counted to see how long she, herself, could hold her breath. It wasn't very long, but maybe the teacher had better lungs. The woman didn't smoke or anything, Tony didn't think. She might smell like Mam in some ways but not like smoking.

How long until the teacher would have drowned?

Tony had gotten to forty-two holding her breath. She'd stood on the slope by the lake and took another breath as the car up-ended and the front began to dive. This time she got to forty-seven. She could hear the screams of the teacher and then the muffled prayer of the kid. The kid's voice was higher in pitch and more piercing to Tony's ear. And, well, sad.

That had shocked Tony the most. The sadness of the

prayer. It wasn't so much the words as the sound of the words. Tony had heard a sound like that long ago. Not a dying groundhog. Not a tortured cat. Something else.

Someone else long ago, though she didn't recall when, or who.

It was the prayer that had changed Tony's mind. She'd rolled the windows down to let the water fill up the car more quickly so the drowning would be faster. At least that was what she'd thought she'd done it for. But then, the open windows where what allowed her to open the car doors at the last moment. Water inside, water outside. She'd learned about that in driver's education at the middle school on one of the days she had attended. Once a car fills with water, the pressure is equalized and the doors will open.

Back in Pippins, the Hot Heads were either basking in the glow of an armed robbery well done, or had been arrested and were sitting in the jail in Emporia waiting to see what would happen to them. Armed robbery and murder. In Virginia that meant a charge of capital murder. A capital murder conviction meant the death penalty. What was the age somebody could fry or get poisoned over at the prison in Jarratt? It was less than eighteen, she knew that much. A boy who'd killed a car dealer up in Richmond had been seventeen at the time and they'd strapped him down and shot his veins full of acid.

Whitey was, what, sixteen? Or was he fifteen? Tony couldn't quite remember. But maybe old enough to execute. Leroy, Little Joe, and Buddy were accomplices. They could get the death penalty, too, especially Leroy, who was the oldest of them all. They would have squealed on Tony if they'd been arrested, too.

"How sweet the sound that saved a wretch like me," sang Blessing at the wheel. Lights from an approaching car swept over his features, etching them with glow and shadow, making him look at once like Jesus and then Satan himself. "I once was lost, but now am found, was blind but now I seeeeeeee."

They might just tell the police I was the one shot the gasoline man, thought Tony. *The gun was my dad's. My prints are all over it. They could say I killed him, then ran off for doing it.*

The plan had been to stir up trouble and make a name for the mysterious gang of Pippins outlaws. So what had happened?

Tony was going to make a phone call to Pippins as soon as she could. The only phone number she knew by heart was Leroy's. He would tell her what had gone down. If he was still at home.

"When we've been there ten thousand years, bright shining as the sun," sang Blessing, "we've no less days to sing his praise as when we first begun." The organ accompaniment on the radio swelled, ebbed, flourished, went silent.

Tony felt sleep tug at her eyes like an insistent hand pulling on a window shade. She touched the pistol through her coat pocket, caressed it. Truck driving. That would be a good job. She would be sixteen soon, and could get her permit. She could drive for Burton's ranch. She could haul hay. Straw. Feed. She could haul cows sometimes, stupid, obedient, and mindless cows. Maybe even a bull on occasion. Now that would be good. That would be a challenge.

That would be good.

She slept.

Chapter Thirty-three

The teacher's arms, which had been wrapped around Mistie's waist, had loosened and fallen to the sides. The lap was not comfortable; the teacher's legs were bony and sharp, the knees cutting beneath Mistie's knees whenever Mistie tried to move around. Daddy's lap was bigger and softer than the teacher's lap, but Mistie didn't like anybody's lap. She wanted to sit on the truck seat.

The girl with the gun was sleeping and snoring softly. The truck driver had turned down the radio and only spoke to himself on occasion when a car darted out in front or somebody in the same lane slammed on the brakes.

They were on a really big road now, with two lanes on each side divided by a strip of grass and sometimes trees. Everybody on their side drove in the same direction. Mistie remembered a road like this, when they had moved from Kentucky. They drove, drove, drove. She hated that road because it seemed like they were never going to stop. There wasn't anything to look at outside the window except trees and distant farms and huge signs. Daddy drove the car. Mama rode in the front and Mistie rode in the back between the boxes they'd packed the week before. Daddy said they had to make tracks since they were breaking their lease. Mistie didn't remember Daddy breaking anything except maybe he meant the door on the stove that night he got mad that the heat-n-serve rolls came out black on the bottom.

During part of the drive Daddy had put his hand on Mama's shoulder, then in her blouse, and she had slapped his hand away and cussed him out. "Yeah?" she had screeched. "Yeah? You think I'm gonna let you get all hot up over me anymore? You think I'm gonna let you get your self in a knot, and let you work it out on me later tonight? You can go to hell, you think that. I ain't never havin' no more of your babies. You see what happens to my babies?" Then she'd cried and held on to the door handle and Daddy had sworn he didn't want her flabby-ass body anyway, and they had driven on and on and on.

Mistie rubbed her eyes and then her crotch, making it warm. She took off the denim jacket, which had crumpled up behind her, and threw it on the floor over the girl's feet. She wriggled her shoulders and her neck. They were tired and they hurt. So did her feet. Part of the way from the camp the teacher had carried her, but most of the way Mistie had had to walk. The girl with the gun cussed at her when she walked too slowly, but her legs would only do what they wanted to do. And that wasn't walk real fast. The three of them had

211

stopped a few times, once to eat some pork and beans and canned corn and another time to poop behind some tall grass, but Mistie wanted to stop and go home.

It was hard to sit up straight on the teacher's lap. Mistie stretched her legs out, trying not to bump the truck driver with her left foot. Then, slowly, she lay over against the girl. Her head came down on the girl's folded arms. The girl didn't move. Mistie waited to see if the girl would wake up and hit her. But she didn't.

Mistie closed her eyes and was dreaming before the sounds of the truck had faded. Princess Silverlace was there, and the two went to play on a sliding board behind the golden castle.

Chapter Thirty-four

She dreamed.

The room was dim, small, and much too warm. There were rows of flat, blacktopped tables with four chairs each, a classroom. On the walls were charts and posters of old men with beards and probing eyes. The walls seeped water, which ran in rivulets to the floor. As if weeping. Or sweating. In the back of the classroom were cages stacked one upon another, filled with animals—birds, hamsters, mice, rats. Baby rhesus monkeys.

The room was inside Old Cabel Hall at the University of Virginia, a building with small, stuffy halls and small, stuffy stairwells. The place smelled old, as though students from two hundred years ago were still agonizing over exams and research papers.

Kate sat at a table near the center of the room next to a small window that had been nailed shut. She had forgotten to complete the reading for the day, and there was to be a quiz. The professor, a gangly man in gray, stood in front discussing a brain diagram shining from a projector. Kate couldn't hear him, but she could see his mouth opening and closing, and could see the other students around her taking furious notes.

Donald was on the other side of the room, nearest the door. He was reading a book. Kate wanted to call out to him but knew the professor would fail her if she did.

"You have to get this class right," said someone next to Kate, and she looked to her left to see Alice. "Psychology one-O-one," Alice continued. "Blow this, blow everything. That's what Freud said."

"It was Jung who said that, not Freud." This was Bill. Alice was sitting in his lap. He had one arm around her waist, the other hand down the front of her embroidered jeans. "You blow up the world with your carelessness."

Kate said, "I care. I just forgot to study last night."

"Pity," said Alice. "To the cage with you."

Everyone in the class turned in their seats, mechanically, at the same moment and the same speed, like wind-up toys whirling about on stands.

"She didn't study," Alice repeated sadly.

Then Kate saw she was indeed inside a cage. It was huge, nearly the size of the classroom itself, the floor wet and soiled and scattered with bits of cotton and feces. Students stood outside the bars, looking in and whispering.

"Let me out," said Kate. "I care!"

The students smiled. Alice shook her head. "Blow this, blow everything. Blown to hell in a handbasket."

A sudden panic clicked in Kate's chest. Her lungs

cramped, and she struggled to keep her trembling legs beneath her. She grabbed the bars and shook them. The people outside burst into laughter.

"Somebody, come on! Donald, let me out!"

Donald, whose face was just visible over the shoulders of those in front of him, said, "No. That is impossible. I made a plea bargain."

"A fine experiment," said a young woman with glasses.

"Yes, we should do well to observe her." It was Deidra Kirtley. She clutched a steno pad to her chest. "Where is Willie Harrold?"

A sliding noise. Above Kate's head, the barred roof of the cage was opening. The ceiling of the room opened, too, and there was the sky, dark and brooding and promising rain. The stench came first, that of rotten fish, of dead things at the bottom of a lake, drifting from the sky and into the cage with Kate. It struck her with the force of a blow, and she was knocked to the floor of the cage.

Beside her fell the body of Willie Harrold. It hit and splattered, rancid flesh ripped free of the bones, shimmering brain matter oozing from cracks in the skull, black blood spurting from eyes and nose. The blue, long-dead lips parted and said, "Happy. Sunny. Snowy. Fucked."

Kate tried to scream. Only a hissing passed her lips.

And it wasn't Willie anymore. It was Mistie Henderson, a small, animated corpse in a filthy pink nightie. "Mama had a baby and its head popped off," said the bloated tongue.

Then it was Donnie, dead in a Rickett-Heyden school jacket, his middle finger up in rigor mortised defiance.

Kate spun to run, and slammed into a towering wire structure in the cage with her. It was a bizarre and horrible woman, a woman fashioned of mesh, her long, twisted arms outstretched, her single pointed steel breast protruding viciously. Black sludge dripped like milk from the tip. The eyes were lidless glass orbs.

Kate backed away from the monstrosity but her heels slipped in the cotton and the filth on the floor. The wire face nodded at her once. The arms reached out, creaking with the effort, and closed in around Kate's body. Kate struggled as the wire-mesh mother dragged her up and into its hideous embrace. The steel nipple pierced her chest.

Kate threw back her head to scream, to beg for help, but her tongue was dead in her mouth. The glass eyes of the mother considered Kate. There was no emotion there, only a void, deep and cold, in which Kate caught a glimpse of her own wire-mesh reflection. Her own steel teeth, her own metallic breasts. Kate's face was pushed down to the nipple, and it was thrust into her mouth.

She began to suck.

Chapter Thirty-five

"Fuckin' A!" said Tony as she threw the duffel bag onto the bed closet to the door. "A real honest-to-God bed!"

The teacher and Baby Doll stood by the dresser that held the television, waiting for Tony to tell them what to do. The teacher's silence since the car went into the lake yesterday was wearing thin. Very thin.

"I get this bed," said Tony. "You two get that one. The Lord works in mysterious ways, don't He?"

Tony had never slept in a motel before, and took it all in with a quick pivot about on her foot. Two double beds, made up with blue and gold spreads. Over the beds, a set of scenes showing fishermen hauling a catch up by nets in the setting sun; Mobile, Blessing had explained as they'd approached the city limits, was located on a harbor on the Gulf of Mexico. It sounded so foreign, the Gulf of Mexico. Maybe they were close to Mexico. Texas was close to Mexico, too.

Tony decided she was going to go see the gulf before

they left Mobile. She had never been to the beach, and those pictures made the gulf look a lot like the ocean.

Between the two beds, a small table with a single drawer and a lamp with a tilted lampshade. Next to the television set was a dresser with a large mirror above it. On the dresser, a small refrigerator. "Man," said Tony. "I could live here." On the far side opposite the door, a small area with another mirror, a sink, and a rack for hanging clothes. Off that, what was likely the toilet, and even a shower, she bet. The heater was on full force, and already Tony was sweating.

Baby Doll sat on the end of the second bed and stared at the television set. The teacher sat down near the headboard and looked at the telephone.

"Oh, no, no," said Tony. She reached down and ripped the phone from the wall. "Absolutely, positutely not." She put the phone under one of the pillows on her bed, then took the pistol from her coat pocket and threw the coat on the chair near the window. Heavy, blue-flowered drapes covered the window. That was excellent. They would stay drawn. Nobody needed to see out. And sure as hell nobody needed to see in.

Bobby "Blessing" Sanford had been the sugar daddy for this room at the Mobile South Motor Inn. They'd driven through the night, across the state of Georgia, then down through Alabama, reaching Mobile by mid-day. Blessing had stopped the rig for a late dinner, breakfast, and lunch, inviting the "family" to join him at the various diners. Tony had declined, saying they would eat from their knapsack because were saving their money for the revival. There would be a love of-fering taken; they didn't want to face the Lord empty-handed. This worked. Blessing paid for all the meals.

Tony and Baby Doll had eaten fairly well. The teacher, still silent, ate very little. When Blessing was outside the cab before their last leg to Mobile, kicking off some dog poop he'd stepped in at the truck stop, Tony had peeked into his glove box and found an envelope with a small stack of bills. She'd taken most but left some so he wouldn't notice right away.

When they reached Mobile—the biggest city Tony had ever seen—Blessing apologized again for only going so far, and offered to pay for their night at the Days Inn. It was nearing eight P.M. Tony didn't argue. She told the man he'd done unto the least of those, just like Jesus had commanded, and Blessing said he'd continue to pray that they made it to Texas safely.

Tony propped up a pillow and lay back against it, the pistol by her side. She tried to pick up the remote control from the bedside table but it was glued down. That was queer. Guess people stole stuff from motel rooms. She punched the power button. The screen flickered to life. It was a menu channel, showing what HBO movies could be rented, and what local channels were available.

Baby Doll pulled her feet up to the bed, and grabbed her toes with her fingers. The teacher folded her hands in her lap and looked at the floor.

Tony flipped through the channels. Maybe there would be some news with word about a murder and robbery in Pippins, Virginia. She made a full circuit, back around to the menu channel and then up again. No news. Baby Doll watched with rapt attention. It even looked as though she was smiling.

"Hey," said Tony, stopping the channel on 5, on which a commercial for a local store—Otto's Hardware—was bragging about their fifty-percent-off-all-bathroom-fixtures sale to an exaggerated melody played by bugles and saxophones. "You like TV, don't you?"

The kid didn't say anything.

"Hey!" said Tony. "I asked you a question. You big on TV? You like it?"

Baby Doll nodded.

"Yeah? What you like to watch?"

She said something, but Tony couldn't hear it over the hardware commercial. She punched the mute button on the remote. "What did you say?"

"Princess Silverlace," said Baby Doll.

"What's that? A show?"

The kid nodded.

"What channel's it on?"

The kid didn't seem to know, or wasn't sure what the question was. Tony stared at the child and wondered what was going on in that bizarre little mind. She pressed the channel changer. Black and white show, a street scene with a kid in a striped shirt, a bike, and a fat, drunk man.

The kid said, quietly, "Andy Griffith."

"Yeah?" Tony looked at the set. The drunk guy and the kid went into the sheriff's office and were greeted by the gangly deputy. Tony pressed the channel changer. Stacks of people atop each other.

The kid said, "Hollywood Squares."

"Yep," said Tony. "That's what that is." Channel changer. Some police thing. The kid said, "Law and Order." Changer. The kid said, "Seinfeld." Changer. "Sponge Bob Square Pants."

Tony rubbed her neck, then her head. She scratched. "Is there any show you don't know?"

The kid didn't say anything. She was gazing at Sponge Bob with something akin to adoration.

Tony left it on the cartoon. She patted the pillow where she'd put the phone. She had not had the chance to call Leroy; there was never a time when they'd been with Blessing that she'd been able to secure the teacher and the kid so she could go off alone. But now there were towels and cords and pillowcases at her disposal.

First things first, however.

"You stink bad," Tony said to the teacher. The teacher looked at her without raising her head. "That's what I hate about women, well, one thing. They fuckin' stink all the time. God isn't Father, like Blessing says. God's a woman, you know that? And a real Bitch at that. If God was a man he wouldn't have fucked the world up so bad. What you think about that?"

The teacher mouthed something that looked like, "I don't know."

"Know why women have higher voices than men do? God made them that way so they'll sound like children to men, so men will want to protect them. Makes me want to puke!"

The teacher looked away from Tony, back to the floor. She didn't seem afraid anymore, she seemed spaced. Maybe water in her lungs had fucked up her mind. Tony kicked the woman's shin with her hiking boot. The woman flinched, but she didn't make a sound.

"Truth or dare?" said Tony. She'd get the teacher out of this daze if she had to beat the shit out of her.

The teacher shrugged, then whispered, "Truth. What the hell."

"Ha!" shouted Tony. "You said hell, a teacher said hell! They're gonna fire your ass for saying hell, if I tell 'em! But they'll fire you for takin' that kid home without permission to give her some clothes, won't they? Too bad, too bad. Okay, truth. You like it when your husband fucks you? You like having someone on top of you, poking you hard and you can't move or anything? You like that?"

The teacher's shoulders lifted and dropped once. A shrug.

"That a yes? I bet it's a yes. Gross. Okay, maybe you like somebody taking over your body and doing what they want with it. But, truth again. What is it like, having a baby? What's it feel like, getting your cunt ripped open by some ugly, wailin' little brat?"

The teacher looked from the floor to Tony. It was as if she had to drag her eyes with her head as she moved it. She said, "I remember joy seeing my son. The pain is forgotten."

Tony's brows drew tight. "How many kids you have?"

"One."

"Just one? A son?"

The teacher nodded, up-down-up, as if someone had her head on a string.

Tony stared at the woman, and, incredulous, said, "You lied to me?"

The teacher's eyes darkened a fraction, as if she had a vague realization that she'd done wrong. Oh, had she ever.

"No," said the teacher. "Did I?"

Tony snatched up the gun and jumped to her feet. She slammed the butt of the gun against the teacher's ear. The teacher wailed and rolled backward, drawing her legs up and covering her head with her hands. "You lied to me! You said you had a daughter and you were taking Baby Doll to give her some clothes!"

The teacher groaned. "No."

"You never lie to me. People don't lie to me! They don't lie to me!" She hit the teacher with the gun, pound, pound, pound, and it felt good. She said, "Get up! Get in the bathroom or I'll shoot you apart! I'll shoot you to pieces, starting with your feet all the way up to your head."

The woman groaned again and rolled over and up. She stumbled toward the bathroom. "Leave me alone. Please."

"You lied to me!"

"I was scared, I . . ." Her words trailed, muddling into incoherent murmurs. Tony pulled the teacher into the bathroom and slammed the door behind her. "I'm gonna tie you up. Keep you where I don't have to look at you."

"I . . . won't lie . . . anymore." There was drool. Disgusting.

"Get in the tub!" Tony slid the shower curtain back as far as it would go. It was a happy shower curtain, covered with smiling fish and crabs and sea horses. Tony slammed the woman in the chest, knocking her back over the edge of the tub. She landed on her ass with a grunt, arms up in a protective stance, head bouncing against the far wall's tile. She remained without moving, stunned or terrified or both. Back in the bedroom, there was canned laughter on the television set. The girl had probably not moved an inch.

A tidy row of bleached, white towels, hand towels, and washcloths were draped on a bar over the toilet. Tony yanked down the largest towel, bit the edge with all the strength in her jaw, and tore the towel down the center. It made two decent-sized strips. She scraped terry lint from her tongue with her teeth.

"Get your clothes off," said Tony. "Stinkin' liar!"

The teacher had found the bump on her head, and was trying to rub it. "What?"

"Now."

The teacher shook her head, swish, swish, slowly, against the far wall tile.

"Don't fuck with me. Get 'em off."

The woman began to breathe funny, heavy, loud, as if she were having a heart attack or a blood clot in the brain or something. But she worked her fingers into the backs of her shoes and worked them off, and then the socks. She grappled for the side of the tub to stand up but couldn't seem to do it. She remained seated to pull off the sweatshirt and then the jeans. She sat, knees up against her chest, in her bra and panties. The breathing noises, raspy and loud, ran a blade up Tony's spine.

"Underwear, too."

The teacher fumbled with the back of her bra and worked the hooks apart. It fell to the slick tub floor. The woman's breasts had dark nipples and stretch marks. A mother's breasts, thought Tony. Deformed from milk and nursing. The teacher slid her panties down, and shook them free of her ankles. Her chest heaved. Her eyes had closed.

"Get up."

The teacher fumbled with the edge of the tub and got her feet under her. She stood, teetering, then leaned on the rear wall.

"Mobile South Motor Inn oughta have lots of nice warm shower water," said Tony. "Hands up to the curtain rod."

The teacher shook her head, her eyes still closed.

Tony grabbed one arm and yanked it upward. The teacher's other arm followed as if with a mind of its own. With one of the towel strips, Tony secured the woman's wrists together and knotted them to the rod.

"Ever see the movie *Scarface*?" asked Tony as she stood back to admire her work. "Mam's boyfriend rented it one time. There was this guy. He was a friend of Al Pacino. He went to a drug deal in some motel room, but the drug deal went bad. This drug dealer with a gun tied Pacino's friend up in the bathtub with his hands on the curtain rod. You see that? God, it was great."

The teacher shook her head.

"You lying? Everybody seen *Scarface*."

"I didn't . . . see it." A noisy gasp. "I don't . . . care for Al Pacino."

"Everybody likes Al Pacino. He's the man. What's wrong with you? Well, anyway, this guy gets tied up in the bathtub and know what they do? They cut off his arms with a chain saw! Cool, huh? Pacino doesn't know what's happening, he's down on the street waiting. But the motel room gets turned into this fucking butcher shop!"

The teacher's eyes opened and stayed open. She looked at her bound wrists and began to struggle, began to kick and twist. The rod creaked but didn't pull loose. It was threaded into the wall and screwed in place. Mobile South Motor Inn had done a nice job choosing and installing the bathroom fixtures. Must have gotten them at Otto's Hardware.

"I don't have a chain saw," said Tony. "God, you're stupid."

The teacher didn't stop twisting. She sounded like the goddamned Elephant Man the way she wheezed and coughed. *I am not an animal, I am a teacher!*

Tony turned on the shower and adjusted the nozzle so it struck the teacher in the head. The water was cold. She turned the knob until it was warm. "See, that's not bad," she said, nodding to herself. "That oughta rinse you off. Get rid of some of that stink. I'm going out. When I get back, I'll let you down. Then we're gonna talk about Baby Doll. About the real reason you had her hiding in the car, why she rubs herself all the time. I bet you know. I know you know. And you ain't gonna lie no more." Snatching up the second strip, Tony worked it roughly into the woman's mouth, forcing it through teeth and over tongue, and tied it at the back, catching strands of flat hair in the knot. The woman gagged, and a whistling breath came through her nose, fast, irregular.

Tony took the gun into the bedroom. The kid was on her side now, her arm beneath her head, watching as a cartoon kitchen sponge explained to a starfish why they should have a fall fish festival. Her legs were locked around each other like a braid of red licorice. One shoe had fallen to the carpeted floor.

"Hey," Tony said. "I'm going out. I gotta tie you up."

The girl didn't sit up. She just held her hands out in Tony's direction without taking her eyes from the screen. Disgusted, Tony dumped a pillow from the case and secured the kid's hands together in front. A second pillowcase bound her ankles. "Those pillowcases aren't too bad, kinda soft, I guess." The girl didn't reply.

"I'll be back. Who said that? What movie? Who said 'I'll be back'?"

The girl looked at Tony and then back at the TV.

"It was Arnold Schwarzenegger. You knew that, huh? You know all those shows on TV."

The girl seemed to smile, but Tony knew it was at the sponge cartoon.

Chapter Thirty-six

Water roared in her bad ear, pounding relentlessly like someone driving a nail into her skull. Her face, damaged by blows and bites, felt as if it were ready to let go of its skin in resignation. Her arms burned with immobility. Her legs ached. She opened her eyes to light and mist, and closed them again. Her tongue fought the intrusive terry and could not push it out.

Over the sound of the water, a slam. A vibration in the floor of the tub. A door closing, somewhere beyond the water.

Her mind moved as if in cold lake water, grabbing at thoughts but coming up with only slippery, rotting impressions.

Cotton on the ground. Blood on her thighs. The copper taste of bile. The second grader in the backseat, sneezing beneath a quilt. Hands between her legs, uninvited, probing, taunting. Her fingerprints on a foyer table. An old brick mansion, void of her son, her husband, herself. Chalk dust on her hands. An accident report on her desk.

She bent her head forward, backward, to the side, but the spray of water was wide and still it struck her head.

Images, tumbling one atop the other in the darkness behind her eyelids.

A puppy trembling in the back of Bill's car on the way to Kate's dorm room.

Donnie at five, sitting with Kate in the living room of their Richmond town house, helping her put together a Christmas box for children in Ethiopia. Pencils, toothbrushes, combs, stickers, crayons. Donnie saying, "I bet those kids'll be really happy when they get this." Kate nodding, smiling. "It's good to help other people. That's the best we can do with our lives, help others." Donnie asked what the Ethiopian children's names were. Kate didn't know.

Donnie firing his rifle at the dead apple tree, and the bark of the trunk opening like a dark, brown flower.

A child in a pink nightie and donated cardigan, licking chocolate from her hands as if it were manna from God.

The mouth of a gun screaming silently at her from the other side of the car.

A teenage girl with the red war-stripes, laughing in the passenger's seat.

The girl. The murderer.

Where was the girl?

Maybe she'd gone off to steal a car. A car, yes, that's where she went. They'd need a car. Kate's car was in a lake somewhere. Where? Where was the lake? Kate couldn't remember.

No, a chain saw. Maybe she's gone to steal a chain saw.

Kate spasmed in the warmth of the water. She opened her eyes again and blinked. Steam rose to her nostrils; mist collected on her eyelashes in heavy beads.

Wake up, wake up!

The water was real. It was now.

The television droned loudly in the bedroom. Scratchy violin music and high-pitched dialogue from actors hired to voice-over in cartoons. Did Mistie go out with the girl? No. No. The girl hated Kate. She hated Mistie. Mistie was in there on one of the beds, watching the cartoon.

Go back to sleep, Kate. It's easier when you're sleeping. The water will go away if you sleep.

Mistie sneezed loudly.

Kate's head whipped up and back, gasping air. The water spray roared against her cheek. She looked at the open door leading to the bedroom. She could see just the very corner of the room, the edge of the dresser on which the television sat. Mistie was on the bed in there, watching TV as Kate hung like a beef carcass in the tub.

Kate drew in the wet air through her mouth. *Wake up, Kate!* Grit and dried sweat ran down her skin to swirl and vanish into the drain. As her breaths steadied, her mind cleared. Vague, nebulous thoughts drew together, took shape.

Bitch.

She was tied in a bathroom in a Mobile, Alabama, motel.

The bitch!

Kate had taken her chance to save Mistie Henderson

from her abusive home, and the goddamn little murdering bitch, on a whim, had snatched it away.

Goddamned little bitch!

On a whim the girl had turned Kate's dream around, smashed it, and had thrown it back in her face. She had nearly killed them both in the lake, and then pulled them back from the brink so she could have something with which to play. Something to entertain her on this trip to Texas.

Wrong. Wrong wrong wrong.

Little shit.

Kate's fists clenched. She bore down with her whole body, lifting her legs to her chest and pulling. The rod bent a little but did not give.

Fucking little shit. Who the hell does she think she is? How dare she do this to me! I will not have this!

She yanked on the rod; she put her feet on the tiled rear wall and drew herself up, but the rod did not fall.

I'm a teacher! I'm Kate McDolen of the Southampton McDolens! She's nothing! Fuck her!

She fought the shower curtain rod, twisting, jerking, slipping on the wet tub and regaining her balance. The rod held tightly. She stopped and waited, gathered her wits and her strength. She pulled again, gritting her teeth into the terry gag as if that would fortify the whole of her body and soul.

The rod bent a bit more, but did not break free of the walls.

Okay.

She clenched her muscles to make them stop struggling.

Just hold it a minute.

231

Her breathing was wild and irregular, but her resolve was not.

Stop and wait.

Outside in the bedroom, it sounded as if Mistie was laughing.

I'll wait, thought Kate. *I'll be here. I'll play her game. But I'll use my sharper wit and my better breeding. I'll kill her if I have to, but she will not win.*

Okay.

Oh, yes.

The warm water began to grow cooler on Kate's neck and shoulder. She shivered, but grit her teeth. Her lip went up in a sneer around the soaked and heavy gag. Oh, when the girl got back they'd have a talk. Oh, yes, they would.

Okay.

Chapter Thirty-seven

The waterfront was not far from the Mobile South Motor Lodge, down a dark and narrow paved road and past a brightly lit seafood restaurant and its parking lot crammed with patrons' automobiles. From inside the restaurant came waves of sound—hoots and hollering and country music from a jukebox. Outside in the lot a young couple leaned against each other and their car, giggling, snuggling.

The sign on top of the restaurant's roof read CATFISH DELITE, TASTY GULF TREATS SINCE 1962. It blinked as if there was a short in it somewhere. For a moment Tony thought of hot-wiring a car from this lot, but it was too close to the motel and the owner would find it in a heartbeat and then they might find Tony and the teacher and Baby Doll, too, and throw them all in some goddamned Alabama lockup.

Tony could smell the fried fish as she passed the restaurant, and her tongue watered. She slowed her pace to savor the smell. She'd had catfish once in her life, but that had been many years ago, when she was six.

She remembered.

Burton had taken her fishing on the Nottoway River in Southampton County. He didn't take Darlene because Darlene had whined that she didn't like hooks and didn't like worms and especially didn't like sitting in the mud and getting her clothes all messed up. But Burton and Tony went that one time, dressed in jeans and boots and packing rods and two lunches in a brown paper grocery bag. What they did was illegal, Burton had told Tony in the truck on the way, because the best fishing spot was on the edge of the McDolen property where the river slowed and deep pools gathered.

"Screw the McDolens," Burton had said as he'd lit his cigar and blown the smoke out the open truck window. It was June, and the day was overcast and hot. "They can kiss my lily white ass, they find us here. They think they own a river? Hell, no, they don't. Nobody owns a river."

Burton had driven off the road to a grassy, hidden spot on McDolen property where clusters of weeping willow trees were punctuated with NO TRESPASSING signs. Tony sat beside her father on the riverbank and dug with her fingers into the soil until she came up with a few grubs, some pill bugs, and one long, red-brown earthworm that crapped black dirt in her hand. Burton showed her how to drive the hook through the body of the grubs. The grubs twisted on the sharp probe, and when Tony asked Burton if it hurt them, he said, "Hell, yeah, it hurts 'em. It's supposed to hurt 'em. But that's why God made 'em."

He'd laughed. She'd laughed. She put the hook through the earthworm, then through it again, so it was impaled in a loop. They'd caught several catfish that afternoon, and taken them home where Burton scraped them clean in an aluminum tub in the backyard while Lorilynn complained from the deck that she'd heard somebody upriver was dumping shit in the Nottoway River and so she wasn't going to eat any of that smelly, diseased catch.

Burton had rolled his eyes as the fish scales flew, and said to Tony, "Got a joke for you. What smells worse than a dead, slimy fish? A live, slimy pussy!" He laughed. Tony laughed, though she thought she knew what the joke meant and it didn't seem funny at the time.

She remembered.

Tony ambled up the graveled lot behind the restaurant, where she paused at the Dumpsters. Light from the rear windows of the restaurant pooled across the lot in a yellow wave and splashed up to the barrels, making it easy to see in the little square side doors. There were some fairly good scrapings there—whole pieces of breaded trout, shrimps glistening with smears of tartar sauce, frog legs deep-fried in cornmeal, rolls barely nibbled on. Back at the motel there were some canned foods in the duffel bag, but none of them had the allure that these odorous bits did. Tony reached in, then pulled her hand back out. She'd reward herself after she found the gulf. She'd pocket as much as she could on her return trip. She'd eat it all in front of the teacher.

The air was warmer and stickier in Alabama than in Virginia. Tony pushed up the sleeves of the WWJD sweatshirt and felt the heavy air sucking her skin. In the darkness on the other side of the street where a streetlight had burned out something fell over, rolled, then stopped. A dog, Tony guessed, sniffing around for cats. Let it come near her, and she'd take care of it like she did the animals on Rainbow Lane. That would be fun. She hadn't taken a dog apart in weeks.

There was a phone booth on the corner of the Catfish Delite parking lot. Tony pushed through the folding glass door and stepped inside. There was no phone book hanging on the chain, and the light in the ceiling didn't work. The phone itself, a clunky silver apparatus, was tacky with bits of chewed gum and other crusted substances. Tony gingerly lifted the receiver, tapped zero, and Leroy's number. After speaking her name on request to the computer-operator, she waited, one foot shaking on the floor, one hand scratching the top of her head. *Come on, come on.*

The line was busy. Tony slammed the receiver down. *That's okay, I know Buddy's number. Nobody talks on the phone at Buddy's house. Nobody likes Buddy or his family so nobody ever calls.*

After three rings, a gruff male voice answered. "Low?" It wasn't Buddy but some other man, one of the uncles, cousins, or in-laws who crashed at Buddy's house on an ongoing, rotating schedule.

"Hey!" Tony tried to interject before anything else was spoken. "Say yes!"

But the man couldn't hear Tony's words or didn't

care that he did, he grumbled at the request to accept charges and the line went dead.

"Screw it," Tony swore. She tried to remember Little Joe's number, but couldn't. It had a nine and five and two and something else. Whitey's phone had been disconnected last month because Whitey's mom was mad about a $458 900 number bill Whitey had racked up on a tarot-reading line and refused to pay the bill.

Tony leaned against the phone booth wall and watched as a car pulled out of the restaurant lot, and another pulled in. She licked the flavor of salty air off her lips and let out a long breath. She dialed Leroy again. Again, busy. She slammed the receiver down and leaned against the booth wall, arms crossed. Who the hell did Leroy's family have to talk to? Maybe Leroy was in jail and they were talking to him. They'd be cussin' on one end of the line while Leroy, on the other, kept his ass to the wall 'cause one of the other inmates, a huge-assed retarded man, thought he was sweetpants. Leroy's mom would cry, of course. Maybe even Leroy would cry. Tony wondered what Leroy crying would sound like.

One, two, three, four, five, six, seven, eight, nine, ten, eleven, twelve . . . Tony counted to one hundred and then tried Leroy's again. Someone answered on the fifth ring. DeeWee.

Okay, DeeWee, don't be a shit, this is Tony calling, you'll hear me say my name, you just say yes.

"Will you accept charges?" asked the computer-operator.

"Uh-huh, okay," said DeeWee. "What's charges mean?"

"DeeWee!" Tony fairly shouted, then lowered her

voice. "DeeWee, it's Tony, hey, what's up?"

"Nothin'," said DeeWee. "Tony, where you at? Leroy said you was gone."

"I am gone, DeeWee. Put Leroy on the phone."

"I think he's watching TV."

"Put him on the phone, DeeWee. Do it."

Pause. "Well, okay, but don't get mad if he gets mad for me bothering him."

A clatter, clunk, silence except for background shuffling and mumbled voices. Then clattering again, a click, and "Fuck it, Tony! Where the hell are you?"

Tony felt her soul soar at the irritation and the intensity of Leroy's voice. Things back home had to be pretty damn good for him to sound like that.

"Can't say where I am, Leroy. But I'm not in Virginia, that's for sure. I'm really far away."

"Where'd you go after . . . after, you know?" The voice lowered. "I thought you got caught or shot or something and taken into custody. You ain't calling from Emporia jail?"

"No. Is that what you hoped would happen? You and Buddy and Whitey and Little Joe all takin' off in the car and leavin' me behind? You hoped I'd get caught and take the fall for your asses?"

"No."

"Why'd you run off without me?"

" 'Cause of what happened in the store, idiot. We didn't have time to wait for you, Tony, you know that! We wait, and somebody would get us all. We knew you'd be okay on your own. You're good at stuff on your own. You'd either shoot or hide, but you wouldn't let nobody take you."

"Oh, yeah?" Maybe they thought that about Tony.

Maybe they'd talked about her like that after the Exxon robbery. She was the toughest of the Hot Heads, after all.

"Yeah," said Leroy. "That's why, since we didn't hear nothin' from you in three days, we thought you was in the jail, getting tortured or something so you'd confess on us."

"I'm not caught."

"Good. Where are you?"

"Told you, I can't tell. But what's the news? Did we make the TV? Radio? We made the newspaper, didn't we?"

"Oh, yeah," said Leroy. "Mrs. Martin was on the TV news two nights in a row now."

Tony felt the chill of excitement run through her veins. "Yeah? What did she say? What did she look like? Was she bawlin'?"

"She looked like shit. She was standin' in the middle of the wrecked-up store with the crap we knocked down all over the place. The reporters had a couple mics in her face and she said, 'They killed him, right in front of me, shot him dead!' They said, 'Who shot him?' and she said, 'Some kid with lipstick on his face!' "

"What'd she say about us, about the rest of us? What about me?"

"Nothin' much about us. Just that we knocked stuff over, tore stuff up, stole some stuff. She mostly talked about Whitey and his gun."

"But I had a gun! I put it in her face, up close! That was me up there with her!"

"Yeah, I know . . ."

"I was the one threatened her, why didn't she tell the

239

news about me threatening her? She only told on Whitey?"

"She didn't exactly tell on him, she told about him, she didn't really know who it was, said it could have been any of a bunch of teenagers who come into the store. Police have been investigatin', going house to house . . ."

"I was the one with bullets in my gun!"

"Whitey had a bullet. He shot that guy."

"But he wasn't supposed to have a bullet. I didn't think there were any bullets in there, they all rolled behind the stove."

A loud sound of exasperation, then, "What? You thought you gave Whitey a gun with no bullets?"

"Just shut up, I didn't think it would matter. I wanted the one with the bullets, I wanted to shoot up the place after scaring Mrs. Martin, but then Whitey shot first."

"Stupid asshole little girl!"

"You wouldn't say that to my face if I was there. You wouldn't dare spit out those words!"

"Yes, I would. You bring a gun you thought had no bullets!"

"Yeah, and it's done! They know anything yet? Who'd the police talk to so far? Are they showing sketches on TV? Drawings of what we looked like?"

"Just one of Whitey, but it don't look like him. Some farmer in a tractor who drove by the Exxon when we were there said he saw a car go out of the lot like a bat out of hell, but didn't know what kind it was, just that it was big. Said the sleet made it hard to see. Thought it was green or light blue."

"They didn't have a sketch of me?"

"No. Get over it. There's a reward for information

about us, though. A hundred thousand dollars if we get caught and convicted. Mrs. Martin quit the store. It's closed until further notice, sign says. Got police tape all over it."

Tony took a deep breath, blew it out on the glass of the phone booth, and drew a frowny face in the steam.

"When you comin' back, Tony?"

"She never mentioned me."

"No. When you comin' back?"

"Probably never. I got places to be. People to be with. Wish I could be there to see everything happenin', but I can't. I'll call you, though, check it out. Check on the progress."

"If they catch Whitey, they'll catch us. He'll talk like a fucking parrot on a stick."

"Maybe. Nobody was supposed to get killed, though. Whitey was such a dumb fuck for that! But fuck it, it's done. And I ain't telling where I am."

"I'll get the phone bill end of the month. I'll know exactly where you're callin' from. Police get the phone record, then they can follow where you're at . . ."

Tony hadn't thought of that. She slammed the receiver down into the cradle and left the booth.

Half a block past the Catfish Delite was another motel, Gulf Towers Motel, and several small houses on both sides of the road, a shadowed alley, a poorly lit intersection. Bugs swarmed around Tony's face, biting flies and some other shit, and she smacked them away. She crossed the intersection and continued down the street.

Maybe they'd see Alabama on the phone bill, but they wouldn't know Texas. It would be okay.

There was a trailer park on the right, the little boxy

homes draped in holiday lights with sparkling trees set in windows. Next to the trailers was a tack and marine equipment shop, a long grassy ball field surrounded by a chain-link fence, and then the end of the road. A solid black privacy fence of wooden slats blocked Tony's view from whatever lay on the other side. Weeds poked their spindly, dry arms through the planks like skeletal prisoners begging release.

A sign, painted in red on the wood, read MARTIN'S MOBILE BAY MARINA. 3429 PERRY ROAD, MOBILE. Tony walked to the barred gate and stared inside. There were boats bobbing on dark water, tied up in what seemed like little stalls. Rows of boats, painted with names that were hard to read in the faint beams from the tall pole lights. Some of the boats had fishing nets stretched to dry across their backs. Others had large seats with harnesses and large poles. These, Tony knew for sure, were for catching and holding on to big fish. No little catfish hooks here. She wondered what they'd use for bait. Eels? Snakes?

There was a thumping behind her, and she turned about to see nothing but shadows, ragged roadside trees, and the dark.

"Get the fuck out of here, whatever you are," she said.

Nothing answered. Nothing moved. *It's just Alabama*, she thought.

Tony wondered if Lamesa was anywhere near the Gulf of Mexico, and if Burton ever got to go fishing. He would own a big boat, of course, bigger than any here at Martin's Marina. Tony and Burton could take a day off from managing the farmhands and go out on

the water and toss back some brews and smoke a few
cigars.

The end of the privacy fence was a half block down
along a hard-packed footpath. Tony took it to the corner. She wanted to put her feet in the gulf and know
what it felt like.

At the end of the marina and the path was a gravely
cul-de-sac and another cluster of small houses. The
first, surrounded by a weedy yard and scrub trees, had
a seagull-decorated mailbox that read, MARTIN, 3427
PERRY ROAD. This had to be the owner of Martin's
Marina. Crappy little house for someone who had such
a big business.

Behind the house was the huge stretch of the gulf,
the color of Mam's morning coffee with lights pulsing
on the surface from the marina and the back porches
of the little houses down the lane. Other lights, farther
out, dipped and swayed on boats and ships. Moonlight,
jagged and blue, streaked the water's surface like lu-
minous claw marks.

Tony sneaked around the Martins' house, between
two boxwood hedges, past a plastic child's slide and
swing set, and down to the water in the rear. The Martins had their own dock, stretching out twenty-some
feet over the water. There were no boats tied to it.

*They must keep their boats in the marina. Afraid
somebody from Virginia will come along and sink it
just for fun. Ha!*

Tony walked onto the dock. It creaked loudly. She
glanced over her shoulder to see that no one in the
family was looking out through their back windows.
No one was.

The dock was warped but solid. At the end was an

Igloo cooler facedown with the lid open and some fishing nets hanging on the posts on either side. Lying by the cooler were three oars, one cracked down the middle and mended with duct tape.

The air was more brisk over the water, and Tony pulled her sleeves down. She stretched her arms out and took in the space and the salt water and the situation. She was the master, she was in control. She was going where she wanted to go, seeing what she wanted to see, making people sing her tune and dance her steps. Fuck them all. She'd set in motion some real trouble back home, and now she could sit back and enjoy it. She was Tony Petinske. Her father was Burton Petinske of Lamesa, Texas. Like the prodigal son in the Bible, which she'd heard about when she was in third grade and went to Bible Class as part of Weekday Religious Education during one school year, Burton would probably kill a fatted calf for her and they'd have a whoop-ass Texas barbecue.

She took the pistol from her jeans pocket and thought of firing one into the water to celebrate. Maybe with luck she'd hit a fish or a crab, if there were crabs in the gulf. But that would waken the natives. She didn't want to push her luck, as lucky as she was. Her head itched again, and she scratched it with the mouth of the gun. What a joke, she thought, to accidentally shoot herself in the brain just to get rid of a few lice. Hell, when she got to Texas she was going to shave her head. Get rid of them all. Who cared in Texas if you were bald, anyway?

"Mam would shit to see me bald," she chuckled. "Darlene would pee her pants to know what I've been doing!"

She lay the gun on the pier, then lowered her jeans and held on to one of the posts. She swung back over the water and let go a stream of hot pee. She then lowered herself and splashed the pee off her privates by cupping water with one hand. It was bitingly cold and felt great. She hoisted up her jeans and turned back toward the yard.

In the yard at the foot of the pier were two boys. One was tall, the other Tony's height. Their arms were crossed. In the moonlight it looked as though both were smiling, though their eyes were not visible beneath the brims of their ball caps.

"Got a cigarette?" called the shorter boy.

Tony's eyes narrowed. Fuck this shit. She said nothing.

"I asked you a question. Ain't polite, not answering."

Tony put her hands on her hips, hands in fists.

"We seen that little pussy of yours, hanging out over the water," said the tall boy. "Oooh, baby, shake that little beaver."

Tony's heart kicked the inside of her chest. She looked at the pistol on the pier.

"Thought you was a boy, with that short hair on your head," said the shorter boy. "But then we seen that pussy. Mmm-hmmm. Nice golden shower, shoulda saved it for us."

"Get out of here, motherfuckers," said Tony.

"Ooh, baby, I love it when you talk dirty," said the tall boy. He chuckled darkly.

"Me too," echoed the other.

Then the tall one was striding forward onto the pier, a near jog, with long, quick steps. Tony dropped to her knees to grab the pistol but her fingers missed and it spun away, across the pier, where it stopped at the edge. She reached for it again with a war whoop of fury, but a foot came down on the back of her hand and another foot kicked the pistol into the dark water. It struck the surface with a *plop* and vanished.

"Fuckers!" screamed Tony. She dove forward, her free arm plunging into the water and snatching but finding nothing but cold wet. "Goddamn motherfucking fuckers!" She rolled over and away from the foot, jerking out from under, then sprang to her feet. Her knife was in her sock. Get it, she'd slice the grins and then the balls off these Alabama bastards.

The shorter boy was beside the taller one now, just feet from where Tony stood. Tony felt the sweat that had erupted on her forehead and her back, tickling, teasing. *These're assholes*, she thought, *these are Buddies and Leroys and Little Joes and Whiteys. These are goddamned DeeWees!* "Get out of my way," she snarled.

"Ooh, a little fightin' girl," said the shorter boy.

"Ain't from around here," said the other. "Talks funny. Where you from, sugar britches?"

Tony backed to the dock's end, one hand out in a fist, and lowered herself slowly to reach the knife.

"Wants to give us a blow job, Ricky," said the tall boy. "Kneeling down, just look at that."

"Yeah," said Ricky.

Tony reached for the cuff of her jeans, slid her fingers underneath and up to the top of the hiking boot. The handle was there, snug, between the sock and the skin.

The tall boy leaped suddenly at Tony and caught a scruff of her short hair in his fingers. "Kiss me, little girl!" He tried to jerk her head back, but she twisted from beneath him and drew the blade out from her sock, then drove it against the plank by her shoe to flick it open.

"Joe, she's got a blade!" cried Ricky.

Joe grabbed at Tony's hair again, but she leaned forward and slashed it across his knee. It cut through cloth, into flesh, back out again. Joe welped, let go of Tony's hair, and snatched at her knife-bearing hand and came up short. "Ricky!"

Ricky, his teeth bared, snatched at Tony's wrist and missed. Tony was on her feet then, leaning forward, carving the air and growling. "Get out of here! Get away from me!"

"She's got the rabies, way she's actin'!" said Ricky. "Damn, she's a mad dog!"

"Back away now!" said Tony. "I'll cut you to bits, you know I will!"

Ricky picked up one of the oars. "Yeah?" he said. "Yours may be sharper but mine's longer." He laughed at himself, pleased with his little joke. "Get it, Joe? Yours may be sharper, but mine's longer!"

Joe tossed up an oar with the toe of his boot as if he were flipping a skateboard, and caught it with both hands. He was breathing heavily. "Don't no bitch hurt me. Don't no bitch never do that to me. Never!"

"Don't no stupid rednecks do nothing to me," said Tony. "You get out of my way, you know what's good for you." She waved the knife, thinking, *My gun's gone, what am I supposed to do without my gun?* "Back off!"

Ricky laughed; Joe didn't. Then Ricky swung his oar at Tony and it caught her on the shoulder with a crack. Pain exploded, but Tony kept her balance and her knife. Joe swung his oar the other direction, and Tony jumped back from it, nearly tipping over the edge of the dock. She grasped a post and pushed herself upright. Then both Joe and Ricky swung their oars at the same time, and they collided with Tony on opposite sides, knocking the breath out of her and driving her forward onto her face. She groaned and scrabbled at the splintery wood to push herself up enough to see. The knife was no longer in her hand.

"Fuck you!" she cried. She hunched herself onto her knees so she could stand. But a foot in her back knocked her down again.

Joe said, "Fuck us? How 'bout fuck you?"

Ricky: "Yeah! Good idea!"

Joe rolled Tony over onto her back. She kicked out with her feet and clawed at his face but Ricky kicked her in the head and her vision was shattered for a few moments. It flew away like pieces of a broken window blowing apart in a tornado. She blinked, squinted, tried to see, but all she could do was feel.

Feel one of the boys unzipping her corduroy pants and tugging them down around her ankles. Feel the other snatching her hands and holding them up over her head, pressing them roughly to the pier and sitting on them with all his weight.

She bucked, but the boy on top of her jammed his knee into her gut and drove her breath out again. She tried to order him off but the words would not come out.

"Show you who's boss!" cried the boy over her, it sounded like Joe. "Cut my leg? I'll show you. I got a big ole poker to stab you with! What'd you say, Ricky, yours may be sharper but mine's longer! That was a good one."

Tony bucked. Another blow to her stomach and the remnants of her last meal with Blessing raced up into her mouth. Liquefied fried chicken and kidney beans. She gagged and spit. Her legs were thrust apart then, and someone climbed between them. There was laughing and panting, and fingers strumming her cunt, her clitoris, and then jabbing into her core.

She screamed and drew her legs together but another fist went into her gut yet again, and again remnants of her last meal rocketed into her mouth, vile and sour.

"Here you go!" Something hard, hard, and fleshy now, wider than fingers, poking at her opening, and then jabbing inside, tearing, hot and persistent. Again and again.

"Me next!" came the voice from above.

"No!" she cried. "Fuckers!" A sob, a scream.

But it went on. And on.

Chapter Thirty-eight

Spongebob was over. *Angry Beavers* were on, chattering and arguing over what they would have for dinner, wood-chip beef on toast or cellulose casserole, whatever that was. Mistie had turned onto her other side when the new show came on. At home in the trailer, Daddy would come and change the channel when *Angry Beavers* started, so this was the first time Mistie got to see the whole thing. If this was a Saturday, *Princess Silverlace* would have been on, but it wasn't a Saturday, Mistie didn't think.

The teacher had gone in the bathroom with the girl a long time ago. The girl had come out and had left but the teacher was still in the bathroom. There was water running in the bathroom. Mistie knew not to go into the bathroom when a grown-up had the water running even if the door was open. One time Mistie had gone in the bathroom when the water was running and Daddy and Mama were in there and although Mistie didn't know what they were doing, they were really mad and chased her out. She got a spanking later that night from Daddy. Her bottom had burned like fire until after Mama went out and then Daddy kissed it to make it better.

Mistie had to go to the bathroom, but not too bad, she could wait a little longer. Maybe the teacher was almost through with her shower.

A commercial came on the television. Pizza Hut, the Edge. Mistie remembered eating at Pizza Hut in Kentucky when Valerie was still alive. There wasn't a Pizza Hut in Pippins, though. She liked Pizza Hut because the waitress was nice and the cups the root beer came in were plastic with dancing pizzas on them, and Valerie and Mistie had gotten to take them home. They cracked later and Mama threw them away.

The commercial ended and the Beavers were back. Mistie scratched her nose with her bound hands, and then rubbed herself. Daddy rubbed her when Mama wasn't home. It was the only time he didn't yell at her, when he was rubbing her.

Mistie smelled the bedspread and then her sweatshirt. She and Valerie and her daddy and mama had stayed in a motel one night after they left Kentucky. No, no, Valerie was not there anymore. The motel room was not as big as this one, and had only one bed. Mistie had to sleep on the floor. Her parents had argued for a long time. Mistie remembered the T-shirt she wore that night. It had a big red flower in the middle of the front that was stiff and smelled funny.

Mistie held her crotch so she didn't have to go so bad.

And the water in the shower kept on running.

251

Chapter Thirty-nine

She remembered.

A cold Christmas. Their first Christmas in Pippins.

Kate, Donald, and Donnie had moved from Alexandria to Southampton County in September, two weeks after Kate had finished her final master's of education course at Georgetown University and had presented her thesis, *A Study on an Apparent Relationship Between Selected Fundamentalist Religious Persuasions and Developmental Delay in the Elementary Public School Student*. The title had scared the shit out of some of the university administration and had brought a chuckle from Donald. The paper explored a connection between offshoot fundamentalist denominations and the higher rate of children in the public school programs who showed symptoms of developmental delay and emotional disturbance. Kate had been discreet and careful; her intent was to get her degree and be done with it, not to stir up any major academic dust. She concluded that it was more the home life and the economic status of the children in these single-church denominations than the religious teachings. Kate didn't believe that was the total truth but a politically correct paper was more in line with what she needed to have to get her degree, and she did win the degree. Signed, sealed, delivered. Put into a nice, oak frame with glare-free glass. Now, Donald could look at her and see two degrees instead of one.

Joy, pride, and excitement had been fading concepts for Kate. Her relationship with her husband had grown distant—slowly yet easily. Kate had grown up in a family of means in Norfolk, so settling in with Donald was comfortable. She knew Wedgwood from Limoges; she didn't have to think about placements of dessert forks and salad plates. She had listened to "Swan Lake" and "The Nutcracker" as a child while Donald had listened to operas and symphony orchestras. Their lives had been so similar they could have been brother and sister, though the McDolens did boast of more assets and more land. It was the familiarity with which Kate had fallen in love, she realized several years into the marriage.

And after several years, it was hard to shake the familiarity off and make the marriage into something different, something exciting and unexpected. Donald liked things as they were. Why would he want anything changed? Kate was smart and had good taste and read books she could discuss with their friends over dinner. She was a caring mother to their new son. They had money with Donald's practice and were destined to make a whole lot more because of his talent and his connections. The little family wouldn't be moving around forever. In fact, Donald's father, his only remaining parent, was in ill health, and it wouldn't be long before the McDolen estate in southern Virginia was ready to change generational hands.

In Alexandria, Kate attended several meetings of a local Amnesty International group, but Donald said he didn't want his clients to think he was a left-winger. She volunteered at a homeless shelter for a few hours a week while Donnie was in school, and even made a good friend with one particularly feisty young mother named Darian who had run away from her abusive husband and was determined to get a job and pull herself and her toddler off the streets. But Donald told Kate gently that such friends were really not friends, they couldn't be, they weren't the same. Not bad, mind you, but not the same. Too different to truly understand. And very likely untrustworthy, for fate smiled upon those who were dependable and hard working. Kate's volunteer work grew spotty until she no longer visited the shelter. Maybe Donald was right. It was certainly easier not to worry about such things. Another two years and Kate felt edgy again, needing something from herself, her husband, the world. She enrolled at George Mason. Donald thought that was a fine idea. Four months before Kate was done with her degree, Donald's father died. The manor in Southampton County was now theirs. They sold their condo, Kate finished her schoolwork, Donnie stomped around and cried that he didn't want to move. And they moved.

Christmas at the McDolen estate was celebrated with a holly wreath on the door, white candles in hurricane lanterns in every window of the sixteen-room house, a small Douglas fir with white lights in the living room with a porcelain nativity scene beneath, and a large blue spruce in the family room. The holly wreath, white candles, Douglas fir, and nativity were there because that was the way Donald's mother and father had always done it. The citizens of Southampton County expected to see that wreath and those lights as they drove up and down Route 58 on their merry holiday ways. It was practically the herald of the season for the cotton-picking masses.

The spruce in the family room was Kate's contribution to Christmas, multicolored, more a happy jumble than a showpiece, covered in lights that twinkled and some that didn't, expensive glass balls, plastic Disney figures, and strands of painted popcorn that Donnie had sewn together when he was four. That was the way Kate's family had always done it.

It was during this festive season, Kate's first at the manor house, that she was introduced to the wealthier citizens of Southampton County. Donald and Kate hosted a "Winter Banquet" to which a select many flocked—Donald's new business friends, old money who had socialized with the McDolens since the 1920s, assorted local politicians, and a spattering of state legislators. It was pleasant enough, but Kate was tired with it after the first hour. Cocktails and small talk were interesting for only so long, and soon she found herself wanting to retire to the family room to watch the blinking rainbow of lights on the spruce tree and curl up under a blanket. Donnie had already disappeared from the scene in his sport coat and tie, up to his room to play his Game Boy.

Kate and Donald had had elegant parties back in Richmond and Alexandria, but nothing to the scale of this bash. At one given time Kate counted seventy-nine guests. There were scads of new names for Kate to remember, longtime family connections to digest, gossip to promise to keep secret, private Southampton in-jokes she tucked away mentally to ask for an explanation from Donald later on.

As Kate tried to keep attention on one woman's rambling—a White Shoulders–scented discourse on the history of her father's tobacco-growing endeavors in Southampton—she found herself thinking about Alice and Bill up in Canada with their pets and their children, in their hippie shirts and hippie beads and myriad causes. For the first time in years, she missed them greatly.

The Southampton School Board superintendent, Stuart Gordonson, arrived a bit late to the McDolen Christmas party; as soon as Donald introduced him to Kate and mentioned her new degree, the man steered her aside and promised her a job if and when she might ever want one.

"We would be thrilled to have a McDolen on our team." Mr. Gordonson had grinned beneath his well-trimmed mustache. "What a feather in our cap, eh?"

Kate thanked him and said she'd let him know.

When the last guest had finally bid the McDolens "Happy Christmas," somewhere around two-thirty in the morning, and Kate and Donald were stacking punch cups on the kitchen counter for the maid to take care of when she arrived in a few hours, Kate mentioned the job offer to Donald. He'd smiled his vague smile and said, "I only introduced you as a courtesy, don't be silly. Stuart would have chastised me if I hadn't. But you aren't seriously considering teaching,

256

are you? There are plenty of other people in this county for that."

He'd stepped up to Kate to put his arms around her, but she'd moved back. "What do you mean?"

Donald chuckled, shook his handsome and prematurely graying head, and said, "Honey, I'm glad you finished your degree. I know you've worked hard. But you weren't seriously considering going into education. I mean . . . honey, Donnie needs you at home. I need you at home. Please don't make me say things that will sound like an old-fashioned chauvinist, but there really is no need for you to teach."

So it would look bad to you, would it? she thought. *Your wife getting minimum pay as a first-year teacher, lugging books to and fro, calling parents to set up conferences, wiping other people's kids' snotty noses. Much too comfy with the regular Joes, Donald?*

"Well," Kate said, "I wouldn't think there would be an opening, anyway. It's the middle of the year."

Donald had kissed her forehead. "True, true." He smiled. "And wasn't tonight just grand? I'm so glad to be home. It will be good for all of us, settled once and for all."

Christmas Day galloped in, and with it a spattering of snow, an emerald ring for Kate, and a rifle for Donnie with a big red bow and a promise from Donald that they would go turkey hunting on New Year's Eve. Donnie, still small for a seventh grader but solid in shoulder and arm, had gawked with amazement and awe at the weapon. Donald had patted his son on the shoulder and said all McDolen boys hunted turkey and game on their land. He explained that hunting helped the McDolen men feel a connection to what they owned. It helped them lay claim to who they were.

Donnie was thrilled. So was Kate. Up until now, Donald had had little time for Donnie. Now, at last, they could try to recapture the father-son bond.

But the connection was a sharp and double-edged one, when all was said and done. Donald, comfortable now in his element, his territory, began to let Donnie get by with things Kate would never have allowed if she'd been a single mother like Darian. He introduced Donnie to cigars, a "McDolen tradition, Kate, only the best blends, of course. God, don't wrinkle your nose. It'll make you look old before your time." Then, of course, the McDolens' favorite beers and wines over dinner and after dinner. Donnie, who had been like Kate in his cautious, shy demeanor, began to embrace his McDolen heritage with gusto.

Donald's attention with Donnie was hit and miss, with his work and his own stable of local buddies, but Donnie discovered quickly that the McDolen name had incredible pull in Southampton. He discovered that when he decided something was in style, the other middle school boys followed suit. They could smell the money on him like dogs after a ham bone, and Donnie loved it.

The rifle that first Christmas had been the beginning of the changes in Kate's son. The beginning of his loss to her. Kate hadn't known on that first Christmas morning as she'd stood outside the sunroom door wiping the cold, wet snow out of her face and laughing as Donnie and Donald had test-fired it against the trunks of the barren trees of the apple orchard, that Donnie wouldn't be living at home much longer. That her shy child would find power and clout as intoxicating as his father's fine wines.

She remembered the cold of the snow. The wet pattering on her cheeks and neck. Donald's shouts, "Yes, that's right, just a bit higher! Pull!" The crack of the discharge. The splintered apple bark.

She remembered.

There was a loud slam. Kate flinched. Her head whipped toward the bathroom door and she saw a shadow pass over the surface of the dresser. The girl was back.

Freezing water was pouring from the shower spigot and down Kate's naked body.

The girl had returned.

Oh, bring her on, Kate thought, her breath picking up again and her arms tightening. She found herself smiling. *Let's have it out.*

Chapter Forty

The girl was back. Mistie jumped when the door slammed. She stared as the girl came in, strode between the bed and the TV, up to the door and back again, then tried to pull the mirror off the wall with a loud grunt. It didn't come, so the girl pulled a drawer out of the dresser and cracked the glass with it. The splinters of glass in the frame looked like the shiny star in Princess Silverlace's crown. The girl paced again, her arms crossed and her eyes straight ahead. She looked as if somebody had put her in a car and rolled it into a lake. She was messed up.

As the girl passed the television the fifth time, she drove her fist into the power button. The TV winked off. Mistie drew herself up and scooched up to the head of the bed.

The girl paced some more. Her eyes were ugly. They looked like pit bull eyes. There was a high school boy who lived at the trailer park who had a pit bull with eyes like that. The dog didn't seem to have any sense except for biting and chopping at everything that went near it on its chain. It seemed more like a machine than a dog.

Then the girl went into the bathroom and the water was turned off.

Chapter Forty-one

The teacher hadn't gone anywhere, big surprise. She was standing in the bathtub, shivering like a wet dog, one foot on top of the other, lips tinged blue, hands above her head and secured with the towel strip. The rod had bent, but was in place. A little bar of paper-wrapped soap had been knocked into the tub and was at the drain hole, gummy and torn. The room wasn't steamy; the water had gone cold, probably a long time ago. Puddles stood on the tile floor.

But there was one disturbing difference. The teacher's head wasn't down. Her gaze was steady and cold as the water, locked on Tony.

Tony turned off the spigot, swiped the knife from her ankle, and lifted it to the teacher's throat. Her body stung and throbbed, and she was going to share all the joy she had to share. "Miss me? Oh, I bet you did. I'm sure you wish you could have gone with me on my little adventure."

"Truth or dare?" said the teacher.

"What?" Tony was incredulous. "What did you say?"

The teacher smiled.

Tony pressed the tip of the blade into the teacher's abdomen, and pushed until she felt the skin give with a silent little *pop*. The teacher's smile tightened into a grimace, but she didn't repeat what she said.

"Oh, tough now?" Tony scoffed. "Enjoy your bath?"

The teacher, eyes locked on Tony's, nodded slowly. "You bet."

"Yeah? Well, you would enjoy what just happened to me. You smelly cunt, I bet you'd get all wet over what I just went through."

The teacher winced, but said nothing.

Tony put the knife on the back of the toilet, kicked off her boots, then peeled off her jeans. The motions nearly made her sick, the sound of the denim sliding over skin. She clenched her teeth and remembered the laughter and the slobbering and the jabbing. She wanted to have them now in this bathroom with their pants down, she wanted to rip their members apart, just like they had ripped her insides. Tony threw her jeans and panties, crusted and hard with the boys' come, into the corner behind the toilet. She stood in just her sweatshirt. "I want you and Baby Doll to see something," she said. "Kid! Get in here!"

"What do you want with her?" asked the teacher.

"I'll show you when I'm good and ready. Kid, now!"

"Mistie, don't come in!" said the teacher.

Tony snatched the knife and drew an inch-long slice across the teacher's stomach. The skin parted smartly. Tony's seventh grade art teacher, Ms. Black, once said Tony could even draw a straight line; well, this one was pretty damn straight. The teacher gasped but didn't cry out. Blood welled, then spilled down to the woman's crotch in the wake of the sheen of shower water. There may have even been tears welling in the woman's eyes, but tears and shower water pretty much matched.

"Kid! In here now!" shouted Tony.

"Mistie, no!" said the teacher.

Tony cut her again, a straight line under the first. A pair of red lips now, drooling. "Shut up, bitch. Mistie!"

The woman sounded like a snake now, hissing. "No, Mistie!"

"What's wrong with you?" snarled Tony. "What's fucked up your brain while I was gone?"

The teacher tipped her head slowly. "Truth?"

"What?"

"Or dare?"

"Truth? I'm gonna show you truth!" Tony knocked down the toilet lid and sat on it, leaned back and opened her legs. *Like those fuckers did, goddamn them, I'd kill 'em, fuckin' kill 'em!* "Wanna see some truth? Watch me!"

Tony turned the knife about, and jammed the handle end into her vagina. Her insides exploded, hot and angry. She scraped with the rough steel against the soft tissue walls, digging, tearing to clean away all traces of the rape. Electrical agony inside, sending her heels into the wet floor and her spine arching against the porcelain toilet lid. *Dig it out! Dig it out!*

Tony turned the knife handle to get a better angle. She dug the space of her womb, her sex, her hands realizing now the urgency of the actions and refusing to let her instincts against destruction stop them. "I'll never be a mother!" she snarled, spittle flying. "I never want nothin' to go here, nothin' to grow here, fuck it all, it's weak, it stinks! That's the truth!"

In the corner of her vision, the teacher staring, her chin resting on the inside of her raised forearm. The stomach streaked red now like the lipstick on Whitey's sweaty face.

She dug. "Mothers are worthless! My fucking mam on her sofa, drinking bug-sprayed beer 'cause she's too lazy to get her own! Baby Doll's mom, who hasn't even put out a report her daughter is missing! Her real mother's the TV, you know that? The damn television, you see how she loves that thing? And you, a fucking teacher and mother, you think that's something great, huh? Nothing but a goddamn brood animal!"

The fireworks in her core, red-hot, white-hot, blue-hot, like cat-clawed moonlight setting fire throughout the gulf of her bones.

"You say you got a kid, a what, daughter, son? Neither, both? What? Fuck you, motherfucker!"

Tears on her face now. *Fuck tears, I hate tears, pussy tears! I don't cry!*

"Fuck you, fuck me, fuck 'em all!"

The knife fell from her hand, clattered on the tile. Tony folded up and over herself, grabbing behind her knees and pushing against the pain. Breathing through locked jaws, she said, "Done now. Done." Blood was warm between her thighs, black-red, rivulets carving down her legs in patterns Ms. Black would have thought expressive.

The bathroom tilted, and Tony went with it. *Ride it out, ride it, squeeze it out, let it run.*

Cramps, then, hard and insistent, nothing like the cramps she had with her period. She growled, hating the cramps, hating what she had there inside her, hoping it was cleaned out enough now to leave her the hell alone.

The teacher, "What happened while you were gone?"

"Fuck you."

"Somebody pissed you off, didn't they? What a constructive way to deal with your anger. Oh, I'm just so impressed."

"Fuck you!"

Tony sat until the cramps subsided, and the blood had slowed and stopped. When she lifted her head from her knees, the room spun, leveled out. She took a breath, and another.

In the bedroom, *I Love Lucy* had begun. And Lucy, as Tony could have predicted, was whining.

Chapter Forty-two

It took the whole of *I Love Lucy* and half of *Gomer Pyle* before the girl forced herself up from the toilet and pulled her jeans back on. She was hurt, badly. She was bleeding.

Big deal. Kate was hurt and bleeding, too.

And all Kate could think was, *Now what, bitch?*

The girl stumbled three times, trying to put her second leg into the jeans. She leaned against the wall, drawing air through her teeth in short bursts, her short dark hair glistening with sweat.

Fall against the toilet lid, come on, you can do it. Crack your skull open. Bash your own brains out, come on.

With the forth attempt the leg went in. Unrolling the toilet paper, she tore off a huge wad and jammed it down into her pants crotch, then hobbled out to the bedroom. There was the sound of the channel being changed to the evening news.

Bitch.

The girl came back into the bathroom, spit blood into the toilet, then looked at Kate.

Yeah, now what? Adrenaline or something else with sharp, biting edges was coursing her blood. Her eyes fluttered shut, then open. The bathroom reeled when they were closed, spun when they were open. Not a hell of a big choice there. It felt as if someone had sanded the enamel off the tips of her teeth. She wanted to bite something, hard.

The girl cut Kate's towel restraints loose with her knife, then brought the knife close to Kate's eyes. Kate kept her mouth shut though her teeth were on edge, ready to strike.

"Get dressed," said the girl. "Then come out."

Kate said nothing. She worked the soaked terry cloth off her wrists and massaged them. Her arm muscles jumped. Her shoulders were stiff and did not come down easily. They complained as she made them obey. Her stomach stung mightily with the cuts.

She waited until the girl left before stepping out of the tub. Her clothes, scattered near the trash can, were soaked. Fuck it, she just couldn't keep clothes dry on this trip. She grabbed a bath towel instead, and wrapped herself in it, folding it across her chest and tucking the edge securely. She draped the wet clothes over the shower rod. There was nothing in the bathroom she could put into her jeans pocket to use to kill the girl. Soap, a tiny bottle of shampoo, and conditioner. A little shower cap, packaged in a little shiny box. A fresh shiver coursed her body. *That's all right, I'll find something soon.* She was caught in a brief and vicious wave of shivers and thought, *I'll never be warm again. I'll stay cold.*

But that's okay. It's good to be cold.

Cold is powerful.

She went into the bedroom.

The girl was standing at a tilt near the door, her fingers clutching the edge of the blue drape. She was likely cramping. Kate wondered how damaged she was. She hoped it was a lot. Maybe she wouldn't be able to go any farther. "Where your fucking clothes?" the girl said.

"Wet."

"No shit. Sit down."

Kate sat beside Mistie. Mistie was tied with pillowcases at her wrists and ankles. The child stared at the blank television screen as if by sheer will she could bring the show back on. The bedspread was crumpled where the girl had flopped back and forth. One pillowcase-less pillow was on the floor.

The girl came up between the beds and slapped Kate across the mouth. Kate's own hand came up to retaliate, but stopped short as the knife slashed the air inches from her nose. The girl turned it slowly in her hand. It winked in the low-wattage light overhead. "Who said you could talk to me in the bathroom? Now, I'm gonna tell you what we're doing next. Tomorrow morning, we're outa this shit hole called Mobile. I'm finding us a car and we're driving straight through to Texas. I'll kill you if you give me any trouble between now and then." She stiffened, caught her breath, as if a wave of pain was passing through her body. "Get those socks you left in the bathroom. Can't leave you loose."

"No," said Kate.

The girl was quick, up on the bed and grabbing at Mistie's hair and jerking her neck back, exposing the soft throat. The blade trembled less than an inch from the skin. Mistie whimpered. "Oh, I think you will. One wrong move, teacher, and we can all sing like Baby Doll, 'Mama had a baby and its head popped off.' "

Kate retrieved the socks from the bathroom floor and sat back on the bed. The socks were still dripping. She wrung them out over the floor, not taking her eyes off the girl as she did.

"Tie your ankles, and Baby Doll'll get your wrists like before."

Within a minute, Kate was immobile in her towel drape and her sock restraints, propped up against the wobbly headboard. Mistie was curled up beside Kate, humming. The girl had used the phone cord, which she'd cut apart, to tie Kate's arms to the headboard. Mistie was tied to Kate's right arm. Her stare was vacant. Kate's insides roiled.

The girl stood back to appreciate her handiwork, and then turned on the television to national news. She climbed onto her own bed, clutched a pillow to her chest, and watched the screen. Every minute or so she touched herself between her legs and cringed. Her foot shook as if it had a motor of its own.

There was a riot reported in Los Angeles, with several teenagers captured for shooting an officer. A fire in Arizona, begun, it was believed, by the incredibly dry conditions over the past month. Thousands of acres already destroyed. A blizzard in North Dakota. A mall Santa in Chicago found guilty of child molestation.

"Yeah, okay," the girl said to the set. "What about Pippins? What about the gasoline man? What about us, huh?" She put a pillow between her knees and let a breath out through her teeth. Oh, yes, she was hurting.

Very, very good.

She went quiet then as a commercial played, then another, another, and the news came back. It was a story about Americans in upstate New York going to Canada for their prescription drugs.

"Virginia's good as Canada!" the girl growled. "Go to Virginia news!"

The national weather report, the dry weather in the Southwest, the snow across the Midwest. Clear and cold in Virginia, cloudy in Alabama and Texas.

The news went off. *Wheel of Fortune* came on. The girl clicked the off button on the remote. She stretched out on her side and looked at the wet spots on the floor where Kate had wrung out the socks. "Tomorrow I'll get a fucking car. Tomorrow, I'll get to Texas. No more of this screwing around."

Kate said, "Truth or dare?"

The girl's head turned in Kate's direction. "You got a death wish?"

"Truth or dare? You like the game, don't you?"

The girl sat up quickly, her focus seeming to go out, then in with the effort. She wiped sweat from her brow with her sweatshirt sleeve. *WWJD?* Kate thought. Well, he wouldn't be gouging himself with a knife handle and cutting up teachers in the shower of the Mobile South Motor Inn. But then again, maybe He would. As a girl, Kate had attended a Presbyterian church with her family in Norfolk; she'd heard how the God of Moses could flip out and go pretty damn nuts when things didn't turn out His way. Like Father, like Son.

271

The girl nodded at the knife by her pillow. "You forget I got that?"

"No, but I've noticed your gun is gone. Truth or dare?"

The girl stared.

"You into your own game? You can dish it out but can't take it?"

Slowly, "There's nothing I can't take."

"Truth or dare, then."

A cough of disbelief, but an expression of curiosity. "Okay, bitch, I'll go for it this once. Dare."

Kate heard her teacher's voice speaking, the voice of calm. She didn't even have to count to ten on this one. *Deidra, if you could see me now. Donald, if you had any idea. This is Willie a hundred times over, and I'm going to win this one.* "You're clearly an independent girl, someone who knows her own mind. You don't need us. I dare you to let us go."

"Wrong!" The girl sat up.

"Okay, fine." Kate felt one eyebrow go up into a benign point, a good addition to the act. Her teeth wanted to chatter, but she locked her jaw muscles. Hissing, then, "All right. I get a truth."

"Yeah? What truth?"

"Why do you hate yourself so much?"

The girl almost smiled. "I don't hate myself, you stupid bitch. I'm the best thing in this motel room."

"What you did to yourself in the bathroom, the way you talk. It's obvious you hate what you are."

The girl shook her head and chuckled darkly. She pulled up her sweatshirt to show an Ace bandage strapped across her breasts. "What I got ain't what I am! See this? If I had the money I'd get 'em cut off.

Fat and skin, that's all they are, but, oh, don't the men think they're something? Looking, wanting to touch, screw what you want, right? You got 'em, Baby Doll's gonna have 'em even if she doesn't want 'em. Think there would be a pill now, one you could take to pop these fuckers down to nothing."

"You wish you were a boy, then?" *Dig harder, Kate. She has a knife. You have a brain.* "There are biological explanations for that, you know. No need to be ashamed."

The sweatshirt came down. "You're ignorant, stupid as a cow! I don't want to be a boy, I just don't want to be a girl. I want to be nothing, just a person. That make sense to your little female mind?"

"Why don't you want to be a girl?"

"You . . . aren't . . . listening!" The girl leaned over and stared at Kate, one hand taking up the knife, the other set of fingers balled into a fist. Then the next moment she drew back slightly, and her tone evened out. Her eyes hitched in a wave of pain. "You're playing with me. You can fuck off."

She rolled from the bed and turned off all the lamps. There was the sound of her dropping to her bed, mumbling something into her pillow. Kate listened until the girl's breathing had changed from consciousness to sleep.

But Kate remained wide awake, riding the turbulent and delicious rush of anger.

I'm going to kill her. Oh, you bet.

Chapter Forty-three

The motel room was hellishly dark. A thin strip of pale light generated from the MOBILE SOUTH sign across the parking lot cut through the center of the wall by the door where the drapes didn't quite meet. The cheap digital alarm clock beside the lamp read two-forty-nine. In the room next door, the television droned and a couple was going at it, given the rhythm of the thumping on the wall. The familiar grunts and little squeals of delight. These people were enjoying it, all right.

Kate thought about Donald. He hadn't touched her since the incident in July. The incident.

Don't think about that. Don't think about your screwups, not now, not now, there's no time, there's no need. You've got a hell of a lot of other more important things to think about.

She shook her head, trying to knock away the sounds next door.

Pants. Squeaks. Moans and giggles.

She remembered.

The last time she and Donald had had sex was in June, a good six months ago, a Sunday afternoon. Donnie was home from Heyden-Ricketts for two weeks, on the stipulation that he would be under his parents' supervision the entire time. Kate didn't know where Donnie was; Donald had let him take the Mercedes riding as long as Donnie promised not to get into any trouble and to be back by dinnertime. Of course, Donnie had promised. "Nothing to worry about, Dad," he'd said. Kate was furious, had scolded Donald for playing so loosely with the rules and expecting things to turn out all right.

They had been in the kitchen, it was sunny that afternoon, with light pouring through the bay window and bouncing along Kate's collection of copperware on the wall rack. Donald had brushed back Kate's hair and tried to brush away her concerns. "He'll be okay," he'd whispered. "Don't be anal, hon. Really." He kissed her. He helped her down to the smooth, tiled floor and made love to her. Screwed her, whatever it was called at the moment. She had watched out the window, watched the goldfinches flutter amid the catalpa trees on the knoll. She did not respond to Donald except to lift her rear when her hiked-up sundress got uncomfortably bulky, but he hadn't noticed.

They were done by the time Donnie returned—he had come back as promised, but two hours late and smelling of gasoline, which he said he'd accidentally spilled on himself while topping off the Mercedes at the Exxon up the road. Kate detected an underscent of pot, but said nothing. Donald didn't seem to notice or didn't want to say he'd been wrong.

It was then she knew she couldn't do it anymore. Couldn't let this man, who cared so little for her concerns, who had long ago forgotten what she was in light of what he wanted her to be, be intimate with her. She'd cried for hours that night, and told Donald it was because Donnie would take the bus back to Philadelphia the next day.

In early July, she came home from a grocery shopping trip to Emporia with a torn blouse and ripped hose. And a story. She had been raped. A man had forced himself into her car and made her drive into the countryside, where he slapped her around and took advantage of her. She hadn't resisted, but had not gone to a hospital and had not called the police. The moment she'd reached the McDolen house she'd showered to wash the man's smell and touch away. Donald had been doting, but had not insisted she tell the police.

"We'll deal with this," he said as he tucked her into bed and kissed her nose. "We can get through this without having to bring the public into our private lives. You were smart, Katie. I love you."

The blouse was burned in the kitchen sink. Donald had brought Kate a snifter of burgundy and had fluffed the pillows.

It worked. Whenever Donald had even looked amorous, Kate had said, "I can't. I just remember him, slapping me, touching me, I'm sorry, Donald," and Donald would back off.

She remembered.

* * *

Wire Mesh Mothers

Next door in the Mobile South Motor Inn the couple giggled and thumped, bang, bang, bang, bang. Newlyweds, maybe, or an unmarried couple. A sound of unabashed joy, thwacking through the motel wall.

For a moment, Kate wished Donald were there. A rush of something, nostalgia perhaps, remembrance of his British Sterling and his warm shoulder.

She shook her head and turned her attention to the girl's shallow, nocturnal breathing on the other bed. Maybe she would rupture, maybe hemorrhage to death. Kate could always hope. The maid would come in, then, and find them tied up. It could be over soon if the little bitch would just up and die.

She offered a prayer to that effect. And then prayed the couple next door would have an argument and stop the infernal fucking.

Chapter Forty-four

Tony woke at three-nineteen according to the motel room's plastic clock, cramping and sweating. She felt her way into the bathroom and sat on the toilet, certain she had only a few minutes to live. But she couldn't die there in a stupid Alabama motel. If she was going to die it would have to be in Texas.

She panted and tried to ride the waves of pain. It was worse than any flu she'd ever had. It was worse than the food poisoning she'd gotten after eating some of Mam's spoiled Thanksgiving turkey. It was worse than any female pain she'd had before. She breathed deeply, slowly, the air hitching in her lungs. She wiped away the clots of blood that oozed from her hole.

The cramps subsided. She wiped the remaining red from between her legs but didn't flush. She didn't want to wake Baby Doll. That kid had been through a lot.

Not that Tony liked her or anything.

Chapter Forty-five

The old Chevy Nova was rusted along the sides, across the roof, and on the driver-side floor, so much that the rubber floor mat sagged in several spots and Kate knew if she pulled it up, she'd be able to see spots of the road beneath them. It was some joke of the gods that it had an engine and transmission decent enough to keep the machine moving forward. They were in Mississippi, driving west on Route 575 near the southern border.

The girl had not died last night. Another joke of the gods. She was alive and kicking and more determined than ever to make Texas. She'd left Kate and Mistie in the motel room in the very early morning and had returned with this vehicle. She didn't say where she'd found it, but Kate guessed some used car lot, from the "inner circle of value" near the back where most shoppers wouldn't bother to look. She'd hot-wired it and brought it back to Mobile South Motor Inn as the sun was coming up. She'd instructed Mistie and Kate to take whatever they could from the place, especially the pillows because they were soft, and all the towels from the bathroom. She ordered Mistie in the backseat, Kate in the driver's seat, and they were good to go.

The girl hadn't died. But Mistie was sick.

Kate had noticed it in the rearview. Mistie's skin was pale, her lips were cracking. She no longer repeated her little poems to herself. She was no longer reaching down with bound hands to rub herself between her legs.

The radio in the Nova didn't work. Neither did the speedometer. Kate drove at what she thought was fifty-five, knowing that if she tried to speed to catch a police officer's attention, the teenager would do her best to take them all down before they were caught.

If she'd only died. But there's still time before she gets to her friends in Texas. I'll keep my eyes open, you betcha. I'll watch for every opportunity. I'm smart. I'm the adult here.

Kate licked her bottom lip, savoring the image of the girl dead on the side of the road.

Mississippi in December was worse than Alabama in December. Kate had the window rolled down to let some of the sticky air in. Kate thought air might help Mistie feel better; what had she eaten yesterday that might have not agreed with her? Kate couldn't remember. When she called back to Mistie to see how she was doing, the girl in the passenger's seat stopped cleaning her fingernails with her knife and said, "Want a third stripe on your stomach? Hey, enough and we'll have, like, an American flag. That's thirteen, right? We can salute you."

Kate didn't answer and the girl didn't seem concerned that she didn't. The wounds on her abdomen were already closing, and it was amazing how little she thought of the discomfort when she had other things to occupy her mind. They drove another twelve miles, cutting through swampy grasslands and small farms dotted with Brahma cattle and snowy white egrets. Mistie slumped in the back, her head rolling to and fro as if dreaming of a tennis match.

"Truth or dare?" Kate asked. She put her left hand out into the wind. She had gotten permission from the girl to tear off her sweatshirt sleeves, and her arms were grateful for the small favor. Her pits smelled, but no longer did Kate feel chagrin. It was almost a good thing, a feral thing. A powerful, woman thing.

"Drop it you know what's good for you," said the girl without emotion.

"Something to pass the time." She liked the sound of her voice; it was gritty, unfamiliar. "I'm bored, I don't know about you."

"You're bored? You're cut and beat, and you're bored?" The girl eyed Kate with lowered lids, then, "Yeah. Why not. Truth."

"Who are the friends you're going to see in Texas?"

"Why?"

Kate shrugged. She didn't really want to know, but getting the girl to relax even a little would help when she had the chance to bash her in the brains with the loose steering wheel once she was able to work it free.

The girl licked sweat from her lip and frowned out the window. She said, "Not friends. I'm going to see my father." She glanced over at Kate as if she thought the revelation was worth a response. Kate did not respond.

The girl continued. "He's a ranch owner, owns almost half of Texas. He's a badass. He sells cattle. He's a drug baron, too, like those guys in Mexico and has more money than God. He kills anybody who gets in his way. Got a slew of bodyguards who catch and torture anyone who my father doesn't like." She looked back out the window.

Kate said nothing.

"He wrote for me to come visit him, so I figured after the gasoline guy got shot, it was as good a time as any."

"Mmm," said Kate.

The girl's head whipped about. "You don't believe me?"

"Why wouldn't I believe you? You seem like the daughter of a drug baron to me."

"You fucking with me?" The girl's nostrils flared, then calmed. "Truth or dare?" she said.

"Truth," said Kate.

"Why you have that kid in the back of your car? You don't have a daughter so it wasn't clothes. And trust me, I got a great dare if you lie this time."

Kate glanced down at the speedometer, forgetting it was broken. The needle rode zero. *Why was Mistie in my car? Yes, Alice and Bill. Ontario. I was taking her to them. She was sexually abused and I was doing a good thing. Saving her from torment. Rescuing the blameless from the furnace.*

"Oh, I wanted to give her a little vacation from school," said Kate. "I was taking her to see a little of Virginia she'd never seen before. Some historical sites for a few days. She is poor, you know. Lives in the trailer park."

"You go off with somebody else's kid and not take

your own? Your son? Forget about him? Or do you keep him locked up?"

"He doesn't live at home."

"Why not?"

"He's off at school. Philadelphia."

"Rich school? Southampton schools ain't good enough for a McDolen?"

"Possibly."

The girl shook her head slowly, accusingly. "Why'd you say that thing about the clothes last time I asked?"

"I was a tad unnerved."

"What the hell does that mean?"

"You had a gun, remember. I was surprised. Caught off guard."

"I don't believe anything you've told me 'bout Baby Doll. They're all lies. You weren't takin' her for no sight-seeing trip."

"Believe what you want. It's true."

"It's not true. Nothing you told me's true. So I got a dare for you."

Yeah, dare me, bitch. Not for much longer. Give it to me, I don't care. I'm biding my time.

"Next town, next phone booth, you're calling your husband and tellin' him what you did."

This wasn't what Kate expected. "What did I do?"

"Got Baby Doll, were skippin' out with her, taking her somewhere to be in a kiddie porn ring. They got those in Richmond, you know. And Washington, D.C. teachers got lots of chances to get kids for kiddie porn rings. Lots of money in it. Teachers do it, and clowns. Perverts."

"I would never . . ."

"Yeah, you would and you will call," said the girl.

"I'm gonna be real close, too, right by the phone. I wanna hear what he's got to say about all this. Just wish I could see his face."

Kate clutched the wobbly steering wheel and tried to pry it off the column. It just kept shaking but didn't come off. "I won't."

"You'll do the dare I tell you to do."

Okay, Kate, Hold on. She won't pick a high-traffic spot. And a phone cord could be an excellent garrote. Countdown to murder. Wasn't there a movie named that somewhere on AMC?

"Sure," said Kate. "I'll take the dare. What the hell."

"Your mouth gettin' trashy, teacher."

"How about that," said Kate. "Wonders never cease."

Chapter Forty-six

Her tummy hurt. She only had her ankles tied together because the girl with the knife—she didn't have a gun anymore—had said, "You'll sit in the back and behave, won't you? If you don't make any trouble I'll let you watch all the TV tonight that you want. Don't know where we're staying, but if there's a TV you can pick, okay?" The girl had even given her two Burger King biscuits instead of just one this morning after they left the motel room. The girl had said, "Got a few bucks from Blessing. So I'll be generous, just this one time. He'd like that."

But now she didn't feel very good. She felt hot and cold all at once, and her arms and legs hurt as if she'd had to run the mile on the school track. She wanted to be home at the trailer. She wanted to lie on the sofa with her head on the football-shaped end pillow, the fuzzy brown one with the black yarn stitches. She wanted to see Princess Silverlace. She didn't like this trip. The teacher was wrong. It wasn't fun, it was terrible. And she was sick.

Chapter Forty-seven

"That's the one!" Tony pointed to a small wall-mounted phone booth outside a Subway in some little town, it didn't matter anymore because it was surprising how little Alabama towns and little Mississippi towns and little Louisiana towns all looked alike. They had crossed the Mississippi River about ten minutes earlier and into Louisiana, just a state away from Texas. The teacher had told her this. At least the bitch was good for something besides driving.

Tony had pressed her nose through the open Nova window as they'd crossed the long bridge high above the broad and muddy water, staring down, thinking of things she'd heard in school about the Mississippi, other than it was spelled "crooked letter, crooked letter." It was the biggest river in the United States. Explorers went up it hundreds of years ago looking for gold. Memphis was on the Mississippi River and that was where Elvis had built Graceland.

Tony had almost told the teacher what she remembered about the Mississippi River but then she stopped herself. That would have been really lame, to let her know she learned something in school where teachers worked.

It was afternoon, midday, and the overcast sky was threatening a shower. Nobody was eating at the Subway. Through the large front window, a bushy-headed sub maker was twirling her hat around on her finger and staring blankly in the direction of outside.

Tony had opened a can of pork and beans from the duffel bag about a half hour before the Mississippi River but it had given her major gas. She couldn't wait to get out and air herself and the Nova. Farting in front of Baby Doll was humiliating. If it'd just been the teacher, she'd farted all day long and locked the woman in the car for an added treat. Tony had had cramps off and on in the Nova, but nothing like last night. She wondered what kind of damage she'd done to herself. If she'd been alone and had a mirror, she would have checked it out. Every so often she would see the reflection of Joe and Ricky on the inside of the windshield, but she would pinch her arm, hard, and the vision would fly away.

"There," she told the teacher. "Get up close, now. Time to call Mr. McDolen with a little confession. What's his name?"

The teacher said, "Donald."

"Lying to me? Donald?"

"No. I don't lie."

"Hmm," said Tony. "Yeah, maybe you're telling the truth. I've heard that name before, Donald McDolen.

It should be Donald McDonald. Or Ronald McDonald. That's better, don't you think?"

The teacher shrugged. "Donald is a fine name. It suits him."

Tony looked over the seat at the kid. "Don't you think her husband's name should be Ronald Mc-Donald?"

The kid looked sick. Before she realized what she was doing, she reached out her hand and touched the girl on the forehead. It was clammy. She patted the face gently, but then jerked her hand back immediately.

"Trying to catch a spider back there," she told the teacher, blowing a loud puff of air through her teeth. "Missed. It hopped away. I think it was really poisonous. Had red spots on it. Was gonna put it down your shirt. You'd like that, I bet."

"Would a spider in my shirt be a dare?"

"No, just a spider in your shirt. And don't cut the motor. It was a bitch to start."

The teacher pulled up to the corner of the Subway shop and put the car in park, the engine still heaving and wheezing. Tony thought the car had been a bad choice. It moved like an old man on a walker. Next time, something smooth and sporty.

"Baby Doll," said Tony, "you get out with me and stand real close so we can be sure the teacher does what she promised to do. We don't want a teacher breaking her promise, do we?" She reached over the back of her seat and popped the back door open, then pushed it with her hand so the kid could crawl out. She held the knife tightly; the way the teacher was acting now, the only thing to keep her in line was Baby Doll's life.

The little kid opened her eyes, and they were puffy

and pink around the edges with crusty stuff. "Get out," said Tony. Baby Doll obeyed, but it was a struggle as she flopped over and tried to work her feet to the ground. Tony hopped out, cut the strip of pillowcase, and drew the kid close with the knife to her ribs. The girl's body was hot through the pink nightie. She'd lost the outerwear way back before the mighty Miss. The gown stuck to her damp body like a wrapper on a melted Hershey bar.

The teacher climbed from the Nova and went to the phone. She was really different since the bathtub last night. She was harder, tougher, not much like a teacher anymore. That was peculiar considering she was wearing two slashes from Tony's knife as well as some facial bruises and bites that were just now fading to green. No matter, Tony was in charge. And this was going to be one kick-ass dare.

"Call collect," said Tony, urging Baby Doll closer to the booth. "He's at work, right? I don't have enough change to plug in the phone."

The teacher picked up the receiver, and stared for a long moment at the short, coiled phone cord as if it were a snake. Then she punched a slew of numbers, then said, "Collect, Kate McDolen." Tony leaned her head in and listened as the phone rang and then a tinny voice said, "McDolen and Associates, Attorneys at Law."

The computerized recording, "This is a collect call from . . . Kate McDolen . . . will you accept charges?"

"Well, oh, all right," said the small voice back in Virginia. "Kate, is that you?"

The teacher glanced at Tony, at Baby Doll drooping on her feet with the knife visible at her side. She crushed the short cord between her fingers, and said, "It's me, Lisa."

"Kate, are you all right? You've never called collect before. You okay? Took me a bit by surprise."

"Don't they know you're gone?" Tony said. "Don't they miss you yet? Get your husband on the line!"

The teacher: "Lisa, I'm fine, just having a little phone trouble. Patch me through to Donald?"

"He's not in."

The teacher's eyes closed, then opened. She grit her teeth. "Is he in court, then?"

"No, just out for lunch. He didn't say where, sorry."

"It's only . . ." The teacher looked at her wrist, but the watch she'd worn was no longer on her wrist, having given up the ghost when embedded with lake slop and left as a parting gift to the director at Camp Lakeview.

"It's a little after eleven, Kate," said Lisa. "Sometimes he does an early lunch. Can I give him a message when he returns? Are you in Emporia?"

The teacher glanced at Tony. Tony snatched the receiver and slammed it into the cradle. She tugged Baby Doll back a few steps. "What's this? Nobody has missed you in three days?"

"My husband thinks I'm on hiatus."

"Oh *what?* I hate that uppity talk bullshit!"

"Hiatus, sabbatical. Vacation for a few days. I told you I was taking Mistie to . . ."

"No, he doesn't think that. Teachers don't take off in the middle of the week. Is he in with you on the kiddie porn ring? Is that the deal?"

"There's no kiddie porn ring. And yes, he thinks I'm on vacation for a while. I told him I needed a break from school just like Mistie did. He cares about poor kids like I do. He's a generous, charitable man."

"Yeah?" demanded Tony. This was no good. "Yeah? Well, you're lying. You call his fucking cell phone. He's gonna hear the truth."

"He doesn't have a cell phone."

"All rich people have cell phones!"

"We don't."

"Even the crack dealer next door to me has a cell phone! Call him."

"He doesn't have a goddamned cell phone. Lay off."

Tony stared at the woman. "Goddamned" now, was it? Tony felt a strange anger hearing such words fall from a teacher's lips. "Well, then, we'll try later. You ain't off the hook. He'll come back from lunch and we'll call again then. Get in the car."

Back in the Nova, the teacher fought the steering wheel like she was angry at the world, or was trying to pull it off, or both. The car popped, roared, and threatened to cut off. Then it locked into gear and pulled away from the Subway where the girl in the window was still spinning her hat and looking as if she wished it were closing time.

Chapter Forty-eight

Mistie threw up on Route 120, soon after passing over Interstate 49 and nestling back into the quiet backland of Louisiana. There was no warning with Mistie, unlike Donnie, who would clutch his gut for a long many minutes saying, "I've gotta puke, it's coming. It's coming!"

It was a soft little "ploop," and then the whimper and the smell. Kate steered to the side of the road and the girl didn't tell her to get back on the road. It was raining, a steady stream of mist-fine drops. The windshield wipers on the Nova worked, amazingly, but they squawked like crows with their tails in a trap. She left the engine running.

"We have to do something," Kate said. She reached back and touched Mistie's cheeks. They were poker-hot. "I'm not sure what's wrong with her."

"You're supposed to know," said the girl.

"Why am I supposed to know it all?"

"You're a mom!"

"You believe women are worthless!"

The girl drove a fist against the dash in exasperation. Then she said, "Get her out."

It didn't take much to carry Mistie from the car. She weighed less than a sack of potatoes. Kate knelt in the wet roadside weeds and tried to shelter her body from the rain. Her own hair was immediately soaked, and the trickles on her bare arms chilling. The girl stood by in the skunk weed, arms crossed, the sleeves from her own WWJD sweatshirt ripped away.

Along the stretch of road were several houses—a white farmhouse on a hill back up the road a few tenths of a mile, and across the road two double-wides on a shared driveway. The rest was pastureland and cows.

"We need help," said Kate. "We need to get Mistie to a doctor right away."

"No way," said the girl. "Absolutely not."

Mistie opened her eyes, squinted, sighed, and closed them. The nightie was coated in remnants of breakfast biscuits and bile. Her skin was pale. Her breathing shallow.

"You little bitch," Kate said, staring up in the rain, "we have to get help!"

The girl slammed her foot into the side of Kate's head, driving Kate to her side, and brandished the knife. "We aren't! We can take care of her, fuck it, she's just sick, for Christ's sake!" She nodded at a barn across the cow field behind them. "There, we take her there!"

Kate was up immediately on her feet, staring into the wild eyes and the flash of the blade. "No, we're through with your pathetic, childish tantrum! Give it up, little girl!" The Nova's engine coughed, and died. There was a hairbreadth of silence.

The girl stood still, whirling one hand in the air. "Come for me. Come on, try it."

Kate hesitated. If she lunged for the girl, she would be stabbed surely, before she could get hold of the weapon. The girl was smart enough not to make the move herself, for in motion, she would be less in control.

"I'm taking Mistie to that house down there," said Kate. "I'm not tied up now. You have no gun. You run after me to cut me with that knife and I'll hear you coming in time to get an arm nick at the most, but then I'll kill you. It's that simple. I'll get your fucking knife and slash your neck wide open. You'll look like you heard the best joke in your life, as big as that grin is going to be."

Heart thundering, her eyes locked on the girl in the rain, Kate squatted down and picked Mistie up under her arms. "Come, honey," she said. *Truth or dare? No, this will be lie or dare. Any lie I give the owners of that house will be believed. I'm a teacher, a teacher with a sick child, kidnapped and taken out of state by a maniac. They'll see my wounds and believe anything I say.*

Kate began backing away from the girl with Mistie's feet dragging the wet weeds.

And then the girl darted forward, not for Kate, but for Mistie, and caught the girl in the shoulder with the knife. A puncture, a blossom of blood. She hopped back as fast as she'd come forward.

"What are you doing?" screamed Kate.

"Stopping you." The girl wiped rain from her nose. "You hold her to move her, your hands are occupied.

You let her down to protect her, and you aren't moving her anymore. Cool, huh?"

"You hurt Mistie!"

"Your fault, not mine."

"She's a child!"

"You didn't think I was able to hurt a child? I was ready to let her drown as easy as I would have let you. So just try me a bit more, teacher. You keep moving her that way and I'll poke her so full of holes before you get her to the house she'll be suckin' up rain like a big, fat old sponge."

Kate wanted to tear the face off the girl. *I will kill you. Give me time.* She looked at the barn across the field.

Mistie was easy to carry through the cow piles and the tall grasses with the girl and her knife trailing behind.

Chapter Forty-nine

The teacher's hands were left free so she could tend the child, but Tony had told the woman to tie her own ankles together with bale string or she'd hobble the child. The teacher didn't much seem to care what happened to her anymore. But the child was Tony's ace in the hole. The teacher cared about Baby Doll. The teacher's ankles were bound neatly with a tidy little knot in the back, as neatly as a teacher who'd been a Girl Scout could do.

The barn was different from the barn the Hot Heads used as a getaway back in Pippins. It was much bigger, and had two sides separated from each other with a supply room. On the side Tony had picked there were eight stalls, a ladder, and a loft. Beneath the sound of the rain on the roof, Tony could hear the skittering of mice in the walls and under the floorboards. The barn wasn't used for tobacco but for animals, and it smelled like it.

Tony had taken the duffel bag from the car. So other than a few farts lingering in the cushions and whatever DNA was in Baby Doll's vomit, and, well, there wasn't much to trace the stolen Nova to them. Well, except for fingerprints and Tony didn't have any on file and she was sure the teacher and Baby Doll didn't. In the country there were always trashed cars and trucks on the sides of roads. They could stay there for weeks, even months, before somebody alerted somebody and had them hauled away or maybe tried to find the people who'd last driven them. Tony wasn't worried about the Nova.

The teacher sat on some straw she'd spread on the floor. Tony was on a bale a couple yards away. She'd found some cool stuff in the supply room—a saw, a pitchfork, an ax. The ax was better than the knife, though she'd put the knife back in its place in her sock for future need. The saw and pitchfork were leaning against a stall door, but the ax was resting on Tony's knee. It was heavy, but would pack a damn good punch. *Manly, yes*, she thought, *but I like it, too.*

It was evening, sometime around eight or nine, Tony guessed. In a dented metal wheelbarrow a small fire burned. It had been the teacher's idea, so they could see what they were doing. There had been old planks and wooden blocks in the storeroom, and they were old and dry enough to burn hot. It was started with straw, then splinters pulled from stall walls, and then the thicker blocks. Tony thought that when she finally reached Burton's ranch in Lamesa, she would know how to build a really good campfire for the cowboys to sit around.

The teacher wore only her bra and jeans. She stroked

Baby Doll's hair and every so often dipped the bottom of her sweatshirt into a pail of rainwater at her feet and wiped the kid's face off. The kid had awakened off and on, and said she wasn't hungry and wondered where her mama was. Tony's gut tightened when the kid asked about her mama. Why hadn't the mama sent out police looking for the kid? Why hadn't her name been on the TV news last night? Just didn't care, clearly. Bitch like Mam.

The teacher began to hum a song, something that sounded like a nursery rhyme. Tony ordered her to stop. She did, but she looked at Tony with eyes that said, "You're mine, girl, you're dead." Tony wouldn't have believed it yesterday. Today, she did.

The firelight played shadows across the floor and the walls and the nooks in the stall doors. Tony had never been in a barn at night. She didn't like it. It was creepy, with most of whatever was in there with them in darkness, things that could watch them while going undetected. Even a flashlight wouldn't have made much difference.

The teacher began to sing again. Again, Tony said, "Shut the hell up!" Baby Doll whined in her sleep, then muttered, "Val."

"Who's Val?" said Tony, but the kid was out in space.

"Truth or dare?" asked the teacher.

"Not now."

"It's your game, and you're in control. Why not take a chance?" The teacher's eyes looked like she was smiling even though the corners of her mouth were turned down. Her skin crawled in the light of the fire.

Tony patted the ax, punctuating her power. "Truth."

"What's your name?"

"Ha!" This truly was funny. They'd spent so much time together and the teacher didn't even know her name. "Okay, truth. It's Tony."

"Tony what?"

"Tony's good enough," said Tony. "If you remembered Spring Fling, you'd know. Too bad. My turn. Truth or dare?"

"Dare."

"No kiddin'?" This was a nice change. "Okay, I want you to lick the bottom of my boot. It's got lots of nice mouse shit on it."

The teacher cocked her head. "I will," she said. "But why did you pick that?"

"Why doesn't matter."

"Why is the only thing that matters."

"You don't make sense. Just lick the fucking boot."

Tony loosened the laces and flipped her foot, tossing the boot at the teacher. The teacher picked it up, ran her tongue down the bottom without a single hesitation, and threw the boot back.

"Sick!" said Tony. "God, I'd never do that!" The teacher was becoming as creepy as the old, dark barn itself.

"Really?" the teacher asked. "So I'm braver than you?"

"Brave's nothing to do with it. Stupid is what it is."

The teacher shrugged, dipped her sweatshirt, and dabbed Baby Doll's neck.

"Truth or dare?" asked the teacher.

Tony hesitated. "Truth again."

"What happened to you last night."

"I meant to say dare."

"No, you didn't. You said truth."

Tony shook her head.

"Okay, dare, then," said the teacher. "Go to the farm-house at the edge of this field. Sneak in, get yourself invited in, whatever. I need some Tylenol, some rubbing alcohol. A thermometer if they have one."

A gray tabby cat appeared near the wheelbarrow, its glassy eyes reflecting yellow. It sniffed at the straw on the floor near Tony's feet. "Get out of here," Tony said. "You got no idea what I do to cats. Psssh!"

The cat scurried off to where it could not be seen.

"Well? Are you going?" asked the teacher.

"I didn't hear what you said," said Tony. "Now just shut up for a while."

"Mistie is really sick. You said dare."

"Maybe I did and maybe I didn't. So just shut up."

She scooted off the straw bale to the floor and leaned against the scratchy surface behind her. Little bits of straw bit into her arms and through the Jesus sweat-shirt. *Jesus, the great protector,* she thought. *Oh, yeah.*

"If you won't go for the things I need for Mistie, then let me go," said the teacher.

Tony leaped up, grabbed the ax, and slammed the blade into the floor inches from the teacher's foot. "Shut up!"

The teacher shut up. Tony bound the woman's hands behind her back with another length of bale string, but left the kid untied. Tony took off her own sweatshirt—screw the teacher, she could do what the teacher did and not care—and rolled it into a pillow-ball, then eased Baby Doll down so her head rested there.

"You ain't gonna run off, now, are you?" Tony asked the child. Baby Doll didn't seem to hear or understand.

She just sighed heavily and whispered something that sounded like, "Bad liver." She was dreaming. *That's good,* Tony thought. If you were really, really sick, you didn't dream. She knew she'd heard that somewhere. If not, she should have because it made sense.

Back against the straw bale, Tony tossed another few blocks of wood into the wheelbarrow. The fire blazed, crackled, and leveled off. Tony kept her gaze on the woman and the kid. She didn't want to see what might be in those dark corners. *Pussy,* she told herself, but it didn't matter. Dark corners could hold things that weren't good. And she had enough that wasn't good without adding to the mix.

She heard a cat's guttural and distant snarl, then only the secret whispers of the dreaming kid and the casual popping of the straw bits in the fire. She scratched her head slowly, as if one wrong move might bring out the devils in the barn.

Chapter Fifty

She dreamed.

She was in a tobacco barn. Leroy and DeeWee were there, hanging like tobacco leaves from the rafters, laughing and swinging and pointing at Tony. Tony lay in the straw, unable to move from the tormenting prickles on her naked body. She tipped her chin up; Mam was holding her arms over her head. She looked down; Burton was holding her legs apart. Something wet and hot was leaking from her privates, trickling along the flesh of her inner thighs like hideous slugs.

"What is happening?" she tried to cry out, but it was a baby's voice that she heard, a babbling garble issuing from her throat.

Mam said, "We'll have this done, don't you worry, Angela."

Burton, who now had a ten-gallon hat perched jauntily atop his dark hair, said, "Got an elm branch for digging. Knife handle just won't grab good. Gonna get those bastards out, hold still."

A searing pain. Tony screamed. Above, in the rafters, Leroy and DeeWee, and now Little Joe and Whitey, flicked dried bird poop at each other and said, "Eat this! Dare, dare!"

Tony tried to sit up, to pull her legs together, but Burton said, "No, don't be such a cow. Hold still."

Mam said, "Honey, I need a beer. When we're done here, would you please get me a beer? My throat's so dry."

Burton tugged at Tony's insides. Tony tried to move with the tug, trying to keep her guts from coming out with the dreadful, powerful suction.

"Hold still!" said Burton. Something in Tony popped and gave way. Burton clucked, and smiled, and held up two wet, writhing earthworms the size of pythons. "Look at this," he said. "Don't take after you at all. Must be their daddy."

She bolted awake.

Fuck!

Breaths. Huh, huh, huh, huh.

Blurry eyes. She wiped them with the heel of her hand. Fucking dream. Who invented fucking dreams? Who the hell thought up such a damn thing?

And she saw the teacher, standing before her with the ax raised above her head, her teeth bared, her lips peeled back, the eyes of Satan himself staring out from the sockets.

Chapter Fifty-one

Mistie heard something, someone, scream, and she tried to open her eyes but they were glued shut. It sounded a little like Mama screaming.

"Valerie!" Mama had screamed, and Daddy had said, "Shut your face, you wanna be thrown in prison?"

"Valerie!" Mama had screamed, and Mistie had cried, a higher sound that blended with Mama's into something like a song. But the screams and the cries were all Mistie recalled, the wailing voices in the kitchen in the apartment in Kentucky.

Daddy had said, "It was a bad liver. We can't help she had a bad liver." And he had buried her somewhere where no one could find out it wasn't a bad liver.

That was all Mistie knew. It was too far away, Kentucky. It was too long ago, Valerie.

The scream came again. Mistie scratched the glue from one eye and looked out in the firelit barn where the teacher was standing over the girl, and it was the girl who was screaming.

Chapter Fifty-two

The teacher arched the ax over and down with a grunt, and as the whistling of the dull blade reached Tony's ears, Tony threw herself backward in a violent tumble, over the sagging straw bale and to the shadowed floor behind. The ax head bit into the straw, a solid whack that split the top half in two.

"Shit!" Tony rolled to her side, scrambled to her feet. The teacher shook the ax like a rabid dog with a groundhog, and pulled it out of the straw. She lifted it up again, both her sweating torso and the old blade catching firelight briefly. The eyes again, dead and terrible.

"Back off, bitch!" screamed Tony.

The teacher walked around the straw bale, her footsteps rhythmic, robotlike. The ax held in position over her head. Tony scrabbled back, slipping in the loose straw, her hands going before her face. "No!"

The teacher's lips opened and closed, speaking something Tony couldn't hear, and then the ax came down again. Tony flopped to the right and the ax struck dead center of the straw where she'd been. Tony scooted away on her knees, panting, snatching for the ax handle before the teacher could wrench it free of the floor.

"Bitch! You fucking shit brain!" Tony caught the slick wood of the handle, the sporadic splinters, but the teacher threw out her foot and caught Tony in the shoulder, knocking her away. Tony lost her breath, caught it, skidding in the needle-sharp straw. The teacher grinned, the flickering fire glow twisting her face into myriad subhuman shapes. She raised the ax and stepped forward.

Tony scooted back on the floor, head reeling. "Don't kill me, you goddamn bitch! Teachers don't kill kids!" The teacher smiled. Tony shoved herself to her feet, ducking just in time to miss the blade as it swung at her head.

The teacher stumbled then, the blow connecting with nothing but air, and she took several weird, skipping steps forward. Air hissed through her teeth with the sound of a car radiator about to blow. Tony shouted, "Ha!" and threw the whole of her weight against the woman. Tony and the teacher sprawled to the floor, Tony on top of the woman, the woman cracking into a stall door. Tony dove for the ax handle, her fingers catching it and locking tightly. She yanked with all her strength, knees bearing down in the straw, body throwing itself back. But the teacher's grasp didn't loosen. She yelped, planted her foot on Tony's chest, and kicked her away. She then sat up and waved the ax.

"Stop it!" Tony cried. "Crazy ass shit!"

Still seated, the teacher swung the ax in evenly measured side sweeps, like a farmer wielding a scythe. Back and forth, swoosh, swoosh, daring Tony to step up and loose her feet from the rest of her body. As the ax kept up its steady sweeps, the teacher braced herself against the stall door and pushed herself, slowly and steadily, to her feet.

"Back off!" screamed Tony. She looked behind her, her eyes probing the darkness for the pitchfork, the saw, something. Something to kill the teacher. Something to save herself.

Baby Doll. Tony saw the little girl lying on the floor, her head cradled in the balled-up sweatshirt. *Baby Doll!*

Tony scooted around the fire-bearing wheelbarrow and dropped down by the child. She picked her up and held her to her chest. *So I catch what she's got,* Tony thought. *Small price.*

The teacher was fully on her feet now, turning like a Disney animation toward Tony and Baby Doll. She strode forward, and stopped. The ax held position over her head.

"Kill me, kill us both," said Tony simply.

"Let her go," the teacher growled.

"Kill me, kill us both."

Baby Doll opened her eyes. She squinted at Tony, then into the shadows beyond the teacher. "Mama had a baby," she whispered.

The teacher stared.

"Put it the fuck down," said Tony.

"I . . . ." began the teacher.

"I ain't letting her go, bitch."

The teacher tilted her head, shut her eyes, opened them, and said, "What?"

"Huh?" echoed Baby Doll.

Tony said nothing. She counted. *One, two, three, four, five, six, seven, eight, nine, ten, eleven . . .*

The teacher looked at Baby Doll, then Tony, then her own upraised arms and the ax handle she clutched. "I . . . ?"

Fourteen, fifteen, sixteen, seventeen, eighteen, nineteen . . .

A strange gasping sound from the teacher. Her mouth opening, snapping shut. The body wavering slightly, the muscles of the arms twitching within the flesh.

Twenty-three, twenty-four, twenty-five, twenty-six, twenty-seven . . .

"Ah," said the teacher. Her tongue appearing briefly at the front of her mouth, disappearing. The ax, still in place overhead, a deadly torch in the hands of a mad Lady Liberty.

There was a rustling sound to Tony's right. She glanced over the same moment the teacher did. There were wide, iridescent eyes in the dark, a crouched body in the straw.

The teacher whooped, spun on her toe, and brought the ax down in a powerful strike. The blade connected, cut through, slammed to a stop in the floor.

The cat's head rolled lazily through the straw and came to a stop against Tony's boot.

Baby Doll stared at it. She reached out one clammy hand to touch the furry ears, the glistening eyes.

And for the first time on the entire, nightmarish trip, the little girl screamed.

Chapter Fifty-three

She remembered.

There was a train track running behind the brick apartment building they lived in when they were in Kentucky. It passed behind the apartment's playground, separated from the children by a tall, chain-link fence and a steep embankment. The train didn't come by often, several times a week, and it was a slow-moving thing most of the time. Once, when Mistie had been in the playground with Mama and Valerie, Mama had watched the train go by and said, "That thing moves like a old man who crapped his drawers!" She'd laughed. Mistie, who had been five at the time, had laughed. Little Valerie, who was two and a half, had giggled shrill and loud.

There were lots of children at the apartment building, three stories' worth of them, and in the summertime the playground was crawling with them because nobody had air-conditioning in their apartments. Mistie didn't remember the names of any of the children who were there, but she remembered the faces, dark and light, chubby and thin, smiling and somber. Every morning of the summer they were there, clustering on the sliding board and cluttered atop the spin-around like Japanese beetles on a rose. They played in the baking-hot sandbox and threw balls at each other until someone finally cried and the mothers told them to be good or they'd have to go inside.

Nobody had any money, much. The mothers and older sisters who sat in the shade of the single tree in the playground were always saying something like that to each other.

"Wish I could get a new car. Not a new one, but a different one. Got a busted transmission in mine and I can't afford a cab to work."

"School's comin' up next month. You ever see a kid with bigger feet than Justin's? Bought him new shoes in June and now he's needin' 'em again for school."

"Randolphs got a window air unit. Gonna run their 'lectric bill up but damn, I wish it was me!"

"Me, too, sister, me, too."

And on it went.

It was mid-August, and after suppertime. Some of the kids had come back down to play while others were settled in their living rooms in front of their televisions. From the playground the blue glows of the sets were visible through the open windows.

Mistie's mama was lying down on her bed because she just found out she was going to have another baby and wasn't happy about it. She told Daddy she was going to get her tubes tied after this one was born. Mistie didn't know what that meant but it sounded bad

310

because Mama had said it through her teeth. Daddy was pissed off and went riding in their Buick. Mama sent Mistie and Valerie out to play in the playground for a while.

"You stay in there and don't go nowhere else," said Mama from her bed. Mistie and Valerie were standing in the doorway to her bedroom, each holding a fruit roll-up left over from supper. "I can trust you to do what I say, can't I, Mistie?"

Mistie nodded. "Yeah, Mama," she said.

"When I call you out this window you come runnin', you hear me? Anybody bother you you come right back up here, you and Valerie, you hear me?"

"Yeah, Mama, okay."

"Okay, then." Mama smiled a little and said, "You're my girls. Watch that slide now, you know how hot it gets in the sun. Burn the skin off the back of your legs, you aren't careful."

"Okay, Mama."

Mistie took Valerie by the hand and led her down to the first floor and then back through the hallway to the rear door of the building. Flies loved the back hall of the first floor because just outside the door was where the residents put their bags and cans of garbage when the Dumpsters were full. The Dumpsters were usually full.

Valerie giggled as several flies found her eyelashes.

"Hey, flies!" demanded Mistie. She flicked her hand at Valerie's face, sending them in a whirl. Mama had spray she could put on the kids to keep the flies and bugs off, but she had forgotten, and Mistie knew it wasn't time to go back and ask for it.

Outside, it wasn't quite as hot as it had been in the

afternoon. It was still light, and the sun was visible beyond the railroad track, sitting atop a distant warehouse like a cat on a fence post.

Mistie put Valerie on the spin-around and pushed it slowly in a circle. Valerie giggled and tried to stand up, but flopped over and laughed again. Then Mistie pushed off and jumped aboard, and the sisters went round and round, looking up at the clouds, watching them spin, too.

The garbage truck came up beside the playground with a hiss and a sound of scraping metal. Some of the little boys stopped to watch, but Mistie only looked at it, then back at Valerie, who was heading for the sliding board.

"Hot, Valerie!" Mistie warned. "Don't burn your legs!"

The garbage truck's steel arms lifted the three Dumpsters in turn, the contents dropping into the huge maw on its back. Then the driver climbed out and opened the gate to the playground and strode to the back door where the extra bags and cans were strewn. He complained loud enough for everyone to hear, though it didn't seem like anyone cared much.

"Put the trash where it belongs next time! I don't get paid extra to lug this stinking crap to my truck!"

One of the teenage baby-sitters, under the tree with a boyfriend, said loud enough for the trash man to hear, "You come when you're supposed to it wouldn't get all overflowing like that!"

No more words were exchanged. The garbage truck wheezed and thumped, then drove away.

Mistie went to the sandbox while Valerie sat on the bottom of the slide and tried to catch a fly. The sandbox was fun, except when one of the stray cats of the neighborhood used it as a litter box. Mistie found a cracked plastic shovel and she began to make a castle. The sand at the top was dry and didn't stick together, but the sand underneath was damp from old rains and stuck together really good. Mistie dug up the wet sand and used her hands to claw all around to make the castle moat. She'd seen a TV show where a queen lived in a castle and the castle had a moat around it, full of snakes and snapping turtles and other things with teeth. It was a funny show, a cartoon, and the prince was so clumsy he kept falling into the moat and the queen kept pulling him out with her silk curtains. After the moat, Mistie formed the castle. A bucket would have been good to use; one little girl who played in the sandbox a lot had a bucket but she'd taken it in. Mistie had to use her hands. But patiently she scooped and patted, pausing on occasion to pick a stone from outside the sandbox to decorate the walls. Some dandelions grew in a grassy path by the sandbox; Mistie popped off the yellow blossoms and covered the top of the castle with them. She sat back on her heels and smiled.

"Valerie, look!" she said, turning toward the slide.

Valerie was not on the bottom of the slide. Mistie hopped to her feet, brushed sand off her knees and her bottom, and glanced around. She didn't see Valerie. "Valerie?" She trotted over to the slide and looked at the ladder, but her sister wasn't there, neither was she sitting in the shade beneath the slide.

Mistie stomped her foot. "Valerie, quit hiding from me!"

Up the bank behind the playground, a lazy freight train ambled by, clacking and clicking. Mistie called over the noise to the baby-sitter under the tree.

"Have you seen Valerie?"

The baby-sitter waved her over, unable to hear over the noise. "What did you say?" said the girl, squinting in the sun. Her boyfriend had his arm around her waist.

Mistie felt funny now. Her mouth was dry and her chest felt as if someone were jumping up and down on it. "Have you seen Valerie?"

The baby-sitter took a drag on her cigarette and passed it to her boyfriend. "Valerie? That little girl with hair like yours? No."

"She's my sister."

"So?" said the boyfriend around the smoke. "You lose your sister, that's your problem, not ours."

The baby-sitter shrugged like she agreed with the boyfriend. Mistie spun on her toe and looked at all four corners of the playground. Amid the few other children, there was no Valerie.

Then she saw the open gate. The garbage man had come for the trash, but had left the chain-link gate wide open. Mistie ran for the gate, laced her fingers through the wire, and stared at the lot where the Dumpsters and the cars were parked. "Valerie!" she called. "You get yourself back here or we're gonna get a whippin'!"

Valerie didn't jump up, laughing, from behind a car. She didn't peer, grinning and giggling, from behind a Dumpster. Mistie went out in the lot, her heart pounding now so hard she could hear it in her ears and feel it in her neck. The lot was hot, still steaming from the afternoon sun; starlings pecked at the dust and squawked at each other.

"Valerie, damn it, come here!" Mistie used her Daddy's word. Daddy could get Valerie to behave when nobody else could. But Valerie didn't come.

Mistie walked across the lot to the grassy embankment. The train had gone on, leaving only its echo. Mistie grabbed hold of brittle bank-side chicory and pulled herself to the track. "Valerie!" She was sweating, and her hair was flat against her neck, but under her skin she felt a quick, passing chill, like the ones she got the moment she hopped out of her evening bath.

Up the line there was a curve where the track rounded to the right behind a five-story cold storage building. Down the line it ran straight for a pretty long ways between rows of other apartment buildings toward the center of the city. Mistie walked up the center of the track, trying to pace her steps with the awkwardly spaced wooden ties. She'd never seen things from this vantage point before; the playground seemed smaller, its grass more spotty and brown. At the bottom of the other side of the embankment, a stream trickled over rocks and broken glass. There were small houses on that side, each with their own fenced yards, clotheslines, doghouses.

"Valerie!"

Mistie held her arms out for balance and walked toward the curve in the track. Mama was not just going to spank them, she was going to take away TV for a long time, and Daddy was going to yell really loud and maybe jerk Mistie's hair like he did before. Maybe Daddy would call the police to come put the two girls in jail. Daddy said police did that to bad little girls who didn't do what they were told. Mistie's eyes welled up at the thought of jail.

She heard a child giggle, and she stopped in her tracks to look down in the direction of the sound. It was a little boy in his backyard, teasing his puppy with a stick. Mistie said, "Shut up!" to the boy.

"You shut up!" called the boy.

Rounding the curve, Mistie could see the track stretching straight again, reaching out to the end of the city. The embankment was taller here, sloping sharply a good twenty-five feet, and covered with gravel instead of grass. The rear lot of the cold storage building was littered with cans and papers and what looked like little balloons. Rusted trash barrels stood upright and lay on their sides. The building's windows were cracked and some were missing the glass entirely. A pile of old clothes lay against one of the upright barrels near the foot of the embankment.

Mistie lost her footing on the ties and stumbled, then caught herself before slipping on the edge of the embankment. She wiped her nose, then sneezed in a sudden whirlwind of dust. "Valerie! Mama's gonna be so mad! Where are you?"

She walked a few more yards down the track and stopped. She turned about, hands on hips, staring down both sides of the embankment. The little boy was still playing with his puppy.

"Hey!" yelled Mistie. "You see a little girl?"

"No!" called the boy. "And I said shut up!"

Mistie looked down at the trash barrels in the back lot of the cold storage building. Maybe Valerie was hiding inside one of the ones that were lying on their side. Back in the apartment, Valerie was always getting into the lower cabinets when Mama left them unlatched. Sitting on her butt, Mistie slid down the gravel with her hands pressed into the gravel so she wouldn't slide too fast. Her palms were cut on jagged pieces of the rock, and at the bottom she paused to spit on them and wipe them off. There were little bits of skin peeled up and little red lines of blood. It hurt, but not as bad as the whipping if she couldn't find Valerie. Her shorts were traced in oil and tar.

"Valerie!" Her voice was wobbly now. She knew she was going to cry and didn't want to. What she wanted was for her bratty baby sister to quit being a baby and hiding when she knew it was time to be home.

Mistie squatted down and peered inside one of the rusted barrels. There was nothing in there but spiders' webs and a rat's nest. She looked in another and found the same. "Yuck!" she said, shivering. She hated bugs.

She looked at the pile of old discarded clothes over by one of the upright barrels. Who would leave their clothes here? Daddy said some boys and girls did a dirty thing where people couldn't see them. The dirty thing meant they took off their clothes. Maybe boys and girls took off their clothes here. But they would get spiders on them, Mistie thought. And the people on the train could look down and see them.

She walked over, her feet slowing as she got closer, because something was odd, something was wrong. Something was familiar.

There were jeans, yes, big old jeans from some man maybe, and a torn blouse and boys' underpants. There was a blanket that was crusted with months' worth of dried, dirty rain. And there was something else, lumped up, twisted, and crumpled, a white shirt drenched in red, a pair of blue shorts.

Mistie began to breathe through her mouth, short, puffy breaths that hurt her throat and her lungs. She couldn't blink. Her arms stung with dread.

317

Uh-oh, no, no . . .

She stopped at the pile and knelt. She touched the back of the T-shirt and found there to be a body within, and the body was warm. She reached over for the little arms that protruded from the sleeves, and rolled the body over. Legs flopped like little rubber dog toys, and one of the sandals was gone from the foot. The arms and legs were raked with scratches.

Mistie stared. The air around her went dark and poisonous. She put her hands to her mouth, trying to cry, trying to speak, trying to shout to Valerie to *get up, get up now, quit playing this stupid game with me!*

Valerie wasn't getting up. Her head was gone.

Mistie found the head in some brush near the embankment. The eyes were open; the neck was ripped and ragged. Mistie cradled it under her shirt and crawled back up to the tracks. She took it home, hoping Mama could fix it. Mama could put it back. Mama could make it right. And that Mama wouldn't spank too very hard.

Chapter Fifty-four

Kate threw the ax as hard as she could across the barn, where it struck the wheelbarrow, turned it over, and skidded into oblivion in the far side shadows. She stared at what was before her, ebbing and flowing in the simmering light from the wood blocks.

The girl. The severed cat head. The screaming child covered in cat's blood.

Kate's fingers were locked in place, paralyzed into position as if around the handle of a demonic ax. Her body was coated in sweat, dream sweat, waking sweat.

She took a step forward, and the girl clutched the child more tightly. The child held the cat's head to her as if it were the grail of God.

And she screamed.

"I . . ." began Kate.

The girl bared her teeth. She stroked the cat's head and wailed as if her soul were being raked over hell's coals. The sound pierced the rafters and echoed along the dark corners of the barn.

"I don't . . ."

"Valerie!" howled the girl.

And then there was a thunderous cracking noise, gunfire, and the voice of a man shouting outside, "Who the hell's in there? Who's in my barn?"

The girl leaped up in a single motion, dragging the child with her. The cat's head flew away. Kate spun about and stared in the direction of the shout.

"Chuck, go around the side!" A man's voice. Furious. "Watch the windows! Could be that gang of rail riders we heard about!"

"Hope so!" came a second voice, younger. "Got a 'ward out on them suckers!"

"Shoot first, questions later!"

"Yeah, bo!"

The burning blocks had lit the nearby straw, and a small blaze was starting to spread its fingers across the floor.

"C'mon!" said the girl, hitching her head toward an open stall. Kate grabbed one of Mistie's arms and the girl took the other, and they carried her off the main floor and into the tiny room where there was a small, latched window. With her free hand Kate knocked the latch open, then shoved the trembling, still crying girl out and into the rainy night. Kate went next, wondering for the briefest moment if the girl might hamstring her as an added bonus, but then she was out, facedown in the soaking weeds, and the girl was behind her.

Her breath in her ears, thundering in sync with the hammering of her heart.

Get up, get up!

She was up, she had Mistie by the forearm, the girl had the other. They were bolting through the steamy rain, across the black waves of grasses and the confused cattle, toward a stretch of forest at the far side of the field.

Behind them, two shouts, on the heels of each other.

"Damn barn's on fire! Get the hose, quick!"

"I see 'em! Out there, out the window! In my sights!"

A strange moment of silence, stretching oddly out across the field behind them, reaching Kate's neck, stroking it with cold nails.

Then a blast, an impact in Kate's left calf, and she went down again into the sharp grasses. No pain for a moment, stretching like the silence, waiting for the precise moment to reveal its full self.

Mistie fell as Kate fell. The girl Tony skidded to a halt and turned about. "Get up!" she ordered. "Get up and run!"

Then the pain exploded, blowing out through the whole of Kate's lower body, fierce, powerful, hideously real. She threw back her head in disbelief. In agony.

"Get the fuck up!"

Hands grappling for Kate's hand, tugging her to her feet, where she tripped, went down, and was dragged back up again. Another blast from behind and a hoot of joy, "They're outa here, by damn! They're faster'n jackrabbits!"

"I can't . . . ," Kate began. The agony scrabbled up through her spine to her head in jagged, sparkling talons. She couldn't form words. She couldn't think words.

"Hell you can't, 'cause I can't carry you!"

Kate bore down with her teeth and her mind, and

made her legs move. Out, forward, out, forward, out, forward. She didn't have hold of Mistie anymore, but she could see the little girl stumbling along beside Tony. The child was no longer screaming.

It was a lifetime before they found the woods and the sagging wire fence that separated it from the cattle field. Tony pushed the top of the fence down with her foot and threw Mistie across. "Over!" she shouted to Kate. Kate crawled over the fence, her wounded leg dragging. Her palms came down in a rain-soaked thistle patch.

Back at the barn, another muffled shot. Distant, incoherent shouts. Kate twisted her head back on her neck to see a faint glowing through the window. *It's going to be a Yule fire.* The first clear thought since she'd gone down. *Poor cows. All that hay.*

Tony caught Kate's upper arm and dragged out of the thistles, across roots and rocks, and along a footpath, cow path, something. Trees then. A lot of them, close together. Tony pushed Kate ahead. Kate let herself be pushed.

And then Kate felt a hand tug her abruptly to a halt, and push her down to her butt. She was propped against the slimy bark of some lumpy Louisiana scrub tree. Kate closed her eyes against the pain. She heard a knife click open.

Damn, she's going to kill me after all. I guess I don't really blame her, not after the ax.

There was a sound of ripping denim.

The sound of rainwater, or was it shower water, in her ear? Thundering, pounding, drilling to her soul.

And then, silence.

Chapter Fifty-five

"Truth or dare?" asked Tony.

The teacher was coming back around, but kept fading in and out, her head thumping against the bark of the tree to which she was tied, her tongue making brief appearances over her teeth. Tony sat beside Baby Doll on top of a flattened nest of some fuzzy-leafed plants, her arms wrapped around her knees. Baby Doll was leaning on her, but she didn't push her off. Tony thought that DeeWee would laugh his retarded ass off seeing Tony in just an Ace bandage and pants, sitting in the wet woods with a teacher in just a bra and pants, propping up a sick kid in a torn-up pink nightgown. He'd talk about it for months. As stupid as he was, certain things stuck in his brain like a thorn.

"You hear me, teacher? I asked you a question."

The teacher didn't say anything, but she moaned and it was a wide-awake moan, not a dreaming moan.

Tony had done doctoring, sort of. Flopped the

teacher over, sliced the jeans leg up the back, and checked out the damage to the woman's calf. It was a flesh wound, really, with no bullet to dig out or anything. But it was raw and nasty looking, with a loose flap of orange skin dangling over the hole. Good thing it'd been a rifle and not a shotgun. The teacher had groaned but didn't wake up, and Tony had cut up the jeans leg for a bandage and tied it like she thought a Girl Scout might.

We look like those beat-up guys on the American Colony Insurance ad, Tony thought. *Only they're carrying a flag, a drum, and a flute. And they're standing up.*

The teacher's eyes opened, and this time there seemed to be some focus. "Mistie . . . ?" she began.

"Here, with me. Got my knife so don't try anything. Shoulda killed your ass when you were out. Truth or dare?"

The teacher sighed, and thumped the back of her head again on the tree trunk. "Not. Now."

"You fucking tried to ax me to death," said Tony.

Eyes closed, opened. The teacher looked up at the sky as if watching for more rain. She shivered, and tried to move her arms. Each hand was outstretched and bound to a low branch with leftover denim strips.

"Look like a fucked-up Jesus there, teacher," said Tony. "Truth or dare?"

"I don't . . . ," said the teacher. "Mistie. Is Mistie all right?"

Tony looked at Baby Doll. She was awake, but silent, curled up into her own knees, leaning on Tony's shoulder. Her pale hair hung in a sheet around her face in a waterfall of yellow. Her body wasn't as hot as it had been, but she still looked sick.

"I was shot," said the teacher, seeming surprised by the sudden realization. She bolted upright against her restraints. "Oh, my God, shot."

"Not anymore," said Tony. "Well, I mean I wrapped it up and all. Just call me Mark Green. I shoulda let you die, shoulda killed you like you tried to kill me."

Tony and the teacher studied each other for a long minute, then the teacher broke the stare. She looked tired, beat.

They'd need some clothes, Tony knew, and soon. Louisiana rain wasn't as cold as Virginia rain, but they sure as hell wouldn't pass through to Texas unnoticed in their underwear.

The teacher tried to move her arms again. She said, "Why didn't you, then?"

"Kill you?"

"Yes."

"Good fucking question. Because I could, I guess. I could, easily, so wasn't any point to it."

"Oh."

"And dying ain't sufferin'. You gotta pay for what you tried to do to me in that barn."

Another long moment of silence. And then Baby Doll whispered, "Truth."

Tony looked at the kid. She brushed the girl's hair back from her face to find a pair of blue eyes watching her. "What did you say, Baby Doll?"

"Truth."

"Not you, I meant the teacher. Truth or dare ain't a game for kids."

Pale, cracking lips, whispered, "Truth. I wanna go home."

Tony shifted on the lumpy, fuzzy plants. She liked the kid better before. She didn't want the kid to be talking. "You be quiet, you ain't well."

"I want to go home. That's the truth."

"Shhh."

"Valerie got killed," said Baby Doll, so softly that the words seemed part of the after-rain breeze. "Valerie didn't have a bad liver. It was her head that got cut off."

"You're sick," said Tony. "Don't talk creepy."

"Who's Valerie?" asked the teacher.

"Baby sister Valerie," said Baby Doll.

"I don't want to hear it," said Tony.

Baby Doll rubbed her mouth, her crotch. She said, "Daddy said Valerie got a bad liver 'cause if we told what happened the social services would put us in jail. In jail for not watching. I was s'pose to watch her. She ran away. Her head got cut off. I think the train did it. It was rolled over in the trash. It had sticks and grass on it."

"Oh, Mistie, dear God," said the teacher softly.

"I forgot," said Baby Doll. "But I remember now. I wanna go home."

"It's okay, honey," said the teacher. "I'm here. You're safe."

Tony laughed. "You think you can make her safe? You've got a hell of a record these past days."

The teacher said nothing. Tony turned to Baby Doll. "Truth, okay?" she prodded. "Why'd the teacher have you in the back of her car? She like to play with you?

326

She takin' you somewhere to play with you and make movies of you without no clothes on?"

Baby Doll frowned, confused.

"To, you know," said Tony. She pointed at her own crotch, pretended to rub it. "She do that to you?"

Baby Doll shook her head.

"Her husband do that to you?"

Baby Doll shook her head.

"Her son?"

A head shake.

"Somebody do that to you. You want to play truth or dare? You gotta tell the truth 'bout this."

"Daddy," said the kid. "Mama didn't want no more kids 'cause they get their heads cut off. She wouldn't let him rub her down there no more. He said I gotta do what Mama wouldn't do so he would be happy."

Tony's skin prickled. Her head itched, and she dug at it. "He fuck you, didn't he?"

Baby Doll didn't seem to know what that meant, and Tony let it go. She stood up, and walked up to the teacher's tree, around it, and back again, kicked wet leaves. She wrapped herself in her arms, tightly. "Your mama didn't stop him?" she asked.

Baby Doll shook her head. "Daddy said don't tell Mama."

"Mistie," said the teacher faintly. "Oh, honey, I thought so."

"You thought so?" Tony strode up to the teacher and struck her soundly across the mouth. "You thought so and you didn't tell anybody?"

The teacher lifted her chin. "You want the truth, here it is. I knew about it. So did most of the school. But no one had made a move to protect Mistie. I decided it was up to me. I was taking her away, I was driving her to Canada. I had her under the quilt so no one would see her. I was rescuing her."

Tony slapped her again for the piss-poor job she'd done at rescuing Baby Doll. Then she straightened and chewed a loose cuticle from her thumb. It tasted like rust. She spat it out. "Why didn't you tell me right off? I'd believed that more than the other shit you tried to feed me."

"I was kidnapping Mistie. You know what that means if I'm caught? Taking a child across state lines in a kidnapping? A teacher doing something like that?"

"I wouldn't have told."

"How would I have known that? You cut me up, beat me, you kicked me, you tried to drown us in the car."

"I wouldn't have told 'cause that's probably the best thing a teacher could do, saving a kid."

"Teachers do a lot of good things, Tony. . . ."

"Most teachers don't do shit!" Tony let out three loud breaths. Her fists clenched in and out. "They don't care about shit! Truth? Okay, while we're at it. I didn't try to drown your ass. I rolled the windows down so I could get you out. That's the truth. You ain't dead, are you?"

"I think you just decided we were better to you alive than dead. We made a tolerable-looking family unit, the three of us."

"I don't kill people!"

"You killed the gasoline man."

"I did not! Whitey did."

The teacher caught her breath. Tony counted seven long heartbeats, and then the teacher said, "You didn't shoot him?"

"Whitey did. And he wasn't suppose to have bullets in his gun, but he did. It was an accident."

The teacher looked away from Tony, and stared out through the forest in the direction of the cattle field and the barn. Tony had stared out that way for more than an hour after they'd climbed the fence, while Baby Doll was curled up and the teacher was still passed out. Tony had been sure the farmer and his troops would come after them with hounds and county sheriffs. But the fire had obviously been their primary issue. They'd put it out before much damage was done. The building was still standing. Hell, they hadn't even called the fire department.

"You didn't kill him?" said the teacher.

"No," said Tony. "But if I really had to kill, I would. Don't ever, ever forget that."

"I won't," said the teacher.

Tony scratched her head. It itched down to the bone over her ears and at the nape of her neck. "We need clothes we going anywhere tomorrow. There's those double-wides not too far from here. I'm gonna see what I can get without nobody knowing. You stay here, watch the kid."

"Her name is Mistie."

"Yeah, Mistie, okay, whatever."

"We need some Tylenol, too, and alcohol."

"Don't push your luck."

"You were good to Mistie, I could see that. Letting her lean on you like that."

"It was an accident," said Tony. "I didn't know she was leanin'." Tony strolled off, but stopped several yards away and called back, "By the way, how the hell'd you get out of those bale strings?"

329

"Backed up to the saw you found in the storeroom," said the teacher. "Had to work myself around like a contortionist in the Cirque Du Soleil but I sawed them apart."

"What the fuck's the cirk duh soulay?"

"Doesn't matter. My ankles were easier after my hands were free."

"I'll never leave you untied again. Next car we get, you drive with your damn hands tied."

"I guessed as much."

"You were going to kill me, you really were."

The teacher's expression unreadable. "Don't be long now. Please."

Please and fuck you, thought Tony.

Chapter Fifty-six

This truck wasn't half as bad as the Nova had been. It was a manual transmission, though, so Tony had tied Kate's left hand to the steering wheel and the right hand to the gearshift with leftovers from Kate's Christian camp director jeans. Kate's calf throbbed mercilessly when she had to press the clutch, but Tony had allowed her to rebandage it, and though excruciating with every move, she thought it would probably heal. But some alcohol, if she could get her hands on some, would ensure that that would happen.

Tony had brought clothes from a dryer in a shed outside one of the double-wides. Overalls for Kate, and a white tank top with stained underarms. Tony had claimed a man's pair of camouflage shorts and a black T-shirt with NAPA emblazoned on the front. For Mistie there was a flower-printed polyester shift, a little short but not too snug around the torso. Tony had also brought an extra shirt so Kate could check and wrap the wound in the back of her leg. But Kate knew better than to thank her. Tony had the drive in her eyes again, the set of brow she'd had back in South Carolina. All she could talk about was Burton and Lamesa and how much money her father had.

East Texas. One-light towns of Fords Corner and Melrose. Tony concluded that this didn't look like Texas, it looked like fucking Louisiana and fucking Mississippi and fucking Alabama. "Texas is a big state," Kate reminded her. "Give it time. There are cattle ranges farther west."

Mistie was between Kate and Tony. Both legs were draped over Tony's lap because Kate refused to let the girl straddle the shift. She was still lethargic, but Kate sensed she was coming around, that she'd suffered from some twenty-four-hour bug that children often got to the terror of their parents and the blessed assurances of their pediatricians. But something to help the fever was still in order. And Kate was ready to offer her right eye for something to bring down the aching in her calf. And her left eye for a real night's sleep.

Tony was playing flip-the-blade with the knife. Every once in a while she'd stop to scratch behind her ears with the blade, then start flipping again. Kate hoped the knife might blow out the window in a gust of Texas wind. But it didn't.

They rolled on another twenty minutes, Kate's leg and stomach growling. They'd eaten nothing since yesterday morning. They had not one cent with which to buy food. Kate had turned on the radio to get her mind off the clammy filth of her body and the tedious drive, but Tony hadn't liked the music—old country, Hank

Williams, Kate thought it was—and made her turn it off.

Traffic picked up on the two-lane, and then the road widened to four lanes. Houses were closer together here, and there were apartment complexes and strip malls. Streetlights were wound with all-weather vinyl holly and big red bows. Store windows boasted holiday sales of everything from riding mowers to parakeets. A green sign reading NACOGDOCHES rushed by on the right. A city this size would have drug stores. If Kate could tidy up her hair and clean up her face, she might make a relatively benign shoplifter.

"Tony," she said. "I want a dare."

Tony stopped flipping the knife. "You can't ask for your own. I gotta do that."

"Then let me tell you what to dare me."

Tony rubbed her chin, her forehead furrowing.

"Dare me to go into a Rite Aid or CVS and get some things we need."

"What the hell we need? Got lots of gas in the tank. Don't seem to be burning any oil."

"Aren't you hungry? I could slip a few things into my pocket, see how big overall pockets are? And I want to get something for Mistie's temperature. And for my leg. And for your hair."

"My hair?"

"You have lice, Tony. Haven't you felt them?"

Tony smacked at her head, then pulled the rearview mirror around and stared at her reflection. "No, I don't! I ain't got the cooties!"

"Whatever you call them, I've seen them crawling in your hair. There's shampoo for that, you know. . . ."

"Goddamn Darlene!"

"Who's Darlene?"

"You want my whole life history? Just find a fucking store and get the damn nit shampoo!"

The first store that looked like it didn't have high-tech antitheft doors was Carlton's Food and Drug, an establishment on a small side road that seemed to have been built some time back in the forties. The bricks were sand colored, the edges of the building rounded. Side windows were made of a mosaic of glass bricks. There were grocery carts crammed together outside the front, likely borrowed from some neighboring grocery store.

"This is good," said Kate. Tony nodded, and Kate pulled into the once-paved parking lot. A few other customer cars were squatting there; one was occupied by a girl of about five and a yapping Pomeranian.

Kate put the truck in park. It idled smoothly. The owner of this would be putting out a bulletin on it, for certain.

Tony pointed the blade at Mistie. "Don't forget who's out here. I'm giving you five minutes exactly. In five minutes, I'm cutting the kid up and taking off."

"I know," said Kate. Tony didn't have a watch but she didn't make mention.

"You tell on us in there," said Tony, "if anybody even looks out here like they think something's going on, I'll bring us all down."

"I'm not going to do that, Tony."

"It's weird when you say my name. Teachers always called me Angela."

"You want me to call you that?"

"No."

"Okay, then, Tony."

"You got five minutes, exactly."

"Yes."

It was difficult to walk without a limp, but Kate tightened her spine and did the best she could. She'd been able to smile through parent conferences, and some were almost as painful as a bullet to the leg. *That's a good one*, she thought. *Ought to call Deidra and tell her about my latest adventure.* A wave of fatigue swept through her body, and she held on to the door's handle, regaining herself, before pushing all the way inside.

The store was alive with an overly warm heat blasting from a ceiling vent and a Zamfir Christmas tape playing on the intercom. A man with a gray beard stood at a candy display, filling a rack up with bags of Christmas-colored Hersheyets and red and green foil-wrapped Kisses. At the front counter, a middle-aged woman was straightening a stack of coupons by the register. She had on a black vest covered with sequined snowflakes. The woman glanced up and smiled. "Merry Christmas!"

Kate nodded. "And to you."

Kate moved up the first aisle, glancing back at the bowed ceiling mirror at the front corner near the door. Turning her body to block view of her hands, she quickly scooped several packs of Lance crackers into the front pocket of her overalls. Then she meandered to the health and beauty aisle. It felt as though her leg was beginning to seep. She hoped not. She opened her pocket to flick in a tube of Suave powder fresh deodorant, a small box of children's chewable Tylenol, and a bottle of rubbing alcohol. There was a sharp pain in her calf, and she stopped, caught her breath, and moved on.

As nonchalantly as she could, she rounded the corner and walked up through the hair products. Rid, for lice. That was what the school kept on hand for outbreaks. She didn't see any. She looked back up the aisle from where she came. Rid, Rid, Rid. She thought the box had a red stop sign on it, but wasn't certain. She looked again. Nothing for Tony's cooties.

"Can I help you find something?" called the woman from the front counter.

"Oh, no, thanks," said Kate. Her voice was surprisingly pleasant and cheerful. "Actually, I'm just taking a break from driving. I needed to stretch my legs a bit. I hope you don't mind if I just look around?"

"No, honey, that's fine," said the woman. "Where you driving to?"

"El Paso," said Kate smoothly. "I'm a teacher from North Carolina. Heading over to see my sister."

"Teacher, huh?" said the woman. "Off for the holidays already? Our kids got another week before school lets out."

There was a small hanging display beside the shampoos, a plastic, toothed rack with folded American Traveler maps tucked in. United States. Southern United States. Texas. Kate tugged a Texas out of its slot, folded it an extra time, and slipped it in the overall pocket. "Oh, well, I teach in a private school. A Christian academy. Our schedule is somewhat different from the schedules of the public schools in our area."

The card and wrapping paper section was past the hair care. Kate stopped in front of a standing display and idly spun the rack about, glancing at the colorful images and flowing script. There was a narrow mirror dividing each section of the rack and it winked at Kate

as it revolved by her, over and over. She caught the
rack and held it still to see herself in the sliver of sil-
vered glass.

My God, she thought.

She stared at the reflection. The thin woman with
the straight auburn hair. The face without makeup, the
baggy overalls and simple undershirt. Eyes a bit dark
and set. Fingernails rough and unpolished.

There's Alice. Kate ran her hand over her cheeks,
over her neck, and down the length of one leg. *Donald
wouldn't recognize me. I look like Alice.*

She stared. She knew. She realized what she had
done had been for herself at first. She had rescued Mistie to rescue herself. To get away from the tedium and
the headaches and loneliness. To take Mistie and drop
her off at a commune for other castoffs and be done
with it.

But not now, she thought. The mouth in the mirror
had no lipstick, no lip liner, and the small wrinkles at
the corners were clearly visible. *I'm not going to take
Mistie to Canada. Mexico is closer. I'll care for her. I'll
mother her. Me. I'll be the Alice in me.*

Yes.

Then something wet slid down the back of her leg to
her shoe. There was blood on the floor. *Damn* she
thought. She rubbed the bottom of the shoe through
the little drops on the floor, smudging them out of focus. She limped to the front door.

"Safe trip!" called the woman.

"God bless," said Kate.

The truck was empty, though the engine was still
humming. The car with the girl and the dog was gone;
the patron had probably been next door at the dry

cleaners. Kate glanced around, more blood drips trickling down to her shoe; the wound was hot and aching.

She saw Mistie and Tony at the outdoor pay phone by the sidewalk. Tony waved Kate over, the receiver in her hand, the knife in the other. Mistie was sitting cross-legged on the concrete slab under the phone box. The little yellow shift was bunched up, showing no panties. Kate stood between Mistie and the street, blocking her from the view of passersby.

"Called my friend Leroy," said Tony. Her voice was stony. Not a good sign. "One eight hundred collect. It works, you know, even though those commercials make you want to barf your beer."

"That's good. Not barfing beer, but getting him on the line," said Kate. "Right?"

"Hot Heads made the news."

"What are hot heads?"

"Whitey got arrested last night."

"Whitey?"

Tony cleared her throat and spat on the ground. "One that killed the gasoline man with my gun. He's on TV, charged with capital murder. They say he's gonna try as an adult. He hasn't confessed but Leroy says it's just time."

Kate knelt beside Mistie and rubbed her head. She reached in her pocket for the box of Tylenol, ripped it open, and took out three pink tablets. "Mistie, can you chew these?" Mistie nodded and put the tablets in her mouth, held them there. "Chew, hon." Mistie chewed.

"Is that what you wanted?" asked Kate, looking up at Tony. She put her hand against the wound in her leg and pressed the denim firmly to slow the blood. "You wanted him to get caught?"

Tony banged the receiver on the steel side of the phone box. The toe of her right boot patted the gravel rapidly. "Yeah. No, not exactly. Asshole!"

"Why?"

"We was supposed to be talked about, wondered about. We was supposed to be worried about, all over the county. We was supposed to be the gang everybody was scared of but nobody knew our names. Like the big gangs in the big places, ones that shoot up stuff and people and write 'don't fuck with us' on walls but nobody knows exactly who did the shoot-ups 'cause they're quick, man, they're smart and they don't get caught. But Whitey shot that bastard and now he's arrested. He's gonna talk you can bet. Bark like a dog. All the Hot Heads going down, except me, 'cause I'm here in fucking Texas."

Kate stood and put her hand on Tony's arm. Tony jerked away. "Why you touching me?" she demanded. "Don't fucking ever do that!"

"He's arrested. Okay. He killed the gasoline man, he should be arrested. Don't you think?"

Tony scratched at the back of her ear. "He'll get the needle up in Jarratt if they try him as an adult, you know. It could have been me. I could have shot him, and got arrested. I could have been the first girl on death row in Virginia. Know that? People don't think girls got it in them, but they do."

Kate spoke slowly. "What is it you want out of all this?"

Tony slammed the receiver down onto the cradle. She put her mouth on her arm and bit. Kate could hear the air drawing through her teeth.

"Don't, Tony."

Tony let go and smiled. Her arm bore the angry and jagged imprint of the teeth, outlined in bright red. The skin was rising in defense of itself, puffing up against the assault. Tony held the arm out to Kate. "Flesh tastes good! Better than mouse shit, I bet! Wanna try? Now if I go down fighting, they'll be able to ID me from my dental records! Ha!"

"Tony, what do you want?"

"I want a dare from you."

Kate shook her head. "Let's get in the truck and go on. I've got a map. We can find Lamesa. It might not be much farther."

"Got a dare for you," said Tony.

"No more dares."

"A dare. I know too much about your fucking life as it is for any more damned truths. So here's the dare. Call your husband. And he better be at the office."

"Tony, let's leave him out of this. You know we aren't into pedophilia rings. You know that was way off base."

The knife appeared, and waggered in the air like a steel mosquito ready for the bite. "Call him. Want me to get him on the line for you? I'll say I'm you. 'Collect call from Mrs. Kate McDolen, rich bitch moron who licks mouse shit!' "

"I will go with you to Lamesa. You don't need to threaten me anymore. I'll drive you to your dad's ranch. But just let Mistie and me alone. Let us go on our way when it's done. There is no reason to call Donald."

"Ronald McDonald!" said Tony. "Call him, bitch, or Mistie's gonna sport a new, deep tattoo." She yanked Mistie back by the arm, and held the girl beside her, knife running through the girl's hair. "How deep 'til

340

you hit bone and come out the other side? My sister Darlene was digging to China. Think she's there yet?"

Kate picked up the phone. Her head itched furiously. She probably had Tony's head lice. One eight hundred collect. She pressed the numbers, waited for instructions, spoke her name. On the back of her left leg, the tickling of blood in a warm pattern down through the stubble of hair. Lisa answered the phone.

"Lisa, it's Kate."

"Collect again? Honey, you are having phone trouble!" A small and distant chuckle. Kate couldn't tell if Lisa was really trying to be funny or if she sensed something was off balance. "How are you?"

"Okay. Lisa, is Donald in?"

"Sure is, Kate. Just hang on one dilly-dally moment."

Kate couldn't say okay. God, but her one leg was throbbing now, and both were shaking. *I don't want to talk to Donald. Maybe he's in the conference room, maybe he's out in the hall. Please, let his voice mail pick up.*

"Hello, Donald McDolen speaking."

"Donald . . ."

"Kate! Where are you? I found your note. God knows I've respected your request to let you be awhile, but I thought you'd at least call, to at least touch base, for Christ's sake. Are you all right?"

Kate looked at Tony, who whispered, "Tell him you kidnapped Mistie. Tell him you're in Texas with one of the Hot Heads, running from the law."

"Kate? Are you still there?"

"I'm here, Donald." *I'm not far from Mexico. No matter what I tell him, Tony doesn't know I'm going to Mexico.* "Here, in Texas."

"Texas? You're kidding, right? What in the world did you think you'd find in Texas?"

"Tell him the town," said Tony.

"Nacogdoches, Texas," said Kate.

"Whatever you say. Is the air good there? All that, what, nice dry heat to clear you head? Is there a counselor there to work on . . . your issue from July?"

Fury flared up the back of Kate's neck. *Son of a bitch! My issue? Am I getting help?*

"No."

"I covered you, Kate," said Donald. She could see him as he told her this, one arm locked over his chest, the elbow of the other resting on top of the balled fist, sitting on the edge of his desk. The gray hair, neatly cut and neatly moussed, now just a little frizzy around the edge with anger. "I called Stuart Gordonson and asked him to let the school know you'd be out a short while. Of course, you didn't say how long, so I felt a bit the fool on that count. Do you blame me for July? Is that it? You punishing me for what someone else did?"

"Not everything is about you, Donald."

"What does that mean, Kate? How does leaving your husband without a word and going to Texas not have some impact on him, pray tell?"

"I'm sorry."

"You're on your way home now, am I right? I can tell Gordon you'll be back this week, yes? By, say, Wednesday at the latest? I can tell Gordon that?"

"Tell him what you did," said Tony. She picked at a front tooth with her knife, wiped the blade on the side of her camouflage shorts, then pointed it back at Mistie. "C'mon, now, you're talking on his dime."

"I . . . I have a girl with me."

342

A pause back across the many miles in Virginia. "A girl. What do you mean?"

He's thinking I've got a lover thought Kate, *some kind of Texas cowgirl lover.* The thought was nearly enough to bring on a dry laugh. Nearly. "A girl from my school. A second-grader."

"Her name," whispered Tony.

"What's her name?" asked Donald.

Mexico, a few hours, tops. We'll be okay, we'll make it. "Mistie Henderson," said Kate.

"Henderson," said Donald. "There was something in the local paper about a Henderson girl not showing up at her trailer park. They weren't sure if she was abducted or a runaway. The residents thought she was a runaway. You . . . have her?"

"I do, Donald. Let me explain . . ."

Then Tony pinched her nose and wailed, "Help! I'm Mistie! She grabbed me and threw me in her white car! Help me!" Then Tony snatched the receiver; slammed it down, and hopped back with a little skip-jump. She laughed loud and long, rocking back like a hyena in a Disney cartoon.

"What did you do that for?" cried Kate. "That's not how it happened!"

"It don't matter how it happened," laughed Tony. "It happened. You're a kidnapper and now your husband knows it, too!"

"He won't believe it. Not the part about throwing her in the car. He'll think I'm the one kidnapped. He'll think I was forced to make the call. Do you know how fake you sounded?"

"But he'll wonder big time! You left him in the first place, didn't you, and wrote a note to tell him you were going? I heard that much. So he's gonna know something's screwed up."

"He won't believe what you said."

"Maybe, maybe not. But the police believed it."

Kate paused, gaped, wiped sweat from her eyes. Her heart stopped one beat, then another, then picked up again. "The police. . . . *believed* it?

"Forgot to tell you. After I talked to Leroy, I called the police. Right here in whatever the hell this town is called, I forgot. It was easy, got an operator, didn't even need the one eight hundred collect. Asked for the city police department. Said my name was Tony and I was with a kid and woman from Pippins, Virginia. Said I'd robbed an Exxon back home and you'd stole a little kid named Mistie. Said they could check up there and know I was right. They wanted to know why I called to confess, and I said what's the fun of nobody knowing? And I hung up real quick."

"Tony, we're *this* close to Lamesa! You could have been with your dad!"

"I still will, but it's better this way!"

"You've lost your mind!"

"You think I ever really had it, bitch?"

Kate looked over her shoulder at the road. How long until they have photos of the missing Mistie from Pippins? How long until they check out the story on the Exxon robbery? "You didn't give them my name?"

"Sure."

This will be FBI. This will be federal. God. God.

"The truck we're driving?"

"I said it was a tan truck. I'm not stupid enough to tell them everything like the license plate or anything, shit, they gotta do some of the work." Tony grinned, wiggled her eyebrows. "Guess we should get going. How far's Lamesa?"

God, we have to hurry!

Inside the truck, Tony slammed the passenger's door behind her, turned on her butt to Kate at the wheel, and held out her hand. "I hope you got something good to eat in that store back there."

Chapter Fifty-seven

The aspirins tasted okay, the crackers tasted okay, and her head didn't ache as much as it had, but Mistie wanted to go home. She was tired and she hated this truck. She wanted to see Mama, to see Daddy. Daddy did stuff she didn't like but she still liked Daddy. He never hit her like one of the old men did his little boy Jake back at MeadowView. Daddy never "punched out her lights" like that other Daddy did his boy.

Mistie rubbed her crotch until it grew real warm. She licked cracker crumbs off her hand and then whined because she was really, really thirsty and the teacher hadn't gotten anything to drink back at that store.

"What's the matter, Mistie?" asked the teacher. She was driving. Her hands were tied up again, one on the wheel and the other on the stick thing on the floor.

"I'm thirsty. I wanna go home."

"I'll look for a water fountain soon, honey. There has to be one in all of Texas, in one of these towns."

"I wanna go home."

"She wants to go home," said the girl with the knife.

"Honey, I can't do that. It would be wrong. I'm going to make the wrong right."

Mistie put her hands over her ears and repeated, "Mama had a baby and its head popped off, Mama had a baby and its head popped off."

"Shh, Mistie, it will be okay," said the teacher.

"Mama had a baby and its head popped off."

"Shhh."

347

Chapter Fifty-eight

Farstone looked like a real Texas town. Tony had her head out the window, blinking in the warm wind and sucking it all in. Clinging to Route 180, the town was three blocks long and four to five blocks wide, with trailers and shacks and two greasy-windowed lounges (the Gila Monster and Blue Star Lounge—21 Over) making up the bulk of the place. This was the kind of town Tony would have expected to see sheriffs with hip holsters and horses tied to hitching posts and tumbleweeds careening along wooden walkways like runaway rabbits. Here, Tony could have expected to see Tony Perkins standing with his arms crossed beneath an elm tree on a high and dusty knoll, one boot propped up against the base of the trunk, his head turned out across the vast stretch of barren land, not a single emotion showing on his face.

There were no gunslinging sheriffs or hitching posts here, but there could have been. The town was dusty and brown and even the air tasted like cattle and barbed wire. The landscape was flat, the dogs sleepy, and the trees bent and haggard. This, Tony knew, was the Wild, Wild West.

"Look," Tony said to Mistie, nudging her with her elbow as they entered the town limits and passed a cluster of little white houses surrounded by billowing clothes on clotheslines. "I think that's a roadrunner out there, see? You like TV, you've seen the roadrunner, right? Beep beep!"

Mistie looked out the window and nodded at the small blur of brown that darted across the rocky ground between the white houses. She didn't seem so sick anymore, not since they'd stopped for a drink from a gas station water hose back about an hour ago in a town called Carbon. The kid had eaten the whole pack of peanut butter crackers the teacher had stolen from the store and then half the crackers from another pack. She had listened with what seemed like a real interest in the stories Tony wove about her father and the Lamesa ranch.

"When we get there," Tony had told the girl, "my dad will probably let you stay a little while. If you're good, though. You can't be fussing or anything, though, you hear me? And you can't be doing that rubbing thing, it's gross. You hear?"

Mistie had nodded.

"He has horses. You ever ride a horse? They're wild, you know? Maybe he has a pony. A pony would be better for you 'cause you're so small."

Mistie had said, "I like ponies. Princess Silverlace has a golden pony."

The stories of the ranch at Lamesa seemed to keep

the kid's mind off being hungry and tired. It was worth it to Tony to bullshit with the kid so she wouldn't start whining again.

There was a stoplight in the center of Farstone, and it was red. The teacher slowed the truck and waited. There were no other vehicles to be seen, save the few parked along the main stretch through town, but here was a stoplight. Texans were funny. It was mid-afternoon, and dry, and very warm. Nobody was outside except some dogs, and they were hiding in the shade under bushes. Maybe this was a town full of Mexicans instead of Texans. Mexicans took siestas.

"Guess some city council had to fight hard to get that stoplight put up," said the teacher.

"Whatever," said Tony. "How far we got left?" Tony nodded at the trip-o-meter. "Look like another hundred thirty miles. Not bad."

A motor scooter with a white-haired old lady at the handlebars putted up the road on the left and stopped at the light across the intersection.

"Now I see why they got the light," said Tony. "Heavy traffic."

"They're looking for us now, you know," said the teacher. "One hundred thirty miles across open land isn't good odds for anyone trying to stay hidden."

"We'll get to the ranch," said Tony. "Texas cops ain't much brighter than Virginia cops, I'll bet. But they know who we are, all right. I bet we'll make the news tonight. Interstate crime. Try that radio again."

The stoplight turned green. The teacher worked the clutch and the gas, grimacing as she did. The truck picked up its pace again. The old lady on her scooter putted past.

"Radio!" said Tony.

The teacher turned on the radio and pushed the search button. Nothing but country music, a pop station, and static. "It's not the top or bottom of the hour," the teacher said. "News comes on then."

"Might be a flash bulletin."

"Well. Maybe."

The teacher settled on the country station, some kind of twangy banjo shit.

They'd left Nacogdoches yesterday, sneaking out of the city by way of every skeezy alley and Dumpster-lined strip mall back lot they could find. Last night had been spent parked behind the crumbling brick snack bar of the Clifton Drive-In, which no longer had a big white screen and no longer had ground-mounted speakers but still boldly proclaimed its name on a sky-high white and blue sign that offered the double-feature of GHOSTBUSTERS and GHOSTBUSTERS II.

Tony had secured the teacher and the kid inside the truck and had gone on a little scavenger hunt. The teacher had said, "I'm not running away, Tony. You no longer need to tie me up. I will go with you to Lamesa. I'll help you get there. I want to go there." Tony'd laughed at the woman, but it was odd because the teacher had really seemed to be telling the truth.

But truth could be lies. It usually was.

She'd hiked only a half mile or so up a dirt side road before finding a small farm with its own gas pump just outside a tractor shed. A collie had run up to her, barking and snarling, but she'd pretended to have something in her hand and the dog had wagged its tail until she jumped on its back and slit its throat. She'd carried a couple gallons back to the truck in a bucket she'd discovered in a toolshed, and made a funnel out of a tattered newspaper she'd peeled from the wall of the snack bar.

In the middle of the night, Tony and the teacher had awakened to the sound of a siren out on the road. Tony had held her breath, counting, not moving even to scratch the lice. The cruiser passed the drive-in, lights flashing, the wailing key of the siren shifting lower as it got farther away.

"After a speeder," Tony'd said.

"Possibly," said the teacher.

They'd awakened hungry. But there was no money, no time, and Tony didn't want to do anything but get to Lamesa. They could eat then. They could fucking wait to eat. The kid whined about wanting something to eat until Tony started telling stories about the ranch.

In the town of Carbon they'd stopped at a Shell station and took turns drinking out of the water hose that was turned on a bed of flowers beside the lot. The water had tasted funny, like it had rocks in it, but it was cold and it was wet.

While Mistie was sucking from the hose, a gangly teenage cowboy pulled up to the tanks and began to fill his pickup with high octane. Tony thought he looked like a real cowboy. She wondered if he knew about Burton Patinske's ranch. He probably did. A girlfriend in the passenger's seat leaned out the window, holding a hot dog dripping in chili. "Bo, want a bite?" she teased.

"Want a bite of you, baby," he said. The girl had laughed, burped around a bite of the dog, and the boy had kissed her full and wet on the lips. Tony had turned away, not wanting to see.

Back in the truck, the teacher mentioned they were down to a quarter tank of gas. Tony brushed it off; a quarter tank of gas in a big old truck like the one they were riding in could likely last to Lamesa. The map said it was about one hundred seventy miles from Carbon. And Tony didn't want to stop one more time, not for shit, not for water, not for God Himself.

Well, except for a stoplight, but that was a done deal, and they were rolling again.

Tony let her fingers play the air of Farstone as the shacks rolled by. "Know what?" she called back inside to Mistie. "If I'd had my gun, I'da shot that roadrunner back there. I hear they taste good as chicken."

"I'm hungry," said Mistie.

"Shit, I was kidding."

As they passed the town limits sign at the western edge of Farstone, the truck coughed, shimmied, and went dead.

"Out of gas," said the teacher. It was nearly a whisper. She sounded horrified.

The truck coasted to a stop in front of a trailer with a business sign by the door that read MADAME ROSE. PALM READER AND ADVISER. CLOSED UNTIL FURTHER NOTICE.

Tony looked at the needle on the gas indicator. It was below E. She looked at the teacher, who didn't look back.

"No shit, out of gas," said Tony. She opened the truck door and stepped down. She scanned the road in both directions. The last thing they needed was some curious mayor or preacher to drive up and ask if they needed assistance. Not that Farstone would have a mayor. It didn't even look like they had a church, unless they prayed in single-wides. "Goddamm it!" said Tony. She drove the bottom of her foot into the side of the truck.

"We're stuck," said the teacher.

"We're not stuck," said Tony. She leaned in with her knife and cut the ties on the teacher's wrists. "Get out."

The teacher stood on the side of the road with her hands on her hips. She looked like one of those women in the pictures Tony had seen at school about the Dust Bowl. Eyes that were cooked dry, dirty arms, skinny legs. Mistie rolled out and leaned back on the truck cab, her hands tucked inside the front of her jumper.

"Let's walk," said Tony.

"Lamesa's a good two hours away by car," said the teacher. "How soon until we'd dehydrate? How easy would it be for us to be caught out in the middle of nowhere? You've made it clear you want the thrill of the chase. I don't."

"I was kidding. God, you think I'm stupid. I'm not stupid."

"We have to get off this main street. Quickly."

They moved down the alley that ran alongside the fortune-teller's trailer and back another block for good measure, then huddled in the ratty grass in the shade of a henhouse. A couple of Hispanic girls walked past in the alley, one holding tightly to the leash of a bouncing shepherd puppy. The girls glanced over, then whispered something and giggled. Tony was sure those girls didn't know who they were. The girls were probably laughing at the teacher's overalls. They were way pathetic.

"I'm going to the lounge," the teacher said with a tip of her head. "You two wait here."

"What you gonna do, whore yourself out for a ride?"

"I don't know what I'll do."

"Damn! That's a hoot!"

"Really, Tony? Call it what you will. Just don't let Mistie out of your sight."

"I don't think I'll let you go. I think you'll be in there sobbin' some story, tellin' them all the bad things I did and how you're all innocent."

The teacher took Tony's chin and Tony didn't pull away. Her fingernails were rough where they'd broken off at different lengths. The woman's breath was rank. "I've made my course. Trust me or not, I will get us to Lamesa."

Tony shrugged, then jerked from the teacher's grasp. "Fine with me. But you got ten minutes, or each minute after that little old Mistie here gets a new piece of a tattoo. I think she'd look cute with a little angel, don't you think? Down her back, between those bony shoulders, give the angel wings, a halo, oh, there's lots of minutes to use up if I need them."

"You won't hurt her," said the teacher. "And I will be back in less than ten."

"We'll see," said Tony.

"You won't hurt her." The teacher was up, and hobbling toward the street.

"We'll see, won't we, Mistie?" Tony said. She looked at the child, who had found a handful of grass with seedpods, and was rocking back and forth and popping the pods off with the wrap and snap of the stems.

Chapter Fifty-nine

"We ain't open yet. It ain't even five yet."

Kate squinted in the darkness, her heard turned toward the sound of the voice.

"I'm sorry," said Kate. "I was just hoping for some help."

"What kind of help?" The voice was male, and decidedly young.

"A ride." God, to say it aloud, in that was the danger. In that the connection could be made if the news had reached this far.

Just get the ride, get out of here.

"Ain't no bus service in Farstone, sorry," said the voice. The darkness of the room began to shimmer away, and in the center of Kate's sight she could see a single shaded lamp sitting atop a bar counter, and a boy behind the bar, counting dollar bills. "No taxi, neither. You ain't from here. You lost?"

Kate could see well enough to walk to the counter

without tripping on table or chair legs. She hoped her limp wasn't terribly obvious, but knew it was. "No, I've run out of gas."

The boy laughed. He was dark skinned, had dark eyes, a head full of thick black hair. He was a little older than Donnie. "That's a bummer," he said. "A goat roper lost in Texas with no gas!"

"Goat roper?"

"Oh," said the boy. He stacked the bills and slipped them into an open cash register drawer. "Don't take offense, it's just something we call people who aren't from here, especially people who are, well, kinda skinny."

"Oh," said Kate. "Okay. No bus. Any gas? Anywhere?"

"Closest gas station is east up one-eighty, town of Albany or west in Anson."

"I can't drive to get gas with no gas." *Kate, keep it easy, don't piss him off.*

"Right there. George Watson got gas up at his ranch for his trucks. But he's not the kind of man you ask for anything."

Kate licked her lips. She slid onto one of the bar stools and caught her head in her hands. She knew she smelled. She hoped the boy had clogged sinuses.

"So, where you trying to get to?" asked the boy.

Say it. "Lamesa."

"Really?"

It was then that Kate saw the open newspaper on the counter by the register. She couldn't read the headlines the way the paper was turned and pooched up at the fold.

"Why Lamesa?"

"I . . . because it's nearly on the other side of the state, right? I make Lamesa and I'm almost to New Mexico. Thought if I could get that far, I could find a motel for the night."

The boy shut the cash register drawer and nodded. He said, "Where you from?"

"North Carolina."

"That's pretty far away."

"You're telling me." She tried to chuckle. It sounded like a gasp. "Can you think of anyone who would be willing to give me a ride to Lamesa?"

"You traveling alone from North Carolina?"

"Why? Does it matter?"

The boy looked over his shoulder. There was a phone mounted on the wall. He shrugged. "I guess it would, if there was only room for one person in the car."

"You have a car? Would you take me? I can't pay, but . . ." *But I'll fuck you for a ride? Hey, baby, take a load of this filthy body and let me tempt you into providing a little shuttle to Lamesa? Stop looking at the phone!*

The lounge door opened with a squeal and Kate looked back into the blinding light of day. She turned away and stared down at the bar. *Don't let him see your face.*

"Hey there, Juan."

Her. Don't let her see your face.

"Hey there, Greta. We aren't open yet."

The boy probably doesn't know jack. I'm jumping at shadows. Thousands of children are abducted each year. And how many do they find? Ten percent? Five? Why couldn't Mistie be one of the lost? The odds are pretty good.

358

The woman walked up to the bar and slid onto the stool three down from Kate. She was in a uniform, but Kate couldn't tell what kind with her peripheral vision. Police, maybe. Security guard. Hostess snack-cake truck driver. "Howdy, ma'am."

She knows who I am, she's making sport of me. People don't really say 'howdy, ma'am!' I have to get out.

"Hello," offered Kate. To Juan, "Listen, thanks anyway but I'll figure something out. Merry Christmas."

"Feliz Navidad," said Juan.

Kate stood and turned. The woman beside her was, indeed, a police officer. Deputy sheriff. She was a large woman with arms that strained at the fabric of her sleeves.

"Ma'am," she said. "That your truck up the ways?"

"Ah," said Kate. What was the right answer? What was the best answer? Her heart began hammering in her chest and in her leg. "Which truck is that?"

Officer Greta chuckled. "Juan, got a beer? I'm off duty. I won't tell your boss you served early."

"Sure," said Juan. He reached under the counter. There was the sound of slushing ice, and then a beer can was plopped onto the bar top. The officer popped the top, and said, "Ma'am? That your truck, the tan one that's out of gas?"

"Yes." A chuckle, way too loud to sound normal. *Get out of here, get out now.*

"Plates say Louisiana."

"Yes. They do."

Juan said, "Thought you were from North Carolina."

No no no no. "I am, originally. Listen, I have to be going."

"How?" said Juan. "You said you'd run out of gas."

Elizabeth Massie

Officer Greta caught Kate by the arm but then let go, as if she realized that was out of order or she'd caught a whiff of Kate's homegrown perfume.

"You can't leave the truck there. Can't abandon vehicles in the limits of Farstone."

Kate's head began to swim. Greta's vague and massive visage bobbed up and down as if nodding. "Okay," she managed, "I'll get it moved."

"Without gas?" said Juan.

"Sit down, ma'am, you don't look well," said Officer Greta.

"I'm fine, just tired," said Kate. She stumbled for the door. *Get out now, find Tony. Find Mistie. Hide. Think it through. There is a solution. You are a teacher. You can fix this.*

She reached the door and pushed out into the light. She blinked madly at the bright assault. In front of the lounge was Officer Greta's car.

Kate caught her breath against the pain in her leg. *Go*, she thought. *Go! Go before Officer Greta realizes who just walked out of the lounge.*

"Ma'am?"

Kate turned about, nearly stumbling on the rough sidewalk.

In the daylight, Greta was a pretty woman with sunburned cheeks and a small nose. She was shaking her head in what seemed like pity. Not sarcasm.

"Ma'am, I believe in doing good for others. My church tells us that. And I like to think I do something worthwhile once a week, besides chasing down kids who break windows and tear up cattle fences. I'm thinking you could use a ride somewhere? To get some gas? I have a can in my cruiser. Anson's got a station. It's not far."

Kate touched her lip with her fingers. "I . . . don't want to take advantage of your kindness." Was this woman laying a trap?

"It's nearly Christmas. Let me do my good deed for the week so I can say I did." Greta winked, smiled. It seemed harmless.

She doesn't know, thought Kate. *Okay. Okay, then.*

"Okay, thanks." *But we have no money for gas. Maybe it'll be a gift, the gas. Don't say you don't have money until the gas is in the truck tank.*

"And don't worry," said Greta as she opened the door for Kate. "I only had three sips of that beer. I'm not intoxicated. I'm off duty, but I am not drunk."

Worry about the money later. One minute at a time. One second.

Greta got in her side and adjusted her rearview. She pulled a cap from the seat and worked it onto her puffy brown hair. "I was kidding. That was a joke. I'm never drunk."

"Oh," said Kate. "Sorry. I mean, that's funny."

The engine revved, and Greta pulled out onto Farstone's Main Street.

"I've got my . . . kids with me," said Kate. "They're up by the truck."

"Why'd you leave them back there? It's too hot to be outside very long."

"Lounge said adults only."

"Oh," said Greta. She smiled. "Right. I forgot. You're a good mom, know that?"

361

Chapter Sixty

Tony couldn't take her eyes off the police scanner on the dash of the deputy's car. The woman said she was off duty, so the scanner was not turned on, but all Tony could think was, *I wonder if we've made it yet? I wonder if we're on that scanner? I want to hear what they're saying!*

They were a few miles west of Farstone, the land before and beside them various shades of gold and bronze, rising slightly in the distance but revealing what Tony guessed were miles and miles of rangeland. She wondered what people here would feel like, driving in Virginia. Would all those trees make them go nuts because they couldn't see past the next curve?

Tony was in the front seat. The teacher and Mistie were in the back. The teacher was smiling her teacher smile and looking like smiling hurt worse than her shot leg.

"You got any doughnuts or doughnut sticks?" asked Tony.

The deputy laughed. "Officers are supposed to be crazy for doughnuts, right?"

"You bet. Got any?"

"Are you all hungry? When did you last have something to eat?"

Tony thought about the red cherry tomatoes and peppers she'd swiped from the fortune-teller's backyard garden. She and Mistie had had a little lunch while counting to ten minutes while the teacher was offering herself up for a ride. Well, Mistie only ate the tomatoes, but Tony had found the peppers to be okay once she spit on them and wiped off the dust.

"We're hungry," said Tony. "Ain't we, sis?" She nudged Mistie over the seat. "My little sis is quiet, but she gets hungry all the time."

Mistie hadn't said a word since getting into the cruiser. She'd just stared at the officer as if she'd never seen such a thing in her life.

"There's a really super diner next to the gas station in Anson," said the officer. "You all can get a tankful for your car, then a tankful for your bellies. Best ribs this side of Fort Worth."

Have we made the news yet? Turn on the scanner!

"Can we listen to that?" Tony pointed to the scanner.

"Honey, I'm off duty, not back on for another two hours. I like a little peace and quiet."

"Please? I never got to hear one before. Just a few minutes? I never been in a cop car before." Tony sensed the teacher in the back, going totally still. This freaked her out.

"Well?"

"Oh, all right. But I'm turning it down. It can cut through my head like a laser sometimes, all that static."

363

She flipped a dial, adjusted the volume, then put both hands back on the steering wheel. Tony turned her ear to the scanner and concentrated.

There was a fluttering, a hum, and a male voice saying something about cows that got out of the fence on the Mendez farm and had caused a motorcycle wreck out on Route 600. Then a code number Tony didn't quite catch, and some garbled follow-up information, "Domestic dispute. Neighbor on Green Avenue heard arguing. Responding to . . ." More static. How in the world were deputies supposed to keep up with stuff they couldn't hear?

The police car rose and fell with the gentle roll of the land. The sky outside was cloudless. It seemed as if Texas were the whole world. Tony liked Texas.

"Had enough?" asked the deputy.

"Another minute, please."

"One more. We'll be in Anson in three."

"Thank you." Tony smiled. Playing the sweet daughter was a hoot. Knowing she was almost at Burton's ranch was so painfully wonderful she could hardly keep it down in her stomach.

Then on the scanner, static, jumbled words, but some quite distinct. "Interstate kidnapping . . . report came in from Nacogdoches . . . one Katherine—Kate—McDolen, age forty-two. One Angela Petinske, age fifteen . . ."

Fuck fuck fuck fuck! Tony didn't know whether to grapple the knob and shut the scanner down or let it run, let the words come, hear it on the air where it made it all real, made it all so goddamned valid . . .

The officer frowned, adjusted the knob. "What is this?"

". . . Moving across Texas, likely to Lamesa where Petinske's father is said to reside . . . eight-year-old Mistie Dawn Henderson, allegedly abducted by McDolen on Tuesday . . . Petinske thought to have . . . in a robbery and murder at an Exxon station in . . ."

The deputy turned off the scanner. Her brows were down, making a stern and uneasy parallel with the brim of her hat. "Where'd you guys say you were from?"

"North Carolina," said the teacher.

Tony said nothing.

"What's your names, anyway? You never did say."

"Jackie," said Tony.

"Mistie?" said the deputy.

"What?" asked Mistie in the back. Then she began to whimper. "Daddy said Valerie had a bad liver. He said her head didn't get cut off. But he said if police found out we'd go to jail. I don't wanna go to jail!"

"Mistie Dawn Henderson?" said the deputy. The voice, thick with a mixture of excitement, terror, determination. "Do you live in Virginia?"

"MeadowView Trailer Park."

"Uh-huh. Well."

Tony saw the deputy look down at the empty gun holster on her side. The gun was probably in the glove box. Tony could get it out real quickly, if it wasn't locked.

"Well, one mile to Anson." The deputy's voice was even and cool, like she was pretending she didn't know shit and was just driving along, happy as a clam. "See it up there? Not much of a town but we like it."

"Yeah," said Tony. "But you ain't gonna see it no more!" She pulled the knife from its place in her sock, and rammed it into the deputy's ribs. The woman's eyes went huge. Both hands came off the steering wheel; one clutching for the leaking red hole in her shirt and the other grasping for the mic on the scanner. Tony grabbed the mic and ripped it from its cord.

"Ahhhhhh!" hissed the deputy.

"Tony, no!" cried the teacher.

Tony dropped the mic on the floor and stomped it as she would stomp a bug, or a girl in the Hot Heads' tobacco barn.

The car spun to the left sharply, hopped up over a lip of rock that lined the highway, and bit the sandy soil of West Texas. It growled across the ground several hundred yards, spraying sand like rainwater. It hurtled up a small, weed-riddled rise, then dropped to the other side, landed at a tilt, and stopped. The engine thundered as if knocked between gears. The deputy panted madly, spittle flying from her mouth. "You . . . oh, God, help me." She lifted her bloodstained hand to Tony. Tony smacked it away.

"Please, get help, don't leave me here," said the deputy. The words was muffled, garbled, like the speaker on the scanner.

"Shut up!" Tony jumped from the car and opened the back door. Mistie stumbled out, ran several steps, and dropped to the sand, crying, "Mama!"

The teacher didn't move. She stared at the deputy's bleeding, groping hands as they fumbled on the dash, on the seat, then the floor, trying to get to the mic to put it back in the socket.

"Out!" yelled Tony. "Fucker, out!" She leaned in and took the teacher's hair and gave it a powerful yank. The teacher crawled out of the backseat. She stood, dumbfounded, by the toppled cruiser.

"There!" said Tony. "There's a ranch, come on! We can hide!"

"You stabbed her," said the teacher.

"She was going to kill us!"

"You don't know that!"

Tony lashed her foot out and caught the teacher in the shin. The woman screamed. It was her bad leg.

"Come *on!*"

With the teacher hobbling and the kid crying, the three scuttled up the long rise in the direction of the buildings of the distant ranch.

Chapter Sixty-one

"It's a mirage," the girl said to Mistie. "Looks like it's right there but it's either really far away or not there at all. I learned that in sixth grade. Believe that? Learned something from a stinking teacher."

Mistie looked where the girl was pointing. It was a farm on a hill. They'd been trying to run to the farm but it was as if the farm knew they were coming and kept backing up. The girl had said, "Almost there," a couple times but they still weren't.

The teacher was crying. She was right behind Mistie and the girl but she didn't talk at all. She just cried.

The ground was rocky and dry and went up and down and up and down. There was some grass growing there, but it was yellow like the hair on Valerie's head. Mistie tried to grab for some but the girl made her run too fast.

At last they reached a dirt road that wound across the dry land toward a large log house, but the girl urged them over the road, down a short slope, then back up to a rail fence. On the other side of the fence were lots of barns and trucks and trailers. Not trailers like at MeadowView but trailers like Mistie had seen taking cows down Route 58 through Pippins. There were some men in cowboy hats standing in the shade of a barn door.

"Quick, over, and in the back of the truck," whispered the girl. "Keep low, crawl if you have to."

Mistie climbed through the fence, the girl and the teacher climbed over. Mistie could hardly breathe for running so much. They had to run at school and she hated it. Running made her pee her pants. She thought she'd peed her pants a few minutes ago, but maybe it was just sweat.

The closest vehicle was a truck with a long, empty trailer behind. The trailer was made of pipes like the gates of cotton farms back in Virginia. The three sneaked over to the side of the truck and the girl slid over to open the side door. Mistie knew the cowboys couldn't see them—they were on the other side of the truck by one of the barns—but she wondered if they could hear her breathing.

The girl climbed in first, then put out her hand to pull in Mistie and the teacher. It took the teacher three times hopping to get up inside.

The trailer was filled with straw, but it smelled like cow poo. The girl lay down flat and covered herself with the straw, then hissed, "Hide!"

Mistie and the teacher lay down. Mistie pulled poo-smelling straw over her head and her body, and wondered what would happen if the cowboys put cows in with them.

Chapter Sixty-two

The cattle trailer stunk, and the floor was soaking wet with urine and manure. Tony held Mistie in her lap and Kate sat directly across from them. It was dark, and the truck was moving.

They'd held still under the straw for what was almost too long to bear. Then Kate had heard some ranch hands come over to the truck, and one said, "Hey, gotta git. Herefords to pick up over in Hobbs. Gotta git 'em and have 'em back to old George by daybreak."

"You ain't cleaned that trailer yet."

"What George don't know his damn Herefords ain't gonna know. Damn, they drink pond water that they're standing there shitting in."

"You got it."

There was a creaking as the hand climbed into the cab, and a grating as he turned on the engine. And then, they were driving off the ranch and heading for Hobbs.

Hobbs, New Mexico. That was west. Kate had

looked it up in the map she had folded in her overall pocket. Route 180 went to Hobbs, after passing directly through Lamesa.

No one had spoken the first few minutes after the truck pulled out of the fenced compound and onto the dirt road. Tony had killed the deputy. Well, she was probably dead. *God, forgive us*, Kate thought. *Greta had done her good weekly deed.*

Mistie had crawled out from her straw when she saw that Tony had done the same, and had snuggled up to the girl. Tony hadn't pushed her away. Kate had checked her leg wound. It had stopped bleeding. At Tony's father's ranch, if they made it, she would clean it out and hope for the best.

Tony's face was hard to see in the darkness. Kate said, "Tony, you okay?"

Tony shrugged. "I didn't want to kill her. She was going to tell on us. I have to get to my dad's."

"It's not long now, we'll probably be in Lamesa in just a matter of minutes."

"I'm watching the road," said Tony.

Kate leaned into the steel ribs of the stock trailer and crossed her arms over her chest.

Tony said, "My dad's the best. He'll hide us. He won't let nobody find us and put us in prison."

"Think so?"

"Know so. He ain't no fucking new nigger. He's got power and people are afraid of him. He ain't no pussy."

"Women aren't the problem, Tony."

"Women suck."

"Look at Greta. She offered to drive us for gas and didn't know who the hell we were."

"She was going to turn us in."

"Before that. She didn't know."

"Maybe."

"Tony, what happened back in Mobile? Why did you . . . hurt yourself . . . with that knife handle?"

"You don't like me to talk dirty in front of Mistie."

"Were you . . . ?"

"Yeah, I was. Two boys down on the gulf. Okay, make you happy?"

"Of course not. But think about this. Look at what they did. They violated you, and they weren't women. Evil has no gender."

"It was my fault. They saw me, what I had, if I just didn't have . . . Fuck it all."

"It's not your fault that they stole something from you."

"Had it stole before. No big deal."

"Really?"

Tony began to rub the top of Mistie's head, and she looked again out to the road. "Mile sign, right there," she said, and her head whipped around as the sign approached and then passed behind them into the night. "Saw it. Three miles to Lamesa."

"That's great."

"There'll be cops crawling all over town. We gotta be more careful than ever."

"We will be." Kate looked at Tony, at Mistie. She said, "You've been really nice to Mistie, Tony. She liked your stories. You'll make a good mother someday, I'll bet."

"Don't ever say that."

"Why not?"

"Mothers are shit. My mother's shit."

"I bet you don't even know your real mother."

"I do. She lays on the sofa and whines."

"You've made your gang your mother, haven't you? A mother is supposed to give you comfort when you're scared and is there when you are lonely."

"Mistie don't have a real mom, either," said Tony. "Can you believe her mama, letting her dad do to her what he's done to her?"

"But whose fault is it? Her mother's or her father's, or maybe both?"

Tony ignored this. "My mother's my gang, okay. Who's your mom, teacher?"

"I had a great mother."

"She dead?"

"No."

"You said had. So, who's your mother now?"

Kate pondered this. It was a valid question. What gave her comfort, what helped her when she was lonely? "Being a McDolen in a place where I have no friends," she said. "Money, I suppose. Position. I got bored with it, frustrated. Things got so wrong, but they weren't as wrong as I thought they were. I was going to save myself with Mistie."

"Fucked it up, huh?"

"Fucked it up."

"Maybe you can stay at the ranch awhile. Can you cook? I don't know if Dad can cook, but maybe he can hire you for a while?"

"Maybe."

Tony studied Kate. "Where *are* you going, then?"

"I want to go home," said Mistie.

"I thought I knew. One step at a time. I have to get with Donnie. To talk."

"I was a mother once," said Tony.

Kate frowned, leaned forward over her knees. The movement stirred up the rancid stench in the straw, and she pinched her nose for a moment. "What?"

"I was a terrible mother. Last year I had two twins. Well, twins are always two, like Jody and Judy."

"Tony, I had no idea."

"Some boy from the high school raped me." The shoulders went up, down, as if it was something forgotten and now remembered in a haze. "Babies were born early, in my house. Mama chased Darlene away, and Jody and Judy, sent 'em up the road for a while, said I had bad flu and they'd get it, too, if they didn't get the hell out of the house."

"Tony . . ."

"Mama said it was my fault they came out so early 'cause I drank beer and hung around with the Hot Heads. The Hot Heads didn't even know I was pregnant. I didn't tell them. They made fun of me 'cause I was getting fat, but I didn't tell. The babies were dead inside me, or Mama killed 'em, or maybe I did when I squeezed them out. I don't know. I even cried, well, just for a minute. Never again." Another shrug. "I never want to be no mama, not one or not like one."

"I'm sorry."

"Don't be. I'm not. I fixed myself back in Mobile, I bet. Won't have to worry 'bout that anymore. Look, Lamesa!"

The truck had rumbled onto a well-lit area with a spattering of suburban businesses; restaurants, car dealerships, a Kmart.

Tony was on her feet, bringing Mistie up with her. She slid open the side door. "As soon as he slows a

little, we're out of here. Don't bust your damn leg open
no more, you hear me?"

"I hear you, Tony."

"We're almost there!"

"That we are."

The truck slowed, wheezed, shifted gears. Tony and
Mistie jumped. Kate took a breath, prayed for strength,
and followed.

Chapter Sixty-three

"Lamesa Boulevard," said Tony, slapping the directory shut and digging at her scalp. They were at a phone behind a Lamesa tire store. The bank clock on the other side of the street read 1:43 A.M. "Eighteen-thirty-seven Lamesa Boulevard. We find that, we find Burton's ranch."

"There might be a map in the front of the phone book," said the teacher. "Look, quickly."

Tony opened the book again, and pawed through the thin pages. Zip codes, emergency number, town map. "How about that." Lamesa Boulvevard, B-5. Tony drew her fingers down across to B, down 5. She paused, and frowned. "This can't be right. It looks like it's in town. A ranch isn't in the middle of any town."

The teacher was standing with Mistie in her arms, glancing back and forth along the dark side street. Mistie had fallen asleep several blocks back. "I don't know, Tony. Maybe it's an old map. Maybe there's a misprint.

But we can't hang here. We have to get to your dad's right away."

Tony nodded. She reached out toward Mistie. "Give her to me for a while." The teacher passed the girl over, gratefully. "But I'm only doing it because you can't walk worth shit," said Tony, "and you'd walk even worse carrying the kid."

"Absolutely. I don't want to slow us down."

"Okay." Tony rubbed her chin, took several steps away from the phone, and glanced at the side street sign. "This is Grove. So Lamesa Boulevard's gotta be that way."

The teacher moved surprisingly fast for someone with a ruptured bullet wound in her leg, but not surprisingly fast for someone who was on the FBI wanted list for kidnapping. The three took the Lamesa streetsides with silent effort, moving along sidewalks when there were sidewalks, dodging parked cars on the roads when there weren't. Tony watched where she was going, she watched her feet. Her toe caught in an uneven lip of concrete and she stumbled, but didn't fall. Mistie breathed softly on Tony's neck.

Tony shifted the child from one hip to the other. *It'd be a bitch to be a mother, having to carry kids around like this all the time.* Cars roared past but didn't slow down, didn't seem concerned or curious. The drivers had their own businesses to attend to. They had homes and families to return to. They had Christmas trees and lights and candles. They had people who were glad they were home, and who didn't want them to leave.

Tony gritted her teeth and forced her feet ahead even more quickly. She had that, too. At 1837 Lamesa Boulevard.

There was heavy wheezing from behind, but Tony didn't look back. The teacher was hurting but there wasn't anything to be done. Not yet.

They crossed an intersection. Another, turning their faces from the bright illumination of the overhead streetlights and into the faint light from the moon. They waited for a red light to stop traffic, and they crossed yet another street. The kid's breath was starting to get on Tony's nerves. In the distance, she thought she could hear the distant whine of a police siren, but it might have only been her own blood fighting its way through the vessels in her skull.

And then she saw the sign, bent, green, white letters. LAMESA BOULEVARD. Crickets hummed in a nearby yard. Tony's heart picked up the rhythm. *We're here!*

"Mistie, wake up," said Tony. She lowered the child to the walk, but the girl's legs buckled under her. "Mistie!" She picked Mistie up under her arms and gave her a little shake. "We're almost there. If you walk, we'll get there quicker! Last one to the ranch is a rotten egg!"

Mistie opened her eyes and shook her head. "We're there?"

"Almost! Can you race me?"

Mistie nodded sleepily.

"Can you?" Tony asked the teacher. The teacher said, "I'll do the best I can."

Lamesa Boulevard was a residential stretch with small yards and even smaller houses. Burton's ranch would be at the end of all this, where the town ended and the Texas wilderness began. Maybe the people in these homes worked on the ranch. Maybe ranches didn't have bunkhouses anymore, they let people have their own houses in town. That made sense. It really wasn't the old cowboy days anymore.

Tony held Mistie's hand and they trotted up the sidewalk, past house after house after house after the entrance to a small RV park after house.

Tony stopped. She let go of Mistie's hand. She looked at the little stone house beside her. The black vinyl numbers on the white, door-side mailbox read *1851*.

No no no no!

The teacher was half a block behind, wheezing audibly. Tony left Mistie on the walk, and ran back. She grabbed the teacher's arm and tried her best not to twist it off. "I think we're lost. We're on the wrong block."

The teacher was sweating heavily. She ran the back of her hand across her forehead and nose. "We are? I don't think so. I've been watching the numbers. That brick house is eighteen-thirty-one. The one next to it is eighteen-thirty-three. Your dad should be the second one after that."

"Should be," said Tony. "Should be, but it ain't."

She retraced her steps and stopped in front of the driveway to the RV park. The entrance was chipped tarmac. It led back to a wide gravelly circle. Around the circle were camper trailers on cement and motor homes with their wheels locked between cinder blocks. Cars in various stages of disrepair were pulled off onto the bald lawn patches between campers.

Mistie was beside Tony now. "Are we through running?" she asked.

A row of galvanized mailboxes were nailed to a post by the entrance. Each had a number painted on the little front doors: 1835, 1837, 1839, 1841, 1842. There were several more; she quit looking.

"Are we through running?" repeated Mistie.

Tony yanked open the mailbox belonging to 1837. There was no mail inside. She slammed the door shut. Hot prickles were jumping under her skin, and she said, "Don't come with me."

She strode forward, every nerve blazing, every hair standing at dreadful attention. A man with a long ponytail and no shirt, squatting by his motor home and banging on a Harley with a wrench, called out, "Hey, there, girl, you lost?"

"Fuck off, grease monkey, it's way past your bedtime," said Tony.

"Oh, yeah, we need another one like you 'round here," said the man.

Tony watched the numbers. They went chronologically around the circle, and she was coming in from the right, the high side. She counted down each shit-ass tin can: 1845, 1843, 1841, 1839.

1837.

It was a camper. A beat-up, sorry-ass, rusting camper with a splintered picnic table near the door. Beside the table sat a woodie wagon with two flat tires.

I could be wrong, Tony told herself. *I ain't wrong much, but I could be wrong. Phone book misprint, the teacher said. Maybe there's more than one Burton Petinske in Lamesa. Maybe he uses this dump as some kind of front, so he can use another name over at the ranch.*

There were lights on in the camper. Well, maybe just one light, the place wasn't big enough to need more than one. Tony stepped up on the block porch and knocked on the door.

"Tony?" The voice was from behind, the teacher's voice.

"Go back to the street," said Tony. "This is just a mistake, that's all."

She pounded her fist on the door, and inside she could hear a grumbling, a thumping, and then the door handle was wiggling back and forth.

Got to be wrong. This is not the right place.

The door jerked open; the whole camper vibrated. Tony held her breath.

There was a man in his undershorts, his hand on the knob and the other hand clutching a beer. A Bud. Mam's favorite kind of beer. He had thick black hair and a black beard. A thin man, he had a major gut that hung over the elastic of the shorts.

"What the hell do you want, little girl?" he growled.

"You know me?"

"Fuck, should I?"

Tony said, "Let me in. Don't make this worse than it is."

"What . . . ?"

Tony pushed her way past the man and slammed the door.

The interior of the trailer wasn't much better than the outside. There was some furniture, a refrigerator and stove, and a table that folded into the wall when it wasn't being used. A bathroom stall door hung open. Tony could see the little shower and the clogged toilet from where she stood.

"Burton."

"What? What do you want?" His eyebrows went up

and down over his face, dark waves on a stormy countenance.

"I'm Angela."

The man froze, then tilted his head. He put his beer down on the folding table. "No shit."

"No shit."

"Love your ranch. Dad."

"My ranch? What are you talking about?"

Tony looked over the table. Hanging on a little wire rack were two guns, a rifle and a revolver. Burton might not have done much, but by damn, he'd replaced the gun he'd lost to Mam.

"Get the hell out of here, Angela," said Burton. "I didn't ask you to come here. I got my own troubles."

"So I'm trouble?"

"Could be! They see me with a kid, they might kick me out. I'm signed up as a single."

"What about your ranch?"

"What ranch?"

"You sent me a birthday card when I was twelve. You wrote on it, 'how you like my ranch?' There was a photo of you on a fence with the ranch behind it!"

Burton sighed and dropped onto a single hardbacked chair by the stove. "Oh, God, Angela. I wasn't drinking then. I had a good job, at a ranch outside of here. The Triple-Bar. Worked there nearly six months. I just called it mine for fun. I liked it. Then I got fired."

"Why?"

"Drinkin'."

Tony's chest hurt. She leaned over to pull in some air, but little came. "I can't believe it. You. God, you lied to me."

"You just misunderstood. Now go home, Angela."

"It's Tony!"

"Get out of here. Go home to your mama."

It was in her hand before she even knew she had jumped on top of the folding table and snatched it down off its rack. And, oh, this one had bullets in it. She *knew*. She could feel them inside like she could feel the little snakelike babies inside her last year. Solid, expectant, anxious to come out. She aimed at Burton, and his eyes grew as round as big, brown longhorn cow piles.

She fired. She fired again. Burton, hit directly in the chest, fell back off his chair to the food-littered floor. He didn't have time to complain about it like the deputy had.

Tony took Burton's beer and poured it over his body. She turned on his gas stove and lit a rolled-up magazine, then moved the torch about the place, touching things she knew would burn right away. The curtains on the window, filmy, cheap things like Mistie's pink nightie. The bedspread on the little love seat. The rug by the sink. Burton's thin-ass boxer shorts. Burton's thick black hair, which puffed and lit and fell to the floor by the dead man's head. A toupee.

Figured.

Chapter Sixty-four

There was a gunshot from inside the camper. Kate cried out, and ran several steps forward, then stopped. Who had the gun? Who was shooting?

"Oh, my God," she whispered.

Mistie began to cry.

A man who had been tinkering on his Harley-Davidson raced over, wiping his face with an oily towel. "That was a shot!" he said. "Who's shootin'?"

Kate said nothing. She listened, but there were no more shots. "Stay there," she ordered Mistie, and slowly approached the cinder block step.

"I wouldn't do that, lady!" said the motorcycle man. "That Petinske fella can be a mean badger when he's drunk."

Neighbors were gathering out on the circular drive, most in various stages of dress. "Somebody call nine-one-one!" said a woman. "That was a gunshot, I heard it!"

"I called already!" said a voice from the doorway of a Wilderness RV. On their way. Ya'll back up, what you got, a death wish?"

"Tony!" screamed Kate.

"Back up, woman, he can come out like a bull any minute!" said the motorcycle man. "We know how he can get!"

"Tony's in there!"

The motorcycle man grabbed Kate by the arm and tried to pull her backward, but she twisted free. "Let go! Tony's in there!"

He threw up his hands in resignation. "Go get her, then, be my guest."

The camper door opened, slowly. At first there were small tendrils of smoke curling out from inside, and then Tony was in the opening, stepping down onto the cinder block step, then down onto the ground, a revolver in her hand.

"Got him good," Tony said simply. There was blood on her hands.

"Tony, what?" Kate took a step forward, and stopped as Tony began swinging the revolver back and forth. "Was it your father?"

Tony's lip curled, a half smile that chilled the back of Kate's neck. "Oh, yeah, it was Burton Petinske. That's who it was." She looked past Kate to the gathering of neighbors, and waved the gun at them. "What the hell you lookin' at? Fuck off! I've killed two today, and I'm just getting started!"

The neighbors flew away from each other like leaves on a winter wind. Some went back to their campers. Others moved behind cars, but continued to watch the spectacle.

"Tony, they've called the police," said Kate. "It's over. Come out with me. We'll tell them what happened, and maybe . . ."

"Ha!" Tony barked. She looked at the barrel of the gun, smiled, then pointed it at Kate. "Men and women," she laughed sourly. "None of them are any good, are they? Mamas, Daddies, they're all fucked up. You're right that it ain't a gender thing. But that don't leave a whole hell of a lot, does it?"

"Not everyone's like that," said Kate. "Not everything."

"You want it in the head or in the chest? I hear new niggers don't want to fuck up their pretty faces when they die, so they would rather have it the chest."

"God, Tony, don't talk like this."

"We're all goin' down, teacher. 'Course, Baby Doll, she's okay. Hey!" Tony turned to the neighbors behind their various cars. "Listen to me, whatever happens, don't let this little kid go back to her mama or daddy. They're fuckin' her up real bad. You hear me? I'm giving a deposition here. It's the truth. You promise me?"

None of the neighbors said a thing. Nobody moved.

Tony shook the gun at one car. "You promise me?"

A little old lady with loose dentures said, "I promise you."

Tony nodded. Then she said, "Mistie, you'll be okay."

Kate looked beside her. Mistie was not there. "Mistie?" she said.

Tony whipped about, staring at the faces of the neighbors, and in the shadows of the scrub trees. "Mistie! Don't you be hiding now!"

Mistie did not answer.

Then Kate noticed the camper door, wide open and the smoke billowing out, harder, faster.

"She went inside!" Kate screamed. Both Kate and Tony ran for the door, but Tony knocked Kate back and Kate landed with a twist of her bad leg. She cried out.

"I'll get her," said Tony, "just stay the fuck back!" She disappeared into the camper.

From behind, a wailing of sirens, the lightning flashes of police lights. Neighbors in the drive hurried out of the way as four cruisers forced their way into the driveway and bucked to a halt. Police heads popped up from both sides of the cars, all holding weapons, all pointing them at Kate and the burning camper.

"Put your hands up and walk this way, slowly!" one uniformed man called.

"Tony's inside, and Mistie!" shouted Kate. "Save them, they're in the fire! Hurry!"

"Hands up, now!"

Kate put her hands up. She noticed her unshaved pits. *Fuck it!*

"Forget me!" screamed Kate. Her food stomped the ground. "Goddamn it, get Mistie and Tony!"

One policeman rushed up and snatched Kate's raised arms. He twisted them abruptly and painfully behind her back. Another officer went to the camper door and kicked it open wider. He coughed in the onslaught of smoke.

"Get out here, now!" he called inside.

New sirens, higher pitched. Red lights instead of blue. A fire engine roaring up beside the police cars.

Suddenly, Tony appeared at the camper door. Her hair was singed, her face blackened. Her voice, raspy with the damage to her lungs. "I can't find her!" she wailed. And then she put one hand to her face and sobbed, while the revolver dangled by her side. "I can't find Mistie! She's dead in there! She's dead 'cause of me!"

"Get down here, now!" said the police by the camper. "That place is an inferno, you don't want to . . ."

"Yes, I do!" said Tony. She threw the revolver as hard as she could throw it. It flipped end over end and landed at the flat tire of Burton's woodie wagon. And then, Tony turned, entered the camper, and slammed the door shut.

"Damn it!" shouted the cop. He leapt onto the block porch and tried the handle. Tony had locked it.

"Tony!" screamed Kate.

"Stupid ass girl," said the motorcycle guy.

"Mistie!" Kate twisted in the grasp of the policeman, and he jerked her arms up behind her, driving a vicious shard of pain through her back. "Get in there!"

Suddenly, the camper windows blew out at nearly the very same moment, like fireworks set on a timer by a master technician. Firemen in full uniform were off their vehicle, scurrying like yellow jackets, hooking a hose to the hydrant at the side of the drive.

Kate dropped to her knees. The police officer yanked her back up. One officer snatched up the revolver Tony had tossed, then said to Kate, "You looking for a kid? She's under there." He pointed beneath the woodie wagon and shook his head. "Bob, get that kid out from under there. You're better with children than I am."

Bob, a young officer with a neatly starched uniform, coaxed Mistie out from under the wagon. She was clutching a handful of dead grass and staring at the ground.

"What's your name?" Bob asked her. But she didn't say a word.

She was put into a separate cruiser from Kate. And they were driven away from the fire and the neighbors and the burning camper trailer and its cinder block step.

Chapter Sixty-five

They got to ride home in an airplane. Mistie had never been in an airplane before. It wasn't really big but the seats were soft and there was a window to look out at the clouds. Mistie had a new dress on, one a police lady had given her back before they'd flown out of Texas. It was pink and frilly, and Mistie knew that Tessa didn't have a dress that pretty. It was a dress that Mistie could wear in a pageant if her mama let her be in a pageant.

The teacher had handcuffs on. She sat across the aisle from Mistie on her own soft seat and watched out the window. Beside her was the policewoman who had given Mistie the pretty dress.

Not long after the plane took off, one lady came up the aisle and asked Mistie what she'd like to have to eat. Mistie shrugged. She said, "Are you going to put us in jail? Valerie had a bad liver. Daddy said that."

"Honey, children don't go to jail," said the lady. Mistie was glad. The lady gave her a hamburger with pickles, french fries, a big Coke with a straw, and some banana pudding. Mistie took off the pickles and put them in the little pocket on the back of the seat in front of her.

"Mistie," said the teacher after Mistie was done eating.

"Don't talk," said the policewoman beside her.

"I have to tell Mistie something."

"You aren't supposed to talk to her. You're in deep trouble, lady. I'd keep my mouth shut."

"I want to tell her I know I won't be a teacher anymore," said the teacher. "But I'll tell them everything I know. I'll make them hear me tell the truth. Too many kids are growing up without good mothers. Without good fathers."

The police lady said, "Be quiet or I'll have to gag you."

"I want to tell Mistie that I'll do everything I can to make it right."

"Bob!" called the police lady. "I need a gag down here!"

The teacher turned and smiled at Mistie. She didn't look scared. She looked happy. She looked like Princess Silverlace when the bad knights had been banished from the kingdom and the good music was playing at the end of the show.

Mistie smiled back.

The
LOST
Jack Ketchum

It was the summer of 1965. Ray, Tim and Jennifer were just three teenage friends hanging out in the campgrounds, drinking a little. But Tim and Jennifer didn't know what their friend Ray had in mind. And if they'd known they wouldn't have thought he was serious. Then they saw what he did to the two girls at the neighboring campsite—and knew he was dead serious.

Four years later, the Sixties are drawing to a close. No one ever charged Ray with the murders in the campgrounds, but there is one cop determined to make him pay. Ray figures he is in the clear. Tim and Jennifer think the worst is behind them, that the horrors are all in the past. They are wrong. The worst is yet to come.

___4876-0 $5.99 US/$6.99 CAN

Quenched

MARY ANN MITCHELL

An evil stalks the clubs and seedy hotels of San Francisco's shadowy underworld. It preys on the unfortunate, the outcasts, the misfits. It is an evil born of the eternal bloodlust of one of the undead, the infamous nobleman known to the ages as . . . the Marquis de Sade. He and his unholy offspring feed upon those who won't be missed, giving full vent to their dark desires and a thirst for blood that can never be sated. Yet while the Marquis amuses himself with the lives of his victims, with their pain and their torture, other vampires—of Sade's own creation—are struggling to adapt to their new lives of eternal night. And as the Marquis will soon learn, hatred and vengeance can be eternal as well—and can lead to terrors even the undead can barely imagine.

___4717-9 $5.50 US/$6.50 CAN

Sips of Blood

MARY ANN MITCHELL

The Marquis de Sade. The very name conjures images of decadence, torture, and dark desires. But even the worst rumors of his evil deeds are mere shades of the truth, for the world doesn't know what the Marquis became—they don't suspect he is one of the undead. And that he lives among us still. His tastes remain the same, only more pronounced. And his desire for blood has become a hunger. Let Mary Ann Mitchell take you into the Marquis's dark world of bondage and sadism, a world where pain and pleasure become one, where domination can lead to damnation. And where enslavement can be forever.

___4555-9 $5.50 US/$6.50 CAN

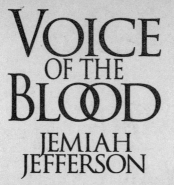

VOICE OF THE BLOOD

JEMIAH JEFFERSON

Ariane is desperate for some change, some excitement to shake things up. She has no idea she is only one step away from a whole new world–a world of darkness and decay, of eternal life and eternal death. But once she falls prey to Ricari she will learn more about this world than she ever dreamt possible. More than anyone should dare to know . . . if they value their soul. For Ricari's is the world of the undead, the vampire, a world far beyond the myths and legends that the living think they know. From the clubs of San Francisco to a deserted Hollywood hotel known as Rotting Hxall, the denizens of this land of darkness hold sway over the night. Bur a seductive and erotic as these predators may be, Ariane will soon discover that a little knowledge can be a very dangerous thing indeed.

___4830-2 $5.99 US/$6.99 CAN

Dorchester Publishing Co., Inc.
P.O. Box 6640
Wayne, PA 19087-8640

Please add $2.50 for shipping and handling for the first book and $.75 for each book thereafter. NY, NYC, and PA residents, please add appropriate sales tax. No cash, stamps, or C.O.D.s. All orders shipped within 6 weeks via postal service book rate. Canadian orders require $2.50 extra postage and must be paid in U.S. dollars through a U.S. banking facility.

Name _____
Address _____
City _____ State _____ Zip _____
I have enclosed $ _____ in payment for the checked book(s).
Payment <u>must</u> accompany all orders. ❏ Please send a free catalog.
    CHECK OUT OUR WEBSITE! www.dorchesterpub.com

Coming in June 2001
from Leisure Books . . .